A Short Period of Exquisite Felicity

A D'Orazio

Meryton Press
OYSTERVILLE, WA

Also by A D'Orazio

The Best Part of Love

This is a work of fiction. Names, characters, places, and incidents are products of the author's imagination or are used fictitiously. Any resemblance to actual events or persons, living or dead, is entirely coincidental.

A SHORT PERIOD OF EXQUISITE FELICITY

Copyright © 2018 by A. D'Orazio

All rights reserved, including the right to reproduce this book, or portions thereof, in any format whatsoever. For information: P.O. Box 34, Oysterville WA 98641

ISBN: 978-1-68131-023-7

Cover design by Zorylee Diaz-Lupitou
Images: 123RF and morguefile.com
Layout by Ellen Pickels

Dedication

To the memory of my beloved Maggie

Chapter One

October 1813, Netherfield Park

Fitzwilliam Darcy was in the midst of reaching for his wine when Jane Bingley announced, "I received a letter from Lizzy today."

His hand jerked at the sound of her name—though to him she was always "Elizabeth"—and before he could stop himself, he had knocked over his recently filled goblet, the wine spilling over the tablecloth.

The resultant bustle distracted everyone from the topic of Elizabeth Bennet. There were numerous exclamations of dismay and concern as an army of servants arrived bearing clean cloths. Plates and glasses were removed and replaced. Fresh wine was poured, and his attire was examined for stains and spots. All were capable about their duties, and soon, both he and the table were set to rights; evidence of his *étourderie* was gone.

How he wished that the stains of his love—and hatred—of Elizabeth Bennet might be as easily removed.

"Forgive me," he murmured to Mrs. Bingley when all had been set to rights. She smiled, for smiling was what she always did, but he knew she was not upset by his blunder.

No, the Bingleys, both of them, were generous to a fault, overlooking all his past injuries to them: that he had contrived to separate them when first they loved one another, that he had made the thinnest of excuses to avoid their wedding, and that he had not seen them for over a year. Indeed, he had scarcely even written to Bingley, just a short letter of congratulation on his marriage and another on the news of the birth of their son.

He would not have come now except that his friend had been unrelenting.

This was to be his last house party in Hertfordshire, and Darcy knew a refusal would likely yield a breach that could never be healed.

Naturally, Darcy asked who else might be present, and Bingley rattled off many names, all eligible ladies and gentlemen of an age to marry. It was *that* sort of party, then; evidently, the Bingleys were to be *that* couple, the ones so overwhelmed by their connubial bliss that they could not rest until they saw their friends settled into the delights of matrimony.

Bingley had come to Darcy at just the right moment. It had been the most melancholy of a prolonged succession of melancholy days. He had been lonely and alone, and he had yearned for something, anything, to take his mind off Elizabeth Bennet. An immediate disinclination to the party had been on his lips, but before making an utterance, he stopped himself with a strange thought: Why not?

Bingley had said nothing of Elizabeth, and Darcy had not asked; however, when his friend left, Darcy immediately began a quick perusal of all the letters Bingley had written to him over the last year, learning that Elizabeth lived in Cheltenham and the Bingleys never saw her. From this, he concluded he was safe—that he would not see her.

He even managed to persuade himself that he was relieved about it.

So here he was at Netherfield, and if she was not present in body, she was certainly alive in his memory. Every corner seemed to hold some recollection of her, but it was his own private torment—at least until now, when her name was spoken aloud.

Miss Bingley was quick to revive her interest in the subject of Elizabeth Bennet. "And how is dear Eliza these days? I do hope she is well."

"She is," said Mrs. Bingley. After a little pause, she added, "She intends to come to us at last."

Darcy was now more a master of himself, and this news of her did not electrify him in the manner the mention of her name had only moments before.

"Oh?" Bless Miss Bingley for her curious, conniving mind. "Will she spend the autumn?"

Bingley interrupted, vigorous and a bit too loud. "No, Caroline, we have asked her to make her home with us, as you well know." He gave his sister a level stare.

Miss Bingley's mouth curled around her reply as if the words were sour. "How delightful."

"She will arrive next week," said Mrs. Bingley with a beatific smile bestowed around the table. "She is wild to meet Baby Thomas."

Thomas was the Bingley's recently born son, a fine, stout little fellow with rosy-pink cheeks and a happy disposition that spoke of his parentage.

Miss Bingley then had much to say about Baby Thomas. Although she thus far had expressed interest in the child only so far as his gowns were concerned, it was evident that she intended to be the favoured auntie. She now began to claim her rights, eager to show herself a doting relation. No matter how young the man, Miss Bingley always would be the rival to Elizabeth Bennet.

Darcy remained silent in the exchange, unequal to the task of speaking of her as an indifferent acquaintance. He could not bear to utter any words of her, and he looked into the faces surrounding him for any sign that they knew what had passed between them. He refused to be drawn in by his curiosity, refused to ask what had become of her and where she had been all this time. Fortunately, he did not have to.

Mrs. Hurst, silent until now, decided to speak. "How shocking it was that she missed the wedding of her dearest sister! I am sure I could not have imagined that the same lady who came through knee-deep mud to attend you while you were sick could miss your wedding."

"Our wedding, as you will recall, was a quiet affair attended by very few," Bingley said, his tone admonishing.

Mrs. Bingley added, "I assure you, Lizzy's illness was grave, else wild horses could not have kept her away."

"Her illness," Miss Bingley trilled, with a sidelong look towards her sister. "Yes, what was the nature of her indisposition? I am not certain that I ever knew. I heard that a distant relation attended to her. I should have thought that, were she so gravely ill, your mother would wish to attend to her."

Mrs. Bingley was making a close study of the plate in front of her even though she had ceased eating. After a gentle clearing of her throat, she said, "It was pneumonia, but the physicians who saw her in London feared it was consumption, and so she went to Cheltenham to obtain the benefit of the waters. Our aunt's sister once had consumption, and she was believed to be the best person to attend to her."

Bingley quickly cleared his throat. "She is quite well now and eager to return to the bosom of her family." He smiled happily around the table.

"Gentleman, shall we forgo our separation tonight? I would much like to remain in the company of the ladies."

Darcy looked around him in astonishment. No one had finished eating, least of all Bingley himself, and he believed that an additional course might have remained as yet unserved. Nevertheless, no one uttered the least word of protest, all of them rising obediently as their host had directed them and moving towards the drawing room.

Miss Bingley was on him almost before he cleared the room, her long thin hand sliding into the crook of his arm. "I am afraid dinner was not much to your liking, sir," she murmured, claiming an intimacy he longed to reprove.

The years of his indifference had done nothing to dispel Miss Bingley's ambitions for him, and he found himself struck by a mad thought. *I should offer for her. Now* that *would show Elizabeth!*

Stupid notion. *Yes, a moment of discomposure for Elizabeth and a lifetime of misery for me.*

He shook his head slightly, but it was enough for Miss Bingley to notice. "I do not doubt you cannot like the notion of more Bennets being set upon us. Indeed, I have not the stomach for them myself. I can only be grateful that Mrs. Bingley does not seem inclined to be with her mother overmuch, for I surely could not abide my brother's home overrun by such a—"

"Mrs. Bennet is his relation now too." Darcy spoke sternly. "By all accounts, since her husband's death, she has led a quiet and unassuming life. It is good that the Collinses have taken her in as they have. I do believe your brother has offered you a separate establishment, has he not?"

His remonstrance quieted Miss Bingley as he hoped it would. She left him quickly as they entered the drawing room, and he was left to his musings about Elizabeth.

It astonished him to think it had been above a year since he had last seen her. A year since he had heard her laughter and witnessed the sparkle in her eyes. A year since he had felt the lightness of her touch on his arm and —dare he think of it?—felt the warmth of her breath against his mouth and tasted the sweetness of her lips.

A year since she had savagely ripped his still-beating heart from his chest and stamped it beneath her dainty little foot.

The mingled sensation of pain and rage that burst through him was almost unbearable, but his countenance revealed nothing, or so he hoped. Surely, he must appear well, for if even the faintest measure of all he felt was to alight upon his features, everyone within view of him would be alarmed.

He still owned the blasted letter that had announced his folly. It was a bit singed in places. After his first reading—nay, his second, for the first was undertaken in sheer disbelief and incomprehension—he had crumpled it, tossing it into the flames of his fireplace. Just as quickly, he had pulled it back, certain he must not have read it aright.

Yet third, fourth, fifth...seventeenth readings had yielded no dissimilar message. Elizabeth Bennet, his betrothed for a hallowed and gossamer week and two days, was his no more.

Another deep sigh escaped him as he turned his head away from the group, ostensibly looking at something, anything, on the back wall of the drawing room.

Miss Bingley was playing the pianoforte. She was a properly accomplished lady and exhibited superbly, her fingering exact. All the notes were played just as they should be, and in just the time they needed to be played. He looked at her with something that strove towards approval, admiring her beauty and her deportment.

Had he proposed to Miss Bingley, he should not have been jilted. Had he proposed to any number of ladies of his acquaintance, it never would have occurred. He never would have found himself twice rejected by a lady so laughably beneath him.

What angered him most was how she had changed him. She had made him believe that to look meanly on those outside his circle was wrong. She had made him believe his principles were good, but that he had followed them in pride and conceit.

That had been stupid. His pride was all he had, and if he looked meanly upon those of a different circle, why then, Miss Elizabeth Bennet had only herself to blame.

THE OCTOBER DAWN WAS BRIGHT WITH SUNSHINE, BUT IT WAS A BRITTLE light with a wind that announced to Darcy that the chill of winter was not long in coming. His horse did not mind; indeed, she seemed to relish the bite in the air, kicking and prancing, hoping for a good dash across the fields that surrounded Netherfield.

Darcy, being an indulgent master, allowed it. Together, they raced across the fields, kicking up clods of dirt and sod, leaping over fences and streams, and Darcy released his mind from the torment of her.

It was cleansing, this ride. There was no woman, duty, or society to attach itself to him; there was only glorious nature, filling his chest and surrounding his senses, driving away any notion of heartbreak.

It could not last.

The horse grew tired, as did the man. They dropped into a canter to return to the stables, but still, he managed to keep his thoughts from moving towards her. When they arrived at the stables, he waved off the groomsman, preferring to enjoy the physical exertion of caring for his horse himself, as well as the benefit of additional time in which his mind was occupied in the routine, and thus away from Elizabeth Bennet.

As he brushed, the refrain that had so assiduously plagued him in the past months made itself heard again. Why? Why did she do it? Was it lies, all lies? Did she despise him at Pemberley as she had despised him at Hunsford? Why did she accept him? Why did she jilt him? On and on, the questions never changed, nor did he ever arrive at a satisfactory answer.

He paused a moment, his hand holding the brush dropping to his side as he leant against the horse's flank. He did not often allow it, but just this once, he permitted the sweetness of the memory to encompass him.

He came around the stables at Pemberley, desperately longing for a cool swim after his long, hot ride, and wishing to make it to the house without encountering the visitors he had been warned were on the grounds. He was too late, though, for they—she—stood before him in the gardens.

She was confused and embarrassed, he was astonished and unkempt, and he left her rather abruptly. After a short, hastily rendered refreshing of his clothing and person, he returned to her. This time, they were both more composed, and he set himself to trying to make amends and show her that he was a better man by her direction.

The result was better than he might have dreamt in his wildest flight of fantasy. She was alternately blushing and sweet, teasing and charming. He came away from her more in love than ever, but with it was something else: hope. He could hardly admit it to himself, but in her eyes, he saw—or believed he saw—the possibility for true regard.

She and Georgiana got on wonderfully when he introduced them the next day, and this prompted a dinner invitation issued by Georgiana at his urging. Elizabeth and her aunt called at Pemberley the day prior to the dinner, and it was in that visit that he saw all he wished for. She flirted with him unmistakably. She held his gaze with those eyes of hers, and he saw the emotion within them.

In thinking back, he could not imagine how he had tolerated such delicious felicity, how he had borne seeing it without leaping into the air and shouting with exultation or without taking her into his arms straightaway. Even now, thinking of that look made his heart race.

That night was sleepless for him. She would be at Pemberley the next day to dine, but it was not enough; he needed more. The Gardiners planned to depart the day after that, so the dinner would be his final opportunity to see her. He could not stand the notion and resolved to pay a call at the inn where they stayed.

There he went the next morning, having hardly slept and rushing his valet through his morning ablutions, changing his coat four times. The Gardiners and Elizabeth were about to walk out just as he arrived, and he asked Mr. Gardiner's permission to attend them.

Elizabeth had taken his arm as they left the inn, their unhurried gait in direct contrast to that of the Gardiners, who moved forward with such haste that it was almost laughable. Mrs. Gardiner was a petite woman and could hardly keep apace of her husband's stride, but she made a valiant effort, creating a suitable distance from her niece and her niece's grateful suitor.

Then Elizabeth said those words that made him certain. She tilted her head to see his face around the edge of her bonnet. "I am pleased you called, Mr. Darcy. I feared I should have little chance to speak to you privately tonight, and there is something I have wished to tell you."

"Pray, what is it?"

"Why, I..." She looked away just a moment and inhaled, perhaps gathering some courage. "I have misjudged you rather severely. I wish to offer my apology as well as my gratitude that you are so kindly willing to overlook my foolishness and begin our acquaintance anew."

"You need not apologise. Your reproofs were warranted. I cannot deny it. As for the situation of myself and George Wickham, I had every opportunity to tell you what had gone between us."

"You did not owe me that," she assured him. "It was your dear sister's reputation, *after all. I cannot blame you for your silence, and I was not correct to judge your actions however I saw fit."*

"My behaviour had given you every reason to believe his lies," he insisted softly.

"Until your letter, perhaps, though your behaviour now attests to my error. I believe you must be among the best men I have ever known."

She blushed very deeply, and it thrilled him.

Hastily, she added, "Forgive me; I am too bold."

He halted and turned to face her. Gathering her hands in his, he pulled them against his chest. She would not look at him but turned her reddened face to the side, her countenance obscured by her bonnet.

It might have been rather precipitous, but his declaration came from his lips before he could even think of it, and his voice emerged resolute and sure as if this had been his plan all along.

"I love you. I have loved you these months, and I have no one to thank but you for the improvement in my character. You showed me how to be the better man that you deserve, and although I know I am yet undeserving, I shall beseech you to accept me."

Faintly, she said, "Accept you?"

"My feelings and wishes have not changed from what they were in April. I love you, I do, as ardently as ever before—nay, more so. Please relieve my suffering and be my wife."

A tear fell from nowhere, landing on his glove and making a dark blotch. He could see how her breathing had quickened, but she would not speak, nay, could not even look at him. A moment of dread filled him until she gasped and began to nod vigorously, finally looking at him, finally managing to say, "Yes. Yes. Yes, Mr. Darcy, yes."

He knew not what happened after that except it was nothing short of divine. He had never before felt such exquisite felicity, walking through Lambton with her, aimless and foolish and happy. In those hours, he had no cares, no worries. There was nothing in Lambton that day but Elizabeth and him and love, filling the roads with their joy. He smiled at every living soul whom he encountered, man and beast alike, and cared not about those who stared at him as if they had never seen him before. He and Elizabeth talked of anything and everything, laughing at the things that had come before and speaking time and again of their affection for one another.

They walked to where the river ran through the town. Standing on the bridge

and gazing down at the water running below, he asked, "...
you think differently of me?"

She turned and looked up at him in a way he would ne...
a century, not ever. In a voice almost inaudible, she said, "...
it began, Mr. Darcy, for I was in the middle before I knew ...
nevertheless, I know my heart now, and it is for you. I love you."

"Elizabeth." His voice was both a gasp and a prayer, and it took all his power to refrain from kissing her there on the bridge. She knew it and reached her gloved hand to her lips, kissing it and caressing his cheek briefly with the tip of her fingers.

Darcy returned to Pemberley later that morning, and it took all of his restraint to appear as he commonly did. Much as he wished to shout his felicity from the rooftop, he would not announce anything until he had secured Mr. Bennet's consent. He could not disrespect the man who would become his father-in-law, no matter how much he wanted his engagement to be known. They planned for him to travel to Hertfordshire once Elizabeth had returned to Longbourn, and then all would be made known.

He had never before, and not since, known the joy he had experienced in those days. Had it all been a lie? How could she have gulled him so thoroughly? Was he truly such a fool to have seen his heart's desire laid before him when, in truth, there was nothing?

That was the only real conclusion he could draw: he saw as he wanted to see. As the weeks and months elapsed, he had even begun to doubt whether any of it actually happened. Perhaps it was nothing more than a foolish dream, a schoolboy's fancy of love.

With a sigh, Darcy finished in the stable. He paused for a moment, feeling the familiar crush of disappointment and despair that always accompanied his return to reality from these temporary sojourns into the happier days preceding his current state. "I still love her," he told the hush of the morning. "I cannot bear the thought of seeing her."

Yet, no matter how much he disliked it, he would see her again quite soon. Her letter had announced her arrival within the week.

He considered leaving. He could, after all; it would not be so very odd. He could claim an urgent matter at Pemberley, something with Georgiana, or he could say nothing at all. Bingley would forgive him; Bingley always gave him.

No matter how he considered it, though, he could not do it. The notion of seeing her might put him at sixes and sevens, might fill him with despair and sorrow, and might rob him of sleep. But still, the alternative—to go away and not see her—was far, far worse.

If I see her, I might at least rest. Perhaps I will put away this infernal longing I have for her and at last be free.

Doubtful, his mind argued. *Very doubtful, but one can hope.*

THE NIGHT BEFORE SHE ARRIVED, DARCY WAS RESTLESS, A CAGED ANIMAL seeking its release. He paced his bedchamber from ten o'clock, not tired, unable to settle into a book, and uninterested in any other diversion. He went to the window, expecting to see a stormy night, lightning, thunder, and wind whipping the denuded branches of the trees in all directions, but there was nothing. A light breeze, disappointing with its lack of ferocity, blew a few leaves astray.

"I am in for an exceedingly long night," he told his mirror. "Sleep is not to be found." For a moment, he considered drinking himself into a stupor but knew such a stupid manoeuvre would not be for good in the end.

Instead, with another look outside, he decided to take a walk. He quickly donned the required clothing from that which his man had laid out for the morrow, and soon slipped from his room, going down a back staircase to the garden where Elizabeth once had declined to walk with him.

His mind slid with ease back into the memory of that day nearly two years ago as he stole from the darkened house.

Miss Bingley entreated him so earnestly to accompany her that he did not feel he could refuse. Within moments, she revealed her design for the walk: to quash any good feeling he held towards Elizabeth Bennet. Had it been obvious even then? Had his growing fascination already revealed itself so much that even Miss Bingley could see it?

She proved to be uncommonly malicious as they walked, an achievement for a lady for whom spite was the common mode.

"I hope you will give your mother-in-law a few hints, when this desirable event takes place, as to the advantage of holding her tongue, and if you can compass it, do cure the younger girls of running after the officers. And, if I may mention so

delicate a subject, endeavour to check that little something bordering on conceit and impertinence that your lady possesses."

"Have you anything else to propose for my domestic felicity?"

"Oh, yes! Do let the portraits of your Uncle and Aunt Philips be placed in the gallery at Pemberley. Put them next to your great uncle, the judge. They are in the same profession, you know, only in different lines. As for your Elizabeth's picture, you must not attempt to have it taken, for what painter could do justice to those beautiful eyes?"

"It would not be easy, indeed, to catch their expression, but their colour and shape and the eyelashes, so remarkably fine, might be copied."

At that inopportune moment, Elizabeth and Mrs. Hurst appeared from another path. He felt his cheeks redden, and he wondered what she had heard.

It was unlikely that she had not heard them. At the time, he had been concerned that she had learnt of his admiration, but now, he believed she had heard Miss Bingley's satire and noted his lack of defence of her.

He shook his head, wondering whether the foundation of her dislike had been laid that day or had merely added to her feelings against him.

It could not have helped when Mrs. Hurst, on seeing her sister with him, immediately abandoned Elizabeth and joined them instead. Elizabeth could not fit in with them and rejected at once his proposal to go someplace where all four could walk together.

"I should not have simply walked away that day," he mused aloud. "In all likelihood, she overheard us speaking of her. Heaven only knows what else she might have overheard at Netherfield. Miss Bingley does not scruple to abuse those she does not like, and I did not defend her for fear of exposing myself. I should have. I should have spoken and made it easier for her."

He shook his head, realising none of it mattered. How many hours had he spent, twisting and turning in his mind the events of the autumn of 1811 and the spring and summer of 1812, looking for the places where he had misstepped? Finding the error could not help. It was over and always had been.

He felt the comfortable, familiar anger rising up within. He stopped on the path, squeezing his eyes closed and gritting his teeth, even as his fist gripped his walking stick so hard that it shivered against the gravel. It would not do; his feelings would not be repressed. The need to shout at her, to proclaim his anguish, was too strong to be denied.

"Dammit!" He swore at the night around him. "I know I did not behave as I ought! I know it!"

He began to pace quickly, stabbing his stick into the dimly lit darkness to punctuate his words. "I acknowledged it long ago, and I changed! I did! For you did I alter myself, wishing to be a man worthy of you, and I believe I had some success. Yet you took that man—the man who wished for no more than to please you and love you and make you happy—and you cut out his heart. You tore me into shreds!"

Darcy stopped, his breath coming fast, and his speech quieting to an angry murmur. "You tore me into sad, uncertain shreds. So you despise me, do you? Well, guess what?"

He paused a moment then shouted, "I despise you too! I despise you more! I despise you with all that I am and all that I ever will be, and I wish, oh how I wish, I might never see you again! I hate you, and I hate everything about you!"

Darcy kicked at a stone on the path. "I hate you, Elizabeth Bennet, and how I wish I had never known you."

Never known her? Could he justly say that?

He stopped, sinking onto a bench, drooping and breathing heavily. Such a statement was patently untrue; he knew that. Despite everything, incredibly, he still was glad to know her. Some absurd part of him would not have relinquished a moment of their acquaintance, no matter what.

And why was that?

He stared into the blackness of the night, not seeing anything before him. "It is because, for however much you hate her…"

Inhaling, he continued, "For however much you hate her, you love her even more. You love her and somewhere…somewhere you have foolish hope that she loves you too. That somehow, some way, this can be fixed."

He sat a moment before uttering an oath. "Damn fool. Look at what she has made you."

He rose, suddenly exhausted, and made his way back into the house. Sorrow was so tiring; he could only hope he would have his anger back to enliven him in the morning.

Chapter Two

Elizabeth's companion had been snoring in the corner of the carriage for the better part of two hours when a strong jolt woke her. Recalling she was not in the privacy of her chambers, she sat up at once, giving Elizabeth a tired smile.

"Forgive me, miss."

"Think nothing of it." Elizabeth waved off her apology. "I wish I could do the same. Nothing whiles away the tiresome hours of travel like repose."

"There is always conversation," said the lady, "if you are so inclined."

"Very well. Of what shall we speak?"

The widowed Mrs. Whiting considered for a moment. "I have never been to Hertfordshire. What can you tell me of it?"

Elizabeth appreciated having something to speak about that required little thought as the carriage moved forward with relentless haste towards a meeting she both dreaded and longed for. She dwelt upon the happy times she had spent in the county, doing all she could to forget the more recent past.

Mr. Bennet had been ill, but far from gravely so, when she departed on a tour of the northern counties with her Aunt and Uncle Gardiner. She would learn later that his decline was rapid, but at the time, her mind was filled: first, with the glad pursuits of a holiday, and second, with falling in love with Mr. Darcy.

The first time she had learnt of the perilous state of Mr. Bennet's health was when Jane had written to tell her about Lydia's elopement with George Wickham. Jane felt certain her father's health could not withstand such a shock, and she wrote to Mr. Gardiner in Derbyshire to beg his assistance in the matter. Mr. Gardiner did all he could and put up an extraordinary sum of money—but Elizabeth was certain neither he nor her aunt ever had any idea of the price Elizabeth had paid.

Mr. Bennet died while Elizabeth was yet in London, doing all she could to secure Lydia's and their family's futures. Elizabeth grieved that she had never been able to say goodbye, but she was comforted in the knowledge that she had—through the sacrifice of her every happiness—kept their family from ruination.

If nothing else, the loss of Mr. Bennet had eclipsed the rumours over Lydia. Their neighbours had been sufficiently kind-hearted to dismiss previous gossip in favour of extending their sympathies to the ladies at Longbourn. Everyone save Elizabeth bore well Mrs. Bennet's raptures for Lydia's "excellent catch."

Lydia, fool that she was, preened with delight over her achievement during a nearly insufferable fortnight in Hertfordshire. Mr. Bennet was apparently long forgotten, for all his wife and youngest child could speak of were wedding clothes, setting up the Wickhams' new home, and the baby that was well on its way. Mrs. Bennet had plans for a grand house in Hertfordshire with a large retinue of servants and elegance in all things; fortunately, Mr. Gardiner was more reasonable.

He assisted the newly married couple in finding a modest but pleasant little house near Cheapside, and he gave Wickham a respectable job in one of his warehouses. It was a patched-up affair, but it seemed that it would do.

Her face must have shown her melancholy for Mrs. Whiting interrupted her reverie. "I understand your father passed rather recently."

"A year ago," Elizabeth answered. "We were fortunate in that his heir took my mother in, and she did not have to leave her home."

"That was very good of him."

"Aye, and I imagine my brother Mr. Bingley also has something to do with maintaining her, though I do not know it for certain."

"Mr. Bingley is your eldest sister's husband?"

"Yes. I have three sisters married and one, Kitty, who is not yet wed."

It had been a surprise to Elizabeth that Mr. and Mrs. Collins had generously offered to keep Mrs. Bennet at Longbourn. They had offered their home to Elizabeth and her sisters as well, but there were a great many changes in fortune ahead for the Bennet ladies.

When Mr. Collins had made it clear that he would suffer no delay in taking possession of his new estate, Lady Catherine was quick to act. She did not wish her parish left unattended and had identified a candidate for the living post-haste. The person she preferred was a man called Parker. He was a serious young man, recently at university where he had distinguished himself well. He was not handsome, but he was kind, if a bit dull, and he wished for a wife to assist him in his duties to the Hunsford parish. Mrs. Collins believed she might have just the lady for him and arranged the introduction.

Mary found nothing to dislike in him, nor he in her, and it was done as easily as that. They married within a month of Mr. Bennet's death. A few tongues wagged, though most understood the practicality of the arrangement.

It was Jane's alteration of circumstance that was most shocking.

One of the first calls of condolence received by the Bennet ladies was from Mr. and Miss Bingley. They came as soon as they heard, paying their regards and explaining their prolonged absence from Netherfield. Mr. Bingley arranged to call again after the burial, inviting Jane to ride in a new curricle he had brought down from London.

When they returned from their ride, Jane told her mother that she had come to an understanding with Mr. Bingley and intended to marry him when her period of mourning had elapsed. Mrs. Bennet did not find that necessary, but Jane insisted.

Mr. Bingley evidently insisted on a few things himself, and thus their son, Thomas, was born in September, only seven months after their nuptials. Elizabeth pursed her lips in surprise when she first learnt of it, but she could not censure Jane. Indeed, had things not occurred as they did, the marriage might have taken place far sooner, but they were certainly not married because of little Thomas. They had married for love, and if a babe born in September was the result, so be it.

"Three sisters married! Your mother has done her duty well. I suppose you are eager to be settled yourself. I daresay you will be next."

Elizabeth could offer no more than a faint smile. *No, I will never marry.*

Despite all the changes, surprises, and turns that had occurred within the Bennet family since August 1812, one surprise remained untold: that Elizabeth had, for nine glorious and beloved days, been betrothed to Mr.

Darcy. Not only betrothed to him, but in love with him—a love that stayed with her still and likely always would.

She winced as she thought of it, squeezing closed her eyes, which usually welled up with tears at the slightest thought of him. Not today, though; today there was too much anxiety and trepidation to weep.

I must be prepared to face his hatred, for surely he will despise me.

She had imagined once before that he would despise her after her first rejection of him at Hunsford, but he had not. He had shocked her when he found her with the Gardiners at Pemberley by greeting her with amiability and kindness and showing her the truth of the man he was: a man with a pure heart and an upright character. The best man ever she had known, then and still.

I do not know that I would want such preference again. This time his ire is well deserved. His spite would match the disgust I hold within myself for having done as I did to him.

She believed herself prepared to face his indifference, perhaps even his cruelty. What haunted her, however, was the thought of braving his sorrow. *That* she could not imagine, nor could she possibly endure it.

Perhaps he has forgot his love for me by now. It is likely a distant, much loathed remembrance, a good meal that has left a foul aftertaste—or distress to the bowels.

Yet as much as she wished it were so, she could not wholly support the notion.

It was an hour and an instant later when the horses slowed to enter the drive at Netherfield Park. Elizabeth's heart leapt fearfully and excitedly as she observed the house that was now her sister's home. It seemed so long ago that they had heard the news of Mr. Bingley having let the place—a lifetime ago.

She had not been there since Jane became mistress; indeed, she would not have come now had she any other choices. But this was the lot of a spinster, so she must grow accustomed to being shifted about to whomever would take her.

He would be within. Her heart beat so hard that it was nearly intolerable. She had no idea how she might be able to greet him with equanimity, not when she wished to throw herself at his feet and beg his forgiveness.

Forgiveness. The notion of it made her laugh at herself, silently and sorrowfully.

"My good opinion once lost is lost forever," echoed from the depths of Elizabeth's thoughts, much as she wished to deny it.

Mr. Darcy's heart was certainly lost to her. Now, the best she could hope for was the manifestation of that designation he had once applied to her: tolerable. She hoped he might tolerate her presence, if only for her to bask in his for at least a short while.

The carriage stopped, and she heard the servants moving about outside. It was time to exit, yet she could not. She looked out the window at the manor house. An eligible purchase offer had been made, and Bingley had the right of first refusal that he exercised after much consideration. He intended to purchase an estate in Yorkshire near Rotherham—thirty miles from Pemberley from what she knew of it. A fine place had recently come up for purchase by a baronet forced to retrench. Elizabeth would join them there and live with them and their children, just as she had always teased Jane that she was likely to do. It would be a good enough life, a starting over. Truly, it was the best she could hope for at this point.

With a deep, fortifying breath, she indicated that she was prepared to leave the carriage. The footman assisted her, no doubt wondering at her cold, trembling hands and the way she stumbled just a bit on stepping down. *Will he await me in the drawing room? Will he be overt in his disdain? Or worse—has he grown indifferent to me, uncaring and unfeeling, able to be easy because my presence means nothing to him?* For his sake, she supposed she hoped for the latter, though it would be extraordinarily painful.

She bid Mrs. Whiting farewell, wishing her safe travels as she continued on to London. Elizabeth's knees fairly shook as she entered the house and was told by Nicholls that the family awaited her in the drawing room. Memories assailed her as she travelled the long hall: the dining room in which she had always been banished to the end of the table with Mr. Hurst, the parlour where they once had read together, and the rooms used for the ball where they had shared a wonderful dance—or a dance that might have been wonderful had she not been so bent on arguing with him. She shook her head, stupid then and still stupid now.

Elizabeth swallowed against her anxiety as the doors were opened and Nicholls announced her. Jane was on her in a trice before she could even look about her. "Lizzy!" Her sister gathered her into a tight hug. "Oh, how wonderful it is to see you at last!"

It was lovely to have an excuse to release some emotion, and if the others in the room—who, when she could bring herself to look, turned out to be only Bingley—believed the tears in her eyes to be solely from the relief of seeing her beloved sister, then it was just as well.

Darcy had decided he would not be on hand to greet her. In this he was resolved. Her letter had indicated that she was to arrive shortly before the dinner hour, and he would find something with which to occupy himself until then. They would meet, distant and indifferent acquaintances, in the presence of friends and relations in the drawing room before dinner.

He spent the day being determinedly busy. He wrote many letters of business, finished a book on new methods of textile production, and wrote a detailed note to his secretary describing the arrangements for the Christmas season as well as Boxing Day.

He rode his horse for a long time and, upon returning to Netherfield, found his practice foils and undertook some fencing exercises. Then he bathed, dressed, and sat by the fire in his bedchamber to begin a new book. Unfortunately, it was dull, and he fell into a light doze.

A gentle knock on his door caused him to jerk awake. With the sense of alarmed chagrin that comes from an unplanned nap—and the subsequent surety upon waking that something of great importance had been neglected—he leapt to his feet and bid whoever had knocked to enter.

It was Fields, his valet. "Sir, they await you to dine."

"Yes, oh, yes, I...please tell them I shall be along immediately." Fields bowed and moved to quit the room, but Darcy halted him. "Fields, ah, is there...has the guest arrived?"

"The guest, sir?"

"A young lady."

"Yes, Miss Elizabeth Bennet arrived this afternoon."

His heart, traitorous and foolish, leapt at the sound of her name. He swallowed with some difficulty. "Thank you."

Fields knew his place, but even so, he gave Darcy a cursory enquiring glance.

After all, Fields knew. It had been he who had awoken early on the day that Darcy sought Miss Bennet's hand in Lambton and patiently endured Darcy's brusque dismissal of several coats before wordlessly handing him a new, freshly brushed one, saying, "A fine coat, sir. Suits your form rather admirably." It was not Fields's way to give an opinion on his master's attire, but Darcy had appreciated it on that day, and he had been far too nervous to think about it overmuch.

Fields had also been there the day he had received her letter and witnessed the dark gloom that had descended upon him for many, many days thereafter. So Fields knew; he knew of Miss Elizabeth Bennet and the significance she held in Darcy's life. But it would never be spoken of.

Darcy scanned the room and was thankful to see a decanter of brandy had been provided at some time during his visit. He was not generally one to imbibe, but he now found it necessary. He poured two fingers, tossed it back quickly, then drank a second just as fast. It did nothing for his nerves.

He moved to the case that he brought with him wherever he went. It contained his keys, money, signet ring, and the letter. Always the letter. Some day he hoped to consign it to the flames—and leave it there—but he had not yet done so, and this night he was grateful. He removed it from the case, allowing it to remain unopened. He did no more than hold it, tracing his fingers over the direction. His name, Pemberley, Derbyshire, all written in her hand.

Gritting his teeth, he brought to the fore of his mind the vision he always had of her writing the letter, no doubt rejoicing in having brought him low and grinning at the notion of his heartache. Complete revenge for his slight of her and her family.

And now he would see her. Would she triumph? Would she gloat? Or worse, would she be pityingly kind?

After a few minutes, Darcy returned the letter to his box and stood. He moved to the mirror and looked at himself. He was a bit pale but otherwise appeared as he always did, his countenance blank of emotion. She was downstairs, and he must meet her with impenetrable solemnity. He could permit himself nothing less than calm disinterest, carefully arranged features, and undismayed hauteur. Fortunately, he was well versed in such disguise. Fortunately, he could appear the opposite of how he truly felt.

ELIZABETH'S HANDS SHOOK AS SHE ATTEMPTED TO FASTEN THE NECKLACE with the small cross that her father had given her. It would not be fastened, choosing instead to snarl in her hair. She pulled it free only to have it fall, useless, to the dressing table in front of her.

Jane had offered her maid to assist Elizabeth as she dressed, but she had declined the offer. She needed these last few moments before they dined—before she would see him—to attempt to regain her composure.

That he had not been in the drawing room earlier was both a relief and a disappointment. A relief because she hated the thought of the scorn she would see in his eyes, and a disappointment because she longed for this first meeting to be over. In any case, it could not be put off any longer. They would meet at dinner unless he intended to hide away in his bedchamber, which she did not think he would do.

A sick, trembling feeling swirled in her gut, and the shaking felt as though it afflicted her insides as well as her hands. More than anything, she just wanted to run away, but she could not.

For the thousandth time, she considered whether she should have told Jane about her changed feelings for Mr. Darcy. She had not ever been able to speak of their painfully short engagement, not even to Jane. By the time she had seen her sister, so much had happened—Lydia's escapade, their father's death, Jane's engagement—she could not imagine what good discussing it would do. And she could not bear to have Jane try to make a good thing of it. She could not stomach any attempt by her sister to disguise the truth of Elizabeth's pain behind a pretty smile and serene countenance.

She picked up her necklace, trying once more to fasten it around her neck. After several fumbling minutes, her efforts proved fruitful, and she rose on unsteady legs, prepared to meet him. Her steps towards the door were hesitant; her mind was desperate to extricate her from this situation, to permit her some excuse to remain in the room for the night. She could not, though, and to do so would solve nothing. She would meet him sometime, and delaying would not improve her spirits nor bolster her courage for the endeavour.

"You did this, Lizzy," she reminded herself. "You made the choice you had to make, and these are the consequences of that choice. It will surely not be so very bad."

Elizabeth arrived in the drawing room having earned no success in her efforts to calm herself before greeting the Bingleys and Darcy. It was with both relief and disappointment that she saw he had not yet joined the party.

Bingley handed her a glass of wine that she took gratefully, grasping it tightly to avoid dropping it. Elizabeth willed herself to be still and placed on her countenance a demeanour of calm complaisance. "Thank you, Charles."

"You are quite welcome." He beamed in return. "It has been some time since you have been in company with Darcy, I think. It must have been that time we were all at Pemberley together, an age ago!"

She tried to look pensive as though the dates, the hours, of those blessed days were not engraved upon her memory. "Yes, I believe it was August of 1812."

"I have scarcely seen Darcy myself since then. How good it is to renew our old friendship!"

This surprised Elizabeth, though on further reflection, she did not think it should have. His spite for her must have extended to all things Bennet, and Bingley was guilty by association.

"You must be relieved to see him now," she said without further thought. She regretted her odd choice of words at once.

"Relieved? Yes, I suppose I am." Bingley nodded, blessedly unconcerned over her phrasing. "To my understanding, he was seen in neither town nor country. Of course, I was rather occupied myself with the business of becoming a husband and father…"

As Bingley rattled on about his life changes, she strove to recover from the painful image that afflicted her. To think of Darcy fixed in his home in Derbyshire filled her with greater sorrow than she could have imagined. Each fresh evidence of the manner in which she had hurt him did this.

Bingley was looking at her expectantly; she had evidently missed a question. "Pray, forgive me. What did you say?"

"It will be an excellent time to renew an old acquaintance for you as well." Bingley was all smiles and Elizabeth studied him carefully. Did he know anything? She did not imagine that Darcy had told him, but perhaps he suspected that something had gone between them.

"Yes, I believe it will," she answered sedately and Bingley, with a cheerful, guileless nod and bow, moved away from her.

Her heart leapt when the door to the drawing room opened, but it proved to be only Miss Bingley sweeping into the room like a duchess. *Bejewelled like a duchess as well.* There had to be some grudging admiration given to her; she was handsome and wore all the latest styles to her advantage, though not to Elizabeth's taste, and she did have a rather graceful and commanding way of comporting herself.

She greeted Elizabeth. "Well, Eliza, you are seen at last. You are so very altered, my dear; the ravages of your illness were great, I fear. But oh, forgive me," she tittered, pressing her fingers to her lips. "I intend no unkindness. You are lovely, just lovely, if a bit frail, and I am quite enraptured with the evidence of your recovered health."

"Thank you, Miss Bingley," Elizabeth acknowledged, suppressing a grin. *Some things never change.* Oh, if only Miss Bingley could know that Elizabeth was no longer her rival. However much Mr. Darcy might disregard Miss Bingley, he certainly despised Elizabeth. For not the first time, she wondered how he might greet her. Would Miss Bingley see how he hated her? Would the entire room know of his loathing?

The door opened again, and Elizabeth's heart once more leapt and began to pound. But no…not Darcy. Bingley had left the room unnoticed by her and now returned. "I spoke to Darcy's man, and evidently, he had fallen asleep by the fire but will join us shortly."

Her nerves were then upon her in full measure, heart racing, hands moist and trembling, every nerve alive to the dreadful anticipation of his presence. Miss Bingley's continued conversation was vapid and dull—something about a little gown she had stitched for Baby Thomas—but Elizabeth was grateful that little response was required. Elizabeth had only to nod in the correct places and make a little noise of pleasure here and there, and Miss Bingley was content.

When, finally, the door opened to admit him, time stood still. The click of the door was like a gunshot and made her head jerk in his direction just as her heart jerked violently within her chest. Elizabeth looked away quickly, too quickly, and moved her head into the most natural posture she could manage. She wondered whether she was deathly pale or red as a cherry; she hoped she would not vomit.

His footsteps echoed as he entered the room with the air of command that he always possessed. As much as she was dismayed by this encounter, it was still a balm to her soul just to see him. His countenance was grave and solemn but so very handsome, and she admired the beauty in his form. As always, his clothing was immaculate and expertly fitted, and he moved with strength and grace, his steps measured and sure.

Yet it is nothing to his character. His true character is above all.

Inasmuch as she wanted to flee, so too did she long to run to him, throw her arms around his neck, and be held by him. She was dizzy and a bit faint; it seemed he was approaching her.

It took an eternity for him to arrive where she stood with Miss Bingley. Her curtsey felt trembling and uncertain, and she could not lower her eyes. Instead, her gaze fixed on him and drank him in, wishing to absorb him and commit every bit of him to memory.

He offered an exceedingly correct bow. "Miss Bennet. How good it is to see you."

"The pleasure is mine, Mr. Darcy."

"I trust that your journey was easy?" His face looked as though the words were bitter in his mouth.

"It was," she replied, desperately trying to subdue the welling of emotion within her. "Very easy."

"Excellent. I understand you have been ill. My best wishes for your recovered health." With that, he bowed again, this one spasmodic and truncated, and turned to join Bingley by the fire.

It is done. We have met, it is finished, and he was not unkind to me. Why then did she want to burst into tears? Why had their polite little exchange felt so painful when she deserved far, far worse?

Dinner was called, and Bingley went to take the arm of his wife to lead her into the dining room. On his way, he stopped, extending his arm towards Miss Bingley. "Come, Caroline," Elizabeth heard him say, and with horror, she realised he meant to compel Darcy to escort her.

She could do nothing for it, but her face began to burn even as Bingley called out, "Darcy, bring Elizabeth in."

The look of distaste on Darcy's face was brief and rapidly replaced by his more stoic demeanour. He said nothing as he returned to her, extending his arm. Elizabeth placed her hand lightly on it, and they began to walk.

What could be said? There was nothing, not with the room of people around them, and so she offered him the best thing she could: her silence.

Elizabeth was so calm, dignified, and graceful, placing her hand on his arm as though she could not bear to touch him. Darcy did not think he could keep his countenance were she to tease him in her usual manner. Surely, she would not dare.

The walk to the dining room was interminable. She said nothing, which brought him both relief and greater anger. *Is this how it will be? Utter silence—no explanation? No attempt to mitigate my ire?* At once, his cravat felt too tight with all the things he wanted to say to her rising up in his throat and choking him.

Once they arrived at the table, he assisted her in sitting, assiduously avoiding any sort of contact, and quickly went to his own place, relieved to have succeeded in this first small challenge to his equanimity.

The first of the courses was laid before them. He had to own, no matter what else her limitations, Mrs. Bennet had always laid a good table, and it seemed this talent extended to her first daughter. Darcy put his full attention on his plate, hoping that he might become like Hurst, indifferent to all around him, diverted in full by culinary pleasure.

He succeeded in some measure. He was aided in the fact that Elizabeth was quiet, much more so than he had ever seen her. *Not so inclined towards teasing when you are forced to bear the society of your victims, are you?*

He afforded her a glance; she was pale, her eyes dull and fixed on the plate before her. *She is embarrassed. Likely, she had not considered the possibility of being in my society ever again.*

For not the first time, he wondered what she thought might happen. She was sure to know that her actions would result in his never-ending spite. He had told her often enough that his good opinion once lost was lost forever. He hoped that if he kept telling himself that—if he repeated over and over again that he had a poor opinion of her— eventually he would believe it himself.

"And how do Mr. and Mrs. Wickham?" Miss Bingley's voice came from the other side of the table.

He startled, hearing the hated name. Mrs. Wickham? Who might that unfortunate creature be?

A sidelong glance at Elizabeth revealed that she too was affected by hearing the name. Her hand shook as she reached for her wineglass, taking a minuscule sip. "They get on very well, Miss Bingley. I thank you for enquiring after them. I will be sure to pass on your regards."

"I hear Mrs. Wickham is again with child." To the indifferent observer, Miss Bingley had the countenance of one who enquired politely after a mutual acquaintance, but Darcy suspected otherwise. There was a glittering meanness in Miss Bingley's eyes that suggested this was some design to shame Elizabeth, though for what purpose he could not imagine.

Elizabeth's eyes were trained on her plate. "No, she is not. Lydia is kept busy with little Emelia, and that is more than enough for now."

"What?" Miss Bingley was a caricature of astonishment. "Surely Mrs. Wickham must have some help?"

"Their income is not sufficient to keep a nursemaid, but her housekeeper does assist her in any way possible."

Jane interrupted, her voice ringing out firm and sure in a manner that Darcy had never heard from her. "No matter how much help there is, a mother is always busy tending to her child. For myself, it is a labour of love."

"Of course, it is," Miss Bingley cooed while her brother laid down his fork and glared at her.

Miss Bingley disregarded her brother and gave Darcy a look, the meaning of which he could not fathom. *Triumph, but for what?*

He put aside thoughts of Miss Bingley's perplexities for now. So Elizabeth's sister married George Wickham? That seemed rather extraordinary; they must have been caught in an assignation and forced to marry. Surely, nothing else could have induced Wickham into matrimony, for the Bennet ladies had no fortune to tempt him.

At once, a feeling of heated nausea gripped him. These thoughts of Elizabeth, Wickham, Miss Lydia Bennet, and even Miss Bingley and her malicious nature, pressed close around him. *Why did I come here? Why, when I could be comfortable at Pemberley?*

"Mrs. Bingley." His voice came out surprisingly loud and sounded almost angry, and he noticed from the corner of his eye that he had caused Elizabeth to startle. The table grew quiet.

"I must be away in a day or so. I had thought I might stay but—"

"What is this?" Bingley cried out in dismay. "Darcy! It has been an age since we have enjoyed one another's society."

"I know, and it is exceedingly disappointing to me as well, but Georgiana needs me to—"

"Did not you say that Miss Darcy is in Kent with Lady Catherine and Lord and Lady Matlock?"

"She is, she is," Darcy stammered. "I thought to join them—"

29

Mr. Hurst spoke for the first time since the soup had been served. "Damn poor turn, Darcy. These fields are near overrun with game, and we need another with us who can clean them up."

"So true." Bingley nodded vigorously. "The sport in Hertfordshire this autumn has been quite beyond compare. Something about the warm spring. A few days cannot hurt can it? I would be most grateful, and our party has not yet truly begun."

All eyes were upon him, like a cage fixing him to his seat. Well, perhaps not all eyes. Elizabeth's remained trained upon her plate, and against every desirable inclination, he felt a wave of longing pass through him. For as much as he wished to run from her, he could not bear to leave her.

"Very well, then. I believe I shall abide by my original plan."

Chapter Three

Elizabeth woke early on her first morning at Netherfield. She was quick to leave her bed, eagerly imagining her re-acquaintance with the beloved woods she had once trod daily. She dressed quickly and simply, and soon found herself leaving the house by one of the side doors.

She paused on the steps, allowing her eyes to roam the landscape. It was a beautiful morning, just short of being chilly. The dew sparkled on the grass, which to Elizabeth's eye, was greener than any she had ever seen, and the hills rolled about gently, welcoming her back to the place where she was loved. Elizabeth inhaled deeply, wanting the air of Hertfordshire to fill her chest and cleanse it of the worries and fears of the past year.

There were so many beloved spots she wished to visit that she stood a moment in indecision—which way to go first? Longbourn, Oakham Mount, the path along the river? She set off at a brisk pace towards Longbourn.

To be here raised her spirits to a level they had not enjoyed in an exceedingly long time. No, she would never be happy in the way she once hoped she would be, but her life would be good. She would be, if not joyous, at least content. She gave a little skip, enjoying the sound of the path beneath her feet.

A different life, but an enjoyable one nevertheless. The notion heartened her. She was resolved that she would never marry. How could she, having known what it was to love and be loved? Anything else would be a pale substitute; any other man would inevitably, continually, fall short. It would not be fair, not to the other man and not to herself. So she would stay with Jane and Bingley, helping them raise their children, sharing their special occasions, and carving out a small piece of their domestic circle for herself. In younger days, she had thought a spinster's life would be positively dreadful, but now it seemed rather pleasant.

It was while she was lost in these musings that Mr. Darcy appeared. There was no sound, no sight to warn her; he was merely there, stepping out from two hedges near the outermost part of the yard and immediately before her, causing her to gasp.

"Oh!" Her hand flew to her heart, and she took a step backwards nearly falling over her own feet. "Mr. Darcy I…I did not see you, sir."

"Forgive me," he said stiffly.

They stood a moment in embarrassment and uncertainty. Her face was on fire, and her heart leapt and stuttered as she shifted uneasily on her feet. She wondered why he did not leave, but he remained, standing in front of her with an inscrutable countenance.

At last, he spoke with some evident discomfort. "The morning is fine. I should have been surprised if you did not take advantage of it."

"Very fine," she agreed with a small smile.

He did not return her smile, slight as it was; he simply stared at her for a moment. "You are fond as ever of walking, I presume."

The way he said it made it seem like a fault. "I do…that is to say, I am. I am fond of walking as ever and have missed these paths."

He continued staring at her, seeming to wish for greater explanation, and she obliged. "Almost all winter—January, February, and most of March—I was confined indoors."

"Why?"

"My illness; it rendered me unable to walk even the shortest distance so… so I am doubly grateful for these rambles now."

There was something in his looks then that passed nearly immediately, something suggesting he would say more, but he did not.

He bowed instead. "Excuse me."

When he had gone, all possibility of pleasure in the day left with him. After some time spent trudging along the path to Longbourn with her eyes fixed on the ground beneath her feet, she thought better of it and turned back to Netherfield.

"Lizzy, tell me what you think of this." Jane came to Elizabeth's apartment almost as soon as she had returned and handed her a paper upon which was written a number of amusements to be enjoyed over the following nights.

"A musical party one night, which I daresay will lead some to dance. You know my husband; he is never in need of much inducement for a country dance. Games are always enjoyable, particularly when some are not as well acquainted as others, and what say you to some theatricals? I know some find it scandalous, but we need not pick anything too daring, and I feel that—"

"Jane." Elizabeth stared at the paper but could not imagine why her sister would go to such lengths for their small party. "This seems excellent fun, but you need not fear for our diversion. We are a small group, and I daresay we are easy enough together to create our own amusements."

Jane stared at her for a moment before the confusion cleared from her brow. "Did I not tell you of my other guests?"

"No. What other guests?"

Jane laid her paper on the bureau and moved to the closet, where she grumbled over the state of organisation found therein. "Did Martha arrange this? I need to speak to her, this is not my idea of order." She began to remove and re-arrange her sister's things. "Just a few guests, that is all."

"What guests?"

"Miss Jenny Haverhill, Miss Olivia Lacey, Lady Sophie Woodbridge." Jane busily folded some shawls. "Mr. Robert Egremont, Sir Edmund Hynde, and Mr. Wallace Rollings."

"And their wives?" Elizabeth gave her sister a pointed look that Jane was ostensibly too busy to notice.

"None of them are married."

Elizabeth groaned loudly, putting as much emphasis on it as she could, and sank into a chair. "Jane, this is not some matchmaking party, surely!"

"No, it is not."

"Why did not you tell me?"

"Am I required to tell you that I have invited people to my home?"

Elizabeth sighed. "Of course not."

"If you will recall, you told me when and how you were to arrive. Naturally, we wished for you as soon as we could have you, but we did not attempt to bring you here at this particular time."

Another grievance had placed itself upon Elizabeth's mind. "And I am the odd lady! Your numbers are thrown because of me!"

"Think nothing of that," said Jane. She finished playing with Elizabeth's clothing and closed the closet door, turning to face her. "Everyone who is coming is quite amiable, and I think we may all anticipate a great deal of diversion."

"I am sure," said Elizabeth faintly. A thousand scenes entered Elizabeth's mind, none of them in the least diverting or agreeable. Darcy with another lady, herself with another gentleman, everyone in the party paired off with someone else while she was conspicuously alone…the risk of mortification seemed rather enormous.

"Why does this distress you so?"

Elizabeth stared out the window and did not reply. Indeed, she could not reply, for nothing she could say would make sense to Jane.

"Lizzy…" Jane had waited until her sister turned her eyes to her. "You must want to marry someday."

Elizabeth gave an indifferent shrug and again looked away.

"I do not understand you."

"I just…I cannot marry someone who I do not love at least a little bit." *And I will never love anyone except Mr. Darcy, who despises me.*

"Knowing the happiness I have with my dear Charles, I would never want anything less for you. But dearest, surely you realise that falling in love does not happen when one is dedicated to solitary rambles and time spent reading? You need to put yourself forward a little."

As if I could possibly consider doing that! Elizabeth only just managed to stop herself from rolling her eyes. "Since our sister's disgrace—"

"Sister's disgrace! Lydia is a respectable married lady now—a mother!"

"When my father died—"

Jane gave Elizabeth a newly perfected, admonishing, motherly sort of look. "Lizzy, stop it. I cannot perceive what it is that ails you so, but enough now. No more being out of countenance. A little friendliness, some measure of your old spirits."

Jane stared expectantly, clearly not intending to be gainsaid, so Elizabeth said, "Very well. I will try my best."

Mr. Rollings was first to arrive at Netherfield two days later. He was a large red-headed gentleman who, despite a considerable fortune, always looked poorly tailored and unkempt. Even now, he entered the drawing room with his shirt tail out and a spot of something brown on his coat.

He was a great friend of Bingley's, who referred to him as "Jolly" Rollings, a nickname Mr. Rollings embraced with enthusiasm. He explained to Elizabeth, "People start out trying to call me Rollings, but soon enough, they slip into Jolly, and I figure it is better than some of the other names that might get attached to me!" He laughed loudly with his hand over his stomach.

Mr. Darcy had not been present when Jolly arrived but came into the drawing room as he was extending his greetings. "Darcy!" Jolly cried out and, to Elizabeth's surprise, embraced him, clapping his back with vigour.

Elizabeth hardly knew what to expect of Darcy in the midst of such a display, but Mr. Darcy's face bore no censure. He seemed rather pleased with the attention, a broad, genuine smile creasing his face as he offered to see Mr. Rollings to his apartment.

They remained there for some time, enough to miss the arrival of the next two guests: Miss Haverhill and Lady Sophie Woodbridge. Miss Haverhill was the beauty of the two, Elizabeth decided as she greeted them. She had hair of a reddish-gold hue and skin that looked like alabaster. She was kind, if a bit removed, when greeting Elizabeth, though Elizabeth noted she was much warmer to Jane.

Lady Sophie was invited at the particular request of Miss Bingley, Elizabeth learnt; evidently, the two were intimates. This was reason enough for Elizabeth to be wary of the lady, and her cool assessment of Netherfield along with several significant looks at Miss Bingley during the introductions (the meaning of which were lost on Elizabeth) put her on her guard.

Sir Edmund Hynde arrived hard on the heels of the two ladies. Elizabeth soon learnt that he boasted the largest fortune of the group, larger even than Mr. Darcy's at twelve thousand a year. Sir Edmund had a deep and abiding passion for all things equine, and he informed Elizabeth of it within four seconds of meeting her. He was disappointed to hear she was not much of a horsewoman and promised, if she would permit him a morning, that he would change her mind.

Mr. Egremont came about an hour before it was time to dine. He was an excessively handsome man, and it was immediately clear to Elizabeth that the ladies of their party noticed it too. Shoulders were straightened and gowns were smoothed when Mr. Egremont appeared. He had a charm about him that was rather intoxicating; there was nothing of either arrogance or artifice in the attentions he paid a lady, be she plain or pleasing. He listened intently, spoke with real warmth and interest, and on the whole, was very nearly irresistible.

They were a merry party at the dinner table that night. Most of the group were well acquainted, and formalities were quickly eschewed in favour of laughter and ease. Even Mr. Darcy relaxed, his posture and demeanour quite different from anything Elizabeth had ever before seen.

Miss Olivia Lacey arrived while they were at the table. Whereas the ladies had straightened and taken note when Mr. Egremont entered, the mere announcement of Miss Lacey's presence at Netherfield caused a surge of enthusiasm among the gentleman. With a quick look, Elizabeth confirmed that even Darcy took interest at Bingley's announcement of the arrival of their final guest. There were glances exchanged between the two gentlemen, and Bingley looked away with a little smile while Darcy appeared to redden just a bit. The suggestion of a blush caused Elizabeth to lower her head, immediately mortified.

When she met Miss Lacey in the drawing room with the other ladies present, she immediately understood her allure. That she was a beauty was undeniable. She had lustrous chestnut curls, large blue eyes, and a figure that was nearly perfect. She had a good fortune and a gentle temper but was a sensible girl as well. Elizabeth conversed with her for only a short while before she felt they might be friends.

"I began to think I might never be allowed out," Miss Lacey said with a little laugh, having told Elizabeth that she was twenty and had only recently enjoyed her first Season. "My mother holds to the notion that an elder sister must be wed before the younger may be seen. Of course, I felt much differently, but the dispute was put aside for the more agreeable occupations of shopping for clothes and planning for balls."

"Your sister has married, then?"

Miss Lacey nodded. "She just married in June, a match that pleased both sets of parents—not an easy thing to accomplish for any young lady. My new brother is the son of Sir Henry Jermyn of Suffolk."

"A good match, indeed."

"And she held a true affection for him. I believe it will be felicitous for them both." Miss Lacey took a tiny sip of her tea. "And now my mother is in a frenzy to see me settled."

Elizabeth laughed ruefully. "A plight I can understand all too well. In fact, I believe I might have it worse than you, for not only is my elder sister married but also two younger than I."

"Heaven forbid! Dear girl, I wonder that you can sit here so calmly." Miss Lacey gave Elizabeth a genuine grin.

"Oh, inside I am a quavering jumble, I assure you." Both ladies laughed.

"Well, you are so beautiful, I do not doubt your success," said Miss Lacey. Elizabeth blushed, but before she could reply, the gentlemen entered.

If Elizabeth had suspected the popularity of Miss Lacey before, she knew it now without a doubt. The gentlemen hastened to be at her side, reminding her of obligations—both real and imagined—to dance, play cards, and to walk or ride. Miss Lacey laughed and spoke amiably to them all but in a manner quite unlike the fawning coquettishness many ladies employed. As Elizabeth watched her converse with the men, it was clear that they not only admired her but genuinely liked her. It might have made Elizabeth hate her if she did not already like her so much herself.

Mr. Darcy did not enter the room with the other gentlemen but came in nearly a full quarter hour later. He did not immediately go to Miss Lacey, a fact that gave Elizabeth unreasonable satisfaction. He instead went to Jane, speaking to her in a low voice for a moment.

But that gave Miss Lacey the opportunity to go to him.

Elizabeth had to look away from the immediate tête-à-tête they formed. It was apparent they knew each other well; Darcy kissed her hand in greeting and guided her over to a settee where they spoke in low tones for nearly half an hour. Elizabeth thought she might be sick from watching them.

It was not long before the cry for music went up. Miss Bingley knew her duty and immediately urged Lady Sophie to take the instrument. With a falsely modest nod, Lady Sophie acquiesced.

She was, as Elizabeth might have suspected, a proficient, as were the ladies who exhibited after her. Miss Haverhill played well and sang even better while Miss Lacey sang with something like chagrin on her countenance and played loudly; it took little wit to deduce that she did not like the sound of her own voice. Miss Bingley was last to exhibit, playing with excessive sentimentality but overall proficiency.

As each lady had given them two songs, the exhibitions took up most of the evening and several of the gentlemen had begun to hide yawns behind closed fists by the time Miss Bingley finished. A light supper had been laid out, and Elizabeth noticed several glancing towards it with interest. Jane's dinner had been excellent, but it had been some hours since they had finished it.

Miss Bingley pursed her lips and preened delicately in response to the smattering of applause she received following her songs. "You are all too kind, I am sure. But I see my sister is going to treat us to more from her excellent cook, so shall we—"

"We have not heard from Miss Bennet." A deep voice, authoritative and just short of censuring, stilled everyone where they sat or stood.

Elizabeth's head jerked towards the settee where Mr. Darcy sat between Jolly and Miss Lacey. They had been a merry party as they sat, speaking quietly amongst themselves and laughing—usually, it seemed, in response to Jolly. Jolly's countenance still bore the vestiges of mirth, showing a slight smile below crinkled eyes and an air of expectation while Miss Lacey's bore the more gentle form of amusement of a demure grin behind her fan.

Mr. Darcy's face had no marks of amusement remaining upon it. He was serious and intent, looking directly at Elizabeth in her solitary chair during the moment of abashed silence that shot through the room.

It was Mr. Egremont who ended the moment of pained mortification. "But, of course, I should love to hear from Miss Bennet." This prompted several of the others to also proclaim their ardent desire to hear yet another lady take the instrument. Elizabeth tried to demur, saying she was sure to have other opportunities, but no one would hear of it.

Mr. Darcy, after his initial request, did not speak again, but his eyes remained on her—she could feel them on her skin—as she protested, acquiesced, and eventually made her way to the instrument. She determinedly looked at the music in front of her as she situated herself.

She wished for nothing more than to hurry through the exercise but knew she must play to the pleasure of Jane's guests. She had less fear for her performance than she might have had in earlier times; she had employed her time diligently in Cheltenham and was thus able to acquit herself nicely at the instrument.

Though in Cheltenham I was never made to practice under the censuring gaze of a man who despised me. She permitted her eyes to peek at him for the briefest of moments while she played.

His face was a mask, showing neither approval nor disapproval. His eyes had not moved nor had his body shifted; his attitude was one of complete and utter absorption in her performance although she knew it was not she who captivated him. She could never be so bold as to think she did; not now, in any case.

She forced her eyes back to her music and kept them there until the end of the song, when she permitted herself one last look in his direction. Then she wished she had not for his face had sagged into something bearing affinity to sorrow.

To make matters worse, he saw her look at him, and sorrow was quickly thrown off in favour of his customary hauteur. He turned diligent eyes on Miss Lacey, who had just begun to speak to him on a subject that would remain a mystery to Elizabeth. He did not so much as glance at her again.

"How lovely her voice is."

Darcy was considerably vexed with himself for having urged Elizabeth to play and sing. And embarrassed as well—what must she think? That he still cared whether she sang or not? How stupid he must seem to her, all but begging her to sing when he should be well pleased to see her silent.

His mortification made him reply to Miss Lacey in severe accents. "She is considerably more practiced than the last time I heard her play."

"So you are well acquainted with Miss Bennet? She seems an amiable girl. I enjoyed speaking to her."

Darcy did not feel he could give any answer that would not betray his true feelings and merely nodded.

"I have never seen her in town. Did she not go for the Season?"

He swallowed; evidently, Miss Lacey would vex him by insisting that he speak on the very subject he would rather not. "I believe her father, when he lived, did not like it."

"With five daughters to marry off, I should think her mother would have insisted on it," she said with a little laugh to show that no censure was intended. "But she told me three of her sisters are married already, so it seems to have done them no ill."

"Save for Mrs. Bingley, none have made matches of any distinction." He spoke before he had time to censure himself. The unanticipated sharpness of such a reply was not lost on the lady; her eyes went wide, then she lowered her gaze to the floor.

He cleared his throat awkwardly but was silent, wholly unable to think of even the most commonplace remark. He was sure his distress showed on his face, but he could say nothing to either explain or disclaim it without revealing too much.

An echo of the past came to him. When Elizabeth had been introduced to Fitzwilliam, she had laughingly said that she and Darcy were not friends. He now used her words with Miss Lacey. "Forgive me. Miss Elizabeth Bennet and I are not the best of friends. Pray, do not think ill of her because of it; there is merely a difference in opinion between us that cannot be overcome."

He forced an indifference to his countenance while Miss Lacey assured him that she understood him completely and would harbour no ill will towards either party because of it.

W<small>HEN THE HALLS OF</small> N<small>ETHERFIELD HAD FALLEN SILENT</small>, M<small>ISS</small> C<small>AROLINE</small> Bingley exited her bedchamber. In one hand, she held a bottle of some fine brandy that Mr. Hurst had given Charles, and in the other, she had a delightfully naughty tome titled *The School of Venus* from Louisa. She tiptoed down the hall, entering the guest wing. At the door of interest, she rapped twice, sharply but softly.

Lady Sophie came to the door immediately. "At last. Come."

With a giggle, Caroline entered and soon the two ladies were comfortable on the rug in front of the fireplace, sipping brandy from teacups (Caroline forgot to bring glasses), and paging through *The School of Venus*.

"I have done that." Lady Sophie pointed to a rather scandalous-looking drawing and Caroline gasped.

"No, you have not!"

"I was engaged once," Lady Sophie reminded her. "One cannot go to one's marriage bed in complete ignorance, you know."

Lady Sophie had been engaged to an older, wealthy gentleman from Kent. Because she was only seventeen at the time, her parents had insisted on a long courtship during which her intended—who claimed he was five and forty (but who most said was actually over fifty)—suffered apoplexy and died. They said a maid found him, but Caroline had heard rumours that the alleged maid was actually his mistress, and the place where she "found" him was in his bed. Moreover, there were rumours that the mistress had put something in his drink to kill him, for she had grown quite mad with jealousy when she heard he was going to marry.

Lady Sophie had emerged from it all with a nice settlement from her intended's estate and the intention to marry for love. She was fond of saying to her friends and acquaintances, "I am one and twenty, I have forty thousand pounds, and if it were not for my nose, I think I should be rather pretty. So I will marry where I like."

"So you let him..." Caroline allowed the question to dangle in the air between them.

"Oh, my dear, of course I did. Would you buy a gown if you did not first see whether the material suited you?"

Caroline laughed. "No, I do not suppose I would. But what if...?"

Lady Sophie understood her. "I do not mean to say a lady should be free with her favours, but once something of an understanding is between you—even if it is as yet unspoken—a little mutual pleasure-seeking is not only acceptable but advisable."

Caroline thought about this, but before she could say more, Lady Sophie closed the book with a decisive thump. "Enough of that. Let us examine the possibilities before us. I think I could be persuaded into a few indiscretions with Darcy—could you?" She giggled, taking another large swallow of the brandy.

Caroline smiled. "My best wishes in that endeavour; I do not think I know of another man who is more prudish."

"A shame." Lady Sophie shook her head sadly. "But he must wish to marry. Is he not thirty? The time is upon him."

"No, he is not yet thirty, but I agree, I think he must soon seek a marriage partner."

"And why not find one here?" Lady Sophie smiled over her teacup. "Your sister has arranged a small party but with excellent choices among the guests."

"You consider Darcy a potential suitor?"

"I consider them *all* potential suitors"

"Even Jolly?"

"But of course! Have you seen his home? Lovely place and quite modern. I should find myself comfortable in it, I think. Hire a good valet to clean him up, and he would do nicely. And what about you? I would presume your sister would like to see you settled?"

Caroline shrugged. "No married lady wants an unmarried sister lingering about, though she is far too sweet to say so. Miss Bennet is to live with us too, so I daresay, we will be subject to a great many of these house parties until both of us are disposed of."

"Miss Bennet is pretty," said Lady Sophie. After a moment, she added, "I noticed Darcy looked at her often, but there seemed to be something of distaste on his countenance. Then again, Darcy often appears to be sucking on something sour."

Caroline laughed and tilted to the side, spilling a bit of her drink onto the counterpane. "That he does, but in this case, I believe he has just cause."

"Oh? Sounds like a story."

"Yes." Caroline nodded vehemently. "Though I cannot say I know what it is."

Lady Sophie stared at her expectantly, the light from the fireplace contriving to lend shadows and angles to her face that made her look almost feral. Caroline smirked at her.

"It was August, a year ago. My brother and I had been invited to Pemberley as we customarily are—"

"Oh, I love Pemberley." Lady Sophie sighed.

Caroline pursed her lips disapprovingly at such a familiar remark, knowing that Lady Sophie had only toured Pemberley's public rooms. "Miss Elizabeth Bennet was in a nearby town called Lambton with her relations. They had been on holiday, and Darcy met them when they toured his grounds.

"He behaved rather strangely while she was there. Why, one evening in the drawing room, he nearly took my head off for saying she looked tan."

"Tan?" Lady Sophie asked. "People often get a little brown on holiday."

"Quite right. I scarcely mentioned it, and he gave me a set down that you could not imagine." Caroline clucked indignantly. "Then she came to dinner, and it took little to understand that there was something between them. Little looks and touches…quite beyond propriety. I half expected an announcement."

"To be sure." Lady Sophie's eyes were wide and alit with scandalised pleasure. "I have never seen him behave so with any lady."

"No, nor I," Caroline agreed. "Then she left, and he sulked about something dreadful! Acted like some green miss whose heart was broken; I hardly knew where to look. I was vastly relieved when my brother shortened our stay, though I was less pleased when he brought us here.

"So, I did believe that his heart was lost to her, much as that notion amazed me. But then he refused to stand up with my brother at his wedding. He has not come to see him until now, and they were such friends before. I cannot imagine what came between them, but there it is, and I have to believe Eliza Bennet is involved in the matter. I think Mr. Darcy hates her."

"Perhaps she refused his offer."

"If it were any other lady, I would agree, but her? Come now. No fortune of her own, and she receives an offer from the likes of him? She would have to have run mad to refuse."

"True." Lady Sophie thought about it more. "Perhaps he learnt something about her to put him off. Some secret that she hid from him."

"Possibly. He has never approved of any of the Miss Bennets. He did all he could to prevent my brother's marriage."

"Is that so? Yet Mr. and Mrs. Bingley appear so well suited."

"Well suited does not always mean suitable," Caroline said, amending her own opinions to those of Mr. Darcy. "It was hardly a good match for Charles, but it is done, and we are all resolved to it. However, it does not follow that we must suffer all Bennets hereafter. Darcy is clearly displeased that Eliza has come; that is all we need to know, is it not?"

Lady Sophie shrugged elaborately. "For whatever mysteries might lie between Darcy and Miss Bennet, I am sure it is no concern of mine. Darcy is there for the taking, and that is *all* I care about."

With a smile, the two ladies clinked their teacups.

Chapter Four

The day after the Netherfield guests' arrival proved rainy, confining everyone indoors. Darcy delighted in it; he needed time to himself, and he claimed to be occupied by estate business. Dinner was the first time he gathered with the others that day.

He entered the drawing room before dinner to find a high-spirited group; the confinement of the day had left them all rather energetic. In one corner, Bingley, Egremont, and Sir Edmund engaged in a debate over some matter of political interest while Jolly entertained Miss Bingley and Lady Sophie with tales of mishap and mischief. Mrs. Bingley spoke to Miss Haverhill and Miss Lacey in low, gentle tones punctuated by soft, ladylike laughter.

Elizabeth sat apart in a little chair by the window, quietly looking out over the lawn with a closed book by her side. Her hands were folded in her lap and her gaze, though directed, seemed absent. An unexpected pang tore through him.

So beautiful. For a moment, he permitted himself to imagine the situation as it might have been. He would have entered with her on his arm, and they would have joined Bingley's group perhaps. She might have smiled at him as he spoke to the other men on the Treaties of Reichenbach, possibly even offering a few opinions of her own. Although military affairs held little interest for her, he could never accuse her of being ignorant of recent events.

The picture was so clear in his mind—her eyes sparkling for him, her cheeks pink, and her whole being radiating confidence—that it startled him to realise she still sat there so withdrawn and quiet. Hardly a picture of triumph.

He took a step towards her, knowing not what he wished to say or do, only to be halted by Lady Sophie. "Darcy, we began to despair of you. What are you about, locked away all day?"

The interruption stopped him from what surely would have been a mistake. "Quite unavoidable, my lady."

She smiled up at him, and he offered a small smile in return that she took as invitation enough to slide her hand into his arm. From his side vision, he noticed that Egremont had detached himself from his little group of gentlemen and approached Elizabeth. Darcy steered Lady Sophie in the opposite direction.

"You must have felt your ears burning last night." Lady Sophie smiled coquettishly at him as they arrived at the windows on the other side of the room.

"Why is that?"

"Miss Bingley and I spoke of you."

"I see."

He pretended to glance at the mantel clock near where Elizabeth sat and saw that Egremont had made her laugh, after which she said something that made him laugh. Anger, familiar and comforting, rose up in his chest.

"Do you not wish to know what we said about you?"

"What?"

"Naughty boy!" she cried. "You have not been attending our conversation."

"Pray, forgive me." He turned so that Elizabeth was removed from his vision. "I am listening to you. You said you spoke of me with Miss Bingley."

"Surely, you wish to know why."

"I believe you wish me to know."

"Perhaps I do." She smiled at him in a sidelong way. She was a pretty girl, not beautiful but handsome enough. She flirted with him, and it was his duty to play to it.

"Pray do not let me suspend your pleasure then; I am keen to oblige you. Do tell me of what you and Miss Bingley spoke."

She pursed her lips. "No, I do not wish you to merely oblige me; I wish for you to yearn to know."

Such silliness! He had never been willing to endure a lady who simpered, but now it was something of a relief. He would never fall in love with a Lady Sophie. He could never have his heart broken by such a creature.

"I cannot be so disagreeable as to dispute you. I yearn to know of what you spoke. Indeed, I shall go mad if you do not tell me."

The flatness of his tone betrayed and, indeed, exaggerated his disinterest, and they both laughed a little. A glance over his shoulder showed that Elizabeth paid them no mind, contenting herself with Egremont and his attentions. They had stopped their chuckling and spoke in an earnest manner, their heads tilted towards one another and bodies close. Almost unconsciously, Darcy found himself leaning closer to Lady Sophie.

"Miss Bingley believes you do not approve of Mrs. Bingley and her sister."

"Quite the contrary."

"So you do approve of them?"

Darcy hesitated only a fraction of a second. "Mrs. Bingley is a fine lady, and I assure you, if I did not approve of the lady unequivocally, I should not place myself within her hospitality. Is this what you and Miss Bingley spoke about? If it was, I must say that it was a wasted conversation. Surely, my opinions, favourable or otherwise, do not merit such attention."

Lady Sophie understood that the subject had been dismissed and adjusted accordingly. "Indeed, that was not our primary subject. We wondered why you remain unmarried."

"Not yet married?" He forced another chuckle. "Am I so old that to remain a bachelor is extraordinary? I am not yet thirty."

"True, but you possess a good fortune, and surely, you desire an heir. Either you never met a suitable lady, or you have been crossed in love." She smiled and leant in. "Poor Darcy. I imagine it to be the latter."

Her comment was unfortunate in its timing, for just then he heard the sound that haunted his dreams: Elizabeth's laugh. He could not stop his eyes from drifting towards her and Egremont, laughing within their cosy little circle.

He pulled his eyes away but not fast enough; Lady Sophie eyed him curiously.

In abrupt tones, he said, "I am much occupied with matters at Pemberley of late."

Lady Sophie turned her eyes to Elizabeth and back to Darcy. "Mm," she said in an agreeing tone. "I am sure you are. No time for diversion—was that how it was?"

"Quite so."

"Well then"—she touched the tip of her tongue lightly to her upper lip—"permit me to make it my sworn duty to see you amply diverted now."

Darcy wished to appear as enchanted by Lady Sophie as Elizabeth appeared interested in Egremont; he soon found he could not. Lady Sophie liked to flirt; she was fond of long, expressive looks, sidelong glances, little taps on his arm with her fan, and appearing to be overcome with mirth. No doubt she understood these postures exhibited her dimples nicely, but he soon realised that tolerating such antics was exhausting.

Darcy found himself between Miss Bingley and Lady Sophie at dinner. It was not a seat that pleased him. He had grown weary of Lady Sophie's attentions, and adding Miss Bingley to the mix could not be to his advantage. Miss Bingley required little in the way of encouragement before she became cloying. The only safety was in silence, though it would condemn him to listen to the pair speak over him on subjects of their choosing: vicious gossip and tiresome *on dits*. His expectations for the evening were poor indeed.

There is one situation in which the requirement for conversation during dinner is lifted: when one's mouth is actively engaged in eating. Mrs. Bingley's table aided him in this; a masterpiece of culinary delights, it contained many of Darcy's favourites, including a beef steak and pigeon pie along with asparagus in a crust.

Darcy undertook his meal with small bites, and he chewed for prolonged periods of time with great deliberation. Any venture of his dining companions into conversation met with a prolonged silence whilst he finished his mouthful, cleared it with a sip of wine, and then said, "What?"

Miss Bingley soon understood his design and was not pleased. She did all she could to rouse his speech.

"How is dear Georgiana? No doubt she is seeing to her wardrobe in town. I am certain no one will have finer clothes than she will, yet only she could wear them with such a becoming air!"

This speech was evidently the cue for Lady Sophie to ask about Georgiana, and she did so with great alacrity. Miss Bingley responded with equal anxiety to please, praising Georgiana as the most charming, most worthy, most accomplished lady who had ever set foot in London.

Darcy grunted in response to these effusions.

As the soup was being removed, he looked down the table at Elizabeth. She was on the other end at Bingley's left. Bingley, Darcy saw, had heartfelt regard for his sister-in-law. There was warmth in his eyes and a smile on his face.

On Elizabeth's other side was Egremont. Egremont's affection was also rather obvious, though of a different variety than Bingley's. A bit of beef lodged in Darcy's throat as he viewed them, and he took a large swallow of wine to remove it.

"I do believe Eliza has earned herself a suitor." Miss Bingley made a little clucking sound. "I am sure I never saw what there was to admire in her. However, she seems to have a way of enrapturing a man." She watched him carefully after this little speech, but he would not give her the satisfaction of showing his true feelings. His eyes and mouth kept to their purpose.

"Shocking speech," said Lady Sophie with a laugh. "Is she not your sister? It is quite unlike you to be unkind to your kin."

Miss Bingley nibbled on a morsel of bread. "Hmm…she is sister to my brother. I suppose I must claim her, though I would wish that the years of our acquaintance had brought with them a subduing of Eliza's animal spirits."

Her eyes slid towards Darcy, but he was unmoved. Let Caroline shred Elizabeth if she liked; it was nothing to him. Resolutely, he spooned a large chunk of boiled potato into his mouth.

Lady Sophie seemed to notice his disinclination for such conversation. "Well, I like her," she declared. "There is something rather agreeable in her air."

"Mr. Darcy has always found it so." Caroline tittered at this, and he shot her an angry look. It was sufficient to quell her. She and Lady Sophie went on to giggle and gossip over others of their acquaintance, persons not at the table. Darcy did the best he could to disregard them as he ate.

Just as he believed he might burst, Bingley rose to his feet, and the table fell silent. "It seems rather difficult to believe, but it has been two years since the first time I ever saw my wife at a little assembly in Meryton. That time seems both a lifetime past and like it was yesterday, but my wife and I thought it might be quite diverting to spend the evening in the same manner that we did that night."

A wave of conversation went around the table. *Bingley and his infernal need to dance!*

"Do you mean here?" Jolly asked. "Or is there an assembly in Meryton?"

"In Meryton!" Bingley cried out. "Will it not be amusing?"

Darcy might happily have killed him were he not suffering from misery of the acutest kind in his gut. For a moment, he considered begging off.

But no, at an assembly he would be made to dance with Miss Bingley, an exertion of half an hour. If he remained at Netherfield, she would certainly stay with him, and he would have to endure her society for several hours. The assembly was undoubtedly the lesser of two evils.

He set off to dress for the amusement, resolved to don his loosest breeches. Alas, his man would prove no use to him, insisting that Darcy wear his most snug ones.

"My grey satin would do nicely," he offered.

"No," said Fields, busily setting out his toilette. "They have suffered an unfortunate tear that I must attend to. My apologies; I overlooked it earlier. The tear is in just such a place as to be hidden from all but the most careful scrutiny, but I fear if they are worn, it will become irreparable."

"Then the cream-coloured?"

Fields gave him an odd look. "The ones you wear in the morning?" His opinion of such a sartorial sin was not hidden, and Darcy bowed to the inevitable.

Fields had a devil of a time buttoning him into the breeches, and Darcy, for the first time of the night but by no means the last, rued his overindulgence at dinner. He uttered a soft grunt as Fields tugged the fabric tight, pinching into his swollen gut most cruelly.

"I fear that I have done your raiment an injustice in the laundry."

"No." Darcy groaned his confession. "I have only myself to blame. I ate far too much this evening at dinner."

"Never mind, sir, we will have you tucked in, and all will be right and tight."

"The tight part of that statement, I cannot doubt," said Darcy, already in a foul humour.

The distress in his gut could only be made worse by the ride to the assembly. It was a distance of merely two miles, and the road was well maintained, but Bingley kept a loose-sprung carriage, and thus the slightest irregularity in the road tossed them all about.

The populace of Meryton was delighted to see them; the Bingleys were now the first family in the district, and as such, their guests were also honoured and revered. Elizabeth was greeted with particular delight; her neighbours had not seen her for many months. Darcy was close enough to overhear as friends eagerly came to her, and she said repeatedly that she was well recovered from the illness she had suffered.

When the ladies finished fussing over Elizabeth, the gentlemen were eager to dance with her, and she was taken away as soon as the first notes sounded. He watched her go, his anger joining the roiling mass of food in his gut to create more distress for him as she danced as merrily as she always had.

Well, perhaps not quite as merrily. It was her eyes, he observed. Though her lips would smile, her eyes simply did not. There was no sparkle of amusement or laughter in them, no matter what the curve of her mouth said.

You are not the injured party, he informed her in his mind as he watched her skipping, circling form move through the pattern. *How dare you appear so miserable?*

He could not observe her any longer and began to move about the room, hoping a little exercise would soon relieve him; instead, it only increased his misery. There was in vogue a particular French pomatum used to fix the hairstyles of both ladies and gentlemen that caused Darcy to either sneeze or form a headache whenever he smelled it. He detected more than a whiff of it on his first tour of the ballroom; evidently, those at the assembly quite preferred it.

He did all he could to avoid it, apprehending that a sneeze could have disastrous consequences for his breeches and himself, but he was required to move away from the wall and dance with Mrs. Hurst. When the dance ended, he escorted her back to her husband, who had retired to a table where the heaviest drinkers of the party were seated. As misfortune would have it, these gentlemen bore heavy applications of the preparation, and the scent was nearly overwhelming.

By some perverse mischance, Hurst, who rarely spoke more than a sentence, suddenly had a long, rambling story to tell, and Darcy was unable to extricate himself. His nose tickled, and he turned his head, but it was of no use. The tickling sensation built until he could abstain no more.

He sneezed.

The first feeling was one of profound relief. As the closures on his breeches gave way, his beleaguered, over-stuffed gut was released, and he was less nauseated and more able to breathe. That satisfaction lasted only a moment; horror dawned as he apprehended that he was about to expose himself in a most rude manner. Darcy held his forearm tightly across his stomach, hoping it would look like he had tucked his hand into his waistcoat in some fashionable sort of attitude. Excusing himself from Hurst and his ilk, he departed, praying for some solution to his problem.

He scurried as elegantly as one can scurry to the window and turned his back to the room, fumbling at his waist and hoping that somehow the situation might correct itself. It did not, and as he was no seamstress (nor did he have thread and needle even if he were), to fix it himself seemed unlikely.

A look about the room offered no hope, and surely, if any lady saw him now, he would be required to offer marriage immediately!

The window held the answer, for framed within it, he saw Bingley's carriage. He sighed with relief; he would return to Netherfield and send the carriage back for the rest of the party. He hurriedly exited the assembly hall, speaking to no one and clutching his clothing as it threatened to leave him.

To his surprise, Bingley stood by his carriage although he did not appear desirous of ending his evening. "Darcy?" His brow furrowed, he came towards his friend. "Are you well?"

Darcy already had one hand on the door. "I…no, I fear I must go back to Netherfield at once."

"But surely you did not—"

Darcy leant into his friend's ear. "I have split my trousers."

"What?" Confusion turned to delight as Bingley took it upon himself to inspect the garment that Darcy vowed would be consigned to the fire as soon as possible. "Well, they do say once a man has hit thirty, he can expect—"

"I am not thirty," Darcy snapped. "I sneezed, and this happened. I believe the buttons must have been loosened, but in any case, I am off for Netherfield."

Bingley clapped him on the back as Darcy opened the door and prepared to enter. "So much the better! I am sorry you cannot stay, but I was loath to see Lizzy off on her own. You will be joining her on the journey."

Inside the carriage, Elizabeth blushed with mortification. She had not been able to hear everything said between the friends, but she understood that Mr. Darcy had an urgent need to return to Netherfield, and until the last moment, he did not realise he would be escorting her. She awaited his reply with dread, for surely he would tell his friend he would not share a private carriage ride with her. But what reason could he give?

Darcy entered the carriage somewhat awkwardly, one arm held firm against his waist. She offered a small, discomfited smile when his gaze met hers, but he looked away, using his free arm to situate himself across from her. Though the shade was drawn, his eyes remained directed at the window as they began to move.

He did not remove his arm from his waist, and after they had travelled for some minutes in silence, she ventured to say, "I hope you have not injured your arm."

The sound of her voice made him startle, but he did not immediately answer. His face rested in shadows, and she could not make him out. Uncertainty drove her to continue speaking. "Mr. Irving, he…many people do not suppose because he is so slight…but indeed, he is quite strong, and he will sometimes challenge newcomers to—"

"Nothing of the sort has happened, I assure you," he pronounced in his haughtiest tones.

Elizabeth dropped her eyes, embarrassed by the strangeness between them that made all attempts at conversation impossible. Humiliated tears stung her eyes, but she blinked them back; under no circumstances would she want Mr. Darcy's pity because she cried.

How dreadful to be in the presence of lost love! I must endure not only the pain of what I lost but also the agony of what might have been. We are not only strangers but enemies. If we had never loved each other, at least we might be friends or amiable acquaintances.

Would she want that? She hardly knew. Some days she wished she had never known him; other days she thought that to have lived her life without her nine days of exquisite felicity would have been no life at all. She sighed.

"My breeches are torn."

Surprised, she looked up. He was staring out the window again although there was surely nothing to see in the passing landscape. His voice had lost its certainty, and he muttered, "Ate too much and then sneezed…tightest trousers I own…fasteners did not…"

An impulse towards violent laughter arose in Elizabeth, but she subdued it. Moments later, Darcy laughed. He laughed rather loudly and in a prolonged manner such that she could not help but join him with a small giggle.

She was quiet long before he was, and when he had finished, she offered, "That must have made for an excessively unpleasant evening. I am sorry you had to suffer it."

"Thank you." They fell into another silence then, as difficult as the others, but Elizabeth imagined that some of the uneasiness between them had gone.

As Netherfield came into sight, Elizabeth realised she faced a possible problem. "I wonder that my brother so easily put me into a carriage with a man having difficulties with his trousers," she said, taking care to speak calmly. It would not do for Mr. Darcy to think her statement carried with it some hidden meaning.

He understood immediately. "These are intended for the fire, Miss Bennet. I would not rouse talk among the servants."

"Surely, your valet is trustworthy."

"You take an eager interest in my attire."

Elizabeth blushed deeply and turned immediately to stare out the window. "Forgive me."

They were in the drive, and the horses were drawing to a stop. Elizabeth knew she ought not to say more, but she did nevertheless. "They are the same that you wore at the first assembly you attended in Hertfordshire, I think."

Mr. Darcy had his back to her as they left the carriage and spoke his answer into a noisy wind. She could not make it out.

DARCY SUCCEEDED IN HIS EFFORT TO REACH HIS BEDCHAMBER WITHOUT detection. He nearly tore the hated breeches from his body and pulled his jacket off just as violently. He stood, breathing heavily, staring at the two garments on the floor.

Elizabeth was incorrect. He had not worn these items in Hertfordshire two autumns past; indeed, he had not even owned them then. When he had worn them was in Kent, on a certain night in the parsonage house at Hunsford. "Cursed. Nothing good can come of wearing you."

A fire was laid, and he bent, holding the breeches near the flames. All that was wanting was for him to release them, and they, with their tendency to bring him misfortune, would be gone.

Yet she had noticed them. The idea pleased him, and he despised himself for being pleased by anything to do with her. With stern resolve, he extended his arm just a bit more, allowing the offending garment to dangle precariously close to destruction.

Somehow, he could not release the breeches. They were made of agony and hope, these dreadful things, and one went hand in hand with another. Acting beyond his reason and his will, his arm retreated, still clutching them. It took him a moment in which he contemplated all manner of weakness

—having the breeches repaired, saving them—but reason won out. He thrust his arm forward, consigning the article to the flames.

He watched until the garment was ash, reminding himself that he must not soften in his feeling towards Elizabeth, no matter how much his heart might want otherwise.

THE DAY FOLLOWING WAS NEARLY PERFECT IN ITS AUTUMN GLORY: BRISK air, blue sky, and shining sun reminding them that it would not always be so. It was a day made for being outside, and Darcy found himself eagerly anticipating a time of gentlemanly pursuits. The other men were of like mind; even Hurst had a quick step and a lively air.

Spirits were high, and the conversation moved easily as they set out into the fields with their guns and the dogs. For some time, talk was of the usual subjects for a shooting party: guns, horses, and the general state of the fields before them compared to their home fields. But Jolly soon became the object of conversation. He had recently commissioned a new carriage, a rather fine landau with every modern convenience and interior luxury.

"The very thing one might present to a future spouse," Egremont hinted.

"Oh yes!" Bingley was quick to pick up on the teasing. "I purchased one quite like it for Mrs. Bingley while we were yet betrothed."

"A single man cannot need such a large conveyance," Hurst opined. "A man that purchases one has a family in his mind."

"I like to travel in comfort," Jolly protested. "Nothing more than that, I assure you!"

"No man likes too much comfort," said Bingley. "A man prefers speed, and a landau will not yield him that."

"Tell us of this lady," said Egremont at the same time that Sir Edmund expressed a wish to know about the horses. Such a fine equipage would not be ordered without a new set of dappled greys, surely.

"There is no lady." Jolly groaned. "Of horseflesh, I am well able to speak, but there is nothing to say of a lady!"

This prompted much good-humoured ribaldry about a secret engagement with a lady of varying reputation depending upon the speaker. At last, Jolly was forced to cry out, "My good lads, had I a lady attached to me, there would be no secret about it!"

Darcy listened to it all with a faint smile touching his lips, though he did not join in their banter. He had lain awake for some time the night prior, thinking of Elizabeth and wondering for the millionth time what to make of it all. His thoughts and the confused melancholy they produced yet lingered.

There was something strange about this business of Wickham's marriage, though Darcy could not say he truly understood it. Something pricked at him—was it intuition or merely a long history with a man who never failed to create problems in Darcy's life? If nothing else, it was shocking to find him married to the youngest Bennet sister.

He could not soon forget that Elizabeth had first held Wickham in tender regard. A remembrance from that hated evening at Hunsford came to his head: *Who that knows what his misfortunes have been can help feeling an interest in him?*

After some time, there was game enough killed, and the gentlemen set off in the direction of the house, the servants behind them bearing their trophies. Darcy, too, lagged a bit, and before long, Bingley dropped back to walk with him.

"Darcy, I cannot tell you how good it is to be in your society once more. Pray, let us not permit such time to elapse again between our visits."

"Bingley, you are too good." To his friend's enquiring look, Darcy added, "I should think you would be quite resolved to have no part of me when I have been such a poor friend to you."

"Ah." Bingley made a dismissive motion with his hand. "Who can think of such things? Better left in the past."

"You seem very happy, and I am delighted for you. I have never been so well pleased to find myself wholly incorrect."

When his friend's agreeable chuckle had died, Darcy spoke again. "I was surprised to hear that Wickham had married."

"You did not know? Yes, he and Lydia were married September last." Bingley chuckled again in a manner that seemed a trifle forced. "They were blessed with Miss Wickham rather quickly—in January. Twelfth night in fact."

"I see."

Bingley made a little grimace but quickly rose to the defence of his brother. "I must say, Wickham has become something of a credit to the family. He works for Mr. Gardiner—you must remember him—and is a fine man of business, or so I am told. They have a charming little house near Cheapside."

"And was his employment part of the inducement into matrimony? A share of Mr. Gardiner's business, perhaps?"

Bingley greeted this enquiry with easy indifference. "I have never been told the whole of it, but I think it is safe to imagine so. In any case, it allows the family to keep an eye on him."

"As well they should. Wickham is not to be trusted, no matter how reformed he might appear."

Bingley gave a little shrug. "He is a married man now. Age might have done for him what no amount of schooling or scolding ever could."

"I thought that Wickham favoured Miss Elizabeth, so I am curious how it is that he is married to her sister."

"Wickham and Lizzy? No, I never saw any of that. Hallo there! Samuel!"

The last was directed at the man carrying their game, to whom Bingley gave unnecessary instruction about where to take the kill. The look on the man's face was respectfully perplexed, but Darcy understood well enough: the subject of Wickham and Elizabeth was not to be discussed. Darcy fell silent; he would not disoblige his friend.

Bingley gave him a smack on the shoulder. "The dampness in the air has given me a chill! Let us find some port and a fire to warm us."

Chapter Five

While the gentlemen occupied themselves with guns and dogs, the ladies received callers from the neighbourhood. First to appear were their nearest neighbours: Mr. and Mrs. Collins of Longbourn. Since her arrival, Elizabeth had seen little of Charlotte—only once and all too briefly—and she awaited the opportunity to speak to her old friend with great eagerness.

She took great pleasure from seeing Charlotte so well in looks. Charlotte wore a becoming gown of jonquil and had her hair styled in a newer, more mature way. She had also a new air about her; she was no longer the wife of a country parson but mistress of one of the principle estates in the area. She was a mother and a wife, and she wore it all in a becoming way.

Charlotte greeted Jane's friends with a dignified ease while Elizabeth held back, awaiting her. When at last Charlotte came to her, the two friends could only smile a moment before indulging themselves in an embrace.

"You are beautiful as ever, Eliza," Charlotte said with a final little kiss to her cheek.

"I fear you are looking at the wrong sister." Elizabeth gave a little laugh. "I shall forgive you, but only if you come here at once and tell me all the neighbourhood gossip."

There was much to be told; Elizabeth had heard some of the latest news but only in the most cursory fashion. Charlotte's brother Charles was recently engaged to a girl from a nearby town, and Mary King had returned to Meryton still unmarried. Sir William Lucas had badly injured his leg in a fall from his horse but did well with his walking stick, and one of Mrs. Long's nieces was married to Mr. Chamberlayne. It was, in all, a satisfying recitation. Elizabeth was pleased to hear that her old friends and acquaintances seemed to be getting on so well.

"And how is my mother? I am surprised she did not come with you today."

"She is unwell," Charlotte replied. "An attack of her nerves." With this bit of information, Charlotte included a rueful smile and a look that Elizabeth did not misunderstand. It was entirely likely that nothing was wrong with her mother save that Mrs. Bennet had yielded to her desire to be cosseted a bit.

"May I be of assistance in some way? Shall I come to her?"

"No, no." Charlotte shook her head firmly. "She has hired a new maid of late, an Irish lady, who has everything well in hand. I think the less made of it, the better."

"If it becomes any sort of trial to you—"

"No, no," Charlotte was quick to assure her. "It does not. It is my pleasure to provide whatever small solace to your mother that I can."

"I cannot feel easy knowing you are doing what my sisters and I ought to do. Pray, tell me Kitty is helpful."

"Kitty is very helpful," Charlotte said firmly. "You need not be anxious. If I need you, I shall send for you; I promise. Will that do?"

Elizabeth agreed, and Charlotte moved away to join Jane in conversation. Elizabeth drifted towards a window, staring out at the fields in the distance, no doubt where the gentlemen were shooting.

The carriage ride she had shared with Mr. Darcy the night prior would not leave her thoughts. She tried to move away from the recollection, forcing herself into contemplation of a book, a conversation with someone, or any other diversion, but it did her no good. Thoughts would intrude like a sweet fog sending in misty tendrils to obscure anything else in her mind.

They had laughed together—awkwardly, it was true, but it had been done —and they had spoken in a manner almost amiable. Could she hope that they might be once again friendly, if not actually friends?

Perhaps if I were to offer an apology… She dared not finish her thought. She should expect nothing of him. She had taken too much already.

Her mind warred with her heart. Her heart wished to approach him, to apologise to him, and to hope in some way to reconcile with him, but her mind knew that such a purpose could not be achieved. It was best to leave him to his own devices. He had tried to depart once he knew she was there, but his friends—her relations—had persuaded him otherwise. It did not mean he was happy to bear her society.

Do not inflict yourself upon him, she admonished herself.

SOME HOURS LATER IN THE DRAWING ROOM, WITH NAUSEA BOILING IN HER gut and her hands clasped together to prevent their shaking, she wished she had heeded her own good advice.

At least I apologised. That is something.

It had seemed fortuitous to find him alone in the drawing room before dinner. He turned to her, his countenance forbidding, and greeted her with a nod that appeared to pain him. Alas, it did not deter her as it should have done. She returned a curtsey on shaking legs after which he turned back to his contemplation of nature as seen through the window.

Elizabeth edged nearer to him on silent feet. When she was about a foot away, she said, "Mr. Darcy," in a voice that was thin and much higher than usual.

He had turned towards her with painstaking slowness, and she moved another step closer despite the lack of warmth in his face. Would that she had taken his silent rebuff!

Alas, she had persisted. "Sir, I…I wish to say that I…"

He cleared his throat and looked down a moment before raising his eyes to view her again. "What?"

She inhaled deeply, holding fast to foolish courage. "I wanted to tell you that I am sorry."

He had merely stared at her.

"That is to say, I know that I have hurt you—"

In a mercilessly civil tone she would never forget, he said, "Indeed, you have not. I am perfectly well."

Perfectly well. Those words rang in her mind even now.

She had stood there, somewhat agape, with her hands clenching against one another, trying not to turn and run. Finally, she broke the dreadful moment. "Very well… Nevertheless, I am sorry."

He nodded again, and she backed away. Relief from the horrible moment came with the announcement of Miss Haverhill. Elizabeth thought she had never been so glad to see someone.

Jolly was hard on Miss Haverhill's heels, entering the room with bonhomie and bluster enough for twelve people. Elizabeth shrank back into the edges of the room where she stood even now, pretending interest in the stack of music by the pianoforte.

She considered feigning illness and withdrawing to her room for the evening, A coward's way out, but Jane would not question it. Jane was ever fearful for her sister's health, believing a relapse was imminent. She had just persuaded herself it was forgivable when suddenly Miss Lacey was at her side.

"Miss Bennet, are you well?"

"I am." She forced a smile to her face. "I am perfectly well." She winced when she realised she had uttered the dreadful phrase aloud.

"Oh, good," said the lady kindly. "You seemed a bit pale suddenly, but you do have such a lovely complexion. I am sure it is no more than that. Shall we sit?"

Elizabeth agreed, and the two ladies moved to a sofa by the fire. "Everyone in Hertfordshire is so very agreeable," said Miss Lacey. "You must have missed them all terribly while you were ill."

"I did," Elizabeth agreed with a faint smile—she was yet recovering her spirits. "I cannot help think, looking back, that to be away from home as I was must have hindered my recovery. Do you miss Kent?"

"I do," said Miss Lacey with a sigh. "My family lives quite near the sea, and I can never quite accustom myself to being without the view of water for too long."

"You need to take care, then, to marry a man with a home by the sea."

The lady laughed. "Or perhaps just one with means enough to take me to see it when my longing has grown intolerable."

Although it was likely unintentional, Miss Lacey cast a surreptitious peek at Darcy when speaking. Elizabeth did as well and found, by the perverseness of mischance, that he was looking at them. Elizabeth hurriedly dropped her gaze, feeling her cheeks flame crimson with embarrassment.

"I understand that you and Mr. Darcy do not get on well."

Surprised, Elizabeth lifted her eyes to Miss Lacey's. "Oh, no, I would not say…that is, did he say that we do not get along?"

"Oh, no, forgive me. I must have mistaken his words. I believe he said something of a difference of opinion."

Elizabeth could not understand herself; her sense of dismay in hearing he had spoken of her to Miss Lacey was unaccountably strong. She fought to retain her equanimity when she really wished to demand all the particulars of any and all discussions they had of her.

She forced herself to laugh lightly. "Mr. Darcy and I have had many differences in our opinions—we have argued many times. Indeed, he once accused me of stating an opinion that was not my own simply to induce an argument with him."

Miss Lacey gasped. "Oh, no! Did he truly? What did you say to that?"

Despite everything, the recollection brought a true smile to Elizabeth's lips. "I believe I laughed and teased him a little about it."

"Tease Mr. Darcy?" Miss Lacey gave the object of their conversation a peek from beneath her lashes. "I do not think I would ever dare."

Miss Lacey has set her sights on Mr. Darcy. Well that could hardly be a surprise. What lady in her right mind would not wish to marry him? Only the silliest kind who thought herself so clever as to dislike him.

Miss Lacey persisted in sneaking coy glances at him, and as Elizabeth watched, she caught him cast a surreptitious look at Miss Lacey. Her heart sank into her house slippers as she imagined the next weeks, watching them make love to one another.

"Excuse me," she said, hurriedly rising. "I think I forgot something in my bedchamber."

NETHERFIELD HAD GUESTS FROM THE NEIGHBOURHOOD TO DINE THAT evening. Mr. and Mrs. Collins were there, along with Sir William and Lady Lucas, Mrs. Bennet, and Kitty. The Gouldings attended, as did the Kings and their niece Mary. They were all pleasant enough, even Mrs. Bennet. Indeed, Darcy was rather shocked by how withdrawn and quiet Mrs. Bennet had become. There would yet be none who called her a wit, but she was quiet and inoffensive, and Darcy thought it a vast improvement.

Darcy had an agreeable companion in Miss Lacey. They had begun in fits and starts—Miss Lacey with several strange and discomfiting remarks, which he later thought might have been meant to tease him. Thankfully, when her remarks were met with his silence, she stopped. From thence, she provided a steady stream of inconsequential chatter. Elizabeth was out of his line of sight; Mrs. Bingley had placed large candelabra with ivy and flowers in the middle of her table, and they obscured everyone except those immediately next to him. It was likely for the best; he knew she had seen him looking at her while she sat with Miss Lacey.

He could not forget her eyes when he had spoken to her in the drawing room. She was struck, not by his hand but by his rejection, and he regretted it deeply. There was in him a desire to protect her even though the only thing against her was his own apparent detachment.

Alone in his bedchamber, he was far from rest and cast about for something to divert him from his thoughts. Fitzwilliam was owed a letter, he remembered. Darcy had neglected his cousin shamefully since coming to Netherfield and so set about the task with eagerness.

Fitzwilliam,

You must forgive my tardiness in writing this letter. As you know, I am at Netherfield visiting Bingley. His circumstances have been altered, but his character has not, and we have been amply entertained.

His new situation suits him well. He and Mrs. Bingley are a happy couple, and their son is a joy to them both. The neighbourhood is glad to have them and, indeed, recognises them as the foremost family. He seems to be a fair master and is well respected by his servants. I daresay his father would be well pleased with his son's establishment as a gentleman.

Darcy paused in his writing, leaning back and considering what to say. His mind ran riot with thoughts of Elizabeth Bennet; indeed, she eclipsed every other thought, feeling, and idea. As such, he had little to say that was truly of interest. He would not rattle away like a fool, yet what could he say? Nothing else mattered but her.

With determination, he threw himself into his task. He mentioned each person in the house with enthusiasm bordering on adoration. He described every round of cards, every dish at dinner, and every shot fired from his gun with a gleeful fervour. What he did not mention was her.

After filling two pages with such rambling, he stopped, satisfied that Fitzwilliam would think he was enjoying himself enormously. The family worried about him; they had seen his melancholy. Although only Georgiana and Fitzwilliam knew any part of what happened, all had worried and rejoiced in the idea that he would attend a country party with numerous unwed ladies.

A Short Period of Exquisite Felicity

He finished the letter:

You have said little of your stay at Felborough. Dare I suppose that Miss Cutler has made a conquest of you?
Miss Elizabeth Bennet is also here at Netherfield.

Sincerely,
FD

He leant back in his chair, wondering what mad impulse led him to tell his cousin that Elizabeth was here.

Although Colonel Fitzwilliam had befriended Elizabeth during their stay at Rosings Park, his friendship quickly soured when Darcy told him what had happened last August. Darcy did not even tell him all of his long, decidedly unromantic, history with her; his cousin knew only that he had offered for Elizabeth, been accepted, and then been rejected. It was enough for Fitzwilliam. He was disappointed she had behaved thusly, and he could make neither rhyme nor reason out of her actions. In any case, his loyalty was to his cousin, and it was a loyalty that grew ever more fierce as he saw Darcy's interminable period of despair over the months.

Fitzwilliam no doubt would berate him for remaining in Elizabeth's presence. He would think him a fool or accuse him of delighting in misery—and perhaps he was correct in that. Fitzwilliam would think it rather pitiable that Darcy had not yet removed from the place, or at the very least, he would wonder why Darcy had not yet demanded the whys and wherefores from her.

The whys and wherefores. Fitzwilliam would have required them of her long ago, but his cousin was a direct, uncomplicated soul. If he wanted something, he got it. If he had a question, he asked it. If he disliked something, he said so, and when he laid his head on his pillow at night, he slept.

Darcy looked over at the pillows on the large comfortable bed; they were undisturbed and likely would remain so.

Fitzwilliam would scoff to learn that some days Darcy wished to know, and other days he was glad he did not. He had not asked her because he feared the answers. He could not bear to know she had never loved him or, even worse, had secretly loved another. At least now he could imagine she had learnt to esteem him, however slim that possibility might be.

But this was a coward's way. He should arrange a private interview with her and force her to say what he needed to hear, no matter how painful it may be.

Perhaps I should depart instead.

What a relief that would be! This scene of torment need not hold him. He had been an exemplary guest. He had danced with the ladies, joined the gentlemen in their shooting, and been as agreeable as he knew how to be. There was no claim of duty left upon him.

A pang smote him at the thought of leaving her, but he knew the pang was born of his weakness. No, it was much better to escape before he permitted his heart to once more make a cake of him. How many times more would he indulge that fickle creature? How much harm would he permit the loathsome organ to bring to him?

He rang for Fields, who attended him within minutes. "Prepare to depart on the morrow and let the stable boys know." Fields bowed and began to quit the room, but Darcy stopped him. "I shall inform the Bingleys myself in the morning. It is late, and I do not wish to wake anyone, but I would like them to hear it from me."

Fields bowed his acknowledgement and was gone. Darcy trusted that his man had understood him—Bingley should not know until it was too late to stop him.

And now to pass the night. Darcy searched about him for the book he had been reading in the afternoon. With a sigh, he realised he had left it in the library.

It had been a pleasant surprise to discover Bingley's library was now far better stocked than on his first visit to Netherfield. He had even discovered several volumes that he owned but had not yet had time to read. Such was the volume he had begun that afternoon, and he eagerly anticipated losing himself in its pages once again.

He strode through the dark halls intent on his mission and entered the library within minutes, eager to retrieve the tome he hoped would help him pass the next solitary hours.

Elizabeth had the same notion, or so he surmised when he found her standing in front of the bookshelves. She startled upon seeing him and nearly dropped the lamp she held. She set it carefully on the table nearest her, and he observed her trembling hand.

"I beg your pardon," he said, bowing stiffly.

"No, I…" She bobbed awkwardly then looked around her, as if hoping the bookshelves might give her some indication of what to say.

Thankfully, his book was immediately apparent on a small side table near a comfortable blue chair where he had whiled away the afternoon. "My book." He gestured at it, displeased to note that his hands also shook a bit. "I left it there."

"Oh." She picked it up and took a step forward to hand it to him. Alas, her diffidence caused her to misjudge, and instead of landing in his hand, the book fell to the floor with a thud that startled them both.

"Oh!" She exclaimed again. "Forgive me, I…"

She bent to retrieve it. By unfortunate coincidence, he did likewise, and their heads collided. Both straightened immediately, each raising a hand to rub the spot where they had struck one another and babbling apologies. Elizabeth was quick to bend again and retrieve the tome where it still lay.

He took it and thanked her. "Is your head—?"

"I am well," she assured him. "Yours?"

"A trifling bump." He hesitated a moment then extended his hand to her.

Her eyebrows flew up for a moment until she arranged herself into a more sedate countenance. Her hand—pale, trembling, and small—came slowly to rest upon his. In a manner most natural, their hands moulded to one another, but he pushed that thought away, leading her to the sofa and sitting down next to her.

For a short while, he did not speak, staring down at the rug beneath their feet. He felt her eyes upon him, no doubt baffled by this alteration in his demeanour towards her. He swallowed loudly and began to speak.

"I thank you for your apology…before…in the drawing room. I did not receive it graciously, and I should have." In a quieter tone, he added, "You know me too well to believe that I am well. I am not—not yet. I was ungenerous, and I am sorry."

"You need not apologise to me," she murmured.

He took a deep breath. "I shall be leaving in the morning and—"

"What? Leaving?" She interrupted him quickly. "Why are you leaving?"

He did not answer, and she pressed him. "Because of me?"

Because I am a helpless moth drawn to your flame, and I fear I shall be incinerated.

He did not reply but rose from the settee and walked a few paces before turning back to look at her.

"It is hard," he began. "Very hard…" He stopped speaking, unable to clearly say what he wished her to know.

"To pretend there is nothing between us," she said when the silence had drawn too long.

"Yes."

"Pray, do not leave on my account." She lowered her head and clasped her hands together, her fingers busily twisting among each other. "Your friend has missed you, and my sister is pleased to have you among her party. I shall go; I must go."

She was an ethereal beauty sitting there, illuminated by the small dim lamp. She seemed so sorrowful with her head lowered. Everything within him revolted against seeing her thusly—she should be in sunshine with laughter dancing in her eyes—and he was struck by the need to fix the situation, to fix whatever ailed her.

"I have already informed my valet."

"I am sure your valet cannot mind if his master has a change in plans." She gave him a beseeching look. "Please stay."

"Elizabeth, I cannot ask you to leave your sister's house."

"I am offering to leave; indeed, I must, for I am needed at Longbourn."

"You must not—"

"Truly," she said in a pleading tone. "My mother is ill and requires my assistance. I intend to leave. There is no sense in both of us leaving, is there?"

His heart longed to approve the scheme even though his mind admonished him to keep his intention to leave. "She seemed perfectly well tonight." He wondered at the little wince she made in response to his words.

"No." Elizabeth slowly twisted her fingers together. "She is melancholic, and I fear it must be a burden for Mr. and Mrs. Collins. I shall be better satisfied if I can see things for myself."

He turned his back on her, unable to continue seeing her diffident posture and her melancholy. He wanted to stay; indeed, he wanted it a great deal. Was he a fool? Should he be leaving her as fast as his horse would take him?

But no. She would go to Longbourn, and he would be at Netherfield. Perhaps in smaller doses, he would learn to be unaffected by her.

"Very well," he said quietly. "I shall stay."

He helped her to rise, and when she stood, he did not drop her hand.

They looked at each other for some time until he finally bowed over her hand, allowing himself one brief graze of his lips against her bare fingers before she left him.

The night wore long on Elizabeth after her meeting with Mr. Darcy. She wanted to cry, she wanted to hope, and she wanted to know the meaning of the kiss she still felt on her hand. It was impossible to think that he was still affected by her—his coldness in the drawing room had served her expectations of him far better—yet it was equally impossible to think him unaffected.

Her arguments with herself left her weak and aching. Inasmuch as she hated to leave, she was eager to see it done, and she went to her sister at the earliest possible time the next morning. Jane was still at her toilette, but she happily invited Elizabeth to join her.

"Just like old times with the two of us together, preparing for the day."

"Not quite the same." Elizabeth looked around Jane's bedchamber. Decorated in rosy hues with green accents, it was a triumph of feminine graciousness, far different from their more austere bedchamber at Longbourn. If nothing else, it was nearly double the size of the bedchamber Jane and Elizabeth had shared. Then again, it was the mistress's chamber; it should be rather grand.

"Have you been enjoying yourself?" Elizabeth saw Jane's devious little smile in the looking glass. "It seems Mr. Egremont has taken a liking to you."

"Mr. Egremont takes a liking to everyone. I would not imagine too much from his attentions."

"He might be a flirt, but even flirts eventually take wives."

"Not all of them."

"I have it on good authority that he does, indeed, seek a wife." Jane twisted in her seat to better view her sister. "Do you think I would invite someone to my house party who only wished to flirt with my guests?"

"I did not realise marital intention was the prerequisite for attendance," Elizabeth teased. "I should not have come myself if I had."

"Oh, Lizzy." Jane sighed into her mirror, having turned back to allow her maid access to the back of her hair. "I have no idea why you speak so. You will wish to marry one day, and in the meanwhile, you should encourage Egremont a little, see what you can make of it."

Elizabeth sighed and said, in an off-handed tone, "I am surprised Mr.

Darcy would come knowing you intended to marry him off."

Jane shrugged. "Even Mr. Darcy must get lonely, I imagine. In any case, he is thirty—is he not?—and it is time. His sister will be out in the spring, and having a wife to help him is surely desirable."

"I think Miss Lacey likes him."

Jane smiled warmly into her mirror. "They would be a handsome couple, would they not? Yes, I would count my efforts quite successful if they made a match of it."

All the more reason for me to leave.

Jane continued, her voice lower, "I know Caroline still thinks she might win him, and her friend Lady Sophie is quite determined as well."

"Then let us persuade Miss Haverhill in his direction, and they can all battle it out." Elizabeth meant her remark to be humorous, but it fell flat. When Jane gave her a curious look over her shoulder and dismissed her maid, Elizabeth knew she was due for some sort of reproof. A scolding? Sisterly confidences? She girded herself for the worst.

Elizabeth sat on her sister's bed, and Jane, heedless of the wrinkles it would cause her gown, climbed up next to her. She studied her sister for a moment before saying, "My husband has wondered…"

"What?"

Jane thought for a moment. "That time you visited Pemberley…before everything with Lydia…"

Elizabeth fixed her eyes on the flowery pattern of Jane's coverlet. She took one finger and began to trace the threads lightly.

"He wondered whether you and Mr. Darcy perhaps…liked one another."

Elizabeth shook her head, congratulating herself on refraining from blushing. "Mr. Darcy and I have never liked each other." *Hate and then love…we never settled for anything as insipid as like.*

"Charles said—" Jane interrupted herself with a laugh. "He said the two of you vanished once for quite some time. He said Darcy mentioned something about showing you his mother's roses, but when you returned… well, let us just say, my dear husband has always expected to be a brother to his friend one day."

Elizabeth laughed weakly. "Your husband is a bit of a matchmaker, I think."

"He does like to see people happy, particularly those he loves."

"Well, Mr. Darcy does not make me happy, and I certainly do not make him so." Elizabeth looked up and forced herself to be brisk. "I did not come in here to discuss my history with Mr. Darcy. I came to say that I am quite worried about Mama, and I think I should go stay with her at Longbourn."

"Worried about Mama? Why?"

"Charlotte said her nerves—"

"Oh, her nerves." Jane rolled her eyes, quite an extraordinary gesture from her. "She has a maid, Kitty, and Charlotte to tend to her nerves. I would not think a thing of that."

"Charlotte is not her daughter, and I do not think it fair that she should have to manage Mama. You know how difficult she can be—I believe I must go to her."

"She came to dinner last night and was perfectly well!"

Those hated words yet again! Elizabeth nearly moaned. "She was in poor spirits."

"Lizzy…" Jane sighed. "I cannot make you stay, but please tell me the true reason you wish to leave."

For a moment, Elizabeth considered confiding in her, but the impulse passed; it was too much to tell and there was no point in telling it. Things were as they were, and no amount of talking about it would change a thing.

"I miss Longbourn. I had not realised how much until I was here."

With another sigh, Jane played her last card. "Mama will not be pleased to think you have quit a situation with so many eligible gentlemen."

"I hope the pleasure of having more people to fuss over her will distract her from that."

With that, both sisters laughed a little, and it was settled.

After a quick breakfast, during which Mr. Darcy, thankfully, did not appear, Elizabeth returned to her bedchamber to help the maids pack her things. It was a short business; she had not been there long enough to situate herself too firmly. By eleven in the morning, she was ready to make the short journey to Longbourn.

The rest of the party had heard the news of her imminent departure and gathered in the drawing room to bid her farewell. She had no idea whether Mr. Darcy would be among them and, indeed, when she entered, he was not. Disappointment caused a lump in her throat, though it was silly. It was likely better that he was not there. If he kissed her fingers again, she knew she would probably do something foolish.

She shook all sorrow aside as she began to make the rounds of those who had gathered.

"I am all anticipation of calling on you at Longbourn," said Miss Lacey with genuine warmth in her eyes. "I would love to see your family home."

"Will they have room for you at Longbourn?" Miss Bingley asked with a look of excessive concern. "I understand they are rather near to bursting already." She looked at Sir Edmund who stood at her side, and she snickered.

Elizabeth found herself quite beyond caring about Miss Bingley and her remarks. "Mrs. Collins has promised me a comfortable bed in the scullery," she replied. Sir Edmund's eyes went wide so she told him, "I am only teasing Miss Bingley a little. She knows that Longbourn is well able to accommodate me."

Sir Edmund had little to say, and the Hursts were likewise unmoved by her departure. Jolly put up a great fuss, promising to wear out his horse on the road between Netherfield and Longbourn. "I shall send my carriage for you anytime," he promised. "I shall come get you myself and walk the distance if need be."

Miss Haverhill said, "How nice to make your acquaintance," as if she would never see Elizabeth again, and Lady Sophie smirked while saying, "I cannot say I regret the improving of our odds around here."

At Elizabeth's tight smile, she was quick to add, "Oh, I say so in jest, of course, but what lady is not relieved to see another beauty gone?" It might have been complimentary save for the note of insincerity in her tone.

Mr. Egremont was last to say good-bye. "Miss Bennet, I cannot deny that you will be sorely missed. I do hope you know I intend to be fierce in competition with Jolly for your attentions. He might walk to Longbourn, but I shall run."

Elizabeth laughed and accepted his bow; then she hugged Jane and kissed Baby Thomas, who sat cooing in her sister's lap.

Bingley would see her to the carriage. He said little as they moved to the front of the house, only reminding her of a dinner a few nights hence when they reached the front door. "They will spare you at Longbourn, I am sure."

"Yes," said Elizabeth. "I do not intend to be a stranger at Netherfield, I assure you."

The day was cold but bright, and the horses were impatient. Bingley handed her into the carriage and set her off with haste and only a few final urgings to return as soon as she could.

Chapter Six

Darcy stood at the window in Bingley's bedchamber, watching the carriage that carried Elizabeth away until it vanished down the lane. He turned from the window slowly and made his way back to his rooms.

You wished her gone.

If only he could excise the portion of himself that missed her, the part of him that longed to run after the carriage and bid her return.

Last night, having left her in the library, Darcy returned to his bedchamber in a state of profound agitation, certain sleep was miles away. To his surprise, he was quick to slumber, but his dreams had been erotic and agonising. He had dreamt of bedding her and of her allowing George Wickham to do the same; he had argued and fought with her; he had been abandoned by her. Worst of all, however, was the dream he had near morning, a peaceful dream of having her at Pemberley as his wife. It was by far the most realistic dream of the night, and when he awoke, he had been disoriented by finding himself at Netherfield—and devastated to recall the actual state of things.

Yet again he was in tumult thanks to Elizabeth Bennet. Would it never end? Was he cursed to spend his life filled with regret for a love that could never be requited? Blast, but he was tired of it!

Forcing himself to appear in reasonably good humour, he took himself from his chamber into the drawing room where he found Miss Lacey and Miss Haverhill sitting together. Both ladies smiled in his direction, and he forced himself to appreciate the pretty, domestic picture they made.

"Join us, Mr. Darcy," said Miss Lacey. "We were just speaking of our plans for the winter."

Darcy took a chair near them. "Ready to be off on the next round of diversions already, are you?"

"No," said Miss Haverhill seriously. "It says nothing to the hospitality of the Bingleys. For myself, I have two possibilities and cannot choose between them."

"Her cousins wish her to go with them to Bath," said Miss Lacey. "But her mother would like her to return home."

They spoke on this subject for a short while. Darcy had no great opinion of Bath—it always seemed populated by the vainest, shallowest of the *ton*—but Miss Haverhill was rather predisposed to it. She soon excused herself, mentioning some correspondence she needed to finish, and Darcy found himself alone with Miss Lacey.

His first inclination was to remove himself, but he pushed that down. He liked Miss Lacey and believed she liked him. *Why not explore it a little and see where it goes? The surest way to forget one woman is to fix your attentions on another.*

"And what are your plans for the winter?" he asked. "Will you return to… Where are you from?"

"Kent, near Margate."

"Oh, yes—Linton Hall I believe?"

She smiled and gave a little nod. "My mother longs to have me home. For as much as she wished my sister married, she misses her now that she has her own establishment."

"Where has she settled?"

"In Old Romney. Her house is Agnes Court." Miss Lacey took a little sip of coffee and dabbed her lips delicately. "Fifty miles away, which seems a great distance to my mother; but my sister has always believed it is not good for a woman to be settled too near her family."

That was it for Darcy; it took no more to remind him of Elizabeth. They had once spoken of the distance Mrs. Collins had settled from the Lucas family. He believed it an easy distance—the very same distance: fifty miles—but Elizabeth had disagreed, saying the limitations in Mr. Collins's means would make travel prohibitive. Stupidly, he had imagined the whole conversation as an indication of her interest in him. He sighed heavily to recall it.

Miss Lacey—for a moment, he forgot she was present—smiled at his sigh. "You must be thinking of your sister. I am sure you are not eager for her to be gone; perhaps she will settle near Pemberley."

Their conversation moved from there. Miss Lacey was eager to hear about Pemberley, a subject on which Darcy could always wax long. His mind, however, could not be diverted. His mouth was engaged in the conversation, but his thoughts were fixed firmly on Elizabeth, Pemberley foremost in his recollections as he described the sights that had most pleased her: the stream, the gardens, and the woods.

"I believe I shall take a turn in the maze," said Miss Lacey, giving him a little look that he knew meant he should ask to accompany her.

"It would be an honour if you would permit me to join you," he said with a beguiling smile, and she assented.

He forced himself to refrain from thinking of Elizabeth as he promenaded Miss Lacey about the maze. Miss Lacey was pleasant to converse with. She was not the sort of lady to merely repeat his opinions, nor did she descend into maliciousness in the guise of wit. There was a genuine goodness about her that he liked, and he knew that if he married her, he would be satisfied with her duty to his estate, to his sister, and to his future children.

He studied her as she spoke, noting her beauty and the elegance with which she moved. It was a dispassionate observation, something wholly unconnected to himself. Miss Lacey did not fire his blood; he could admit she was handsome, he could even contemplate marriage to her, but it did not thrill him as Elizabeth did.

No, no, no. Elizabeth's absence was meant to help him forget her, but it only made him miss her. He had not accounted for how she would haunt the place, nor how the other ladies would be so pale and dull in comparison to her.

It was both a blessing and a curse for Elizabeth to be back at Longbourn. The reassurances of familiarity were there alongside the marks of how much had changed. Her father's library had become Mr. Collins's sanctuary, and although he had altered little, the essence of her father was long gone. Mr. Bennet's library had always been in a state of comfortable disorder, with books opened and strewn about the room alongside half-drunk cups of coffee or tea. Mr. Collins, on the other hand, had everything neatly shelved (most likely because he rarely read anything), and there was a strange pungent smell throughout.

In her letters while she was yet at Cheltenham, Elizabeth had urged Charlotte to situate Mrs. Bennet in the dowager's cottage. It was a well-appointed little house, and although it was not nearly as large as the main house, there was still ample space for a widow and one daughter. Elizabeth was mortified to discover that, not only had her mother insisted on remaining in the main house, she had not even surrendered the mistress's bedchamber to Charlotte.

Mrs. Bennet was resting in her chamber when Elizabeth arrived with her things. She gave a disapproving huff when she saw her daughter. "Jane has a house full of eligible gentlemen, yet here you are."

"I heard you were feeling poorly," said Elizabeth with a conciliatory smile. "I wanted to do what I could for you."

Mrs. Bennet huffed again. "A daughter's place is with her mother, but I should like to see you married. It is not right that you should have two younger sisters already settled…"

It was a harangue Elizabeth had heard many times before; indeed, Mrs. Bennet had written the same feelings in nearly every letter. She thought it a disgrace that Elizabeth was not already married and believed Elizabeth should be ashamed because two of her younger sisters—even Mary, who no one ever thought would find a husband—had settled before her. Nothing more was required of Elizabeth than to look suitably chagrined and nod her head at appropriate junctures; Mrs. Bennet lost enthusiasm for the subject soon enough.

When she had finished ringing a peal over Elizabeth, Mrs. Bennet wished to hear the news from Netherfield. She was most concerned that Baby Thomas was draining away Jane's youthful bloom, and Elizabeth assured her it was not so. "She is as lovely as always, Mama, and Bingley is as much in love with her as he ever was."

"She has done her duty by him," said Mrs. Bennet. "That is something. These great men want an heir, Lizzy, and you will do well to remember that."

When Elizabeth had listened to as much as she could tolerate and had done as much as she could to see her mother diverted, she went into the drawing room where she knew Charlotte liked to sit. Here she could see much improvement over the previous furnishings.

Charlotte favoured a simpler style than Mrs. Bennet, and the former mistress's large overstuffed sofas and chairs (too many of them) had been replaced with fewer, smaller pieces. The old paper on the walls—a mass of floral print favouring dark blue, purple, and green—had been done over with a yellow paper with light pink flowers. It was feminine and cheerful. Elizabeth liked it exceedingly well and was quick to compliment her friend on the changes.

"I was about to go into the woods to gather some pine cones for an arrangement in here. Come out with me," Charlotte bid her. "You can tell me more about Mr. Egremont."

"Mr. Egremont?" Elizabeth laughed. "I assure you, there is nothing to tell. He is a flirt, and he indulged in his characteristic behaviour with me as well as with every other lady, including Jane and Mrs. Hurst."

The two ladies rose and retrieved their gloves and bonnets. "I have it on good authority that he has singled you out for his attentions."

Elizabeth shook her head. "He did not. He is a kind, amiable gentleman, and there is no more to it than that."

Charlotte would not be denied her share of the gossip as she gathered pine cones and colourful fallen leaves. No matter Elizabeth's protests, she insisted on seeing blooming love affairs in every conversation Elizabeth related to her.

Elizabeth had bent to pick up a particularly large pine cone when Charlotte asked, "And what of Mr. Darcy? Jane says his eyes are still for you."

Elizabeth straightened and began a close examination of the pine cone. "Jane is quite wrong."

"Is she?" Elizabeth could feel Charlotte's eyes upon her. "I believed he might have formed an attachment to you while we were in Kent…when you came to us last spring."

"I know you thought so." Elizabeth smiled at her teasingly. "You were wrong then, and you are wrong now."

"Miss de Bourgh noticed it as well."

"I wonder whatever became of their supposed engagement," Elizabeth mused aloud, wishing to change the subject. "Above a year has gone by; surely, Lady Catherine wants to see her settled soon."

"Lady Catherine still holds to the hope that Pemberley and Rosings will be one day united. I have heard Mr. Darcy will go to Kent after he is done at Netherfield. Perhaps it is his intention to propose then."

Charlotte was looking at her closely, and Elizabeth shrugged lightly. "Anything is possible, is it not? I cannot think why he has waited so long."

"No, nor can I, but it seems he intends to settle the business shortly. Mr. Bingley has said that Mr. Darcy means to have a bride for himself, and soon."

He has been ready to marry for above a year. Elizabeth spoke as indifferently as she could manage. "Does he? There are many charming young ladies of good fortune among Jane's party. If he is determined to choose a wife, I daresay he cannot go amiss with one of them."

"Yet you have come here?" Charlotte gave her a sidelong look that was only half teasing. "Do you have no wish to be among the selections?"

Elizabeth knew not how to reply to such a statement. No, she did not wish to vie for Mr. Darcy's attention, but it did not follow that she did not want him. "I missed Longbourn, and I did not like the notion that you should bear the burden of Mama's care."

Charlotte, in a manner most vexing, appeared unconvinced. Elizabeth allowed some of her frustration to seep into her voice when she continued. "Mr. Darcy and I, as always, do little more than argue. I should not be surprised if he finds me the most loathsome creature among his acquaintance."

"Now there is a change!" Charlotte chuckled lightly. "You used to say that you found him odious and disagreeable, and now you speak more to what *he* thinks of *you!* I wonder what has occasioned such an alteration."

The band of anxiety, which had been tight around her chest for above a year, constricted momentarily into grief. Elizabeth sighed to release it. "Do not make something from nothing, I implore you."

IN THE DAYS FOLLOWING ELIZABETH'S DEPARTURE FROM NETHERFIELD, there occurred a pairing of sorts among the eligible ladies and gentlemen of the party. The Bingleys and the Hursts looked upon it all with amusement and a degree of satisfaction.

Miss Bingley had set her sights on Sir Edmund, which was no great surprise as he had both a title and the largest fortune. Egremont was liberal with his attentions to all the ladies, but he appeared to be narrowing the field to Miss Haverhill even though Elizabeth had seemed his favourite before she left. Jolly was serving as an unwitting second fiddle for Lady Sophie—or perhaps he was aware of his standing and unconcerned by it.

It was no great mystery to Darcy that Lady Sophie had set her cap for him; indeed, she was clear enough with her flirtations and intentions. Darcy found himself, however, more inclined towards Miss Lacey. Each day, he spent more time with her, time that passed in a sufficiently agreeable manner. If it happened that he failed to think of her when she was not directly before him, so be it. She suffered no discouragement because of his abstractedness.

Lady Sophie did not like his attentions to Miss Lacey, and a contest of sorts had arisen between them. If he walked with Miss Lacey, he would be asked to walk with Lady Sophie. If he spoke too long with Lady Sophie, he would find Miss Lacey gently inserting herself into the conversation. Nothing was too overt or offensive—both ladies were too well bred for that —but the intentions on both sides were clear.

Such manoeuvres were tiresome, and he began to grow fearful that one of them would soon have expectations of him. His heart remained true to Elizabeth, even though his mind did not like it. One mention of her was enough to render him silent and grave for the rest of the night. When he went to bed, he dreamt of her, and when he awoke, his first thought was of her. These sorts of dreams were not new; it had been thus for some time. He could only hope that it would eventually improve, though it did not seem it ever would.

"We are engaged for dinner at a place called Lucas Lodge," said Miss Haverhill as they gathered in the drawing room one afternoon. Several of the gentlemen, having awakened early for a long ride over the countryside, had been dozing in their chairs. Darcy had been contenting himself with a book. "I do not think I know that family."

Darcy listened to see how the conversation among the ladies would go. Their hosts were not present, and he wondered what opinions might come out that would not otherwise be uttered. He kept his eyes trained on his book in hopes that the others would not note his interest.

"You do," said Lady Sophie, rolling her eyes. "Mrs. Collins is a daughter of that house."

"Ah! So we shall see Miss Bennet again!" Miss Lacey exclaimed warmly. "How good that will be."

Lady Sophie shrugged and sent a little look to Miss Bingley, who was eager with her spite. "Absolutely enthralling, I am sure. Although some of our party may be less than pleased to see her."

Darcy gave no sign that he heard.

"Some of the party felt her presence so entirely insupportable that she needed to be sent away."

Darcy still did not look up. "Miss Bennet returned to Longbourn to care for her mother," he said in a flat tone.

"Hmm," said Miss Bingley in a tone that was falsely agreeing. "I suppose a houseful of servants and maids, Miss Catherine Bennet, and Mrs. Collins were unable to fulfil that duty?"

"I think it admirable that Miss Bennet should feel her place is at her mother's side. I have always admired someone whose first object is their duty." He sent Miss Bingley a look that was not quite glaring, all the while wondering why he, of all people, should defend Elizabeth.

The Netherfield party entered Lucas Lodge with no little amount of ceremony. Elizabeth knew the Bingleys did not wish it for themselves; nevertheless, to have so many distinguished guests in his home excited Sir William's love of grandeur, and he would make as much of it as he could.

Bingley entered first with Lady Sophie on his arm, at ease with his share of the attention and eager, as always, for an evening among friends. Jane followed with Sir Edmund and looked as beautiful as ever. Jolly was behind them, seeming unusually subdued, with Miss Haverhill on his arm, and Darcy was next with Miss Lacey. Caroline and Mr. Egremont entered last, but Elizabeth's eyes remained on Darcy and Miss Lacey.

They formed a handsome pair and walked comfortably arm in arm, looking easy together. Elizabeth noticed particularly how the creases of anxiety that had marked Darcy's handsome face of late seemed to have left him. He moved with comfortable grace, chuckling lightly at something Miss Lacey said before pausing to greet his hosts.

Elizabeth swallowed and turned away, instinctively seeking the comfort of Charlotte. She did not move quickly enough, however, and before she knew it, they stood before her. Mr. Darcy with Miss Lacey on his arm—a more dreadful sight she had never seen.

Miss Lacey warmly greeted Elizabeth. "Miss Bennet. How good to see you. How is your mother?"

"She is doing well," Elizabeth said, forcing a smile to her lips. "I thank you. She thought of coming tonight, but in the end, the idea of dressing defeated her energies. We are no longer in mourning, but she still feels the loss of my father keenly."

"As do you, I am sure," said Mr. Darcy. "Forgive me. I do not believe I have as yet extended my condolences."

Elizabeth looked up to see a surprising warmth in his eyes that matched the sympathy in his tone. It nearly brought tears to her eyes, and her throat tightened with it. "Thank you. I…it has been above a year now. I had thought I would be more recovered from it by now, but…I…it is difficult."

His gaze was kindly and fixed on her countenance. "Some losses require more than a year. Some losses affect you all your life long."

Elizabeth understood he spoke of more than the loss of her father, and she took a deep breath to quell the rising sorrow in her chest. "I am afraid you are correct. There are some losses that change you forever."

"That is true," he murmured.

"Poor dear," said Miss Lacey in a bright, over-solicitous tone. "You must have been very close to him."

Elizabeth startled, having almost forgotten Miss Lacey stood with them, and her words broke the spell Darcy had cast over her. She realised that the other lady still stood firmly attached to him, looking for all the world as though she were already his wife.

A moment later, Lady Sophie joined them, having detached herself from her escort. "Dear Miss Bennet! We have been miserable without you at Netherfield!"

"Miserable?" Elizabeth gave Lady Sophie an uncertain smile, for once happy to see the lady. "I hope not, for it does not speak well of my sister's ability as your host."

"Oh your sister is charming, and I could just stare at Baby Thomas all day long." Lady Sophie slid a look at Darcy, and Elizabeth nearly laughed aloud at such a manoeuvre. Evidently she wished Mr. Darcy to know that she was well prepared for motherhood.

"As could I," said Miss Lacey. "I just dote on children."

"No one loves children as much as I do," Lady Sophie proclaimed. "If I do not have at least ten, I shall die trying."

"Ten might be too many for me," said Miss Lacey with a gentle smile. "I should not like my husband to be neglected, as I fear might be the case in a house with ten children."

Lady Sophie, having been adeptly vanquished, turned to Elizabeth. "What of you, Miss Bennet? Seeing your sister must make you long for a family of your own, does it not?"

The conversation, which had begun in a tolerable fashion, was suddenly rendered painfully uncomfortable. Elizabeth felt her face flame. Had Lady Sophie wished to humiliate her, she could not have done better than to raise the spectre of the failed engagement between Elizabeth and Darcy. She hazarded a glance at him; his face had lost all warmth, and he stared in stony silence at his feet.

She had no idea what to say and made some inane remark about everyone wishing for a home and family, and Miss Lacey—perhaps sensing her discomfiture or perhaps not—tugged Darcy away to greet someone on the other side of the room. Lady Sophie followed after them, leaving Elizabeth alone.

Yes, Elizabeth did indeed want a family. She wanted the family who lived in her mind, a family she had made on the long, lonely days spent before a roaring fire in Cheltenham with a poultice on her chest. A tall boy with Darcy's curls and a girl who liked to catch frogs and play in the pond. A husband with whom she could laugh, tease, and talk of books and whatever else crossed her mind. It was difficult to accept the truth: this family could never be. She missed not only Darcy but all the hopes and dreams of the life she would have had with him.

"Enough of that now," she murmured to herself, watching as Miss Lacey listened intently to something Darcy was telling her. "There is no use thinking of what is lost."

As the evening wore on, Elizabeth recovered her spirits sufficiently to admit to some amusement at Darcy's plight. By some perverseness of mischance at dinner, he was seated between the two ladies who wished to have him. Elizabeth watched him turn his head side to side as first one lady and then the other tugged him into conversation. She pitied him for the ache that he must surely have felt in his neck by the end of the meal.

Lady Sophie was often aided and abetted in her efforts by Miss Bingley who, having turned her attentions to Sir Edmund, was no longer a rival. When Lady Sophie was asked to exhibit at the instrument, Miss Bingley urged Mr. Darcy to turn the pages for her. He did, albeit with a look of dutiful mortification on his face.

Miss Lacey had the advantage of some measure of his preference. Nearly as soon as Lady Sophie finished playing, Miss Lacey took her place. She did not insist on Darcy turning her pages—nay, she was far too refined for such machinations. Instead, she smiled sweetly up at him and said something charming; he smiled with genuine pleasure, and that was that. At the instrument he remained, happily turning pages.

Lady Sophia disliked that display of affection almost as much as Elizabeth did. She hastened to him when Miss Lacey was finished, insisting he accompany her to a nearby settee. Elizabeth had to admit that he seemed to have a great deal to say to her. He did not exhibit the ease that he had with Miss Lacey, but it was evident he was enjoying himself.

At no time did Elizabeth find his eyes upon her, and she did confirm it as frequently as was possible without making a simpleton of herself.

DARCY WAS STRANGELY GRATEFUL FOR THE ANTICS OF MISS LACEY AND Lady Sophie. Neither lady was so determined as to embarrass him, and fixing his mind on encouraging both and neither at the same time was a distraction from what truly bothered him: Elizabeth.

Her beauty alarmed him. He did not know whether time or experience had altered her, but whatever it was had done her well. Her face was less youthful, yet that which was lovely in her before was now more defined. He had seen it at Netherfield, but tonight she exuded allure, and he could not deny the powerful effect it had on him.

Darcy excused himself from Lady Sophie and Miss Lacey and made a perambulation about the drawing room. His eyes drifted around as he strolled, seeming not to see Elizabeth—yet seeing quite well—as she spoke to Egremont on one side of the room.

He came to a stop near one of the back walls, a place where he could see her without appearing to. Her melancholy affected him deeply even as he tried to be unaffected by everything to do with her. She had certainly been kind to him since her arrival—kind and complaisant—but he longed to see a bit of her impishness and teasing spirit. Egremont was readily engaged by her; Darcy could see it in the way he hung on her every word. Yet the man did not know, could not even imagine, the way she was when in her usual spirits.

Darcy knew his rage had abandoned him, leaving sorrow and regret in its place. Who could be angry at one so beloved, one who was so obviously gripped by despair? He had not before considered how much she had lost—some through her own choices—nevertheless, she certainly must have her regrets.

Some part of him must have decided to go to her. He made several halting steps in her direction without being conscious that he was doing so, but once he became aware, it seemed only right and natural.

However, Mr. Collins came to arrest his progress. Darcy knew not whether he should shove the man aside or thank him for his intervention.

Since reacquainting himself with Mr. Collins, Darcy believed the man had become slightly less fatuous, though his sense of importance had swelled. This change appeared due, at least in part, to becoming a landed gentleman; he seemed to feel his new rank rather keenly. Collins spoke to him with far too much familiarity, leaning in close enough that Darcy's nose wrinkled from the cloying, yeasty smell of him.

Collins went so far as to place his hand on Darcy's arm. "I received a letter just last week that was written in a most elegant hand, clearly stating the nobility of the writer. It was, as you might have guessed, from your own dear aunt."

From thence, Collins began to give, in minute detail, information on people and things Darcy had no inclination to hear. He relaxed into the prattle, only half hearing; his eyes and mind were fixed on Elizabeth.

Egremont had gone, and she was strangely alone on a settee in the midst of the crowd with her eyes fixed on her hands in her lap. On one side of her, Mrs. Collins leant away to speak to her mother, and on the other side, Mr. Hurst had fallen asleep.

Collins rattled away while Darcy silently urged her to raise her eyes and look at him; finally, she did.

She met his gaze immediately. With strange consternation, his eyes darted away. When he looked back, her eyes were again on her lap.

He kept his gaze upon her, and soon enough, her eyes returned to study him, but she looked away almost immediately. Not many moments passed, and again, her gaze was upon him. This time, it appeared she was suppressing a mortified smile when she lowered her eyes to her lap. Did she blush? It seemed to him that she did, at least a little. He could not help but break into a smile; he was still able to make her blush, for whatever that was worth.

"Yes," said Mr. Collins eagerly. "I knew such news as this could only delight you. Yes, it is true, your dear aunt has offered to come to Hertfordshire and provide her most generous assistance to me at Longbourn. Her condescension knows no equal."

Chapter Seven

Had it been in any way true, the imminent arrival of Lady Catherine would be sufficient inducement for Darcy to flee Netherfield. However, as was learnt by further questions and an inspection of his aunt's letter, it was more a wish of Mr. Collins than a plan of Lady Catherine to come to Hertfordshire; therefore, Darcy remained.

There was rain for several days following the party at Lucas Lodge, and it was during one such day that the door to the drawing room opened, and none other than his cousin Colonel Fitzwilliam was announced.

Of the party, Fitzwilliam was acquainted with all of the men except Sir Edmund. They had been at the same school, and several had even been in the same house. Fitzwilliam was well regarded, and he entered the room to much acclaim. He went around teasing and greeting, slapping backs, and shouting out enquiries for health and family.

At last, he arrived at Darcy. "There is my cousin. How are you?"

"What are you doing here?" asked Darcy in surprise. Fitzwilliam did not answer in a straightforward manner, turning his back on Darcy in favour of his host.

"Bingley, I pray you will permit me to trespass on your hospitality. I had thought that I might stay at the local inn, but I must say, if the one I passed is the only one, it seemed dreadful."

"I would not hear of your sleeping at the inn," Bingley proclaimed. "You must stay here; there is ample room."

"And ladies in abundance," Jolly remarked under his breath.

Mrs. Bingley was rapidly applied to, and to no one's surprise, she gave her warmest welcome to the newest member of the party. Darcy had to admire her serenity; an unanticipated guest did not seem to trouble her in the least. Within moments, she had dispatched the housekeeper with instructions for Fitzwilliam's comfort, and not long after that, he was pleasurably ensconced in a room next to Darcy's with a warm drink in his hand and a blazing fire in his hearth.

Darcy entered once he was certain his cousin was settled. Fitzwilliam offered a genial albeit tired smile from his position in a chair by the fire. "Darcy, I am dead with exhaustion. I have been in Nottingham and made Hertfordshire in two days."

"In this weather? Why such haste?"

Fitzwilliam grinned. "Should I not be eager to see my cousin? But let me tell you of Nottingham. My father has learnt of a small estate near Cotgrave. Twenty-five thousand pounds, and with some attention, it could be brought up nicely. There are some nearby mining interests as well. I rode up to see the place. It is not large—nothing to Pemberley, of course—but charming."

"How is the house?"

"Lovely. The inside is a bit dated, but there has not been a mistress for some time, or so I am told. Nothing is in disrepair."

"The price seems uncommonly low."

"The present owner is a gentleman of fifty or so who inherited it when his father died. He wants only enough to cover the debts and be done with the place quickly; he favours living in town."

Darcy smiled at his cousin. "Will you sell your commission?"

Fitzwilliam shifted in his seat before admitting, "I think I just might. I do believe that I surprise myself by saying so. I never imagined I would retire my post until either the war was done or I was."

"A new estate does require a master to tend it."

"Yes, and no one feels more strongly on the subject than my father. His reasons for ending my military life and adopting the country life were numerous and spoken with vigour."

"They wish to see their son firmly planted on English soil. Who can blame them?"

"They tell me I have served well and done my duty to my country and my king. This little thing"—he gestured at his left arm where a gunshot wound still healed—"frightened them."

"A bit to the side and it would have been no small thing."

"I know," Fitzwilliam admitted. He paused a moment, swirling the liquid in his glass and seeming lost in thought. "It is not as easy as one might think in this uncertain time. You must understand, Darcy…the dread of war… is a peculiar, exhilarating dread. I have never before felt as alive as I have when facing death. When I am there, toe to toe with the enemy, I am part of something significant, something larger than mere existence. The very purpose of a man is to defend what is his, to protect it and keep it safe. I am not sure I can resign that for a life of quietly tending my fields and having dinner at my neighbours' houses."

Darcy nodded. "It is not quite as dull as all that, but I do apprehend you. You have enjoyed a steady diet of excitement these past years, and the notion of settling down has come on you suddenly. I do not deny it will require an adjustment, but I do think it needful."

"More than you know. My parents have a sum set aside that they will give me once I sell my commission. They are buying me off, and I find myself not unwilling to be purchased. I shall be well occupied with all that I must learn and do. I do not presume to know the half of it.

"You will do well enough," Darcy assured him. "You have a good head for numbers and a tendency towards diligence. Naturally, if there is anything at all that I can do for you, I beg you would permit me to help."

The fire cracked and hissed, and Fitzwilliam watched the flames for a moment. "I must admit, thinking of it has made me feel that to undergo such a task…not alone…might do very well for me."

"Yes, and that is why I offer my service should anything—"

Fitzwilliam chuckled. "I do not mean the assistance of a cousin."

"Then what do you mean?"

Fitzwilliam flushed red. "A wife, Darcy. I am thinking of a wife."

"Oh!" Darcy chuckled. "Allow me to be quite frank, sir, and withdraw the offer of my services in this regard. Is there a particular lady who has caught your interest?"

"Not as yet, but this letter I had from you was filled with effusions for all the ladies in your company. I had to come immediately and try my hand at winning one."

Darcy rolled his eyes, knowing his cousin teased him, and offered as much in return. "Miss Bingley remains unwed, and her fortune would no doubt be of good use to you as you set up your house."

Fitzwilliam guffawed. "Good lord, Darcy! Do you think I have no sense? Had I a bent towards tormenting myself, there are many ladies of the *ton* who would suit me." He paused and then said seriously, "No, it is not for *me* to punish myself. I shall leave it to *others* to torture themselves in the name of love."

Darcy heaved a great sigh. "Is that your purpose here?"

"I admit I was alarmed to think of you under the same roof as Miss Bennet. But she is not now here?"

"She decamped to Longbourn a few days ago."

"Why did she do that? Did you frighten her off with a few of your blistering scowls?"

Darcy shook his head. "How it came about does not signify. She left, and I stayed."

It was Fitzwilliam's turn to heave a sigh. He finished by lying back in his chair and staring at the ceiling as though seeking guidance from the heavens. "I have half a mind to get you drunk and toss you in the carriage for home. Pemberley, I think. London is too near."

"I cannot do that. Bingley is a good friend, and I deserted him once before. I shall not do so again. I must learn to tolerate her, for she will live with him until she marries."

Fitzwilliam shook his head, his gaze still fixed on the ceiling. "Darcy, I do not comprehend you. You could have any number of ladies, including one of these whom you lauded so eloquently in your letter. Miss Olivia Lacey would be an excellent possibility, and Miss Haverhill is a noted beauty."

"Miss Haverhill does not speak. The chairs have more to say for themselves."

"When did you become so fond of conversation?"

Darcy stood and went to the fire. He took up the poker and jabbed at the logs a few times. "Two people inclined towards silence would make for a painfully dull family circle."

"Very well, forget Miss Haverhill. Lady Sophie Woodbridge comes from an excellent family. She would be a credit to you."

"Her attentions are laid bare towards every man in the room."

"Ah well. Perhaps I shall save her for me. So Miss Lacey it is! A fine choice."

Darcy turned back to his cousin and rolled his eyes. "I like Miss Lacey, but I cannot see myself married to her."

"No one can imagine themselves married to a lady until they have gone and got leg-shackled to her," Fitzwilliam protested. "You find a girl you like well enough, and the rest comes later. Love comes gradually; that is just the way it is."

Darcy shook his head as stared into the flames. "Not always. Sometimes you meet a girl, and she reaches into your chest and claims your heart and soul, and no matter what else happens, you cannot seem to get it back."

Fitzwilliam groaned. "Surely, you do not still love her?"

Darcy made no reply.

Fitzwilliam muttered some imprecation under his breath, still staring at the ceiling above him. "How can you love a woman who has done to you as Miss Elizabeth Bennet has? She is cruel, unfeeling, and unjust."

"She is none of those things. She is…generous and kind and—"

"Generous and kind?" Fitzwilliam moaned at the ceiling. "More like unprincipled and barbarous."

"You do not understand her as I do—"

"For the love of all things holy, why are you defending her?" Fitzwilliam sat up and fixed him with a look of stern reproof.

The flames of the fire jumped while Darcy considered his cousin's question.

"I can never forget how I found you last September," Fitzwilliam said quietly. "You sent Georgiana to my mother without a word of explanation. No one heard from you for weeks, and Mrs. Reynolds was sending letters to my mother's housekeeper begging for help. You were prowling your house all night long, not eating, not sleeping…you were near collapse by the time I arrived."

The truth was that Darcy scarcely remembered that time. The entire autumn was a jumble of wet, grey days and dark, lonely nights. Darcy spent his time wishing he could cry or scream or rip open his chest and lance the painful wound in his heart. He dimly recalled Fitzwilliam arriving and forcing him to drink some remedy Mrs. Reynolds had concocted and then sleeping for what seemed an exceptionally long time. When he eventually awoke, Fitzwilliam sat him down and forced him to speak, to tell everything there was to know—or at least as much as Darcy could bear to say.

Darcy believed that conversation, awful and painful as it was, had been the first step in a healing process—an exorcism of sorts. Now he realised that he had merely whitewashed a rotting plank. The pain was still there; it was just concealed behind the guise of a functioning, reasonably good-spirited gentleman.

"Being in the company of Miss Elizabeth Bennet can only do you harm. I beg you to leave with me. Tomorrow morning, first light. Pemberley, London, Italy… I am at your disposal."

He waited, staring at Darcy as Darcy stared at the flames dancing before him.

"I insist you leave with me, Darcy."

Darcy slowly shook his head. "Forgive me, but I…I cannot."

"Cannot?" Fitzwilliam leant towards him. "Or will not?"

After a time, Darcy said, "Both."

Fitzwilliam replied with another loud groan, accompanied by throwing his hands in the air.

Darcy gave him a wry grin. "You know, I have rarely seen such feeling exhibited outside a London opera hall. Have you considered a career on stage?"

"Laugh as you wish, but this has all the marks of a Shakespearean tragedy. Tell me: How much misery will you permit this woman to inflict upon you before you are done with her for good?"

Darcy poked at a log with the toe of his boot, keeping his foot as close to the flames as he dared. "I have not the affinity for anguish that you suppose I do."

"Then what? What do you need to put this whole thing behind you and move on?"

Darcy considered that for a bit, watching the flames as the warmth on his foot grew uncomfortably hot. At the moment it did, he stepped back.

"I shall leave you to slumber."

"I am not done talking about this."

Darcy gave his cousin a weak smile. "No, I had not supposed you were."

DARCY AND FITZWILLIAM WERE BOTH AWAKE AT AN EARLY HOUR, AND BY eight in the morning, they were astride their horses, facing the November chill as they galloped across the fields around Netherfield. For some time, they behaved as boys: pushing themselves and their animals at a breakneck pace, and shouting and laughing at one another as the clods of dirt flew up behind them.

After a time, they dropped to a more leisurely pace. Darcy looked over the fields and gently rolling hills before him. November presented a particular starkness. Though not yet winter, a feeling of impending death was spread out before them. The harvested fields were grey-brown, and the trees were caught in their relentless march towards gloom. It was a cruel beauty.

Shaking his mind from such depressive observations, he showed Fitzwilliam some of the more notable features of the land they surveyed, such as the town of Meryton and the various manor houses and estates.

Eventually, they came to a stop at the crest of Oakham Mount. Hertfordshire spread out around them, and they sat in contemplation of it. "You did not mention that estate." Fitzwilliam gestured to the northeast.

"Mr. Collins, whom you must remember, has recently taken possession. It is called Longbourn"

"Ah! Dear Mr. Collins!" Fitzwilliam laughed. "How keen you must have been to renew that acquaintance!"

"I must own that being a landowner has changed him. He is not quite as foolish, though he remains excessively verbose. By all accounts, he has done Longbourn some good."

Fitzwilliam nodded, his eyes on the vista before him. "The home of Miss Elizabeth Bennet."

"Former home, but yes."

"And she is staying there now?" Fitzwilliam regarded Darcy with scepticism. "Even nearer than I had supposed. How long a ride—twenty minutes?"

"If you wish to tire your horse. It is three miles."

"An easy walk."

"What is your meaning?" Darcy asked.

"None, just that she is nearby. Easily accessible if one desired access."

"I do not wish access to her; else, I should not have asked her to leave."

"You asked her to leave?"

"No." Darcy looked down at his saddle and rubbed at a little mark with his thumb. "Well, yes, you might say so."

Fitzwilliam watched him for a moment. "I am glad for her sake that you did, for if I had my way, I might grab her and shake her until some explanation for her cruelty came free."

"I am of a mind to do that myself," Darcy admitted. "Though I suspect her answer will cause me great sorrow, even more than already afflicts me."

"How could that be possible?"

For a moment, Darcy did not answer. "We should move the horses. It will not do to let them stand, not on a cold day such as this."

They turned the horses, putting their backs to the view of Longbourn. They began at a slow pace, the animals picking their way down the path.

"She once cared for George Wickham—loved him, I think."

"Then she is even more a simpleton than I supposed."

"Might I remind you that Georgiana also fancied herself in love with him?"

"Might I remind you that Georgiana was fifteen?"

Darcy waved his hand tiredly. "What I know is that she loved Wickham, yet somehow, last September, Wickham married her younger sister. About the same time, I was jilted. I know not how these things connect, but I suspect quite strongly that they do."

"Wickham is married to a former Miss Bennet?"

"The youngest, Miss Lydia Bennet. She is younger than Georgiana and far, far sillier."

"But the Bennet girls have no portion if I remember correctly."

"No, they do not."

"Then how did this girl persuade Wickham into matrimony?"

"He works for their uncle. I imagine money changed hands and probably a bit of their uncle's business."

After a few minutes spent under the sound of horses' hooves, Fitzwilliam asked, "So your belief is that Miss Elizabeth Bennet still harboured a tendre for him but accepted you nevertheless…then jilted you?"

"I know it makes little sense."

Another pause ensued until Fitzwilliam asked, "And now she is come to live with the Bingleys? Was she at Longbourn before that?"

"For a time she was in Cheltenham at the home of a widowed sister of her aunt Mrs. Gardiner."

"Cheltenham? What was she doing there?"

"She was ill; they feared it was consumption. But it was pneumonia, and she is recovered."

"Ah."

Darcy glanced over at his cousin who was staring at the path in front of him, clearly deep in thought. Suddenly, he shook himself and turned his head to meet Darcy's gaze.

"What are you thinking?"

Fitzwilliam disregarded him for the sake of another question. "How long was she in Cheltenham?"

"What does that signify?"

"Indulge my curiosity."

Darcy shrugged. "I do not know when she went there—last autumn I believe—but she was there until she came to Netherfield so a twelve-month… maybe more."

"Rather a long time to trespass on the hospitality of some distant relation."

"Perhaps the lady required a companion."

"Or perhaps Miss Bennet required a place of seclusion."

Darcy looked over at him again. "I am not sure I comprehend you."

"In general," said Fitzwilliam, "there is but one reason young ladies are remanded into the care of distant relations in other counties."

It took Darcy a moment to understand him. "You do not accuse me—"

"No, I accuse *you* of nothing."

Comprehension struck Darcy in a manner that was physically painful. He gripped the reins of his horse tightly, so much that his fingers cramped. "If I were not on this animal," he said in a low tone, "you would find yourself on the ground with an aching jaw."

"Does not George Wickham commonly leave a trail of despoiled maidens behind him? It would certainly not be his first by-blow, to be sure."

A series of small recollections intruded in a most unpleasant fashion: Miss Bingley's trilling question—"*What was the nature of her indisposition?*"—the awkwardness of Bingley during conversations pertaining to Wickham, and lastly, Elizabeth's own admission that she had been "confined"' indoors for most of the winter. An interesting word choice.

In the midst of such swirling torment, he told his cousin, "Wickham and his wife have a daughter, born in January."

To this, Fitzwilliam offered no comment.

"I shall not believe it," Darcy declared. "No. It is completely nonsensical. If the Bennets required him to marry a daughter, why not the one he ruined?"

"Perhaps he ruined them both," Fitzwilliam quipped, far too easily for Darcy's appreciation. Darcy gave him a fierce glare that subdued him. "I cannot say. Perhaps Miss Elizabeth refused to marry him? Perhaps he was in love with the younger one?"

"I suppose he might have taken up with her sister whilst Elizabeth was in Kent," Darcy said. Thinking of this, he added, "If my understanding of these matters is correct, then she did not heed a word of my letter and threw herself into his arms right after returning from Rosings."

Too late, Darcy realised what he had said, for inasmuch as Fitzwilliam knew about the circumstances of Darcy's jilting, he did not know about Hunsford.

It was too much to hope that Fitzwilliam would not notice. "Letter? What letter?"

Darcy did not reply immediately, and Fitzwilliam pressed him. "Pray tell me you did not respond to the letter where she released you?"

"I did not."

"Thank God for that much. So what did you write to her?"

Darcy stared straight ahead. "Last April, when we were all in Kent—you must recall it—I proposed to her."

"Proposed marriage? Last April?"

Darcy nodded. "I had fooled myself into believing she was aware of my interest and anticipated my addresses, but in retrospect, it seems I caught her wholly by surprise."

Darcy could see by Fitzwilliam's countenance that he had also caught his cousin by surprise. His mouth hung slack, but he closed it to ask, "And did she…?"

"Obviously, she refused me, but it was not merely a 'no.' Indeed, we argued rather bitterly. She had many grievances to air—her hatred of me was well deserved, I must own."

"Based on how you had behaved in Hertfordshire the autumn prior?" It was now Darcy's turn to be surprised, and his cousin chuckled.

"Oh, I gathered some idea of it during our conversations at Rosings. Rather beastly, were you?"

Darcy chuckled ruefully. "Her ire was not unfounded. I began our acquaintance by slighting her at an assembly and did not improve much from there. Then our friend Wickham came to Meryton and did what he could to turn her against me. In retrospect, it seems like the stupidest thing in the world that I thought her attached to me. I was completely in error yet never so sure of myself.

"As you might guess, I was exceedingly angry and humiliated by her refusal, and in a dreadful bitterness of spirit, I wrote a letter to refute her charges against me. That letter included the truth of my dealings with Wickham. You will recall that I urged you to speak to her of the matter should she ask you."

Fitzwilliam expressed his shock through a low whistle. "I am all astonishment, yet it does make sense. I remember your request that I speak to her—I thought it quite strange—and I recall the excessively long journey back to London with you in a dark humour. I had no idea you suffered in the throes of heartbreak."

Darcy shrugged. "In retrospect, such considerations seem almost romantic. Then, once my anger had been tempered, I at least had the idea of something to do, something to rectify the situation. I tended to her complaints; I corrected those defects in pride and conceit to which she had objected. I strove with all I was to become a man worthy of her love."

He sighed. "Yet even as I did, even as I tried to improve myself, to become a man worthy of her, she ran to Wickham. It makes me nearly sick to think of it."

"Perhaps he seduced her or imposed himself on her."

Darcy merely nodded by way of acknowledgement.

The men fell into silence again as they moved forward slowly on the horses. After a few minutes, Fitzwilliam remarked, "You must have believed her feelings for you had altered when you saw her at Pemberley."

The sweetness of the memory overcame him, and Darcy had to close his eyes for a moment, his mind filled with the sunshine of that August morning, the feel of her hand on his arm, the look in her eyes as she told him all he had ever wished to hear her say.

Lost in his recollections, he spoke without intention. "We were in love, the stuff of poetry and song, and it was exquisite. It was beyond a doubt the happiest time of my life—that day and the days that followed—in which everything I held in my heart for her was reflected in hers for me."

He paused a moment, recalling himself to the present. "Or so I believed. It seems most likely that it was a case of seeing what I wished to see."

Each gentleman lapsed into his own thoughts for a time, broken only when they arrived at a fork in the path. One would take them farther afield; the other would return them to Netherfield. They chose Netherfield.

Upon handing over their animals to the lad in the stable yard, Fitzwilliam said, "I have always admired Miss Bennet, and I cannot think her cunning or fickle. I think it possible she merely found herself in an untenable position and wished to release you from any part of it."

"Perhaps so," said Darcy. "I suppose what I really must do is ask her. Sit her down and force her to tell me. I think it is likely the only way I shall ever be released from this madness."

He had turned to look at his cousin while he spoke and saw the fleeting but disapproving look that moved across his face.

"You think it unwise?"

"I cannot see what good it would do you," said Fitzwilliam carefully.

"It would release me from the anguish of—"

"Release you from one anguish only to send you into the next. No matter her reason, the fact remains that she jilted you. She did not hold you in enough esteem to treat you as a husband—or a lover for that matter. Can there be any just cause?"

Darcy did not reply to that.

As they walked back towards the house, Fitzwilliam laid his hand on Darcy's arm. "Come away," he urged. "Let us tell the Bingleys now that we shall depart on the morrow."

For a moment, Darcy considered it. Certainly the most sensible thing was to leave and never again see her. To move on, to find another, to marry, to live. It would do him best, yet it would not do at all.

If someone had asked him a month or even a fortnight ago, he would have said with certainty that the idea of Elizabeth Bennet in his life repulsed him. He would have agreed earnestly that he was resolved to live his life without her, and he welcomed the notion of never seeing her again, no matter the cause of her faithlessness.

But not now.

Now he felt that ache—the same ache he felt after his first visit to Netherfield. He departed that November day certain he would never see her again and feeling a part of his soul had gone missing because of it. The same ache was felt as he departed Rosings five months later, knowing she despised him and once again certain that he would never see her again. Since meeting her in the autumn of 1811, the ache had been ever present—save for those nine short days last August.

To leave now, perhaps never to see her again, seemed an impossibility. To forgive her? Also impossible.

But when would this accursed ache be gone?

Feeling his cousin's eyes upon him, he muttered, "No, not yet."

Chapter Eight

On entering Netherfield, Darcy and Fitzwilliam parted, retiring to their respective chambers. Fitzwilliam, accustomed to a military schedule, was nearly mad with hunger and made a quick business of making himself presentable to company. Mere minutes later, he was within the breakfast room, making free with the selections.

"The good colonel," said Egremont as he entered, giving Fitzwilliam a genial slap on the back. "Ah, but Mrs. Bingley does know how to feed her guests, does she not?"

Fitzwilliam grinned happily. "I scarcely know what to eat first."

"Good food and lovely ladies," Egremont said as he filled his plate. "Now what is this I hear about you trying to make Darcy depart?"

"It does seem rather foolish, does it not?" Both gentlemen settled into seats with their filled plates and waited as a footman filled cups of coffee for them. "But Darcy is rather determined to remain, so I can have no objection."

"You are a welcome addition, sir, though with one lady gone off and two others intent on your cousin, our numbers are not as they should be! But the shooting has been good, so that is always something."

"Two ladies for Darcy! No wonder he wishes to stay." Fitzwilliam chuckled. "And what of you, good sir? Are there any I should defer to your capable flirtation?"

Egremont groaned as he stirred cream into his coffee. "I am under some considerable inducement to marry. My mother is tired of dandling grandnieces and grandnephews on her knee and insists on having a few of her own to cosset."

"And do any of the present company suit you?"

"Miss Elizabeth Bennet is a lovely girl."

"Miss Elizabeth Bennet?" Fitzwilliam considered it for a moment, pleasure commingled with relief spreading through his chest. "A fine choice indeed, but only for a man who felt himself capable of enjoying beauty, wit, and intelligence combined."

Egremont chuckled. "I do fancy myself able to meet the difficult task. I heard she and Darcy do not get on well. Why is that?"

"She and Darcy?" Fitzwilliam carefully lifted his napkin and wiped his mouth. "Oh, I think he might have once said something she did not like at an assembly. Refused to stand up with her, perhaps? I cannot recall the exact details. 'Tis nothing, I assure you."

"Ah." Egremont dismissed it easily. "It would have been far more suitable to my purpose had she remained, but her mother took ill."

Fitzwilliam grimaced theatrically. "Bit of bad luck, that. But surely you may call on her? I saw the house today while we rode. It cannot be but a mile or so."

"Three," said Egremont ruefully.

"Three? Why that is nothing. You should call on her, perhaps even this morning."

"Perhaps I shall." The gentlemen grinned at one another, both satisfied with the conversation. "I do not think Mrs. Bingley has any amusements planned for the afternoon."

"Mrs. Bingley has kept her guests well occupied?"

"Very well indeed." Egremont raised his brows. "Her ideas of amusement are excessively wholesome I fear, likely too sweet for soldiers like you and libertines such as I."

"Oh, no." Fitzwilliam laughed. "Lots of poetry reading and concertos?"

"And charades...let us not forget the charades."

"I think, between us"—Fitzwilliam leant in and spoke in a lower tone—"we could likely find a way to bring some excitement to the party."

"That would be excellent indeed." Egremont thought for a moment. "Say, were you at that house party at Horner's Abbey..."

"I was not, but I have heard the stories—a bit of legend, that! Though likely a bit too much for these ladies, at least for the first night."

"True," Egremont agreed. "But perhaps a little kissing would do."

"Kissing games," said Fitzwilliam. "Just the thing."

CAROLINE BINGLEY SAT AT HER DRESSING TABLE, WELL PLEASED WITH WHAT the looking glass had to show. She had a new gown in a lovely shade of saffron that set off her complexion rather nicely. It was an expensive gown, particularly for a morning dress, but well worth every farthing if it induced Sir Edmund to propose.

A knock came at her bedchamber door, and Lady Sophie permitted herself entry. "You are looking very pretty."

"I thank you," said Caroline, adjusting a stray curl on her forehead. "I do think it suits me."

Lady Sophie seated herself on Caroline's bed but did not speak.

"Excuse us, Martine." No matter what Jane said, Caroline thought it was insupportable to refer to the maid by the common, English name of Martha. Caroline would call her Martine to make her seem French even though she was not. Martha understood, nodded, and left them.

"What is it?" Caroline asked.

"What is what?"

"It seems you have some news? Has Darcy proposed to you over his porridge this morning?" Caroline tittered, causing Lady Sophie to frown.

"I begin to think it a futile endeavour, and when you hear what I have learnt, you might agree with me."

Caroline leant closer to the mirror. It seemed she had the threat of a blemish on her chin, which was excessively vexing. She poked at it with her finger. "Pray, tell me."

"Colonel Fitzwilliam is all man, is he not?" Lady Sophie gave her friend a smirk. "I do enjoy the good use of regimentals."

"Second son. Unless those regimentals can pay the jewellers, I have no use for them."

"Oh, he is not as penniless as most—not if my maid knows anything about it."

"What could your maid possibly know about the colonel?"

Lady Sophie twirled a curl by her neck. "Seems the colonel is ready for a wife."

Caroline lifted a brow and considered the colonel for a brief moment.

"Your father would like to see you as part of that family."

"That he would."

"But will you give up so soon on Darcy?"

"I do not think Darcy can be persuaded into acting as soon as his cousin could." Lady Sophie pouted. "I need a husband. Even the most restrictive husband is more obliging than a father."

"Certainly more obliging than *your* father! Well, then, Miss Lacey, Darcy is yours to vex." Caroline smiled as she stared at herself in her looking glass. "And I shall remain in good hope that Sir Edmund will be persuaded in my direction very soon."

"Perhaps even today," Lady Sophie suggested. "You are so very well in looks."

At this, Caroline was induced to begin a litany of complaints against herself: her bosom was too flat, her complexion was too dull, her hair was not arranged well, and her jewellery was tarnished. It was all calculated, of course, to make Lady Sophie compliment everything and assure her of her beauty. After ten minutes spent in such agreeable occupation, Caroline was satisfied, and the two ladies descended to the breakfast room.

SEVERAL TIMES THAT DAY, DARCY FOUND HIS COUSIN'S EYES UPON HIM, and he did not have to think long to understand why. Whatever thoughts he had, Fitzwilliam kept them to himself, at least until the afternoon when all had retired to dress for dinner.

Having above an hour before dinner would be served, Darcy stretched out on the bed, thinking longingly of a nap. As tired as he was and as poorly as he had slept the previous night, he knew he could not sleep. The exhaustion he felt was not one cured by closing one's eyes.

His mind, as always, was filled with Elizabeth Bennet. *Why does she not love me? Why did she jilt me? What is she doing at this very moment?* Endless questions. Was Wickham the answer? Was this something else in his life that Wickham had destroyed? Or had she decided she simply did not love him? Perhaps he was inherently unlovable.

Into such musings, the entrance of his cousin was profoundly relieving.

"Jolly is a decent fellow. Egremont too, once he is done flirting with the ladies."

Darcy agreed with a faint noise as his cousin took a seat in the chair by the fireplace. "Have you found a wife yet?"

Fitzwilliam chuckled. "No, have you?"

"Yes."

Fitzwilliam straightened. "Indeed? So will…oh." Realisation took the starch from him immediately. "Darcy, you need to put this behind you."

"And so I am," Darcy retorted. "I have scarcely spoken to the woman."

"In any case, I believe the order of the evening will be of use to you in that endeavour."

"Oh? I understood it to be a rather quiet evening."

"It might start that way, but I believe things will take a little turn once the Bingleys retire." Fitzwilliam rubbed his hands together and grinned.

Darcy felt a pulse of alarm and sat up. "What do you mean?"

"A few little kissing games." Fitzwilliam turned to study his cousin's face carefully. "Nothing of any consequence, so do not set your back up nor think for a moment you may excuse yourself. I insist on your presence."

"I would not behave so dishonourably—"

"It is only a few kisses, Darcy."

"The ladies will expect—"

"Nothing," said Fitzwilliam firmly. "The ladies understand it is merely a bit of fun, with nothing meant by any of it."

"Then what is the point?" Darcy cried out in exasperation. "Why shall we play silly games more suited to green lads than grown gentlemen?"

"The same reason we used to gallop our horses on the Rowsley Road and swing out over the ravine on that rope we tied up—for the thrill of it." Fitzwilliam grinned. "Of course, in this case, you will be unlikely to break your neck."

"No, but I might like to wring yours," Darcy snapped.

"Mine? Why?"

"Do not think I do not see this as your handiwork." Darcy glared as fiercely as he was able. "The last thing I should need is to have some father or brother accuse me of using his daughter ill and force me into a marriage to one of these…these…"

"These eminently suitable, charming, pretty young ladies? A dreadful fate indeed. However," Fitzwilliam held up one finger, "the rules of the game are always set into place before any of us indulge. Any lady who feels ill-used may excuse herself."

"And any gentleman will be afforded the same privilege, I presume," Darcy retorted. "Do not count me among your numbers. I shall not do it. I am a man of honour."

"You are precisely the person who needs to do this," Fitzwilliam countered. "And if you will kindly remove that horrifying look from your countenance, I shall tell you why."

Darcy took a deep breath and did as he was bid.

"Honour is an excellent thing," said Fitzwilliam. "I commend you for it, for you are truly exemplary in this quality. However, you are a man of nearly thirty—thirty!—and as near a virgin as anyone I know."

Darcy's scowl returned. "I am certainly not—"

"Yes, I know. I was there if you will recall, but that was many, many years ago. And what since? How many women, paid or otherwise?"

Darcy was silent.

"Have you even kissed anyone? Besides her?" The word dripped with contempt as it left Fitzwilliam's lips.

Darcy did not answer.

"Even honourable gentlemen have needs, Darcy, and yours have gone unanswered for far too long. For whatever else I might say about her, Elizabeth Bennet has allurements that—"

"Watch yourself," Darcy warned.

"She is a seductress," Fitzwilliam insisted. "A siren, luring men to their death against the rocks."

"Stop that."

"Did not I feel it myself?" Fitzwilliam pressed his hand to his chest. "I do not censure you for feeling what she intended you to feel. I only mean to say that a little light-hearted fun with another woman will…help. An antidote, if you will, to the poison she has placed in your body and soul."

Fitzwilliam rose and came to lay his hand on Darcy's shoulder. "Trust me, you need this."

Darcy shook off his hand. "No one needs to dally with a woman."

"As our old friend Aristophanes would tell us, 'if this dog do you bite, soon as out of your bed, take a hair of the tail the next day.' So there you have it—a bit of tail is all you need." He gave a bawdy laugh.

Darcy felt a revolted shudder pass through him even as he found himself considering the idea. Perhaps Fitzwilliam was correct. Had he not thought, if he fell in love with another, that he would finally be free?

"If you cannot extricate yourself," Fitzwilliam said ominously, "you might as well write to Lady Catherine directly, and tell her to set a date for you and Anne to marry. You must conquer this. It has gone on long enough."

Darcy fell back against his pillow with a light thud. It was true. He needed to be free, even if he did not truly wish it. He could not fall in love, but perhaps he could like someone enough to forget love ever mattered.

In a grudging tone, he said, "I shall play your silly game, but when I wish it, I shall leave."

Fitzwilliam clapped him on the back. "I promise you—you will not want to."

When Mrs. Bingley rose and bid them all good night, there was little response from the group in the drawing room. Bingley was urged to follow her, and after several lacklustre protestations, he did, saying his farewells with a sheepish grin. Mr. Hurst was already asleep, and Miss Bingley, after several pointed glances from the others, persuaded her sister to take him to their apartment.

For about half an hour after they had gone, the assembled group continued as they were. Miss Bingley spoke to Lady Sophie in low tones, and Miss Haverhill sighed over a romance novel she was reading. Miss Lacey was at the pianoforte, playing softly while Jolly, Egremont, Fitzwilliam, and Sir Edmund busied themselves with cards. Darcy struggled to write a letter to Georgiana.

When the last hand of cards was played, the men at the table rose. "So," Egremont said with a grin, "shall we get to it?"

"My man wondered at a second shave," said Sir Edmund. "I do hope the servants will not talk."

"The servants have already talked," Jolly proclaimed with a slap to his friend's back. "Another reason to envy us, my man."

Miss Lacey rose from the pianoforte, a deep blush already affecting her, and Miss Bingley exchanged a look with Miss Haverhill, which prompted both to giggle. Then everybody spoke at once, assuring each other of absolute discretion, the need to avoid scandal, and the like.

Jolly soon clapped his hands, bringing them all to silence and summoning them to the card table. However, fitting nine persons around one card table was impossible. The gentlemen had a discussion of the logistics of it, which led to the discovery that the table could be expanded. This arrangement yielded six places, which was better, but all were nearly in one another's laps.

Darcy sat as far back as he could without being too obvious, but still his leg touched Miss Lacey's to one side and his cousin's to the other.

"So the game is Naughty Lottery," said Egremont. "Plays just as it always does save that the fish you win are used to purchase favours, from a kiss at the table to time in the servants' closet."

"So we are all harlots in this game?" Darcy asked. Jolly laughed loudly, but everyone else disregarded him, choosing instead to bicker over the "prices" assigned to each successive prize.

"Pairing off is strictly forbidden," Jolly announced. "The odds favour the ladies, so we shall all expect fair treatment."

"Except that the odds do not favour the ladies," Lady Sophie replied. "For there are five of you and four of us. A gentleman will be able to choose more often than a lady—but then again, so it often is." The other ladies laughed and agreed with her, and the first hand was dealt.

The knot in Darcy's stomach tightened as the play began. For the first few rounds, it was all innocent enough. Fitzwilliam was the first to be awarded a kiss from Jolly, who affected an air of innocence and protested that no one said one must restrict their prizes to the opposite sex. Fitzwilliam startled him when it was next his turn, leaning in and telling him to purse his lips but at the last choosing to give a kiss to Lady Sophie. Darcy won several hands but chose not to use his fish, quietly setting them to the side and hoping the game would be over before he was made to use them.

Despite her protestations that fortune would favour the gentleman, Lady Sophie benefitted from a great deal of good fortune throughout the game. Darcy observed with increasing alarm that Lady Sophie, unlike the others, chose not to spend her fish immediately. Evidently, she wished to save them for the big prize, which was time spent in the servants' closet with someone of her choosing.

At last, with a grand flourish, she dropped a fish onto her pile and drawled, "Well, men, it seems I have ten fish."

"A grand prize!" Jolly roared with laughter. "Who will be the lucky fellow?"

Lady Sophie rose, taking her ten fish and tossing them into the spent pile. Darcy watched as she gave an impudent, examining look across all the gentlemen. "Hmm," she said, placing her finger to her lips. "Who here looks like he knows what he is about?"

Fitzwilliam and Jolly were both quick to protest her doubt, while Egremont sat there with a grin and Darcy restrained his impulse to walk out. Lady Sophie rested her eyes on Darcy for a long moment, moved to Egremont, and returned to Darcy. *Is she hoping to excite my ardour? Tiresome woman.*

Lady Sophie finally extended her arm to Egremont. "Come, Robert. Heaven knows we have played these sorts of games often enough, and I do believe you owe me a favour."

"Seems you will be doing *him* a favour," Fitzwilliam muttered. Cheers and jeers were called out while the other three ladies hid scandalised grins and darted looks at one another. Egremont offered Lady Sophie his arm, and they strolled over to the end of the room where a small door was concealed behind a screen. They went around the screen, and a second later, the click of a door closing was heard.

Miss Bingley giggled into the silence. "And do we all just…we sit here and wait for them to…"

"Indeed, we do," said Jolly, relaxing against the back of his seat. "And we pray to God that they take too long, requiring us to burst in on them."

"Oh, I could never!" Miss Lacey exclaimed. Two pink spots had bloomed on her cheeks.

"Oh, I certainly could," said Sir Edmund. "Egremont has it coming."

Lady Sophie and Egremont returned in a disappointingly short time bearing satisfied smirks upon their faces. Neither spoke a word as they returned to the table, both aware they were under close examination by their friends. Egremont helped Lady Sophie sit, and the game resumed.

Sir Edmund and Miss Bingley were next to retire to the servants' closet, and both looked well pleased to go. Unlike Lady Sophie and Egremont, they were gone for some time, long enough that shouts and chants began to go up. Jolly had just risen to knock on the door when it opened (the screen having since been moved), and the pair exited. Miss Bingley had an astounded, happy look, and Sir Edmund appeared to be thinking of something besides horseflesh for once.

Darcy began to relax. Despite Jolly's warnings, it did seem that some pairings had been defined, and this little game was a farce designed to permit these pairs to kiss. It was all in good fun, and he realised he need not be uneasy.

Then in a timid, self-conscious manner, Miss Lacey spoke. "It seems I have collected ten fish."

Giggles and cheers broke out along with urging from various people to choose this person or not. She smiled and shook her head, laughing as she spoke. "No, no, I have already made my choice. Mr. Darcy—will you join me in the servants' closet?"

Chapter Nine

Darcy was excessively aware of his cousin's eyes upon him as he reluctantly rose from his seat. How deeply he regretted playing this infernal game! But it was too late to repent his choice now. Every feeling within him revolted at the idea of kissing Miss Lacey, but to refuse would humiliate her.

If I have learnt one thing, it is that to humiliate a lady is excessively unwise. A gentleman does not embarrass a lady, no matter the circumstance.

He forced himself to his feet, resigned to the task before him; for a moment, he was still, unable to compel himself forward. *Come, Darcy. You are master of an estate since the age of two-and-twenty. You have suffered far more challenging tasks than this.*

He felt the eyes of the room boring into his back. Miss Lacey cast playfully bashful looks behind her as she led him on the interminable journey across the room. She stopped before the door; it seemed he was expected to open it for them, and so he did, reaching across her, turning the latch, and opening the door.

They entered the small space, and Darcy closed the door behind them. It was dark, the only bit of light coming from the crack between the door and the floor. For a moment, there was nothing but silence.

Miss Lacey laughed nervously, and Darcy startled, having not realised that she was so near.

"I…this feels a bit strange."

"It does," he agreed quietly. "Fear not, for I expect nothing. You need not—"

"I think I might like to," she admitted. Her voice grew a bit nervous as she whispered, "I never have."

"Oh." Shame and guilt seared him. Surely, he could not be Miss Lacey's first kiss when he was so entirely uninterested in her. Was he? Indeed, he was. She held no claim on his heart. It would be unfair to kiss her knowing he was in love with another.

"Miss Lacey, I have to tell—" Miss Lacey rose on her toes and kissed him quickly on his cheek and then even more rapidly on the side of his mouth. She moved back as silence, heavier and darker than the closet, fell on them.

"Was that…did I do that well?" Anticipation lit her voice. It was evident she wished him to continue what she had begun.

"Yes." The word came out in a hoarse croak. He thought he might be ill.

She pressed near to him again. "Would you like to—"

No, I would not. Not in the least. Darcy had just made the discovery that, without some measure of affection, kissing was as disgusting an occupation as could be imagined. Suddenly, he felt himself suffocating in the darkness; the walls were close and the air even closer. He fumbled behind him, seeking the latch as he attempted to draw a deep breath.

"Ah, no, I cannot…I…"

"Darcy," she breathed, and he felt her press her bosom into his chest. "Fitzwilliam…"

He pulled back but discovered there was nowhere to go even as Miss Lacey pushed closer to him. With relief, he heard jeers and calls from the room without. The rest of their party had grown impatient for their turns in the servants' closet.

Miss Lacey made a little protesting sound. "We have scarcely had a minute in here!"

Darcy's hand landed upon the latch, and he immediately opened the door. "After you."

Their return to the table was no less painful than their removal. Darcy assiduously avoided Fitzwilliam's look of leering anticipation as he assisted Miss Lacey back to her chair and regained his seat. His fish remained where he had left them neatly stacked, all ten of them. Play resumed and soon Fitzwilliam was off to the closet with Lady Sophie. For that, Darcy would thank him heartily although it did not appear too much of a sacrifice for either of them.

A Short Period of Exquisite Felicity

Fitzwilliam and Lady Sophie remained within so long that Jolly was required to go bang on the door. He tried to open it, but it seemed that someone of considerable strength was holding it closed. At last, the couple was induced to come out by the cheers and calls of their fellow players. When they emerged, Lady Sophie's bodice appeared a bit askew, and she looked at Fitzwilliam with a distinct light of intrigue in her eyes. Fitzwilliam, too, appeared a bit affected by Lady Sophie.

A strange melancholy settled on Darcy as he sat with one hand resting on his fish and the other holding his cards. How easy it seemed for others to meet someone and form an attachment! Yet how difficult his own affairs of the heart had been. Why could he not be easier? He liked Miss Lacey; she was sensible, kind, and handsome, and he believed she would be a suitable match in all respects. But the idea of marrying her, kissing her, and begetting children with her thoroughly disgusted him.

How different it had been with Elizabeth. He did not often permit himself to remember, for remembrance brought him pain. But perhaps just this once he would allow it, permit himself to revisit that hot August day with the smell of late summer in the air and the feel of Elizabeth on his arm.

How good, how right, it felt to have her walking close beside him. She chattered away about some such nothing—her visit to Blenheim? Something about the Peaks? It did not signify. And then she had seen the roses—his mother's roses—and he was merely thankful that they continued to prosper year after year. Elizabeth gasped when she saw them, her delight so vivid that he made her a promise then and there.

"I shall see to it that you have a posy of them in your chamber every morning."

She smiled. "It would seem a shame to tear some poor maid from her duties just to cut flowers for me."

"Who said anything about a maid?" He had gently touched her cheek with the tip of his finger. "I shall see to it myself."

Her smile grew even larger. "Sir, I must warn you: you show every sign of being an indulgent husband."

"Oh dear. What if you should become insufferably spoilt?" he teased.

"It is of grave concern," she teased in return. She edged nearer, her face tilted towards his in a charmingly tempting manner. "I suppose, however, if I spoil you in return, the effect may be lessened."

> *"How will you spoil me?" He pressed as close to her as he dared and then some.*
>
> *She lowered her eyes and peeped up at him through her lashes. "Why, in any way you would like me to."*
>
> *His skin seemed to come alive, prickling and warm. His heart pounded, and his head swam. He worried for none of that though, for it was his lips that led the charge, lowering to her, kissing her first gently and then deeply, the true kiss of a lover.*

He shook himself free of his memories, absently rubbing at his arms. The shadow of a smile lingered on his lips, and he forced himself to regain a more sober countenance. He glanced around to see whether anyone had observed him.

Miss Lacey was three chairs away, watching him; she gave a little wink, and he nearly groaned, realising she had misunderstood the object of his reverie. *I assure you, madam, I did not think of you.*

When he looked back, her eyes were still on him, and she glanced pointedly at his pile of fish. He gave her a smile that felt tight and pained on his lips; then he lowered his eyes. He did not look at her again, and thankfully, the game ended soon after.

LIFE AT LONGBOURN WAS SEDATE AND ORDERLY. MR. COLLINS SPENT HIS days among the tenants and on the land, no doubt still acquainting himself with the workings of the estate. Charlotte kept herself busy by visiting the neighbours she had known since girlhood. Mrs. Bennet was oft in her chambers with Mrs. Philips; no one knew what they found to amuse themselves for so many long hours, but as they disturbed no one, it did not warrant much consideration.

The only person who truly minded the tedium was Kitty, but even she was enlivened in anticipation of their brother Bingley hosting a ball.

When Elizabeth learnt of it, she hoped it would be a quiet affair, something she could easily eschew. But such hopes could only be in vain with Mr. Bingley planning the event. Musicians from London were engaged, and notes had gone around to every family in Meryton and quite a few in London. The thoughts of nearly every lady were filled with notions of which gown, shoes, and ribbons might be worn and dreams of this dance partner or that.

For Elizabeth, such fancies were more like fears. She did not fear Mr.

Darcy would be rude to her, but she did dread his cold civility. She feared hoping he would ask her to dance, and she feared the sorrow she must feel when he inevitably did not. Most of all, she could not abide the idea of watching him dance with someone else.

On the morning of the event, she went to her mother's bedchamber. It was Mrs. Bennet's habit to linger in bed with tea and a muffin, and her daughters had long known this was the time they would find her most agreeable. Kitty entered hard on her sister's heels, no doubt with some application of her own.

Elizabeth took a moment to arrange her mother's pillows more comfortably behind her and laid a shawl across her shoulders. As she smoothed it, she said, as though the thought had just occurred to her, "Mama, I believe I should remain home with you tonight."

"Home?" Mrs. Bennet cast Elizabeth a look meant to wither. "Why should you remain home?"

Elizabeth perched on the bed by her side as Kitty settled on the other side. "Someone should be here for you."

"Certainly not! Remain home when all those eligible gentlemen are at Netherfield? I cannot comprehend why you are even here! You should be there, putting yourself in front of Bingley's friends!"

"They were not for me," Elizabeth said in an unconvincing manner.

"Not for you? Of course they are for you! Now, I insist you put yourself forward a bit. You cannot expect to live on the charity of Mr. Collins forever."

"Certainly not," Elizabeth teased weakly, "I intend to live on Mr. Bingley's charity."

Kitty giggled, but Mrs. Bennet was not amused. "You are going to that ball, and you will do your best to dance and enchant someone—this Egremont fellow perhaps."

Elizabeth had not expected to be successful, but it still dampened her spirits to have lost the battle so quickly. "Mr. Egremont is a determined flirt, and no lady is left wanting for his attentions. There is nothing of significance there."

"Make of it what you can," her mother advised. "I do not care how you do it. Jane would not have invited you if she did not think you wished to marry."

"I cannot marry." The words came out before Elizabeth could stop herself.

"Cannot marry?" Mrs. Bennet cried out. "Why ever not?"

Elizabeth could not answer her. The truth—that her heart inextricably belonged to Darcy—would not be believed, and no other reason would do.

"See here, Miss Lizzy," her mother began, and Elizabeth knew from long experience that any tirade begun in such a manner could never end well for her.

"I am only teasing, Mama," she said hurriedly. "A little joke."

But Mrs. Bennet was not done with her reprimand, telling Elizabeth she had no compassion for her nerves, and Elizabeth, hoping to console, resigned herself to attending the ball.

Following her more successful application for new ribbons, Kitty followed Elizabeth to her bedchamber. Elizabeth's room boasted a long window that, by virtue of the light, served as a tall looking glass. She did not particularly care for such a view, but Kitty would often take the opportunity to observe herself twirling and preening.

Elizabeth rolled her eyes as her sister flirted with an imaginary suitor, lowering her lashes and pouting her lips. "It is only a country dance, Kitty, given by our brother and sister. There is no cause to be so eager."

"There *is* a cause to be eager," Kitty replied, practising a smile she no doubt hoped was mysterious. "Rich gentlemen all about the place! Do you think I should wear my yellow gown? I have picked out the hem with blue thread very nicely, I think, and I do believe Lydia would—"

"Let us not do anything that Lydia would do." The reply came much more sharply than Elizabeth intended, and she sank into the seat by her dressing table, abashed. "Forgive me, Kitty."

Kitty stopped her antics and regarded her sister with unusual compassion. "Why do you not wish to go tonight?"

"I am not inclined to dance, that is all. It does not matter; Mama would not hear of my staying back."

Kitty went to her, laying a hand on her back. If Elizabeth lifted her eyes, she would see her sister reflected in the glass, but she did not do so. "Mama only wants you to be well, to be what you used to be. We all do."

"What I used to be? What do you mean?"

There was a pause as Kitty seemed loath to say what was on her mind. "You are different, Lizzy. You do not laugh and tease as you used to, and sometimes you still seem sad."

Elizabeth ran her finger along the edge of the dressing table, feeling all the little marks left behind by five young girls and the families before them. How could she explain to her young sister that love—deep, abiding love—had left upon her heart the same sort of nicks and gouges that marred her little table?

"Does being here at Longbourn refresh your grief?"

As good a reason as any other. "Yes, I confess it does a bit."

Kitty smiled with relief. "I have grown accustomed to Longbourn being different from when Papa was alive. I forget all these changes are new to you."

"Yes," Elizabeth agreed, though, in truth, she scarcely thought about her father. It seemed that Netherfield and a certain gentleman therein would consume her. Would it improve when he left? The notion left her hollow and blank.

And now she would be required to go to Netherfield and watch him with Miss Lacey, dancing and perhaps even falling in love with her. She would watch Jane and Bingley, their felicity on full display, and the other young couples, pretty and gay and unencumbered by the secrets and lies that still haunted her.

"Perhaps you should go see him," Kitty suggested. For a brief, horrid moment, Elizabeth believed she meant Darcy. Then she collected her wits and understood her sister.

"Papa?"

"Yes. Have you been there since your return?"

"No," she admitted. "No, I have not."

"Go," Kitty urged. "It seems it will pain you, but strangely, it is oddly comforting. You should go now to return in time to dress for the ball!"

Kitty would not be gainsaid, so Elizabeth agreed. It seemed she would have no choice but to see her father at last. "I am sure the walk will do me some good."

THE MORNING FOLLOWING THE KISSING GAMES, FITZWILLIAM DESCENDED into the breakfast room at an uncommonly late hour. Darcy chided him gently for it.

"It seems the adjustment to the dull routine of a gentleman might be easier for you than anticipated."

Fitzwilliam chuckled as he poured himself coffee. "Tedium is not without some advantages." He selected a muffin from the basket on the table, managing to consume nearly half of it in one bite, and drinking much of his coffee in one gulp. In mere moments, he was finished with breakfast.

"Get your hat," he told Darcy.

"My hat?"

"We are going for a walk to Meryton with the ladies."

Darcy looked out the window. It appeared to be a fine day for November, and a walk might have been pleasant under other circumstances. But ladies? He believed he knew which ladies Fitzwilliam might have engaged for the excursion.

"Thank you, but I do not think—"

"I have promised Miss Lacey and Lady Sophie we shall escort them. Now come."

Darcy felt a pit of dread form in his stomach. "Ask Jolly to go with you."

Fitzwilliam gave him a severe look.

"I shall not raise Miss Lacey's expectations."

"No?" Fitzwilliam selected another muffin and bit into it with the ferocity of a lion. "Why not?"

"Why are you so intent on forwarding an attachment between us?"

Fitzwilliam shrugged. "I like Miss Lacey."

"I do too. Like her. Not love her."

"Of course you do not love her." Fitzwilliam's irritation turned into a soothing calm. "Not yet. You need to spend time with her. You must have enjoyed kissing her?"

On this subject, Darcy would not speak. "Get someone else to go."

"I promised her *you* would come; indeed, I might have suggested it was your idea. Now get your overcoat and hat; we are for Meryton."

Darcy stood angrily but did not move. "You have grown insufferable in your attempts to make a match for Miss Lacey and me."

"Perhaps I have," said Fitzwilliam with a cocksure grin. "But I know you are too much of a gentleman to embarrass her because of it."

Darcy hesitated.

"After all, it is not her fault that I am making you angry. Why disappoint her? Come along and let this be the end of it."

Darcy sighed. "Very well, but only so I do not humiliate her."

DARCY RESENTFULLY DONNED HIS GREATCOAT AND HAT AND AWAITED THE descent of the ladies into the vestibule. Had any excuse to avoid this excursion presented itself, he would have seized it gladly; but alas, it did not.

Lady Sophie minced and smirked her way down the stairs, while Miss Lacey smiled openly at Darcy as she pulled on her gloves. Fitzwilliam offered Lady Sophie his arm and led her out the door. With little ado, Miss Lacey slid her hand around Darcy's upper arm and followed suit. It was a presumption he could not like, but he obligingly arranged his arm to support hers, and away they went.

"Do you enjoy a walk in cold weather, Mr. Darcy?"

"I enjoy being out of doors no matter the weather." He was determined to be civil but not encouraging. There was a real danger that his attentions could raise her expectations were he incautious.

They went down the lane from Netherfield, chatting idly about the weather and their preferences for it. Those subjects led to a conversation about the forthcoming festive season. Just when she mentioned her father's large Twelfth Night gathering in London, Fitzwilliam suddenly exclaimed, "Oh no! I forgot the very letter I intended to post. Sophie, be a love and come back with me to retrieve it."

Darcy immediately understood the scheme. "We can all go back."

"Nonsense!" Fitzwilliam was moving Lady Sophie away at a rapid pace. "Lady Sophie does not mind; do you?"

"Well, I—"

"Here we go then! Just walk slowly, Darcy, and we shall be back with you in a short time—minutes, I am sure."

He and Lady Sophie retreated with haste, and Darcy was left alone with Miss Lacey, who appeared delighted by the turn of events. With a rueful smile, he surrendered to his fate and indicated the lane. "Shall we continue?"

They began, as Fitzwilliam had suggested, at a slow pace that matched the rate of their conversation. Darcy was too much occupied with the thoughts in his head and his fears for whether he would ever be able to love another woman, while Miss Lacey, he would later realise, was forming a resolution to speak.

They were halfway to Meryton when she suddenly stopped. She turned to face Darcy with two bright spots on her cheeks that could not be attributed to the chill in the air. "Sir, if you would so oblige me, I fear I must speak to you. It may be somewhat ill-judged to speak frankly of the matter, but I can think of no other way."

"Of course," he said, sounding stiff and cold even to his own ear. "Please continue."

He stared down at her as she twisted her hands and pressed her lips together. "I fear I have earned your disapproval by my participation in the game last night."

"Why do you think so?"

She gave a pained little smile. "Our former ease has gone, and it grieves me. I suppose you are repulsed by my boldness in kissing you as I did."

"No, no," he assured her. "Nothing could be further from the truth."

"Then what is it?"

"It is nothing at all, I assure you." They stood for a moment in silence. She did not believe him, and he felt badly for it. He might not be in love with her, but neither did he wish to offend her.

She turned away and again moved towards Meryton, her head bowed and her hands clasped in front of her. He followed slowly, watching her back, the weight of the silence between them growing more oppressive with each step.

They were within view of the churchyard in Meryton when he spoke. "Miss Lacey."

She turned back and faced him.

"Pray, forgive me for not have spoken sooner. I must reassure you, there is nothing you did last night that offended me. If I am somewhat melancholy, it is only due to…" What reason to give for the deep sorrow which plagued him?

"Fatigue," he concluded feebly.

For some reason, she believed him, and a smile broke over her face. "And I as well! I cannot think how I shall manage to keep awake through a ball."

"Nor I," he agreed. Then, because she gazed up at him so expectantly and he knew he had offended her, he said, "Will you do me the honour of dancing with me tonight?"

"Yes," she said in a gasping, excited tone. "Yes, sir, I thank you. The first set is yours, I have promised it to no other!" She gave a delighted, girlish giggle and drew in beside him.

First set? But no, I…ah blast it, what does it matter? Darcy did what he could to play along and seem pleased by the notion of dancing with her.

At this most inopportune of moments, a movement a few feet away caught his eye. A mourner who had been kneeling at a nearby grave rose, and with a start, he realised it was Elizabeth. To escape the meeting was impossible; she had seen them and now stared at them with wide eyes and a pale countenance. It suddenly seemed that he stood far too close to Miss Lacey, and he leapt back with a rapidity that was likely more damning than helpful.

"Miss Bennet!" Miss Lacey greeted her with a face wreathed in smiles. "How do you do?" She contrived to move them towards Elizabeth while simultaneously keeping Darcy close to her side. Elizabeth took one or two reluctant steps away from the grave and onto the path.

"Miss Lacey, Mr. Darcy." She curtseyed, keeping her face lowered. "How good to see you."

"And you." Miss Lacey smiled warmly and reached to take her hands. "You have been missed at Netherfield. What do you do here?"

Elizabeth glanced down towards the grave, and Miss Lacey's eyes followed it. "You have found me paying my respects to my father," she replied just as Miss Lacey exclaimed over her stupidity.

"Pray, forgive us for interrupting you. We should have seen that you did not wish to be disturbed." She smiled up at Darcy, and he found he did not like being included in her "us" and "we." He looked away.

Elizabeth shook her head. "Some things are best disturbed. But do not let me intrude upon your walk."

"I do hope we shall see you at the ball tonight," said Miss Lacey eagerly. "Mr. Darcy and I were just arranging our dances."

It hardly seemed possible, yet Elizabeth's face appeared even more pained than it had before. Something in her demeanour appeared to shrink in on itself. Darcy was assailed by a protective rage on her behalf.

"Do not permit me to detain you," she said softly.

She took it for some romantic interlude, this stupid walk on which he found himself. And no wonder, given what Miss Lacey had done—insufferable presumption! "We were with Fitzwilliam," Darcy announced abruptly. "He went back to find a letter. I expect he will be along shortly."

"I have not seen him." Elizabeth lifted her eyes to his, and he saw they were deadened by anguish, caused by what she thought she saw before her.

Do you regret me? Do you love me still? She did; he could read it easily in her eyes. It confounded every notion he held of her. Words and questions rushed to his lips, but he bit them back; it was not the time to speak of these things, not with Miss Lacey hanging onto his arm as though she owned it.

The lady tugged at him. "We should leave Miss Bennet to her time with her father." He reluctantly went along with her, leaving Elizabeth alone in the graveyard.

Against every better inclination, he glanced back as they made their way down the lane. She remained where they had left her, her eyes following them and her hands twisting themselves into knots at her middle. When she noticed him looking, she lowered her head immediately, her hands dropping to her sides.

It was a deeply affecting image that would not leave him on the way home. Elizabeth seeming so pale and fragile, left behind in her sorrow, whilst he was merrily on his way with Miss Lacey. He thought of Fitzwilliam's words several nights prior: the very purpose of a man is to defend what is his, to protect it and keep it safe. Did not he wish for that? To protect what was his? To defend her and keep her safe?

Yet he could not. *She is not yours*, he reminded himself. That idea fuelled his rage and made it burn hotly, albeit impotently, in his chest.

The return walk was interminable. Miss Lacey, having comfortably attributed his silence to his supposed fatigue, regaled him with a few stories and did her best to keep pace with him. He arrived at Netherfield in a fury sufficient to box his cousin's ears were he given the opportunity to do so.

Fitzwilliam and Lady Sophie were sitting comfortably before a fire in the drawing room. The colonel cried out, "There you are! We wondered where you had gone."

Darcy was stone-faced and unyielding to the furtive grin Miss Lacey shot at him. "Yes, well…you are as poor chaperones for us as we have proved for you."

As if we need a chaperone!

He glared at his cousin while Miss Lacey prattled away about their walk until he finally was able to retreat to his bedchamber. As he expected, his cousin was hard on his heels, knocking only moments later.

"That Lady Sophie," said Fitzwilliam with a grin and a rueful shake of his head. "Quite the minx. I daresay she wished to continue our most agreeable activity from last night. I could scarcely persuade her to come to that little copse of trees by the—"

"I hardly wish to know about that." Darcy glared at his cousin.

"You are surely not angry that she has turned her eye to me? I was the most persuasive I could be in that dark little closet last night—one cannot blame a woman for being quite undone." He chuckled.

"I did not take kindly to being abandoned."

"I did not abandon you. We returned and then I was not able to find—"

"That is all very well for you, but perhaps I had no wish to be left alone with Miss Lacey!"

"Why not? Why would not you wish to be left alone with a beautiful woman?"

"Because she is beginning to make presumptions," cried Darcy. "Presumptions of a something far more than I am willing to entertain. She nearly kissed me! On the lane, in the middle of town, right in front of God and Elizabeth."

Fitzwilliam laughed. "I should like to see what happened if she had. I can only imagine Miss Bennet's face."

Darcy cursed and went to the window where he gazed out on the landscape. The image rose again in his mind, the pained look on Elizabeth's face as she looked after him. "She was mortified and quite distressed to see us standing so close together."

"I am sure she was. The big fish has slipped her hook."

"She was never like that," he retorted sharply. "If she had wanted me for my fortune, we should have been married above a year now."

Just as sharply, Fitzwilliam countered, "No, she did not want you for your large fortune, she wanted Wickham for his large—"

"Watch yourself." Darcy turned and scowled fiercely. "Why is it so impossible for you to believe she might have once loved me; indeed, that she might love me still?"

"Perhaps she does—but even so, I do not much care for her manner of loving people. Not when the people in question are the very ones I love too, and I must watch them be angry and sorrowful for over a year. That sort of love she may keep to herself."

"If she does still love me," said Darcy, the novel idea taking shape in his mind. "If she does...then I must...I must try to speak to her...I must—"

"Darcy." Fitzwilliam's utterance was half stern and half pleading. "You must put Elizabeth Bennet behind you. There is no gain in continuing in this manner for a woman who has betrayed you!"

Darcy gave him a cold stare.

"'Tis true. You are not the Darcy I have always known—moping about after this woman who is so laughably beneath you. I'm finding you rather pathetic, if you must know." He shrugged. "I speak as I find."

Darcy crossed the room in two quick paces. He could not say how it all began, but soon enough, he and his cousin were engaged in the sort of scuffle they had not had since they were schoolboys. As they had back then, they fought in a furtive manner: Darcy hissed that he would like to see Fitzwilliam try to take him from Netherfield, and Fitzwilliam muttered vague threats about tying Darcy to a horse cart. Both men proffered little shoves and half-hearted punches in areas least likely to produce noticeable injury.

Their dispute died quickly, and soon both men were regarding each other in a shamefaced manner. "A thousand apologies," Fitzwilliam murmured, straightening his coat.

"Perhaps a thousand of them, but I do not believe even one. You are not sorry."

"I am sorry that I am making you angry. I hate to see you like this; you are uncertain and unhappy. The truth is, the only person I have ever seen affect you so was George Wickham."

"And it is George Wickham now too, in a manner of speaking."

"When Elizabeth Bennet is behind you," said Fitzwilliam softly, "so, too, will George Wickham be gone forever. Let us leave Hertfordshire. Time and distance—"

"Will do nothing for me," Darcy replied. "I have already had above a year with both, and as I learnt immediately when she arrived, it mattered not. I need to speak to her."

Fitzwilliam shook his head. "What good can come from it?"

"Resolution," Darcy said softly. "Perhaps even…"

"What?"

Darcy ran his hand through his hair, disarranging what had already been rather dishevelled. "There is some part of me that hopes we might yet be reconciled. I have tried to remove it, to forget it and wish it away. Perhaps I must give it its due and address it by speaking to her directly."

"Reconciled!" The expression on his cousin's face left Darcy in no doubt of how much the notion disgusted him. "I shall not permit you to harm yourself, Darcy, no matter what I must do to save you. I intend to carry my point in this."

Darcy regarded him for a moment. Fitzwilliam stood with his hands balled at his sides and a determined set to his jaw. Darcy's anger melted a little as he considered that his cousin would do anything to see him removed from that which pained him.

He smiled faintly. "You know you sound precisely like Lady Catherine when you say that."

Chapter Ten

The mile between the Meryton churchyard and Longbourn took Elizabeth above half an hour to travel. She found herself on several occasions standing stock-still on the road and staring at nothing; then, with effort, she would make herself begin walking again. Her thoughts, it seemed, were so weighty that they had the capacity to stop her movement.

She had known from the day she wrote her letter that Darcy would marry another lady, perhaps even fall in love with her. What she never anticipated was having to watch it. In her mind, they would meet again when they were older, forty or fifty perhaps. She would be the maiden aunt of Bingley's children, and he would be an elegant older gentleman surrounded by his sons and daughters, his wife a shadowy grey figure beside him. In this vision, Elizabeth would fear nothing save for a mild pang of regret.

To watch him falling in love with a beautiful, charming lady was another matter entirely. This sensation was no mild pang; it was agony.

She arrived back at Longbourn and immediately went to her bedchamber. A gown was laid out on her bed—a beautiful gown of palest rose picked out in a silvery thread. Lydia had abandoned it at Longbourn, proclaiming it ugly and virginal although it had been meant as part of her wedding clothes. She had snickered that it would do very well for Kitty, but Kitty, Lydia's follower in all things, protested immediately that she also thought it ugly. Elizabeth thought quite the opposite, and after some altering (she was neither as tall nor as stout as her youngest sister), she felt the gown suited her rather well.

Elizabeth stared at it for a moment before snatching it up, caring not that she crushed it in hands that were likely none too clean after kneeling by her father's grave. She threw it unceremoniously to the floor and kicked it away. Then she sank onto the bed, resting her face in her hands.

Pink was such a wretchedly hopeful colour. What good did a pretty gown do a lady who was destined to live her life alone and unloved?

Elizabeth owned another rose-coloured gown. She had worn it the day he found her at Pemberley, the day he had greeted her with such unexpected kindness. The day when she realised he was more dear to her than she had imagined possible.

None of that mattered now. What mattered was that she was to go to a ball and watch him make love to another lady, a lady who would bring neither ignominy nor shame to him, who would not jilt him, and who would marry him, live with him, and have all the comfort of his presence for the rest of her life. With a sigh, she lifted her head and opened her eyes to stare at the gown.

In her present state, it might suit her better to don one of the gowns she had worn to mourn her father. But she could not imagine her mother would countenance such a gesture; therefore, she slid off the bed and knelt to pick up the gown. She laid it out on the bed again, smoothing its wrinkles and brushing at a bit of dirt.

The dress was ready to be worn, and she would wear it. Her hope in so doing was to put him out of her mind for good. It seemed impossible, but she would try.

Mr. Collins decided it was eminently suitable for him to escort the younger ladies of the house to the Netherfield ball. Charlotte, having recently confirmed she was increasing, had no vigour for the amusement and happily relinquished the duty to her husband. Mr. Collins had a new carriage to take them, large and luxurious and far above anything her father had ever owned. Elizabeth wondered how he afforded it but then decided it was none of her business.

Everything was similar to the first ball at Netherfield, the one time she had ever danced with Mr. Darcy. She would not permit herself to think of that dance now; to do so could only raise false hopes within her. How different it would be now if only he would design to ask her again!

Jane and Bingley were handsome and felicitous, greeting their guests with good cheer. Elizabeth kissed Jane on the cheek, allowed Bingley to kiss hers, and moved into the rooms set aside for dancing. They were already crowded with people, and she allowed her eyes to scan the room, not wishing to be pathetically obvious in her search for him.

So engaged, she nearly ran into Mr. Egremont, who offered an amiable greeting. "Miss Bennet. How do you do?"

"I am well, sir." She smiled and curtseyed. "I hope you have been keeping yourselves well and amused here at Netherfield."

"Well enough," he said with a charming grin. "Dare I suppose it was me you were looking for just now?"

She laughed, feeling herself colour. "Was it so obvious that I was looking for someone?"

"Obviously, you wished to find me." The grin never left his face, and he leant into her. "Your plan was to put yourself before me so that I would ask you to dance the first set."

"Is that so? How bold I am!"

"Quite so," he agreed. "But fear not; I shall indeed ask you. Miss Bennet, may I have the pleasure of your hand for the first set?"

"You are too good, sir. Naturally, I shall accept as this was my design all along."

He chuckled in a delighted manner. "I shall return to you shortly. I daresay the musicians are nearly done with their shrieks and shrills."

Elizabeth felt an uncommon degree of gratitude for Mr. Egremont; it was a comfort to know she had a partner for the first dance. She would not sit, rejected and alone, and if it could not be the man with whom she truly wished to dance, she had no doubt Egremont would prove an agreeable partner.

That man appeared almost as if she had summoned him. He descended the stairs with Colonel Fitzwilliam. Darcy walked slightly ahead of his cousin with his head angled backwards speaking to him; thus, he did not see Elizabeth immediately. Her eyes swept over him; she had never seen a man look as fine as Mr. Darcy looked in his evening attire. He was almost too handsome to be borne. Her heart quickened, and a flush of heat engulfed her.

He finished speaking and turned his head away from his cousin. His eyes moved over the vestibule and immediately found hers. Their gazes locked each upon the other.

A frisson of half alarm and half thrill went through her. He caught her staring with her want of him in clear display, but she did not much care—not yet. All that she cared about was the fact that she was in a moment with him, both of them communing in this small way. She watched as his eyes took her in; she pleased him—she could tell that much—and it brought a faint smile to her lips. Darcy reached the bottom step, and for a brief mad moment, she wondered whether she could induce him to come to her. Her lips curved into a faint smile, and she flushed when she perceived a warmth for her in his eyes.

The moment ended when Miss Lacey appeared from nowhere, cheeks already pink with enthusiasm, and attached herself to his arm. Darcy looked down at her with a smile that, to Elizabeth's eye, looked rather tender. It was the death of whatever vain hope had grown inside of her in the past moments, and she swallowed hard. Carefully, she forced herself to turn away and walk with as sedate an air as possible out of the area.

"I intend to solicit her hand for a set," said Darcy over his shoulder to his cousin as the two men descended the stairs into the vestibule.

"*Her?* Surely you do not mean...?"

"Save yourself the bother of attempting to dissuade me. My mind is settled on the matter."

"Darcy." Fitzwilliam moaned the name more than said it. "Come now. You must..."

Fitzwilliam said more—Darcy heard his cousin speaking even if the meaning of his utterance was lost—but it could not signify. She was there, standing in the vestibule as if she awaited him, and she was lovely. Her eyes were upon him, and he could not deny that there was frank admiration in them. He could only suppose it was mirrored in his own, because in a trice, the past was erased. His heart went soft, and he knew he would go to her, not only in body but in mind and spirit. Anger? He had no anger. All would be forgot; all had been forgiven.

"And I was led to believe it was the ladies who spent too much time at their toilette." Miss Lacey interrupted his reverie with a little laugh, moving close to him just as he landed on the bottom stair. He turned his eyes to her, still lost in thoughts of Elizabeth. "I began to think you intended to remain in your bedchamber."

"Ah." Darcy felt as stupid as he ever had; Miss Lacey seemed like a leering stranger to him, a rude intruder thrust into a pleasant colloquy. He was struck by the compelling impulse to walk away.

Fitzwilliam put a hand on his back. "I believe Darcy had a nap," he announced in a forceful voice. "Still a bit tired, eh, Darcy?"

"I did as well," she confided, moving even closer to the two gentlemen. "Unless fatherhood has altered his custom, I daresay, we can expect Mr. Bingley to keep us dancing until dawn."

Darcy saw with disappointment that Elizabeth had left, but it was no matter. He would ask her to dance later, and the devil take the hindmost for it.

Mr. Egremont was a charming partner, but Elizabeth found his affected gallantry rather tiresome. His compliments lacked the unstudied air that would have made them feel genuine. No matter that; she tolerated him with good grace and as much of her sparkle as she could manage.

Mr. Darcy and Miss Lacey appeared to enjoy their dance together. Smiles and laughter were in abundance from both parties, and they conversed with the ease of intimacy. It gave Elizabeth a sick feeling in her stomach, and she soon resolved to pay no heed to them as best she could.

"I understand you are soon to be in London," said Egremont. "Bingley said you would all be there some months."

"Yes," Elizabeth agreed with a faint smile. "I do not think he is able to take possession of Beckett Park until the summer."

"You will be able to enjoy the Season, then."

Elizabeth agreed with a smile and a nod.

"Do you like London?"

"What time I have spent there, I have enjoyed, although I cannot imagine it being my permanent home." She smiled at him. "I find myself in need of a good country ramble when I have tarried too long in town."

"Ah well, good on you, then. For myself, I am always bored silly when I am too long in the country."

While they danced, they talked easily about subjects of little consequence to either of them. Elizabeth was as fond of sketching character as ever, but Mr. Egremont made himself easy to discern. She might smile and laugh with him, but there was little of true substance to be found. She could not dislike him, but neither could she love him.

How could she love anyone when her heart was already given to another?

The dance ended, and she looked around. Darcy and Miss Lacey were off to the right, thus she would go left. "Mr. Egremont, might I prevail upon you to escort me to the punch bowl?"

"With pleasure." He bowed.

Too late, Elizabeth realised that the other couple had changed direction. It seemed they, too, were intent on some punch. Elizabeth attempted to gently persuade Mr. Egremont to another direction, but he would not be moved, promenading them in a rather determined manner right into the path of Mr. Darcy and Miss Lacey.

Miss Lacey called out, "Mr. Egremont, have you come to join me for our dance?"

She halted, forcing Darcy to halt as well. With a coquettish smile that somehow managed to encompass both men, she said, "You are impatient to claim me, I see, but I fear I am dreadfully thirsty."

"As are we all," he replied genially. There was nothing for it; they went to the punch bowl as a group with Mr. Egremont and Miss Lacey carrying the conversation while Darcy and Elizabeth moved silently at their sides.

Punch was poured and given to both ladies. Elizabeth seized her cup gratefully, wishing for something, anything to carry her off. There was little time to tarry, for the strains of the next set were heard, and Egremont soon drained his cup with a flourish and extended his arm to Miss Lacey. "Off we go. Miss Bennet, it was a pleasure."

They went on their merry way, and the two left behind were abandoned in an anxious silence. Elizabeth studied the cup in her hand, willing her feet to leave him but quite unable to do so. She glanced up to see him staring at her—not the intent gaze he once had, but something more troubled and confused. He looked away as soon as he saw her observation. She decided she must remove herself from him.

"Excuse me."

"Would you like…"

She looked at him curiously, but he shook his head, motioning that she should continue on her way. She did, walking across the room in what felt like a most conspicuous manner. She had no idea in what direction she went, insensible of everything but the anxiety of being near him. With relief, she noticed Jane speaking to Mrs. Hurst at the side of the room and hastened towards them.

Thankfully, the two ladies were deep in conversation, and after a few obligatory remarks, they were content to leave Elizabeth to her thoughts. Her imagination tormented her, forcing her to relive Mr. Darcy's dance with Miss Lacey and embellishing the tenderness she had seen between them.

She hit upon the idea of going to one of the unused bedchambers and resting for a bit. She considered telling Jane she was ill, but Jane could not be counted on to be discreet. She would raise a hue and cry, perhaps even sending for the apothecary, so Elizabeth decided she would merely slip away.

Alas, it could not be. Jolly arrived to ask her to dance, and after him, Sir Edmund. She supposed both dances passed in an agreeable manner, but her mind was filled with nothing more than Darcy's eyes, troubled and sad upon her. She knew he would despise her forever; she had known it for some time. Nevertheless, she hated to be reminded of it.

By the time the supper set was called, she was again in her chair by the edge of the dance floor. She groaned, thinking she had only endured half the night so far and wished more of it behind her. She did not have a partner, which was unlucky for it meant she had no one to escort her to dinner. Mr. Darcy was again among the dancers, this time with Lady Sophie, who evidently pleased him much less than Miss Lacey had.

"Oh, dear Eliza, why do not you dance?" Miss Bingley arrived in a whirl of feathers and silk, sinking into the chair next to Elizabeth with a contented sigh. "I am positively fatigued by my exertions tonight! I have not had a moment to breathe!"

"I am fatigued myself," Elizabeth owned.

"All the better for me," said Miss Bingley with a glittering smile. "I shall have an agreeable companion while I enjoy my own brief respite."

Elizabeth nodded, feeling tired and wan.

"They make a handsome pair, do they not?" Miss Bingley indicated the dance floor where Mr. Darcy moved grimly around the happily bobbing Lady Sophie. "Ah, but I fear she has lost that race."

"What do you mean?" Elizabeth did her best to sound indifferent in her enquiry.

"Nothing official, only that he seems quite taken with Miss Lacey."

Elizabeth noticed that Miss Bingley watched her from the corner of her eye and gave a slight smile. "How nice for them both."

Miss Bingley tittered, holding her fan up over her face. "I even saw them sneaking off for a kiss the other night—if you can imagine the very proper Mr. Darcy doing such a thing."

A white-hot pain stabbed into Elizabeth's gut. She did her best to appear sedate though she knew such a tumult of emotion could not be wholly concealed, certainly not from someone like Miss Bingley who was so keen to discover it. "How…how amusing."

"Indeed." Miss Bingley giggled in an affected manner. "Quite scandalous. However, if nothing more, my dear Sophie has the comfort of knowing she has not made a fool of herself. At least *she* has other possibilities well in hand."

The meaning of Miss Bingley's inflexion was not lost on Elizabeth who only agreed faintly, "Yes, I am sure she has many suitors."

"The colonel can scarcely leave her side for a moment! But a lady such as Sophie, so well-bred and from such a well-known family, would be a match even the Earl of Matlock would approve."

Elizabeth did not answer; not knowing any of the persons involved, she could not comment. In any case, her mind was too full of imagining Miss Lacey kissing Darcy. The pain that attended such notions nearly took her breath away. She watched him, remembering his mouth on hers, the taste of him, and the feel of his hands on her back and waist. Did he press Miss Lacey against his chest with one hand on her back while the other wound its way into her hair? Did he move his fingers in a slow, delicate caress against the skin of Miss Lacey's neck? Did he tell Miss Lacey she had the most beautiful eyes he had ever seen?

Bile choked her throat, and for a moment, she was dangerously close to throwing up. Elizabeth bit her lip and stared at the floor in front of her toes. She could not cry, not now—not in front of Miss Bingley.

At supper, Elizabeth sat next to Mrs. Long at a table of matrons and chaperones. Mrs. Long had a goodly amount of neighbourhood gossip to relate; never mind that Elizabeth had heard all of it before—some of it several times over. Nevertheless, she listened again to who was married to whom, who had given birth, what servants were stealing, and why the butcher's daughter had gone away so suddenly.

It was dull but familiar, and Elizabeth was able to keep up her end of the conversation with little effort while watching the table where sat Mr. Darcy, Miss Lacey, Lady Sophie, Colonel Fitzwilliam, Jolly, and Miss Haverhill. Theirs was a table of high spirits and good humour, it seemed, and if Jolly occasionally grew too loud and rumbustious for polite society, no one appeared to mind.

Throughout, the refrain repeated itself: *he kissed her.*

Although Darcy had escorted Lady Sophie in, Miss Lacey had somehow contrived to be next to him. She appeared as she had before: contented and cosy, sitting too close, and murmuring asides for his ears only. It made Elizabeth positively ill to watch it, yet she could not look away. The beginnings of a headache flickered within her temples.

Elizabeth had arranged a dance with young Mr. Goulding for after supper, and when that had concluded, she was content to sit out the next few, finding an out-of-the-way chair on which to settle and be alone with her thoughts. She had hoped to hide there for the rest of the ball, but Jane would not have it.

"Lizzy, have you danced at all since supper?" Jane sank into the chair next to her sister with a delicate sigh. "Are you feeling well?"

Elizabeth disregarded the former question and seized gratefully onto the latter as an excuse for her indolence. "I am a little tired," she prevaricated. "I thought it prudent to be cautious."

"Well, of course," said Jane impatiently. "But with so many gentlemen around, I think you should dance at least a few dances. Mama will be angry to hear that you sat in a corner all night."

"I danced nearly all the dances before supper and with Mr. Goulding afterwards," Elizabeth said indignantly. "And how will Mama hear anything unless you tell her?"

"Unless *I* tell her?" Jane gave Elizabeth a look. "Have you forgotten you are surrounded by voluntary spies?"

Elizabeth forced herself to chuckle. Jane referred to a saying that Mr. Bennet once heard and adopted with great alacrity: every man is surrounded by a neighbourhood of voluntary spies. It was certainly true in the environs of Meryton. "It is true, I suppose; you are the least of my worries. Very well; the next man to ask me will be given a positive answer."

"Good." Jane gave a little pat to her hand.

On the other side of the room, it appeared that Mr. Darcy was in an argument of some sort with Colonel Fitzwilliam. Neither man was ill-bred enough to show their ire to one another, but it was clear enough to the sisters: the colonel's neck was flushed, and Darcy was speaking through clenched teeth.

"I wonder what that is about," Jane said quietly.

"I could not begin to imagine."

Jane giggled. "Perhaps Colonel Fitzwilliam had the audacity to ask Miss Lacey for a set, and Mr. Darcy does not like it. He would prefer her to sit and talk to him."

"Perhaps so," Elizabeth said in a voice that was tight and shook just a little.

Jane looked at her curiously. "Lizzy, what is wrong with you?"

"Nothing."

"No, it is not nothing." Jane put a hand to Elizabeth's head. Elizabeth knew she did not have a fever and Jane did too, though she pursed her lips and made a good show of concern. "I believe you have a slight fever."

Elizabeth pushed her sister's hand away. "Perhaps I should retire upstairs for a bit."

Victory was within her grasp. Jane appeared willing to allow her younger sister to depart and had just opened her mouth to say so when a gentleman appeared.

His hand outstretched in anticipation of an affirmative reply, Mr. Darcy said, "Miss Bennet, will you do me the honour of dancing the next with me?"

Unprepared and surprised as she was, she stared at him for a moment too long. It was sufficient for him to frown, and his hand began to withdraw.

She forced herself to speak. "I cannot…I had not supposed I would—"

"Lizzy," Jane spoke almost imperceptibly, but Elizabeth heard and understood her meaning. She had promised her sister she would dance with the next man who asked, and here was the test of her determination. To her left, she almost felt Mrs. Long's ears prick up, listening.

Elizabeth took a deep breath, resolved. "I thank you, sir," she said. His hand reached towards her once again, and she laid her hand in his and rose to her feet, feeling unsteady. They walked towards the dancers, Elizabeth feeling acutely aware of him beside her.

When they had taken their place within the set, she looked at him. Months ago, she would have expected to see his dark eyes intent upon her, but now he merely stared unhappily at his own feet. Perhaps whatever mad impulse that caused him to ask her to dance had dissipated, leaving him remorseful and wishing she would excuse him. The idea that he repented his request made her sink, and she wished there was some graceful means to extricate herself.

The beginning of the dance did not change her opinion. He moved steadily but without enjoyment, and he avoided looking at her. The dance would go on interminably it seemed, particularly given the number of couples.

She resolved to speak. Other couples had glanced at them curiously, no doubt feeling the ponderous silence in their midst. She waited until it was their time to remain still while the other dancers whirled and bobbed gaily around them. Mr. Darcy stared into the air, and she stared at him. How much she wished to be at least his friend!

"We should have some conversation, Mr. Darcy."

His eyes jerked towards hers, and he seemed almost amazed to see her there.

She tried giving him a small smile. "We must seem odd, standing here so silently."

She had hoped to allude to previous, happier times, but he appeared displeased.

"Very well," he said in sharp tones. "I suppose I shall first observe that, although you happily accepted the attentions of every other man in the room, it appeared uncommonly difficult for me to secure your agreement."

"I…no. I was merely surprised. I am glad to dance with you, sir."

He frowned in reply and began asking her strange, seemingly unconnected questions. Many times he seemed not to believe her answers, such as when he asked how often she went to London, and she replied that she had not been there for above a twelve-month.

"Above a twelve-month?"

"I was in Cheltenham since last autumn, and now I am here."

He frowned. "I can scarce credit that."

Her brow furrowed. "I cannot see why. There have been many times in my life when I would go a year and more without being in London."

"I should think you would want to see…to see the Wickhams."

"I most certainly do not," she replied coldly.

She could not comprehend his ire, but the longer they danced and the more questions he asked, the greater seemed his displeasure. At last, she was resolved to say something about it. They had just undertaken a somewhat serious argument regarding the symptoms and signs of consumption. Mr. Darcy, it seemed, did not appreciate the opinion that, at times, consumption arrived with the absence of a fever.

"Sir."

He met her gaze with eyes that were dead of all expression. "What?"

She kept her countenance neutral and calm. "I fear you wish to be dancing with someone else."

"If I did wish it, I should have asked someone else. You are by no means the only lady present."

She glanced around her. At the moment, no one paid them the least attention. "I was surprised you asked me."

Very abruptly, he said, "I need to speak to you. There are things between us that must be said."

"Oh." A pulse of fear went through her, but she hid it behind a small, conciliatory smile. "Very well."

"It is nothing to smile about." She had angered him it seemed, and he spoke coldly. "I assure you, this is not a conversation that will provoke one of the many laughs you have had at my expense."

"I have no wish to laugh at you," she protested. They were once again moving through the pattern, and as such, their conversation was fractured and spoken in hushed, hissed tones. "I told you once that I have no desire to ridicule what is wise and good, and I do think"—she paused and swallowed, uncertain how he would take her compliment—"I do think you are both."

His eyes flashed, dark and angry. "I remember the conversation, and I recall telling you I made it my practice to avoid those weaknesses that often turn men into objects of ridicule. Yet I succumbed to you. You are my weakness, and I am now ridiculous."

How he does despise me. "How fortunate, then, that we have arrived at the end of our dance; you need not tolerate my society a moment longer."

She curtseyed in a hurried, inelegant manner and turned away from him. Her first wish was that he would stop her, but he did not, and she walked quickly away, plunging against the tide of couples moving to join the dancers. Tears flooded her eyes, prohibiting her from seeing where she was going; she blinked them back furiously, her vision clearing just in time to show her she was nearer to outside than in. Longbourn. She would go home.

Her decision required no thought. Elizabeth had not wanted to come tonight, and now she had argued with Mr. Darcy. Remaining here was insupportable. She knew she should excuse herself or go to Jane or do something sensible, but it was impossible. Foolish or not, she would give in to her desires, which compelled her to leave Netherfield and make her way back to Longbourn.

She slipped through a side door, certain no one had seen her, and she was relieved to be free of the burden of the ball. The November wind and the darkness of the night soon made her aware of her folly, but she proceeded without caution, somehow finding the path leading to Longbourn. She moved at the greatest speed she could manage, a speed borne from her desire to escape but also to help her stay warm.

She had just begun to congratulate herself on the escape when from the darkness came a male voice.

"Miss Bennet!"

Chapter Eleven

"Miss Bennet! Elizabeth!" Elizabeth disregarded him, accelerating her pace as she moved away from the path and taking a shortcut that led her more quickly to the lane. She heard his footsteps quicken accordingly, so she walked even faster, the wind whipping against her skirts.

"Stop!"

"Go back to the ball!" she shouted over her shoulder, but she knew not whether he heard; her words might have been lost to the wind that whipped her cries from her lips. In any case, he did not answer but further increased his pace.

"Stop!"

"No!"

Reaching down, she gathered her skirts into her hands and began to run, cursing her light dancing slippers. She began at a trot but soon gained speed, hearing him close behind.

"You are being a fool! Stop!"

"I have no wish to argue with you!" she shouted, suddenly wishing for nothing more than to be in his arms. The wind caused tears to stream down her cheeks, but she paid them no heed and ran faster, seeking distance from her longing for him.

He had the advantage of longer legs and was nearly upon her when she attempted to confound him by diving into what appeared to be a tightly grown hedge. She knew it was not. It was a path disguised by overgrowth that she knew well from childhood. The branches scratched at her a bit, but she kept going faster yet, seeking what advantage she could. Her legs and lungs began to burn from her exertions even as her nose ran from the cold air.

A rustling from behind told her Mr. Darcy had followed her into the hedge, but he had not the advantage of youthful adventures to direct him as she did. Elizabeth heard more than a few grunts and gasped oaths as the branches snapped and whipped around him.

"Please go back!" she shouted.

"No!"

"Please!"

And then she misjudged, stumbling over a root, her dance slippers proving poor protection for a run through the rough, darkened countryside. Mr. Darcy suddenly appeared and caught her, preventing her fall.

He grabbed her roughly and pulled her against him. In a voice as rough as his touch, he barked out, "What on earth are you doing?"

"What are you doing?" she hurled back.

"Saving you from your folly!"

"I do not need saving, least of all by you."

"Yes," he replied with fire in his voice. "Yes, I am aware of how little you need me. Nevertheless, I would not have you scampering about the countryside on a cold November night. Should you manage to get to Longbourn without being killed by highwaymen, you would likely catch your death of a cold."

She jerked away from him. "Highwaymen are few near Meryton. We are too far off the London road to be profitable for such scoundrels."

"You are mistaken if you think I will allow you to walk away."

"You are mistaken if you think I am sufficiently in your power to allow you any influence over my actions."

With two quick paces, he covered the short distance she had gained. He grabbed her arm, pulling her back to his chest. She stared up at him, and he met her look with ferocity. "Trust me; I know you are not in my power. I am well aware of your indifference."

"I think we both know," Elizabeth admitted, swallowing the lump in her throat, "that I have never been indifferent to you. I have hated you, been angry at you, loved you, admired you, and enjoyed your company. Never, though, have I been indifferent to you."

He dropped her arm. "You never loved me."

She looked into his eyes while the wind bit their cheeks and made them both shiver. "Yes," she said softly. "Yes, I did…I do."

"You have a rather miserable idea of what it is to love someone, then."

She drew a deep, defeated breath. "I have no wish to argue with you. I give you leave to call tomorrow and say whatever you would like to me. Pray, go back to the ball; Miss Lacey no doubt wonders what has become of you."

He studied her, his eyes grave and intent. "What have you to say about Miss Lacey?"

Elizabeth lifted her chin, wishing to appear indifferent. "Miss Bingley told me you kissed her."

He seemed to sag a little, losing a bit of his righteous fury. "Yes, I did," he admitted. "I did kiss her."

"Then I must suppose your offer for her is forthcoming."

"What if it is? Were you hoping I would offer for you again and give you the opportunity to break my heart a third time?"

His manner lacked the affront that his words suggested and made her ache deep within herself. "I never intended to hurt you," she said quietly.

The wind howled and moaned around them, yet they did not move. Elizabeth shivered while watching Darcy look off at something only he could see for several excruciating moments. "You are a madness to me," he said at last. "I have thought of nothing else but you for above two years. You have seen me to the highest highs and the lowest lows."

"I am sorry." She reached out and touched his sleeve lightly. "I truly am."

He looked at her and seemed to draw himself up, squaring his shoulders. "I need to know why."

His countenance made her shake; the cold wind of November was nothing to the chill in his aspect. She nodded. "Very well. Um…now?"

"Not now. I would not have you die of exposure. I shall call on you tomorrow. For now, let us return to the ball."

When they returned to Netherfield, Darcy permitted her to enter first, and he followed moments later. He both hoped and feared that she might have awaited him in the hall, desirous of continuing their discussion, but it would seem the only person who wanted to talk to him was his cousin.

Fitzwilliam stood in a wide stance just inside the vestibule, his hands folded behind his back. He shook his head when he saw Darcy. "Am I not a buggering Frog?"

"I am sure I have no idea." Darcy attempted to push by, but Fitzwilliam did not permit him passage. "Are you?"

"What can you possibly be about, sneaking outside with her?"

"I did not *sneak* anywhere with her," Darcy retorted. "I noticed she went outside, and I suspected she intended to return to Longbourn. 'Tis three miles, and I thought it unwise in this cold, so I went after her to tell her so."

"Let her freeze to death; it is none of your concern!" cried Fitzwilliam. "Lest you forget, she willingly surrendered all claims to your compassion some time ago."

"She will always have my compassion," Darcy said with a soft sigh, "much as I wish to deny it. Now, if you would please excuse me, I am tired and would like to retire."

"I just spoke to Fields and asked him to pack your trunks."

"Rather presumptuous of you. I do not intend to leave."

"I intend to make you." His cousin stared at him with steely blue eyes that left Darcy in no doubt of his determination.

"I need to speak to her," Darcy insisted. "I want to hear it. I need to hear it to put this past me."

For a moment, they stared at one another until Fitzwilliam said, "Very well. Call on her in the morning, and we shall depart as soon as we can afterwards."

Darcy replied drily, "I thank you for your permission, sir; however, *I* shall decide when I should like to leave."

"Why would you wish to remain? Surely, not for her!"

Darcy realised the notion was not as absurd as it once had been. There was a part of him that wished all could be explained away. *She loves me. Did she not say so? And there was truth in her looks when she said it.*

And she was jealous of Miss Lacey. Was it wrong of him to delight in that?

Softly, he said, "I do not answer to you, Fitzwilliam. I shall stay as long as I want for any reason I choose."

Fitzwilliam considered his reply for some time before saying, "You know I have only your best interests at heart."

Darcy looked around him at Bingley's home, where felicity resided and love abounded. "Sometimes even the most intimate friend does not know what is best."

A Short Period of Exquisite Felicity

Fitzwilliam acknowledged that with a nod. "I shall concede that point, but there is nothing more to be done tonight. What say you to some drinks with the other men in the billiards room?"

"Now?" Darcy pulled his watch from his pocket.

Fitzwilliam clapped him on the back. "The hardy among us like to see things through to the dawn. A few drinks should help you sleep."

Elizabeth was relieved they had managed to return to Netherfield with evidently no one aware that they had slipped off together. Neither of them needed to be accused of an assignation, though she did think rather longingly that it might be nice if someone forced them to marry because of it.

Mr. Collins had been well past ready to leave when she returned and scolded her for vanishing, but he had not appeared to suspect anything amiss. His irritation was borne of sleepiness. Elizabeth had not seen Darcy again before she left.

To sleep was impossible. She tried for an hour and then resolved herself to seeing the sunrise. She went to her window, settling on its seat. It was a cosy spot, cushioned by pillows she had made and with her books in shelves beside the window. She took up a book but did not open it and, instead, stared out at the night for what seemed like hours.

He had come after her. Though the words they had exchanged were angry, the thought warmed her. Of their meeting tomorrow, she could not think; it made her tremble to imagine it, long belated though it was.

The winds had subsided, and hints of light from the forthcoming dawn had begun to illuminate the meadow. There was an ethereal peace to it, and Elizabeth found pleasure in permitting her eyes to wander the familiar sights partly shrouded in darkness.

When first she saw movement in the lane, she thought she must surely be imagining it. But no—it continued up the lane until she could see a horse and a rider. An express? Her heart leapt; in her experience, an express brought nothing but bad news.

But the rider seemed to be in no hurry to deliver it. As he drew closer, he appeared to list to the side a bit, and the horse's gait went from canter to trot to plodding. When he was close enough, Elizabeth could see that the horse was a fine steed, large and elegant, and the rider had a fine figure and noble bearing. No, it was not an express rider, and she had an alarming suspicion who it was.

What can he be about? It is hardly time for a ride.

She hurriedly pulled on a dressing gown and crept on silent feet down the hall. She descended into the vestibule and slipped outside without drawing any notice.

The man—who now she could see was Mr. Darcy even though his features were partly obscured by the shadows of the night—had just drawn up to the gate. Elizabeth watched as he rose in the saddle, evidently meaning to dismount. He swung his leg down, and his body left the saddle...and there was a terrible thud. With a gasp, she ran to him, seeing he had fallen to the ground. One foot was caught in the stirrup where it hung for a moment before the weight of his prone body tugged it free.

The horse, most fortunately, did not rear up though it moved restlessly, tossing its mane and craning its head to see what was attached to it. She grasped its reins, tugging it to the fence where she tied it securely before returning to Darcy, who appeared to be unconscious.

It did not require much examination to determine the cause of his fall. The odour of the brandy and ale he had consumed rose up from him.

Something in the lane had caused a wound across his forehead that slowly wept a rivulet of dark blood. It needed cleaning, but Elizabeth was loath to leave him on the road while she went for her remedies. She ran her hands over his form, putting aside her maidenly sensibilities to determine whether he suffered any broken bones. Fortunately, he did not, and she pulled at him gently, moving him a little in hopes of rousing him. At last, she was rewarded with a faint moan.

"Mr. Darcy? Come, sir, you have fallen. Allow me to attend the wound on your head."

He moaned slightly but did not open his eyes.

She tugged at him a bit more, eventually managing to move him into a more upright position, propped against her knee. She spoke to him loudly, wishing to wake him. It surely could not be good for him to be on the cold ground. "Mr. Darcy, come with me to the house so I may cleanse your wound."

He groaned again.

"Mr. Darcy? Mr. Darcy? Come now."

He opened his eyes just a little. "What are you doing here?"

"You are at Longbourn." She pulled at him, trying to encourage him to get on his feet. "You came here on horseback."

His voice was angry and low, and he jerked his arm away from her, declining her assistance. "Yes, quite right. Time for some answers, Elizabeth."

"You may have as many answers as you like, but first, we must tend to your wounds."

She paused while he slowly rose to his feet, swaying dizzily for a few moments until he gained some semblance of balance. He staggered forward, and she took his arm, forcing him to put it around her shoulders for support. This time, he allowed her to help.

He leant heavily on her, and she struggled beneath his weight as they made their way to the servants' door at a snail's pace. Before too many minutes passed, she had to stop and catch her breath. "A moment please, Mr. Darcy."

He paused obediently, standing and swaying as he stared at her. The cut on his head continued to bleed, a dark rivulet of blood wending its way down his cheek. He moved as if to wipe it on his sleeve.

"Do not!" she exclaimed. She reached into his pocket, where earlier she had seen that he kept his handkerchief. She extracted it and began to dab at the wound. "Let us go into the house. I must clean this, else it will surely fester."

He laughed darkly. "Perhaps I shall die—the ultimate punishment for my sin of loving you."

She had no idea what to say to that. "Come to the house, and allow me to care for you...for your injury." He begrudgingly placed his arm around her again, and together they began to walk. For several moments, they did not speak; their energies were directed towards movement.

Abruptly he stopped, turning and swaying a bit until he faced her. "Did you wish to make me love you so you could reject me as I rejected you on the first night of our acquaintance?"

"Of course not."

"Did you wish to see my pride awarded with a fall?"

"No." He stared at her, so she said again, "No."

He continued to stare, cold and motionless, and inasmuch as she could not fathom him in the daylight, in the wee small hours it was much worse. She broke their strained moment, taking his arm and tugging him, inducing him to enter the house. He complied silently.

Mr. Darcy said no more as she quietly took him into the kitchen, locating

Mrs. Hill's remedies and bandages as well as some water. She began to clean the wound, which thankfully was not deep, though it was long, extending well into his scalp.

She had hoped to avoid the notice of the house, but alas, Mrs. Hill, who was acutely attuned to any activity within her domain, arrived soon after Elizabeth began her ministrations.

"Miss Lizzy! Oh, such a fright you gave me!"

"Forgive me, Hill." Elizabeth smiled and tried to appear as though nothing unusual was happening. Mr. Darcy attempted to rise, but she laid her arm on his to restrain him. "Mr. Darcy had an accident on his horse."

Mrs. Hill looked out the window with her eyebrows raised but said nothing, instead moving to assist. She saw to Mr. Darcy's horse first and then returned, removing the bloodied cloths and cleaning up the space.

Mr. Darcy at last broke his prolonged silence. "I must return to Netherfield. I beg your pardon for having so importuned you both."

It was a dignified, well-mannered speech, but it was delivered in a benumbed and clumsy manner that betrayed his true state. Mrs. Hill looked at Elizabeth in alarm. "Forgive me, but he seems a bit…out of countenance."

"Yes, I know," Elizabeth murmured. "Mr. Darcy, I fear more ill might befall you should you attempt to return to Netherfield just now. Rest a bit, and then you may go."

"No, no, I am quite well." He rose and began to move, immediately hitting a basket of coal and nearly falling over it. Elizabeth was there at once, steadying him and making him sit again.

"Sir, I must insist that you remain. Hill has a room prepared for your convenience, and your horse is in the stables. We shall send a note to your cousin later in the morning." Mr. Darcy noted his approval of this plan with a faint nod.

"Miss Lizzy, would you like me to have Mr. Godwin attend him?"

Elizabeth paused a moment then turned, giving Mrs. Hill a significant look. Mr. Godwin was Mr. Collins's valet and, as such, was nearly the last person on earth that Elizabeth would wish to know of this—save for Mr. Collins himself. Heaven only knew how he might manage the situation, but humiliation and lack of discretion were sure to be the best part of it.

"No, I think it might be best if only you and I know of this…this episode. I would not like to embarrass Mr. Darcy for what is surely most uncharacteristic behaviour."

Hill nodded and curtseyed to Elizabeth. "You may be assured of my silence. I do not think anyone needs to know."

Elizabeth smiled, knowing she could trust the woman who had cared for her since childhood. She kissed her dear old cheek and whispered, "Thank you. Please return to your bed. I shall see to Mr. Darcy."

If Hill found Elizabeth's actions shocking, she nevertheless did as bid. When she had gone, Elizabeth turned to Mr. Darcy, ensuring that the sticking plaster she had applied to his head was secure.

It happened so quickly that she was in the middle of it before she knew what it was about. Mr. Darcy pulled her down onto his lap, encircling her tightly in his arms and kissing her with great fervour. She did not resist; her mouth opened to him, and her arms went around him, clinging to him just as tightly as he did to her.

There was a desperation in the manner in which she kissed him; she wished to taste him, consume him, and make him a part of her. On his part, there was roughness. He bruised and abraded her skin, but she did not mind in the least. There was a hateful quality to his desire—but it was desire nevertheless.

The violent storm of passion dissipated as suddenly as it had come. Elizabeth remained in Mr. Darcy's lap for just a moment before gently extricating herself and standing. She looked down at him in the kitchen chair, and he was watching her intently. He spoke not a word.

"Come, let me show you to the guest chamber." She turned and began to walk, noting with relief that Mr. Darcy rose and followed her. He maintained a steady but slightly weaving gait on their journey. Neither of them spoke, but Elizabeth, for once, was grateful for his silence, wishing for as much circumspection as possible as they moved through the darkened house.

When they arrived at the room, she silently pushed open the door and stood back. He entered, stumbling across the threshold.

She spoke quietly. "There are water and towels, and the chest has extra blankets should you require them."

He turned at the sound of her voice, saying nothing, just staring at her with black eyes and a blank face. There was nothing of welcome nor warmth in him, but she was drawn towards him nevertheless.

He must have understood what she was about; he did not shrink from her as she stood on her toes, placing her lips on his and renewing the kiss she had begun minutes earlier. He placed one large, warm hand on her back, steadying her as he returned her affection. He was not rough this time, but gentle, his lips an unexpectedly sweet caress.

"Did you love me?" he murmured, his voice low and rumbling against her lips.

"Yes," she whispered back. "Yes."

"Do you still?" His thumb traced a circle on her back, burning into her and making her feel unaccountably warm.

"I do," she murmured. "I love you."

He groaned, his lips remaining on hers and murmuring something unintelligible. Although she could not be sure, it was not likely any sort of endearment.

"Hush," she said. "We shall talk tomorrow."

IN THE MORNING, DARCY BLESSED THE HEAVY CURTAINS THAT KEPT THE bedchamber as dark as night even though it added to his confusion about his whereabouts. With a silent groan of dismay, he remembered he had ridden to Longbourn.

He had just begun to wonder what would be best to do—quietly return to Netherfield? Seek Elizabeth?—when the door opened. The light caused a bolt of searing pain to shoot through his head. He winced and turned away, though the sight of Fitzwilliam entering the room was welcomed. For a moment, his cousin stood silently staring at him.

"I am grateful," said Fitzwilliam in a measured tone, "that you are not dead."

"Forgive me if I alarmed you. Damn Hurst and his Madeira."

"I do not know that it was the Madeira as much as the gin. Or the brandy. Or perhaps the combination of them all." Fitzwilliam stood by the bed and frowned. "But let us get you out of here."

He leant in, putting his shoulder under Darcy's and heaving him upward. Darcy sat for a moment not moving. The motion required to achieve a seated position had made his nausea increase, and he believed he might be sick. He sat for a moment with his face in his hands, willing his stomach to remain where it was.

"Your trunks are packed. Everything is ready for us to depart."

"I cannot." Darcy's voice was muffled. "I must speak to her, and I am in no state to do so now." He lifted his head and looked into his cousin's disgusted eyes. "She loves me, Fitzwilliam. She said so last—"

"You were as thoroughly foxed as I have ever seen you. How do you know what she said?"

"She said it before I was drunk. As well as after."

Fitzwilliam began to pace, making little grunts of annoyance.

"What if he took advantage of her? Hurt her in some way, and perhaps that is why—"

"Are you going to marry a woman who has lost her virtue to George Wickham?" Fitzwilliam spoke harshly. "Has it come to that? The mistress of Pemberley should be George Wickham's leavings? Pardon me, but I think I hear the sound of your father tossing about in his grave."

"Perhaps," said Darcy quietly but firmly. "Perhaps it must be so."

"You have lost your mind. Now get up; we need to get you out of here."

"You cannot comprehend—"

"I comprehend all I need!" Fitzwilliam hissed loudly. He closed his eyes a moment and took a deep breath. "Forgive me; I do not intend to have an argument with you. Let us go. As you have said, you are in no state to have this conversation with her now. It has waited this long, and a little while longer will not hurt anyone."

ELIZABETH SENT UP A SILENT PRAYER OF THANKS THAT MR. COLLINS accepted without question the story that Mr. Darcy had fallen from his horse early in the morning and came to Longbourn to rest. She supposed it was not wholly a lie; after all, it had been after the midnight hour when Mr. Darcy arrived and therefore it was morning in the broadest sense of the word.

Mr. Collins sent word to Netherfield, and soon Colonel Fitzwilliam arrived in Mr. Darcy's carriage to fetch him. Elizabeth heard the bustle from her bedchamber, trying her best to stay there. Alas, she could not, and she went outside to speak to the gentlemen.

Mr. Darcy was seated in his carriage when she left the house, but his cousin remained like a sentinel. He closed the door firmly and took a step away from the carriage when she approached.

"Colonel Fitzwilliam." He stared at her coolly. "I wonder whether I might enquire as to the state of Mr. Darcy's health."

"A minute, please." Colonel Fitzwilliam opened the carriage door and ducked his head inside. He muttered something Elizabeth could not hear. He extricated himself, closed the door again, and told the coachman to go on.

"Some rest, and he will be returned to good health, I think." Fitzwilliam paused a moment then added, "Some rest and, I hope, some distance."

"Distance?"

"I intend to make him go away, within the hour if I can."

"Go away? From Hertfordshire?"

"Away from *you*."

The venom with which he spoke shook her. "Colonel Fitzwilliam, we were friends once, and I am grieved that you now greet me with such animosity."

"Someone who hurts a person I love in the manner you have hurt Darcy can only be henceforth my enemy." He shrugged. "Forgive me; I am steeped in loyalty."

"It is not your loyalty I question, only your civility. In any case, I wished to enquire after him, and you have answered me. There needs to be nothing further between us." She turned towards the house.

"Actually, I do think there needs to be one thing more between us. Will you join me?" With a slight gesture, he indicated the wilderness across the lane from Longbourn.

With a growing sense of unease, she agreed.

Chapter Twelve

A few minutes later, Elizabeth and Colonel Fitzwilliam were strolling together in the wilderness. He did not offer his arm, but she would not have taken it if he had. This was no friendly call, and she had no doubt that the conversation would be unpleasant.

After some time spent listening to the sound of his boots crushing the fallen leaves on the path, he said, "I am struggling to find some delicate way to say what I must. I fear I must be frank and pray that your feminine sensibilities can bear the shock."

"I have no doubt they can."

"Very good." He kept his head lowered with his eyes fixed before him. Elizabeth looked over at him frequently, unable to imagine what he must know or suspect.

"He thinks when he offered for you at Lambton that you loved him." The colonel's voice dripped with scepticism. "He thinks you love him still."

When she did not immediately reply, he gave her a hard stare. Although she felt anything but composed, she managed to give him a cool nod in response.

The colonel sniffed in a manner unmistakably derisive. "Lies."

"I had not realised *you* were an authority on my thoughts and feelings."

"I *am* an authority on your actions, or at least those actions that affected my cousin a twelve-month ago."

Her heart began to pound, and she took several moments to calm herself. When she regained her equanimity, she replied, "I do not deny I hurt him, but neither shall I deny that I did—and still do—love him."

"I do not think you comprehend the meaning of that word, but regardless, I cannot imagine what you hope to gain by telling him so."

"I do not hope to gain anything."

Colonel Fitzwilliam shot her an angry glance. "Then why say it?"

"I wanted him to know." She returned a matching look, refusing to be cowed by him.

"I believe you like to imagine that Darcy is in your power. I believe it grieves you to think that he might fall in love with someone else." The colonel stopped and turned to face her, staring at her mercilessly. "You have made your choices, and as such, any alliance between you is impossible. Indeed, I cannot think any decent man would have you as his wife."

"I have no intention to marry. I shall live out my days with Mr. and Mrs. Bingley."

"They are too good, taking you into their home." His tone was deceptively uninterested. "That is no concern of mine, however. My concern is for Darcy. What can you hope to gain by continuing to weave your web around him?"

"I am not weaving—"

"Darcy is weakened by you, and I intend to be his strength. Do you understand me?"

She crossed her arms over her chest. "I do not weave any web around him. I have scarcely spoken to him since he has been in Hertfordshire, and I left Netherfield when he asked me to."

"I do not want you to tell him that you want him, nor should you say you love him."

She forced a merry laugh. "If he asks me if I love him, he will hear a truthful answer, and indeed, he did ask me. I did not declare myself to him unprovoked, nor would I."

The colonel gave her a long, appraising look, and their conversation paused for several minutes. She had nearly declared herself victorious when he spoke again, touching his tongue to his lips as if he savoured the words as he spoke them. "Leave Darcy alone and we do not have a problem between us. However, if you continue to plague him with your declarations and your wiles, I shall not hesitate to expose you. I think that must be plain enough for your comprehension?"

"Expose me?"

"Your connexion with George Wickham." He quirked a brow at her. "I think you comprehend me."

"George Wickham is my sister's husband."

"I think we both know the truth of the matter is not nearly as simple as that."

He turned, indicating he would return her to the house, and she went ahead of him, pressing her lips together to avoid exposing the emotion within her. *What did he know?* The anxiety that had long been her constant companion was still with her—she had been lowly and meek since that fateful day in August of 1812—but somewhere within resided the spirit of the Elizabeth Bennet she once had been. *That* Elizabeth Bennet railed against the unfairness of suffering over and over again for Lydia's mistakes. She wanted to scream at the colonel, to hit him and tell him he was being cruel and unfeeling. What right had he to loathe her? What right had anyone? She had done what was necessary to save her family. Was that worthy of scorn?

Abruptly, she turned on him. He halted quickly, just scarcely able to avoid colliding with her. "Excuse—"

"Not everything is as it appears on the surface, Colonel Fitzwilliam. I shall thank you to kindly remember that. I do not know what is known and unknown to you, but pray understand this: there are two sides to every story. Do not dare sit in judgment of me; you are not in possession of all the facts."

"Am I not? Perhaps you should further enlighten me." His eyes were hard upon her. "I cannot think you have anything to say that will vindicate your cruel treatment of a man of good character, but please give it a try."

With that, the burst of former spirit left her. Yes, she was treated unfairly, but so had she treated Mr. Darcy in a cruel and unjust manner. He had also suffered for Lydia's folly; he simply had no idea of the cause.

"The tale is not yours to hear. The only person who has a right to know has never asked."

"Very well, but allow me to make a promise to you." The colonel stared at her as he must have stared down his enemy on the battlefield, his eyes cold, hard, and unyielding. She had no doubt that, given the opportunity, he would enjoy slaying her.

"What?"

"An alliance between you is impossible. Never consider it. I shall go to my grave making you suffer. He might forgive you, but I shall not—not now, not ever. Stay away from him."

"You might wish to remember that you are his cousin, not his keeper," she said, but her ire had been spent. She felt a warm tear slide down her cheek, and she knew she must escape him. He had made it known that he had no sympathy for her, and she would not permit him to see her cry. She turned and ran into the house, leaving the colonel and his hatred behind her.

Darcy took to his bed for nearly three hours, which was quite unprecedented behaviour for him. When he woke, he had cotton wool in his mouth, but his headache was a little better, so he supposed it had been for good. Looking at the mantel clock, he determined they would not be able to make it to London that day, and he was strangely glad that Fitzwilliam's plan to hie him off had been thwarted.

Fields came immediately when Darcy rang, bearing powders and the promise of a bath. Both did remarkable work in restoring Darcy to a semblance of his customary vigour—in body if not in mind. With his headache abated, he could not long excuse himself from reflecting on his mortifying behaviour the previous night.

Fitzwilliam thought him utterly idiotic for wishing to dance with her, but the truth was that he had wanted some time, no matter how small, in which she belonged to him. So he claimed her and they danced. Her initial meekness had been a source of vexation—where was her wit, the sparkle that he longed for?—yet when she spoke, that vexed him too. How dare she speak as though nothing lay amiss between them?

He hardly even knew what he wanted from her anymore; he knew only that he did not have it.

His state of inebriation had been somewhat intentional, shameful as it was to admit. He had easily seen that Fitzwilliam wanted him drunk, and he allowed it. He had wished for oblivion, a stupor that would numb him from the pain of thinking of her and make him forget how much he wanted her. Alas, somewhere in the haze of too much drink, he had evidently decided to go to her and make a fool of himself.

His fingers rose as if by their own will and lightly touched the cut on his head. For a moment, he lost himself in the memory of the way she had cared for him and tended his wounds. Would that she could do the same for the hole in his heart!

And their kisses! The first was meant to claim her, to brand her, and the second was meant to…to what? To show her that despite everything, she was still dear to him. He groaned, ashamed and embarrassed by his own foolishness.

Fields entered to help him from his bath and mentioned that Fitzwilliam wished to wait upon him at his earliest convenience. "Tell him I would like a walk," said Darcy. A quick glance outside showed that daylight yet remained. Perhaps even enough that he could call at Longbourn? "A short walk," he added.

Although he might not have chosen such an activity for himself, Fitzwilliam obliged Darcy's wish. "Rather fond of the cold these days, Darcy?" asked his cousin when he joined him in the vestibule some minutes later.

"It is not so cold." Darcy tugged on his gloves. "The air will do me good, I hope. How are you looking so vigorous?"

"I had only one drink to your three." Fitzwilliam grinned broadly. "Feeling a bit rode over, are you?"

"Quite so." Darcy chuckled ruefully. "But much improved now that I have slept."

The gentlemen set off into the maze, strolling the paths that were by now well known to Darcy. "I must thank you for coming to retrieve me. I was asleep as soon as I sat. I do not even recall you joining me in the carriage."

"I walked back." After a moment's hesitation, Fitzwilliam added, "I stayed behind to talk to her."

"Why?"

"Because I knew you wished for answers, and I saw that you were in no state to obtain them."

"What did you say to her?" Several moments passed. "Fitzwilliam, I insist you tell me at once what you said to her. You had no right to interfere."

"I did not interfere." Fitzwilliam turned to Darcy and sighed. He lifted his hat and scratched his head a moment. Settling it back on his head, he said, "Well…perhaps I did, just a bit, but Darcy, I have only your interests at heart. I love you like a brother—nay, I love you more than my brother —and I cannot like how this woman leads you about."

"She does not lead me about."

"Think of what she has done to you! And you follow after her like…like a hound sniffing after a bitch in heat! It is not the behaviour of a man of your station."

Darcy scowled with his haughtiest glare. "I certainly do not."

"Then why did you ride over there in the middle of the night?"

Darcy turned his face, staring out at nothing. "She loves me."

"Love! I assure you, the lady knows nothing of the affliction. In any case, what good will it do you if it can only bring you pain?"

Darcy did not answer for a moment. At last, he responded carefully, "I thank you for serving me as my confidante in this matter; however, I neither require your assistance nor welcome your interference."

"I think you still love her," Fitzwilliam accused him quietly.

Darcy permitted his silence to confirm his cousin's fears. Fitzwilliam understood him and sighed in disgust.

"Tell me this. Save for one short period in which you were betrothed, has loving her ever made you happy?"

Darcy had no good answer for that. He stared at the path beneath his feet, grinding his walking stick into the stones.

"Sometimes you marry the one you love," said Fitzwilliam, "and sometimes you love the one you married. Either way, it ends the same. Save yourself the heartache of Elizabeth Bennet; I implore you."

Darcy looked up, fixing his cousin with a searching look. "What did she say to you? Of what did you speak?"

"The weather, Darcy, what do you think?" Fitzwilliam rolled his eyes. "I spoke to her of you and the circumstances around the pair of you."

"You asked her about…about…?"

"Yes."

"Did she—" He stopped. "Was it Wickham? Was it…was it as we—"

Fitzwilliam laid a hand on his shoulder, giving him a comforting squeeze. After a mightily heaved breath, he said, "She could not deny it."

Darcy forcefully expelled the breath he did not realise he had been holding. After a moment, he said, softly, "There it is, then."

Fitzwilliam clapped him on the shoulder. The two gentlemen walked on together for some time, their pace slow and their thoughts, at least for Darcy, burdensome. As the house came into view, Fitzwilliam spoke.

"First light tomorrow?"

Darcy thought about it for a long moment, stopping on the path and turning towards his cousin. "I need to talk to her."

"I did talk to her. I told you what she said."

Darcy shook his head. "No. If what you say is true, then he must have imposed himself on her! I have resented her all this time when she was the victim of grievous injury. I should have enquired as to the truth of the matter. The burden of guilt is mine to bear—perhaps even more than hers."

"How so?"

"Because I knew what he was! I could have stopped it."

Fitzwilliam crossed his arms over his chest. "The verity of that statement is questionable, but I shall not debate you in favour of asking you this: Then what?"

"I do not follow."

"Once you hear it from her, then what will you do about it? The pair of you are standing there, and she has confessed all…and then you walk away? You propose to her again? What?"

Darcy removed his hat and rubbed his hands through his hair roughly. Thinking, considering, pondering—that always had been his way. Elizabeth changed everything about him, including this new tendency to act from his heart and impulse rather than by slow, careful reason. What did he want from her? The truth…but was he ready to reconcile with her? To walk away from her?

Fitzwilliam continued to speak. "No matter what, Darcy, I cannot forget that she accepted you and then left you. As your betrothed, she owed you something, an explanation. If she were in trouble, it should have been set before you—do not you think so?"

"Mm."

"Tell me what sort of marriage would come with a lady who took things on herself, who believed herself the head of the family." Fitzwilliam shook his head. "Not a marriage I would like. No, when I am married, my wife will bring her problems to me, not scuttle off to do whatever she thinks ought to be done."

"We were not yet married."

"Engaged is as good as married in such instances as these."

Why did not she come to me? If such was the case—if Wickham somehow had imposed himself on her—I might have helped. I might have killed the blackguard, but that would surely be a favour to society.

"We would not have been betrothed when…when it happened."

"She should have told you," said Fitzwilliam firmly. Evidently, on this point, he would not be swayed.

Darcy began to walk again with his cousin a step behind. As much as he wished it, he could not disagree with Fitzwilliam. One fact remained incontrovertible: whatever had caused her change of heart, whatever evil had befallen her, Elizabeth chose to hide it from him despite her promise to be his wife. Her honesty and candour had failed her at the time when it ought to have been most evident.

He sighed heavily. Every time he thought he knew his mind in this matter, something else would arise to confound and confuse him. How he hated it! Uncertainty was something he had never known before the fateful autumn of 1811, but since then, it had become his constant companion.

"Georgiana is no doubt eager to have you back in London."

"Yes," Darcy agreed in a faint tone. "I had thought she would wish to go to Matlock with you, but she wants to remain in town." Thinking of Georgiana brought another concern to the fore. "I am sure it need not be said that I do not wish Georgiana to hear anything to do with Miss Bennet."

"Naturally," said Fitzwilliam through a yawn. "But does Georgiana know—"

"She knows that I proposed to Miss Bennet and that Miss Bennet…well…that Miss Bennet clearly is not married to me. There need be nothing else."

After a moment, Darcy added, "I had to tell Georgiana something. She was at Pemberley; she met Miss Bennet…she saw how I made a fool of myself. When it all went off, I sent Georgiana to stay at Matlock, and she required some explanation."

"I have never discussed the situation with Georgiana. How did she take it?"

Darcy twisted his mouth a moment. "She despises Miss Bennet. She had much to say until I asked her to stop, and I told her the very mention of Elizabeth Bennet brought me grief. Then she ceased to speak of it, but I do not mistake her silence to mean that her heart has softened."

"Why should it? That woman has treated you in a most infamous manner. A woman so beneath you with nothing to offer, not even fidelity and trust."

A few steps more, and Fitzwilliam added, "Only consider that Georgiana —and, I must own, the rest of us too—would not acknowledge her. Not her, not Wickham, not any connexion thereof. Is she really worth it, Darcy? There are an abundance of women you could marry, but you have only one sister and a few cousins, people who have loved you since the day you or they were born."

Darcy met his declaration with silence.

A Short Period of Exquisite Felicity

"And I need not mention what would come of the Darcy name if the truth came out, which it inevitably would. Wickham would no doubt threaten you endlessly. Between this and the matter at Ramsgate, I daresay he would think he owned you."

"Enough." Darcy knew he sounded as weary as he felt. "I am still too beset by last night's indulgences to sort all this."

"So let us depart. Take some time to think of it, and once you are certain of your way, you may return to it in London."

"In London?"

"Yes." Fitzwilliam smiled at him, and Darcy took it for reassurance. "The Bingleys go to London with Miss Bennet in January. If you insist on speaking to her, why not do it then? After you have had time to consider everything."

HE WAS GONE. ALTHOUGH SHE HAD EXPECTED IT, ELIZABETH FELT THE loss rather keenly. Some part of her had hoped they still might speak, might somehow resolve what lay between them. Evidently, it was not to be so, and she resigned herself to his loss all over again.

The days moved along at a snail's pace, so slowly that Elizabeth felt she could scarcely bear it at times. She took to remaining abed long into the morning, wishing the days to be shorter, but then she was unable to sleep at night, lying awake and thinking of him.

The guests who had been at Netherfield departed in the last days of November and then, with painstaking deliberateness, November became December. Eventually, Elizabeth made preparations to remove to London with Jane and Mr. Bingley. She returned to Netherfield in time to help Jane close up the house for good, and it was a relief to have something—small tasks assigned to her by Jane—on which to rest her mind.

With their things sent ahead, the Netherfield party spent Christmas and Boxing Day at Longbourn. Longbourn was thusly filled to the brim with happy chatter as Baby Thomas delighted them all with his antics.

Elizabeth sat amid all the revelry, a silent, watchful presence. It reminded her of something Mr. Darcy had once said: *"I cannot catch their tone of conversation or appear interested in their concerns, as I often see done."* Yes, she knew precisely what that meant now, sitting among her family like a stranger in a strange land, seeing and hearing but not comprehending or feeling. Their conversation puzzled her, and their gaiety made her sad.

They set off on 28 December for London, Elizabeth feeling simultaneously relieved to be leaving yet dreading to be gone. She reminded herself often that such was the fate of a spinster; she did not decide her own course but relied on the kindness of her relations to keep her.

The house that Bingley let in London was on Davies Street, sufficiently fashionable for Miss Bingley's tastes and pretensions while close enough to Hyde Park for Elizabeth's walks. It was a good size for them all, though Miss Bingley immediately protested that Elizabeth had the superior apartment. She said Elizabeth's was larger and more richly decorated, and as the elder of the two, she believed it should be hers to choose.

"Take it if you would like," Elizabeth replied listlessly. "I am sure I do not care either way."

"Caroline, we thought you might like the view of the street," Jane said, hastening to intervene. "And the fireplace is larger too. I know how you tend to take a chill. The room is not much larger at all, and Elizabeth's has a little seat beneath the window where she might like to read."

But Caroline, having decided upon a preference, would not be moved, and Elizabeth, still uncaring, gave way to her although Bingley and Jane were both prepared to insist on her behalf. "It really does not matter to me," she said, and it was the truth. Indeed, she hardly even wanted to read these days; nothing was able to hold her interest for more than a paragraph or two.

The first full day in town was cold, grey, and windy, but Elizabeth found herself desirous of a short walk. This would be her home for some months, and she thought to familiarise herself with the area as soon as she could. Jane argued against it but soon was distracted by the servants needing this or asking that, and before too much could be said, Elizabeth dressed warmly against the wind and slipped out a side door.

On later reflection, she supposed she might have anticipated seeing him. In a place such as London—with a population of one million, if the latest census could be believed—one naturally would see the very person one wished to avoid.

It was a bit of good fortune that she managed to avoid his notice. She was gazing with frank curiosity on the grand houses in Grosvenor Street, permitting herself the indulgence of wondering whether one of them was his. He was walking towards her but with his head lowered to avoid the wind. For a moment, she was stock still, praying he would not see her.

A moment later, he entered what Elizabeth thought was the loveliest of all the houses she had been surveying. She released a breath of relief as the door closed behind him, and she knew she would escape unseen with nothing more than hotly blushed cheeks to admonish her for her stupidity.

She stood for a moment, knowing she should leave, but she remained in contemplation of the house. She could have called it her own now, that stately, beautiful home on Grosvenor Street. She might have awaited him by a roaring fire as he returned from his club or a morning call, and he would have come in, telling her how cold it was. It would have been their second Christmas as a married couple, but perhaps they would be yet at Pemberley, not even in town at all.

Such musings could not help her; indeed, she wished Mr. Darcy were at Pemberley and not in London where she might see him at any time. For not the first time, she considered telling her sister and Mr. Bingley everything in hopes they would avoid his society. But no, that would be unfair. He was Mr. Bingley's friend, and Mr. Bingley's friend he should remain.

The ache of her hands, chilled despite her gloves, reminded her it was time to go, and she quickened her step, noting miserably that it was a short distance back to Davies Street.

It was a distance too short to be of any use in avoiding temptation. Elizabeth found herself returning to his street often, far too often, despite the warnings she gave herself with regularity. She persuaded herself that by going at odd hours—usually before breakfast—she would never be caught.

Until she was.

Mr. Darcy did not see her; she supposed there was some small mercy in that. She was standing in unconcealed admiration of the place when a gentleman strode up to the door with great haste. Because he was not in regimentals, it took her a moment to recognise Colonel Fitzwilliam. And by the time she had, he was staring right at her.

She jerked her face downward a moment too late, praying in vain that her bonnet concealed her. She turned and began walking—fast but not too fast—and did not dare glance backwards until she believed she was safe.

She was not. The colonel stood yet on Darcy's step, staring at her. She could not make out his expression, but it was likely censuring.

Chapter Thirteen

Colonel Fitzwilliam stood in silent indignation watching the back of Miss Elizabeth Bennet as she hurried away in shame. Swallowing his pique, he adopted a cheerful front as he went to join his youngest cousin at breakfast.

Georgiana smiled as he entered and took a place at the table next to her. He chewed absently on bacon and drank coffee while she told him all that had transpired in her life during the three days since he had seen her: one friend's sister became engaged and another's mother died suddenly, a disaster occurred at the dressmaker when a favourite dress was made up entirely in the wrong style, and she was quite at ends with the way her brother continued to sulk about the house.

"Does he? Does he tell you what plagues him?"

"No. He is not angry or unkind, merely abstracted, and I cannot think what weighs on him so!"

"It is nothing about you," he assured her. "You need fear nothing for your own concerns."

"So you know what troubles him. I thought you must."

"I cannot say for certain, but I wager I know the heart of it." He shrugged. "Dare I suppose his abstractedness has gone on since our return from Hertfordshire?"

"To some extent, yes, though it has been much worse in the past week."

Since the Bingley party has been in town. Fitzwilliam nodded. "That makes sense."

He did not look at her; she stared at him as if she wished to use the force of her blue-eyed gaze to bore the information out of his brain. He sipped his coffee and ate his bacon with carefully contrived serenity until Georgiana could tolerate no more.

"You both treat me like a child!" She rose and tossed her napkin onto the table. "I am permitted to suffer the agony beside him; thus, I think I have the right to comprehend what it is about!"

"Your brother's affairs are not mine to tell, sweetling," Fitzwilliam insisted.

"Then *you* stay in this house and watch him fret and stew," she retorted. "'Tis maddening!"

She started to walk away, but Fitzwilliam grabbed her hand. "I can see it grieves you."

It took a moment for her pique to abate, but after some moments, she relented. "It does. I only want to help him overcome his melancholy."

Fitzwilliam sighed. "And he requires all the help we can give, as this particular affliction insists on revisiting him."

"Oh no!" Georgiana's eyes were wide with fear. "Is it something to do with Mr. Wickham?"

"Yes and no."

Georgiana sagged in her chair, raising her hand to cover her face. "My sins will forever haunt me, I fear."

"It is nothing to do with you."

"I am sure it must," she said with a gentle sob. "Is he threatening my brother again?"

"No, no, nothing like that."

"Then what?" she cried with shining eyes. "If it is not for me and my foolish reputation, then what could it be?"

Fitzwilliam studied her a moment. It did not escape his notice that Georgiana was still deeply affected by every mention of Wickham's name. The merest reference sent her into an agitation of fear and self-castigation. If he told her nothing now, she would worry endlessly just when they needed her attention turned to the forthcoming Season.

In the face of his silence, she sighed and cast her eyes down at her lap. "I did not expect you to tell me."

They stayed thusly for several moments: Georgiana with her shoulders bowed and head turned, and Fitzwilliam watching her while finishing his coffee and eating one last slice of bacon.

"Very well, but naturally you heard not a word from me."

"Naturally," she agreed with a small smile. Keeping her wary eyes on him, she straightened and smoothed her skirts.

"I cannot be free with the particulars because, in fact, I do not know every one, but it has to do with George Wickham and Miss Elizabeth Bennet."

For a moment, she was baffled, then comprehension struck. "Not—"

"You of all people must know how persuasive Wickham is; and she did, according to your brother, once love him."

Georgiana swallowed hard. "Mr. Wickham is an artful sort and well able to please where he likes."

"As is she."

"She is?"

"Within mere days at Netherfield, your brother was completely bound in her chains." Fitzwilliam shook his head sadly. "I would give anything I have to extricate him from her grasp, particularly as I have cause to believe that she repents her actions."

"She does?"

"She does. But I believe it goes without saying that he cannot marry a woman who has borne George Wickham's child, particularly when we both know so well how cunning Wickham is and that he would use any excuse to extort money from your brother and make him miserable."

"She...she had his child?" Georgiana's eyes were wide with horror, and her mouth hung agape.

Fitzwilliam held up a finger. "I said no more than what I said, but you may infer from it as you like. You are nearly grown now, and you surely must be aware of the way things are at times."

"Yes, yes."

"In any case, Wickham is now married to her sister. Being with Elizabeth Bennet means Darcy would never be free of the reprobate. I should think both of us would do nearly anything and stop at nothing to make certain that should never happen."

"Indeed," she agreed earnestly. Hesitantly, she added, "Perhaps if another lady were to take his fancy..."

"Perhaps," Fitzwilliam agreed thoughtfully. After a moment, he snapped his fingers. "Miss Lacey! He was rather taken with her at Netherfield. Do you know whether he has called on her of late?"

"I…I believe he has."

"Splendid. Perhaps you should call on her too. Do you know her? Never mind that, I shall introduce you." He gave her a conspiratorial grin. "She would be perfect for him."

As December bled slowly into January, Darcy's regret for having neglected to speak to Elizabeth could only increase. The conversation he wished they had would not leave his mind, though he was never able to settle on a result. Would they end as friends? Would it be their last conversation?

So much of the past months had been spent in despising her that he had not previously considered any possibility of reconciliation—or the consequences of such. It was not an easy matter to ponder. What would it mean to forgive her? To love her again? Could he accept and forget what she had done? Worse still, what advantage might this give to Wickham?

But against all this, his want for her remained. He wanted her in his life no matter how much argued against it. It was an impossible dilemma and one he was not yet prepared to resolve regardless of how many sleepless winter nights were spent tossing about thinking of it.

His distraction further increased once the date arrived for the Bingley party to be in town. When a sufficient number of days had passed, and Darcy knew he could appear merely polite (rather than too eager and anxious), he made a morning call to Davies Street.

Bingley was not at home, and much to his chagrin, Darcy was received by only Mrs. Bingley and Miss Bingley. The two ladies occupied chairs across from a settee in which he seated himself. When tea arrived, Miss Bingley made much of her belief that she knew how he liked his prepared, but she did not. He preferred it without cream or milk, unlike how she served it to him. He took a sip or two to be polite then pushed it away.

They spoke of the weather—it was cold, as it tended to be in January—and of the festive season. Bingley had delighted the ladies of his household with many little trinkets and baubles, and they had much to say about his generous nature.

"He does love to shop, certainly more so than many gentlemen," Darcy agreed.

Conversation languished after this, and Miss Bingley sought to fill the time by repeating uninteresting gossip that was unlikely to be true about people he could scarcely abide. She had just begun what promised to be a prolonged dissertation on Mr. Walter Pickering and the autumn hunting party he had hosted in Sussex, when the door opened and Elizabeth entered.

For a moment he was struck dumb, staring at her with his heart pounding so hard that it seemed it would leap from his chest. A moment too late, he rose politely and bowed to her.

Someone must have warned her of his presence for she did not seem surprised to see him and made every effort to excuse herself. "Forgive me, Jane. I do not mean to intrude, but I wanted to let you know I had returned."

"Come sit, Lizzy," urged Mrs. Bingley. "Have a bit of tea to warm yourself."

The settee where Darcy sat was closest to the fire; the only other chair was at some remove from the group. Elizabeth hesitated, glancing at him. He offered a faint smile and made a gesture with his hand at the place next to him. She came slowly, appearing uncertain but not unwilling.

When she was situated next to him, Miss Bingley leant forward, her teeth bared in a feigned smile. "You must have been down in Gracechurch Street this morning. Tell me, how are Mrs. Wickham and Mrs. Gardiner today?"

She pronounced "Wickham" with a grand flourish, but Elizabeth kept her composure. "No, I have not been to Gracechurch Street."

"Tomorrow, then," Miss Bingley insisted. "I know you cannot bear to be long parted from them."

It was calculated meanness, but Mrs. Bingley interceded, asking Darcy about his sister; this sent Miss Bingley into raptures about Georgiana and turned her attention elsewhere.

Elizabeth was quiet through most of the conversation, leaning forward and pouring herself a cup of tea. As she did, she noticed the cup Darcy had pushed away. Without a word, she obtained a new cup and fixed him tea in precisely the way he liked it. Discreetly, she moved it in front of him, not looking to see his grateful smile.

When the tea was gone, he rose to leave. The small party moved into the vestibule where, alas, a door had been left slightly ajar. The resulting cold was nearly unbearable for the ladies. Mrs. Bingley shivered and mentioned something about her housekeeper, and Miss Bingley bid him farewell in hurried tones. Thus he was left alone with Elizabeth.

"Thank you for the tea," he said in a low tone. "Miss Bingley has not yet learnt my preference, not that I would wish her to know."

Although her countenance for these many months had been meek and pale, for a moment, the Elizabeth Bennet he once knew—the true Elizabeth Bennet—came through. She gave him the impish smile that always portended some teasing, and her eyes lit for a moment. "I did once intend to marry you. To learn your preference in drink was of no little import."

Her words caused him to catch his breath; he was thrilled, alarmed, and joyous all at once. She had no such happy response, appearing to repent of her levity almost immediately. Colour flooded her face, and she gave him a stricken look, murmuring, "Forgive me." Then he could not stop her, and she rushed off, but it hardly signified as his carriage drew up moments later.

He did not breathe until he was seated in his carriage, and then he released his breath all at once. Her words, he would not soon forget: *"I did once intend to marry you."*

She could have no notion of how her words affected him; the scales had fallen from his eyes. *My life without her makes no sense.*

For so long, he had been angry and sad, plagued by a confusion that rendered him motionless and helpless. He had not yet given up all of it, but for the first time in many, many months, he was certain that he would at long last forgive her and do whatever he needed to retain her in his life.

The two most important facts remained: she loved him, and she had intended to marry him. This dreadful situation in which both of them were entombed was neither her design nor her desire.

He forced himself to *truly* imagine the worst. *She had Wickham's child. Can I forgive that? Can I forget it? I must. I can. I shall.*

The idea filled him with as much terror as elation. It was alarming to comprehend her holding such dominion over him that he would forgive her nearly anything.

Do I not need air to breathe and water to drink? Food to eat and sleep at night? So, too, do I need her.

"I shall have her once again," he vowed, watching out the carriage window as Bingley's house fell away from his sight.

A SURPRISE AWAITED HIM AT HOME: MISS LACEY AND HER SISTER, LADY Jermyn, were sitting with Georgiana. He was not aware that the two ladies knew his sister but was relieved to see her making friends.

As had been the case at Netherfield, he found Miss Lacey, whilst agreeable when directly in front of him, was easy to forget when she was not. He had called on her as he would any acquaintance, but nothing was meant by it. At least *he* intended nothing, and he dearly hoped that she did not have a different understanding.

He paused outside the drawing room door, waving away his man. The ladies seemed to be having a pleasurable time within, judging by their gentle laughter and gay conversation. It made him smile as he opened the door and entered.

"Ladies, do not permit me to disturb you. I merely wished to offer my greetings."

The ladies rose and greeted him prettily, urging him to join them for a few minutes; he felt it impolite to refuse. He went to sit in an empty chair, but Georgiana, who had been seated beside Miss Lacey, offered him a broad smile and reached it first, leaving only her previous space available. Darcy nearly groaned aloud at the plainness of such actions. His smile stiffened into a grimace, but he did as he must and joined Miss Lacey on the settee.

"I hope you will not think me bold, sir," said Miss Lacey. "Miss Darcy has told me just how you like your tea. May I?" She indicated a pot before her.

"I thank you, but I am not in need—"

"Dear brother, tea will be just the thing to warm you, will it not?" Georgiana pushed the teapot towards Miss Lacey. "Do pour, Miss Lacey, I thank you."

Reluctantly, he acquiesced.

The ladies did not remain overlong. Darcy made quick work of his tea, speaking as little as possible while remaining civil. His sister made several clumsy attempts to force him into a private tête-à-tête with Miss Lacey, but he stubbornly refused to be drawn in.

When he was finished with his tea, the ladies rose to take their leave, making plans and promises to meet another day for shopping. "Mr. Darcy, I understand you are to join us for dinner a few days hence?" Lady Jermyn smiled. "At my father's home, that is."

Darcy felt himself redden. Was he? Had he missed an invitation? He had no recollection of such an engagement.

"We received your note just yesterday," said Miss Lacey.

Yesterday? "Ah…yes. Yes, of course."

"I am all anticipation," said Miss Lacey with pink cheeks and a gentle smile. "It will be a lovely evening, I know it already."

He accompanied his sister to see their guests to their carriage and stood with her in the hall. When the carriage began to move away, Georgiana turned to him with glowing eyes. "Such amiable ladies! I am already excessively fond of them."

"I did not realise you were acquainted, but they are excellent ladies to count among your circle."

"Colonel Fitzwilliam introduced us," she informed him happily.

At once, a number of things became clear to him. "Pray, do not become a matchmaker, Georgiana. It is an insult to all parties."

"A matchmaker?" Her eyes flew wide. "Oh, Brother, I never meant to—"

"No." He held up his hand. "I see Fitzwilliam put you up to this, for I know you would never subscribe to such obvious manoeuvres on your own. Am I correct in supposing it was also Fitzwilliam who replied to the note for dinner?"

She hung her head. "Brother, do consider that my cousin and I wish only to see you happy, and we perceive that Miss Lacey is the best one for the job."

"*I* am the best person for the job of seeing myself happy," said Darcy with gentle sternness. "I do not require the assistance of our officious cousin, so please do tell him that he should direct his attentions to his own affairs."

She lifted her head. "Oh, I could never say that."

"Tell him it came from me." Darcy turned and took several steps towards the direction of his study.

"H-Have you seen her?"

The halting manner in which Georgiana asked made Darcy immediately aware of whom she spoke, but he did not acknowledge it. He turned with one brow raised. "Miss Lacey? Yes, I saw her only minutes ago. You were there."

Georgiana did not respond to his jest, but her eyes searched his face intently.

"I do not owe you or Fitzwilliam any accounting of the people I see and the places I visit."

They stood for several moments, Darcy refusing to answer his sister, even as she served as his cousin's proxy. "Permit me the respect of domain over my own affairs, dearest." He hoped the endearment softened the warning he felt required to deliver.

By the blush that rose to her cheeks, he saw his message was understood.

He regretted causing her pain but knew the message must begin now. He would do as he wished in this matter of Elizabeth Bennet with no regard to the interference of others.

Georgiana hung her head. "Yes, Brother."

He regretted subduing her and offered a small olive branch. "Bingley is my friend, and it is inevitable that I should have seen her while calling on him."

This small confidence warmed her a little. She lifted her head and offered a wan smile. "Of course."

"Come," he said with a conciliatory smile. "Did you not have a painting you wished to show me?"

MRS. WICKHAM, YOUNG AND SILLY AS SHE WAS, REFUSED TO ALTER HER dress for such inconsequential matters as weather; therefore, in January, she wore a light muslin that clung to her figure, eschewed a shawl, and stoked the fires to the point of her husband's suffocation. It was oppressive and made more so by the coterie of equally silly, pretty young things who were constantly in and out of the small but handsomely fitted house on Fenchurch Street. Wickham thought he could scarcely manage to swallow some breakfast before they set upon him, and at times, he merely longed to escape.

Alas, he had been late about his business the previous night and consequently spent too much of the morning abed. By the time he arrived in the breakfast parlour, there were already three of them, each more foolish than the next. Two were married, the third was not, likely due to the absence of any appreciable bosom and a high-pitched voice that pierced a man's ear.

The ladies had gathered, it seemed, to discuss this problem: Miss Cobham was now twenty-two and reaching the point of desperation.

"My sister did not marry until three and twenty," he heard Lydia say as he opened the door to the breakfast room. "I should have died had I reached such an age without a husband!"

"With such a husband as yours, I do not wonder that you snatched him up." It was at this unlucky moment that he entered. The ladies, however, were not embarrassed to be found at such a subject; indeed, they looked him over in a way that made him wish he were wearing his great coat.

Lydia giggled and rose, planting an elaborate, damp kiss on his cheek. He smiled at her and made a courtly bow to them all; after all, Lydia's friends today might be his lovers tomorrow. "Good morning, ladies."

"We are discussing Miss Cobham's difficulties in finding a suitable husband," said Lydia with a wink. "Alas, all the good men already have been taken."

"Such fools in this town." Wickham gave his most charming grin. "I should think they would be lined up outside your door, Miss Cobham."

"What about you, Mr. Wickham?" asked Mrs. Stone. "Have you a handsome brother or two stashed away somewhere who are in need of a wife?"

The ladies shrieked with laughter over this, and Wickham formed his wince into a grin. "Alas, I do not. I boast no near relations, or at least none willing to claim me."

This made them all shriek again, and Wickham tossed down his coffee, filled with a sudden determination to leave them as quickly as possible. Surely, he could buy a bun or something here or there if he were hungry later. Lydia asked where he was going, and he told her to the booksellers; only Lydia would be silly enough to think him in earnest.

The blast of cold winter air on his face as he stepped onto the street was a relief. He wandered the streets for a time, stopping here and there, at last finding himself at Lloyd's coffee house for a snack.

He picked up a discarded newspaper and read for a time before becoming aware that someone was watching him. He gave a surreptitious glance around and immediately perceived his observer. When the man saw that he had been spotted, he rose, taking his cup, and went to join Wickham.

Wickham offered no greeting, chewing and offering merely the most disgusted look he could summon to his countenance. His companion did likewise.

"What do you want?" Wickham asked finally. "I should think all needful association between us is at its end."

"I have learnt to keep you in my sights," the gentleman replied.

Wickham rolled his eyes. "Yes, well, I am not quite as fond of having you in mine, so do leave me."

"Rather impolitic, are you not? And I have come to offer a kindness."

"Everything does have a first time, I suppose. What?"

In reply, the gentleman withdrew a purse from his coat and tossed it on the table.

Wickham's eyebrows shot up. He opened the purse and counted. Surely, he was wrong. He counted again then lifted his eyes to the man across the table. "Why?"

"Why what?"

"What do you want of me?"

"Consider it a reminder."

"You must think me quite forgetful."

"When one builds a wall," replied the gentleman, "it serves well to fortify it now and again."

To this, Wickham would only smirk as he gave the purse a last look before tucking it into his pocket. "Then you may consider me fortified…though if you would like absolute—"

"No." The gentleman held up a hand. "You already have all I am offering."

"You cannot blame a man for trying." Wickham drained his cup and rose. "I am finished here and shall bid you adieu."

"I wish I could be finished with you as well." The gentleman sneered.

"Your choice," said Wickham. "Not mine." So saying, he strode from the shop.

Chapter Fourteen

"Well, there he is at last." Colonel Fitzwilliam, sitting with Darcy and Lord Matlock at their club, spotted his elder brother, Viscount Saye, approaching their table.

"Were you expecting me sooner?" Saye grinned and, tossing himself into a chair, ordered a generous repast before turning his attention to his companions.

His father frowned over his newspaper. "I did not like the sounds of that argument last night."

"Then perhaps you should have not listened."

"You argued with Lady Saye?" Colonel Fitzwilliam asked with interest. It was a source of never-ending wonder to both Fitzwilliam and Darcy that Viscount Saye had, against all probability, married a woman he not only loved but doted on to an almost comical degree. Neither could comprehend how the former Miss Goddard had managed to tie one of the most noted rakes of the *ton* so firmly to her apron strings; but she had, and Saye often professed himself delighted to be in residence there.

"She"—he pressed his hand to his chest with a flourish—"argued with me."

"What did you do?" asked Darcy.

"It must have been quite dreadful," Lord Matlock remarked. "Lady Saye has such a sweet temper."

Saye rolled his eyes and spoke to the ceiling above him. "One might expect to gain some sympathy among the society of gentleman, but evidently it is not to be."

Colonel Fitzwilliam echoed his cousin. "So? What did you do?"

"I gave her money!" Saye threw his hands up. "Are not women the most contrary creatures?"

"She was angry because you gave her money?" asked Darcy doubtfully. "That makes no sense."

"And as Lady Saye is a woman of sense, I must say there is more to this story," Fitzwilliam concluded with a grin. "Was the money a payment of some sort?"

With all eyes upon him, the viscount was forced to explain.

"She learnt of a particular evening sometime past when I was relieved of a sum she thought above my touch. Above a year ago! Silly girl—what can it signify whether or not I lost seven thousand pounds so long ago? I put the money back, which drew her notice to it, and so it went."

"Seven thousand pounds!" Lord Matlock exclaimed.

"How on earth did you contrive to lose such a sum?" Darcy asked.

"For some people, seven thousand pounds is a fortune," Lord Matlock replied sternly.

"And I thank God every day I am not one of them," Saye replied blithely. "If you would like to know the where and how, you will need to ask my brother; indeed, the seven thousand pounds went to his credit."

All eyes turned to the colonel, who lifted his glass. "I needed the money."

Darcy wrinkled his brow, wondering why Fitzwilliam was so desperate for seven thousand pounds as to fleece his own brother for it.

"In any case, it seems she has forgiven you," Fitzwilliam said, "as I did not find you in your chamber this morning, and your bed appeared undisturbed."

"She has forgiven me indeed," Saye agreed with an arrogant smirk. "Then again, resisting my charms never has been her strength."

"Spare us knowledge of the details," cried Fitzwilliam in jest.

"Even if you did know them," said Saye with a flourish, "I am certain you would not understand half of them."

Saye's food arrived, which required good-natured jests from his brother about what had raised such an appetite. When that was done, Darcy decided to depart, asking Fitzwilliam to accompany him to the door.

"Why did you require so much money?"

"What?"

"Seven thousand pounds is a great deal of money."

"Not when one is seeking to buy a house," Fitzwilliam replied. "Then it is a mere trifle."

"Above a year ago? I thought you had only seen the place in Cotgrave—"

"Darcy, Darcy!" Fitzwilliam interrupted him. "If you would like a look at my books, I can grant you entry to them later. Saye had it to spare; think nothing of it."

Embarrassed, Darcy felt himself redden. "Of course. Forgive me. But that is not why I wished to speak to you. I understand I am engaged to dine with the Laceys this evening."

The smile left Fitzwilliam's face. "How nice for you."

"You reply to my invitations now?"

"I did." His jaw was thrust forward in the way he had always done when attempting to be unrepentant.

"If you ever do so again—" Darcy began.

"Going after Miss Bennet again, are we? Your present misery is insufficient?"

Darcy stopped walking, and they stood in the vestibule of the club. "I beg your pardon?"

"Georgiana told me you went to Bingley's place."

"Do not conscript Georgiana to your purpose."

"She is a willing aide. She, even more than I, wishes to see you settled with someone who is not vile and mercenary."

"Excellent. Miss Bennet is neither. I am glad to see we are all of one accord."

Fitzwilliam glared at his cousin. "How many times must I save your pompous rump before you begin to save yourself?"

"I neither require nor wish for your help. Indeed, I firmly insist that you remove yourself from my affairs immediately before I am required to cut you off. I mean it, Fitzwilliam. No more. I am a man full grown, and I shall do as I see fit."

He did not await his cousin's response but pushed open the door and went off into the cold day.

JANE, EVEN CONFINED BY THEIR FATHER'S CIRCUMSTANCES, HAD ALWAYS loved to shop. As Mrs. Bingley, there was little to stop her, and she anticipated an excursion with happy vigour, insisting Elizabeth and Caroline attend her almost daily.

Although only the beginning of January, Harding Howell was crowded with ladies who had their minds fixed on the forthcoming gaieties of the London Season. For some time, Elizabeth contented herself with watching them pore excitedly over the newly arrived silks and muslins, hearing only bits and pieces of the chatter arising as sleeve length, overlays, and bonnet possibilities were discussed.

Caroline saw Lady Sophie and was immediately off, leaving Elizabeth to reassure Jane over her potential purchases. Even when she shopped in Meryton with its limited selection of fabrics and ribbons, Jane had endless patience for examining, considering, and discussing the choices for her dress. Now in London, with such an array before her, it was nearly impossible for Jane to come to a decision. Elizabeth tolerated it for a little while, but she soon had to admit that the charms of the shops were wearing thin.

She began to wander about, more interested in the sights and sounds around her than in the fashions and accoutrements. While thusly engaged, she saw Miss Darcy and Miss Lacey strolling a short distance away and moving in her direction.

On later consideration, Elizabeth could only suppose that Darcy's relative ease during their meeting at the Bingleys' home had made her presume that Miss Darcy would be happy to greet her. Miss Lacey smiled as they approached, and Elizabeth moved towards them with no hesitation.

Something drew Miss Darcy's notice to Elizabeth when she was still several paces away. She stopped walking and her blue eyes locked with Elizabeth's. Elizabeth offered a small, amiable smile. Miss Darcy did not return it but kept her gaze, sedate and inscrutable, on Elizabeth.

Miss Darcy's stillness made Miss Lacey stop too, and she might have said something, Elizabeth was not sure. Just as Elizabeth opened her mouth to extend her greetings, Miss Darcy slowly and deliberately turned her head.

Miss Lacey gasped, and her hand flew to cover her mouth. The persons nearest to the group turned to look at them, and someone barked a shocked laugh. A murmur rippled through the group. "The cut direct!"

Elizabeth's face flamed with mortification, and she took an inadvertent step backwards. She stood for a moment, stupid in her shock and unable to command herself to retreat. Thankfully, she recovered her wits seconds later and turned away from the ladies—one shocked and one still standing with her head turned awkwardly away—and fled. Miss Lacey called after her, but Elizabeth paid no notice.

A Short Period of Exquisite Felicity

Elizabeth wanted nothing more than to escape the store, but she was resolved to behave rationally. She laid her cold fingers on her burning cheeks and went to find her sister. Fortune smiled on her; Jane had managed to place an order, and although she might have liked to stay longer, she consented to return to the house. There was a brief delay as Jane sent her footman to find Caroline. He returned with the message that Miss Bingley would travel home with Lady Sophie.

"Oh, I do hope I shall not live to repent that muslin," Jane fretted happily once they were seated in Bingley's carriage. "Do you think it will make up nicely? Perhaps I should have gone with the tambour muslin?"

"The tambour was nice," Elizabeth remarked woodenly, her heart still racing in her chest.

"Are you certain I should not have purchased the plainer one? The colour was prettier on me, I thought, a more pale yellow than the tambour. I do not think the brown hues are as flattering to me."

"Mm," said Elizabeth.

"Although the tambour would have turned out nicely, I think, and I could have put the lighter lace on that one, so what was near my face was less brown. Would that have been the superior choice?"

There was a brief silence until Elizabeth reminded herself that she needed to speak. "No, I like what you selected."

Jane continued to fret and fuss until Elizabeth snapped, "Jane, I do not imply any reservation over your choices. I am feeling unwell."

"Oh no!" Jane was immediately aghast. "What is wrong?"

Tears sprung into Elizabeth's eyes, much to her horror. She had no wish to cry, particularly because relating the story would require much more explanation than she wanted to give at the present.

"I have a bad headache," she offered.

"Oh! Poor thing!" Jane moved to sit next to her sister and laid a hand on her head. "Why, I believe you might have a fever too! Why did you not say something? We shall get you home and straight into your bed."

Although she was not the least bit ill, the idea of playing sick was tempting, and Elizabeth surrendered gratefully to it. They arrived back at the Bingleys' house, and Elizabeth was immediately the object of much cosseting. She was soon in bed with a book, a hot brick at her feet, and a poultice on her chest. (She could not say how it happened, but somehow Jane had arrived at the conclusion that her pneumonia was returned.)

At last, Jane and her housekeeper were gone, and Elizabeth was left in solitude. She sat for a moment, eyes closed, reliving the horrible moment. She thought she might never be able to forget the horror when Miss Darcy had turned her head and cut her so plainly and so dramatically.

She wished she could hate the girl or think her vile, but unfortunately, she knew the truth of the matter. Miss Darcy was a dear, sweet girl who, like Colonel Fitzwilliam, despised her for what she did to Darcy. She loved her brother beyond reason and no doubt thought Elizabeth was the most evil person for having hurt him.

Elizabeth wondered what the other ladies present thought of it and whether any of them had any idea why Miss Darcy behaved as she did. She supposed they would be told; it likely did not matter anyway.

When Elizabeth was gone, Miss Lacey immediately turned her attention to Miss Darcy who, once her courage had left her, appeared green and somewhat ill.

"Miss Darcy, are you well?" She took her arm and propelled her to a more private spot. She had no idea what lay between the two ladies but understood it was likely not something good. It was at this inauspicious moment that Miss Bingley and Lady Sophie appeared.

Miss Darcy stared at them with wide, helpless eyes, seeming astonished by her own actions and unsure what should be next done. "Did you…was Miss Bennet…?" She trailed off.

"Miss Bennet?" asked Miss Bingley. "Eliza Bennet?"

"She cut her," Miss Lacey murmured.

"Cut her?" Lady Sophie exclaimed.

"Indeed," Miss Lacey murmured.

Miss Darcy threw her hands up over her face. "My brother is going to be so angry with me."

The ladies exchanged uneasy glances all around. Darcy's loathing of scenes and gossip was well known.

"I am sure no one saw," said Miss Bingley in a voice that lacked conviction.

"Why tell him?" asked Lady Sophie. "It will only concern him, and I do not think he and Miss Bennet are such friends that *she* would tell him."

"What if one of his friends tells him?" Belatedly, Miss Darcy looked around her. Most of those who had watched were returned to their shopping, though the more bold among them continued to glance at the four ladies.

"No one noticed," said Lady Sophie. "And if they did, who is Miss Bennet to them? No one, I assure you."

Despite their reassurance, Miss Darcy grew ever more fearful and fretful, and Miss Lacey announced she would accompany her home. They bid the others adieu and went on their way.

Miss Lacey considered her young friend carefully as they tucked themselves into the carriage and began the journey home. She was not yet well acquainted with Miss Darcy, but her opinion was such that she would not have expected the girl to give someone the cut direct. Miss Darcy always seemed sweet and rather shy. Surely something extremely dreadful must have happened for her to despise Miss Bennet enough to do something so drastic.

Miss Darcy looked up from where she was sniffing deep within the squabs. "Miss Lacey, I must beg your pardon for bringing infamy into our excursion. I never meant to ruin our day."

"Think nothing of that. I am only sorry for your distress."

"Thank you." The girl wept quietly into her handkerchief for several minutes before saying, "I despise Miss Elizabeth Bennet."

"I had presumed as much." Miss Lacey smiled and leant over to give Miss Darcy's hand a pat. "I know you are far too elegant to have undertaken such action without a just cause."

"My brother is my only family, as you know. Indeed, he very nearly raised me."

"Your brother is a good man."

"His happiness is as dear to me as my own—nay, perhaps even more."

"It is true that we may often forgive the slights against ourselves more readily than those against a loved one." Miss Lacey considered a moment before adding, "From your words, I must surmise it is your brother whom Miss Bennet has harmed rather than you."

Miss Darcy nodded miserably.

From thence, it seemed no more would be said. The carriage rolled on with each of its occupants lost in her own thoughts until Miss Darcy burst out, "He thought that she loved him! Indeed, she said it outright to him and then…then she would not marry him. Fitzwilliam thinks that…he thinks it was another man, a most unsuitable sort of…but no, I should not say so. I…never mind that."

Pity filled Miss Lacey's bosom. She had seen in Darcy a reluctance towards romance, but she could not have suspected it was born of a broken heart. This cast her own plans and aspirations in a different light.

"How dreadful," she said gently. "Your brother told me there was a difference of opinion between them; it seems it was much more than that."

Miss Darcy uttered a short, bitter laugh. "Yes, you might say so, if a broken engagement can be seen as a mere difference of opinion."

They arrived at Darcy's house, and Miss Darcy moved to depart the carriage. "Miss Lacey?"

"Yes, dear?"

"My brother plans to dine with your family this evening, does he not?"

"He does." Miss Lacey smiled warmly. "Do not fear, I shall not feel compelled to discuss the circumstances—"

"Oh no!" Miss Darcy exclaimed. "No, I can never keep anything from him. I shall confess all. He has shown me mercy for far worse than this."

"He is an exemplary brother and guardian, then."

"The very best." Miss Darcy smiled. "I only meant to implore you to be good to him. He deserves far better than he has got."

Miss Lacey nodded vigorously. "I have every intention of it."

It was no little source of vexation to realise that the party at the Laceys' home was an intimate gathering; some might have even thought it a family party. Besides Darcy, all were relations: the elder Mr. and Mrs. Lacey, Miss Lacey, Lady Jermyn and her husband, Sir Henry, and the younger Mr. Lacey and his wife. There were also two married cousins with their wives.

The meaning of an invitation to such a dinner gave Darcy considerable unease as it spoke to a far greater intimacy with the Laceys than he desired. He had feared raising Miss Lacey's expectations, yet it seemed he had. His discomfort rendered him even more taciturn than was his wont.

The Laceys were by and large an easy, amiable group, and if they noticed Darcy's awkwardness, they were kind enough to compensate for him. To her credit, Miss Lacey did not simper or fawn over him, which was a relief. There was no lack of good conversation either in the drawing room or at the dinner table, and the meal was plentiful and delicious; nevertheless, Darcy counted the moments until he could depart.

When the ladies left the gentlemen, the younger Mr. Lacey was quick to sit beside Darcy. He was an artless man, intelligent and likeable. He was of an age with Darcy and had been at the same schools. While they had not been intimates, he was still someone Darcy respected and regarded highly. He had married shortly after university and was already the father of two children. That, along with some precocious hair loss, left Darcy feeling as though he was speaking to one much older than he.

"I must tell you how pleasant it is to have you here. You make a fine addition to our group, and I hope it is the first of many such evenings."

"Thank you," said Darcy, with no further response to the implication presented.

A political argument had begun on the other side of the table, heated but in a respectful manner. Lacey, seeing the other men were well occupied, lowered his voice and spoke to Darcy in confidence. "My sister is quite fond of you. She enjoyed the party at Netherfield very well."

"Yes, well..." Darcy scrambled a moment, wishing to discourage but not offend. "She is a charming girl. I have no doubt she will be surrounded by suitors this Season."

Lacey chuckled, but warily. "The business of seeing my elder sister settled exhausted us all. I would not mind if Olivia had things resolved before Easter."

Darcy picked up the glass that had been set before him. It was an enticing-looking port, and he swirled it around a moment before he spoke quietly but firmly. "I do hope I have not behaved in such a way as to give Miss Lacey expectations I am not at all prepared to fulfil."

Lacey considered him seriously. "Darcy, you are ever the soul of discretion, and I cannot fault anything that has passed between you and my sister. At this time, I would say the fancies my sister holds are more hopes than expectations, but do not think them less dear to her because of it."

"I see." Darcy took a look around the table, seeing that the other men were still wholly engaged in their conversation. "I shall be frank, then, and ask why you are having this discussion with me."

"Well...you like her, and she likes you." Lacey smiled awkwardly. "But I do understand why there might be hesitation."

Some premonition made Darcy's gut clench at these words, and he took a careful sip of the port. "Hesitation? I do not understand you, sir."

"Pray, do not think ill of my sister," said Lacey in a lowered voice. "She has learnt of your recent disappointment...the broken engagement. It must have been kept very quiet."

Darcy's face flamed, and he swallowed with difficulty. "A broken engagement? Who told her that?"

"I presumed you confided in her. Perhaps as an explanation of sorts for any reluctance towards—"

"I told her no such thing," Darcy snapped.

Lacey paused a moment, aware that his guest had grown vexed. He glanced at the other men who, fortunately, were still much engaged with their own interests. "She related none of the particulars to me. She said only that things had gone off after an understanding had been reached."

Darcy felt his jaw clench almost unconsciously. In a deliberate manner, he said, "I would never confide any such thing in your sister. As her brother, you should urge her to exercise caution in the relating of scandalous tales."

"Naturally," Lacey agreed. A faint flush had risen on the man's cheeks, and he raised a finger to his cravat, seeming to restrain himself from giving it a tug. "Let us speak of pleasanter things, shall we? The war, perhaps, or should we discuss the Corn Laws?"

"I should prefer to speak to Miss Lacey."

Miss Lacey was retrieved from the drawing room by her brother, and the small group of three took themselves to the elder Mr. Lacey's book room. When the door closed behind them, Miss Lacey turned to Darcy with a composed demeanour but frightened eyes.

"My family has offered no offence, I hope, sir."

"You must know how excessively vexing it is to hear that one's most private affairs are being bandied about in drawing rooms," Darcy replied in dark tones. "Your brother said that you told him I had suffered a broken engagement."

"Well...yes, I did." Miss Lacey offered a trembling smile. "I...forgive me. I was with Miss Darcy today at Harding Howell when she...when she cut Miss Bennet, and naturally Miss Darcy felt obliged—"

"What?" For a brief moment the room swam, and Darcy reached blindly to grip the back of the chair nearest him. "She did what?"

"When she...when she cut..." Miss Lacey stammered, shooting fearful glances at her brother. "She said she intended to tell you—"

"She cut Miss Bennet? At Harding Howell?" Darcy knew he sounded stupid, but he could not imagine Georgiana doing any such thing. "I know nothing of the matter. Georgiana took to her bedchamber earlier today and has not been seen since. I beg you to tell me what happened."

"Tell him, Olivia," urged Lacey.

Miss Lacey straightened and drew a tremulous breath. She summed it up neatly for him, but the bare facts could not disguise the horror of what his sister had done right in front of what might have been the whole of the *ton*. He closed his eyes for a moment, unable to countenance what pain and humiliation Elizabeth must have suffered. He vowed that Georgiana would pay for this—Georgiana and Fitzwilliam both, for he did not doubt his cousin's hand in this for an instant.

And in that moment, he realised he was lost, more lost than even he knew. He would ever be Elizabeth's defender and protector; he would ever be Elizabeth's lover.

With a start, he realised he was still with the two Laceys, and they were both watching him intently. "I need to go," he said abruptly. "Please give my apologies to your mother."

Mr. and Miss Lacey both cried out their protests, but he waved them off. "A moment, please, sir," begged Miss Lacey. "I must speak to you."

She gave her brother a look. He coughed and looked silly for a moment before announcing that he needed to fetch something for their father and leaving the room. He began to close the door until Darcy's pointed look reminded him not to.

"I am so very sorry," said Miss Lacey earnestly.

"No, no, it is nothing you have done. Forgive me if I...if I have misled you with regard to my feelings and attentions."

The light in her eyes dimmed. "Misled me?"

"There can never be anything more than friendship between us," he said gently.

"Because of Miss Bennet?"

He paused a moment, hesitant to confide in another lady what was surely the truth. But she was not an uninterested party; her hopes were suffering even now.

"Alas, no matter how I have tried to outrun it, my heart is hers. I could not in good conscience marry another without my heart to offer."

Miss Lacey looked down.

"Forgive me. I am only just understanding it myself."

He could read her disappointment, but it was to her credit that she did not grow spiteful or pout. Instead, she raised her head. "I understand, and I wish you the best, sir."

He nodded and took her hand, bowing over it. "Thank you. I wish you the same."

Darcy thought he must surely have frightened his servants with his quick pace and dark countenance when he returned home from the Laceys'. To the first footman he saw, he said, "Bring Miss Darcy to me in my study." The man nodded and ran off.

Georgiana must have had some idea of the reckoning she was due, for she was already damp-eyed and contrite when she entered his study.

"Brother? Did you—"

"Yes, I did," he said shortly. "Did you give Miss Elizabeth Bennet the cut direct at Harding Howell?"

"I…" Her eyes flew wide, and she twisted her hands together in front of her. She seemed incapable of finishing the sentence.

"Let me be clear on this point, Georgiana. Such behaviour is not the behaviour of a Darcy, and I shall not tolerate it. You are not some cork-brained society trollop but a lady of distinction and wit, and I expect you to behave accordingly—with dignity and graciousness."

Georgiana began with a slow weep that rapidly became outraged sobbing. "*She* is the cork-brained trollop, and she is not worthy of your ardent defence of her. She deserves to be publicly humiliated for what she did to you."

"Well, it seems," Darcy pronounced coldly, "that she was."

"It is not enough! It is nothing compared to what she has done to you!"

"You have no idea what she has been through! Do not dare judge her!" He spoke in a loud and unrestrained manner that he regretted immediately, though he could not deny his sentiments.

Georgiana responded by crying even harder, her face twisted into a caricature of agony.

Darcy responded in the only way he could; he went to her, offered his handkerchief, led her to a chair, and rested one hand on her shoulder while she wept. She wept for some time—much longer, he thought, than was warranted by the situation.

"Georgiana, calm yourself. There is no need for this unseemly display."

She sniffed and snivelled, trying valiantly to stop her tears, but they seeped from her eyes despite the effort. "Forgive me," she cried. "I cannot bear to disappoint you!"

"You have disappointed me," said Darcy severely. "I cannot like such behaviour—no matter whom the recipient—but I particularly despise it against the woman I love."

Georgiana gave a dry, heaving shudder. "I know that you once loved her—"

"Not loved. *Love*. I shall not stand for your hurting her." He closed his eyes for a moment against the import of the statement.

She turned damp eyes upon him. "So you will forgive her?"

After a moment, he nodded. "I shall."

"Even though she…?"

"No matter what she has done. After all, is that not the meaning of love? That it surpasses every objection against it?"

Georgiana slowly wiped her eyes with Darcy's handkerchief. "I…I do not know. I do not know that I could forgive such a thing."

"Well." Darcy was brisk, straightening and moving to look at her more directly. "At the present moment, we need to concern ourselves with this: Will she forgive you? We shall go to the Bingleys' house in the morning and seek an audience with her."

"I suspected as much." Georgiana sighed. "Very well. In the morning, then."

Chapter Fifteen

In the first moment after she awoke, Elizabeth did not remember. Then the whole humiliating spectacle came back to her at once: the painful angle of Miss Darcy's neck, the titters of the ladies around them, her horror as she understood what was happening, and the sick feeling of mortification that swept through her.

Did Darcy know what his sister had done? Had he encouraged it? Did he wish for it? She would certainly understand if he had, but that did not mean she thought it was just.

Impatiently, she shoved the covers aside and stood. How she wished she could have silenced the stupid chattering hens at Harding Howell! She had more character in her foot than most of them had in their entire bodies, and she should not be the object of their derision. To imagine them going from drawing room to drawing room, speaking of her mortification and laughing or pitying her! It sickened her.

For not the first time, she regretted deeply that she and Darcy had not the chance to speak to one another about the truth of the situation. No matter what he thought, she believed him to be fair. She might have formed hasty judgments against him in the past, but he had not done so to her. He would have heard her explanation and done what he could to ease the suffering she had endured. She would not say she wished for his love—no, even in her angry state she knew she had surrendered that for good—but he would perhaps have pity on her and stop any gossip that went about.

Caroline was confident that Sir Edmund's offer was forthcoming, and as such, she required another day in the shops to select the perfect material for the perfect gown in which to accept the offer.

"Will not you come with us, Lizzy?" Jane asked. "You scarcely bought a thing yesterday!"

"No, no," Elizabeth demurred. "No, I cannot."

"You cannot wish to stay here all day, can you? Surely, you must want to go out and see—"

"Let us leave her to shift for herself," Caroline interjected swiftly. "Our Eliza does like a good book, and I believe I saw a new one, did I not?"

Caroline gave her a sympathetic little wink and smile. Elizabeth knew it was driven by pity, but she was not above taking any kindness, no matter how forced.

"Yes," Elizabeth agreed. "I am wild to read it."

Jane protested a little while longer and reluctantly offered to remain at home, which Elizabeth assured her was not necessary.

Finally, the house was empty, but Elizabeth found her book—not new at all, but one she had read several times—could not hold her attention. Neither could the pianoforte nor a letter to her mother; thoughts of yesterday and her mortification would consume her.

They were so much in her mind, she almost expected it when the housekeeper entered to announce that Mr. and Miss Darcy desired an audience with her. A pang of anxiety went through her; the visit would not be pleasant.

"I shall see them in here."

The housekeeper nodded and left, returning with the guests only moments later. They performed the required ceremonies of polite society in silence, Elizabeth observing Mr. Darcy's unusual pallor and the grim set to his jaw as well as Miss Darcy's red eyes and shaking hands. She offered them both a seat, after which Darcy gave his sister a stern look.

Miss Darcy could not look up from her lap. "Th-thank you for receiving us."

Elizabeth acknowledged her with a nod.

"It is indeed generous of you," said Mr. Darcy in a voice far too loud. It made his sister jump and become shiny-eyed, though she held back her tears bravely.

"Think nothing of it, sir."

No one spoke for a moment, and Mr. Darcy bent his head towards his sister, hissing something at her. Whatever he hoped to gain, he did not. Miss

Darcy merely turned her eyes towards Elizabeth and stammered something unintelligible as her tears began to flow. Mr. Darcy hissed again to no avail.

"I am grieved," he said at last, with unconcealed impatience, "to learn of my sister's rudeness, of your injury at her hand. I shall not permit her to depart this place until she renders you a proper apology."

To this, Georgiana wept more. Elizabeth watched her for some minutes, soon realising no good would come until Miss Darcy had enough composure to utter the words her brother wished her to say. "Mr. Darcy, perhaps you would wish to wait for us in Mr. Bingley's study?"

She surprised them both. Georgiana ceased weeping to stare fearfully at her, and Darcy appeared dubious. Elizabeth urged him again. "Excuse us for just a moment, sir, and perhaps Miss Darcy will be better able to speak."

He rose from his seat slowly. Elizabeth stood with him and led him to the hall, pointing to the door of Bingley's study. He went on apprehensive feet, glancing back continually, but at last he was gone. Elizabeth closed the drawing room door and joined Miss Darcy on the sofa.

Miss Darcy clasped her hands together tightly and stared wide-eyed at Elizabeth. Elizabeth regarded her with equal intentness, feeling a mixture of irritation, pity and understanding. After a short while, when it was clear the girl would remain silent, she spoke. "While I can neither like nor approve of your actions yesterday, I cannot deny that I have earned your spite."

This small concession appeared to steel Miss Darcy's resolve. She sat straighter, and dabbed at her eyes and nose with her handkerchief. "I am deeply sorry for humiliating you."

"As I am sorry for the pain I have caused you. Perhaps one day we can both learn to forgive—"

"I am sorry, but I cannot. I am sorry for what I did but…but that…" Miss Darcy stopped speaking, shaking her head as if to warn herself against what she wished to say. She stared at the rug beneath her feet, her breath fast and shallow, with evidence of a great tumult on her countenance.

Elizabeth knew what must weigh on the girl, and although it was not a subject of which she enjoyed speaking, Miss Darcy was not a disinterested party. "I know I have hurt him," she said quietly. "If not for utter desperation, I may assure you—"

"But you loved him," said Miss Darcy accusingly. "I know you did."

"Your brother? Yes, I—"

Miss Darcy shook her head vehemently, the curls at her temples bouncing. "No, not my brother. Mr. Wickham. You loved Mr. Wickham, did you not?"

"Mr. Wickham? No! I…no, I never—"

"Did he tell you he loved you? Did he say he wished to marry you?" The words burst from Miss Darcy's lips as though she had no control over them.

"Mr. Wickham and I were never anything more than friends."

Miss Darcy seemed not to have heard her. "He must have. Surely, you would not…not unless he had promised to…to marry you. Did he?"

"I do not understand what you are asking me."

"I know about you and George Wickham."

Elizabeth leant forward as if it would help her understand Miss Darcy's words. "You know *what* about me and George Wickham?"

"I know he seduced you, and you found yourself in…in a difficulty."

"What?" Elizabeth suddenly felt as if her corset was pressing the life out of her. The room swam about her, and her breath came in gasps. "I beg your pardon?"

Miss Darcy looked at her with a shade of uncertainty passing over her face. "You threw over my brother because you were in love with George Wickham and you…you had his child."

Elizabeth gaped at her for a moment. "What would make you think that?"

"Fitzwilliam told me—"

If she said more, Elizabeth did not hear it. She was on her feet, striding quickly towards the hall and finding herself at Bingley's study within seconds. With one arm, she thrust the door wide, causing it to bounce against the wall and leave a small dent.

Darcy stood by the window, a book in his hand. The sound of the door being opened with such vigour startled him, and he snapped the book closed as he turned to Elizabeth.

"*George Wickham*? Are you *mad*? What did you…who else have you told these lies?"

"Lies? What—"

"Of course they were lies! Seduced by George Wickham?" Elizabeth gave a brittle, angry laugh. "I suppose you think Emelia is *my* child?"

After a moment, he said, "Given the timing and length of your sojourn at Cheltenham, yes, I did think it possible."

Elizabeth gasped again and, for a moment, believed she might faint. The rage within her was nearly uncontrollable. She wished to hit him, to throw things at him, to scream as loud as she could.

"Get out!" Her voice was trembling and low. "Get out immediately, and do not ever darken this door again."

Darcy set the book down on Bingley's desk with a thump. "No."

"No?"

"I am not going anywhere."

Miss Darcy appeared at the door, her face white and her eyes wide. "Georgiana, leave and close the door," Darcy instructed, and she retreated immediately.

Elizabeth moved closer, placing herself nearly toe-to-toe with him. "A gentleman would not remain where he was unwanted, and you, sir, are most decidedly unwanted."

"Oh, I know that." His lip curled around the words. "But it seems you owe me an explanation."

"I owe you nothing! Anyone who would think such things of me—"

He stepped closer, stabbing a finger towards her. "You wrote me a scanty bit of nothing, taking away what I had believed, until then, was love. I hardly knew what to think of anything!"

"Oh, do not dare blame me!"

"I was forced to contrive in my own mind explanations for your cruelty. When I came to Netherfield and learnt of your illness, it seemed likely —at least to me—that your sister's child was yours. Yours and Wickham's." With stiff condescension he added, "Of all people, I do comprehend how a proper young lady might find herself under the power of a reprobate like George Wickham."

She was so amazed that she spoke without thinking. "It astonishes me to imagine I once loved you. I believed you had altered after Hunsford, but I see now that I was greatly mistaken. You remain arrogant, conceited, and disdainful of the feelings of others."

She saw a flush of anger come into his cheeks, though he controlled himself, pressing his lips together tightly for a moment. "I apologise for my conclusions, but in the absence of truth, of any explanation whatsoever, I had to suppose as I would."

"*This* was all you could imagine? You might have asked me! It is true, I did not offer an explanation, but neither did you ask for one!"

"Very well," he said, his countenance pale. He took several breaths, staring at her, before asking, "Why?"

She was enraged, and her first idea was to retort that it was too late, that he did not deserve the truth; but he did. Indeed, she relished the notion of telling him so that he might feel the weight of his own error much more keenly.

She did all she could to calm herself, to don some cloak of equanimity, no matter the distress it might cover. She turned away from him and went to the window. Staring out at the street below while taking deep breaths, she awaited the return of her heartbeat to its usual pace. When it had, she took a seat and indicated he should do likewise. After a moment, he did.

"I fear the truth will be something of a disappointment after these fanciful notions you have devised." She tried to sound scornful and brave, but in truth, she could not.

"I would like to know." He took a deep breath, appearing to gather his courage. She wondered what he might anticipate hearing that could be worse than what he had already thought.

"When the regiment removed from Meryton that spring, Lydia went to Brighton as the particular friend of Mrs. Forster. I did not think it prudent but…never mind that. I think it likely she went to Brighton with the design of making George Wickham marry her."

"She loved him?"

"She was with child," Elizabeth replied bluntly. "Lydia—not me. No one knew it at the time. Even Lydia herself might not have been certain, but I do think she went to Brighton determined to come home married. From what I know of the story, after some weeks at Brighton, Mr. Wickham began to understand her intentions. Maybe by then the babe had quickened? I hardly know—that part of the story is not something that has ever interested me.

"What I do know is that Mr. Wickham attempted to slip away from her, but she learnt of his plans and hid herself in his carriage as he went away. She left her friends thinking he was taking her to Gretna Green, but they somehow lost themselves in London, unwed but living as if they were."

She paused a moment, sinking her head in her hand before straightening and continuing her tale.

"When the express from Colonel Forster arrived at Longbourn, it was Jane who had the unhappy task of receiving it. She perceived at once that my father should not be told. He was exceedingly ill, and she believed, rightly, that such a shock could mean his demise.

"That morning in Lambton when you came to the inn, I had received two letters from Jane. You arrived just as they were delivered, and I happily put them aside, thinking they would not contain anything more than the usual chatter of assemblies, friends, and gossip. I did not read them until we returned later that night after we had dined at Pemberley.

"It was a shock," said Elizabeth. "I did not then know that Lydia was increasing; I thought she was eloping—putting herself in George Wickham's power—and this was shocking enough. Jane begged my uncle's urgent assistance. We were gone from the inn within the hour."

"You were yet at Lambton when this happened? Why did you not tell me?" He appeared astonished. "I could have gone with you, nay, I would have ridden ahead and—"

"I had some vain hope that I might conceal it from you." She lowered her gaze to her lap. "I hoped this further evidence of family weakness might never be known to you, that you would know it only as a hasty marriage that happened before ours."

This seemed a source of astonishment to him; when she dared look at him, his mouth was agape and his brow was furrowed. "Mr. Gardiner was the one who found them in London?"

"Along with an agent acting on his behalf."

"So was it Mr. Gardiner who paid Wickham to marry her?" Her brows flew up with surprise, causing Darcy to give a bitter laugh. "I know Wickham too well to imagine he did it for any sense of honour. There are likely daughters and sons throughout the empire that can claim the parentage of George Wickham even if he would not likewise claim them."

"It took some time to find them—time and, yes, money to persuade Mr. Wickham to do what was right by her, but in the end, he did agree. After several long days of fear, worry, and anguish, we had some small hope of a happy end to the matter."

"You knew there was to be a child?"

"My aunt and uncle wished to keep it from me, but Lydia revealed it one morning. It was to my immense relief that all the plans had been settled. The wedding was only a few days hence, and it seemed we would just barely escape our ruination. I was immeasurably glad when it was done. Even though I did not like to see Lydia bound to such a man at sixteen, it was the right thing to do and therefore best done as quickly as possible."

A short silence fell while Darcy considered what he had been told. At last, the obvious question came to him. "What does any of this have to do with you and me?"

Sudden and abrupt nausea afflicted Elizabeth, and a metallic taste rose in her mouth. It had always been thus, ever since that day in the Gardiners' front parlour. She hated thinking of it and loathed talking about it, but she knew she must.

Elizabeth returned to the window and stared outside as she related her story. It was a cold day in January with a wind that could slice a person in two, but for her, it was again that hot, stifling day in late August with not a breath of air to be found.

Lydia had been alternately querulous and tearful that day until, at last, Aunt Gardiner had suggested a shopping excursion to divert her. My aunt blamed bridal nerves, but I thought it was more likely the effect of being a spoilt young miss with a mind completely lacking in reason and good sense. I could not bear the notion of another day spent picking over fabrics and accoutrements; Lydia had adopted such airs, one would think she was marrying a duke. So I remained at home alone while they went out.

I was reading when I heard him in the front hall, and I presumed he would leave when he realised Lydia was not there. Alas, no; moments later, Mr. Wickham was shown into the drawing room where I sat. He looked every inch a man without a care in the world, his expression so unaffected, so arrogant, I could hardly bear it.

By this time, the arrangements had all been laid. Lydia was increasing, and this reprobate was the cause. He had hotly denied the charge until it was made clear that money and employment would be his, provided he did as he ought and marry her. It would be a patched-up business, but Lydia—and by extension, our family—would narrowly escape ruination.

"I am afraid I must disappoint you this afternoon. My sister is gone to the warehouses with my aunt for wedding clothes."

"I think we both know that I care not a bit where your sister is at present. Indeed," he chuckled, "I am rather relieved she chose someone else to amuse her for the afternoon."

I could not like hearing him disparage her. It seemed to me that he could at least keep the appearance of an eager bridegroom. "That is no way to speak of the woman you will soon call your wife."

"Will I? I daresay that is up to you, dear madam."

"My uncle already gave you a small fortune, Mr. Wickham. I assure you, no other man would be so forbearing towards someone who behaved as shockingly and without scruple—"

"I always did find your impertinent spirit rather charming, Lizzy."

He delighted in taking the privilege of a brother, and I believe he knew that it vexed me.

"You should sign the agreement as you told my uncle you would."

"Ah, the agreement. I learnt some information that changes the agreement a bit." He shook a finger at me. "You, my dear, were not forthcoming."

A cold prickle of alarm traced my spine. "Me?"

"It is a pity when one who is almost family must learn of these things through other people. It is hurtful, indeed, that I should not know that my almost-sister is bound to my oldest friend."

Dread sank through me. I tried to seem calm but stammered as I lied to him. "I-I have no idea what you mean, sir."

"Come, come," He scolded me. "Such disguise does not suit you."

"It is no disguise."

He rose, enjoying his moment of suspense. He took a turn about the room while I watched, waiting for him to speak.

"I do not suppose you know I have a brother."

"A brother?" I asked. "No. I know little about you, yet it is more than I care to know."

My insult could not injure him, and indeed, he grinned at me. "Is that any way to treat someone who holds your family's future in his hands? In any case, you might say he is my half-brother. After my father died, my mother married his father, a Mr. Wilton, who runs the Old White Horse Inn at Lambton. Fine man, fine, fine man indeed.

"I do believe your family found the inn suitable, did they not?" He smirked at me. "How did you enjoy your stay? Mr. Gardiner thought it pleasing, but perhaps not as much as you did."

"It was lovely."

"My brother—young Wilton—assists his father when he is able by doing little things here and there around the inn. He was serving as a footman when you *were in residence with the Gardiners. 'Tis a small world, is it not?"*

He paused and asked me for some refreshment. I denied him—no use in pretending that this was a friendly call.

He went back to his seat. "To wit, I received a letter from Wilton just last night and learnt, most astonishingly, that the grand Mr. Fitzwilliam Darcy arrived in a hurry one morning—quite too early for polite callers, by the by—and took a certain young lady on a walk through the town. Being the resourceful lad he is, he followed, only to learn the great gentleman had matrimony on his mind. Moreover, the lady—who heretofore had expressed an immense disgust for said gentleman—accepted him! Very surprising, very surprising indeed.

"Now who do you suppose this fortunate young lady was? And I say 'fortunate' not in terms of the character of her betrothed but, rather, in regard to his fortune."

"Mr. Wickham, the terms of the agreement are settled. If you imagine I shall ask Mr. Darcy to add to your ill-gotten gain, then you are sorely mistaken. He would not part with a farthing on your behalf. In my estimation, he has given you far too much already."

"You wound me. However, I do not wish for Darcy's farthings. No, what I wish for is far, far more dear to him."

His disgusting, lecherous gaze travelled slowly and lingered over me. I wanted to shudder and recoil; however, I did what I could to appear unaffected. "You wish to find yourself on the end of Mr. Darcy's sword, then? I assure you, such an insult will not go unanswered, and should you choose to make the attempt to debase his intended with your foul—"

"You flatter yourself." He chuckled. "Your sister has given me my fill of Bennet women, and I am determined to avoid any lady with a surfeit of conversation in the future. Oh, you might favour different subjects, but I see you are much like Lydia in this regard. Pray, remember this: when a man wishes to attend to his needs, the last thing he wants is a long discussion about it."

"What do you want, then? More money? A place in society? Mr. Darcy will afford you neither."

He examined his nails, saying nothing; he clearly enjoyed toying with me.

"What, Mr. Wickham? You hold the superior place, or at least, you imagine you do. What will satisfy you and make you sign this agreement, that we might be finished with this unpleasant business?"

There was a pause, then Mr. Wickham stared at me; his impertinence and levity were gone, replaced by cruel, serpentine solemnity. "Darcy told you, I think, of all that has passed between us."

"He told me that you were paid handsomely to release any claim to the living at Kympton and received an additional sum to preserve Miss Darcy's reputation. You were paid more than you deserved, Mr. Wickham, by all accounts."

"Monetary gain was only part of it. My wish was for revenge, and in that, I was denied. Darcy still lives as a king, wealthy and well regarded, while I scrape by as best I can. He suffered not at all, while for me, each day is a struggle."

"You place yourself within your own struggle. You squandered every advantage given you."

Wickham shrugged. "Perhaps so. But I would like Darcy, for once, to taste bitterness. You will aid me in that."

"No, I shall not," I said immediately. "I love him. I cannot deny I once disliked him, but that time is long past."

The smirk had returned. "Ah, so you do love him? Better and better. I do hope you told him so?"

I did not gratify him with an answer.

"So let me tell you how it must be now: I shall sign this agreement of your uncle's and do all that is specified therein—and for no further sum than is already promised me—with one additional consideration."

"Which is?"

Wickham smiled again, a cold, mean smile. "You must break his heart. Jilt him. Leave him alone, bereft, and wishing he had never, ever laid eyes upon you."

I refused immediately. "Never. I shall never do any such thing."

"You would choose your own desires over those of your entire family? But you are a clever girl; surely, you understand your engagement is doomed."

He rose to his feet and began to pace, lecturing me as a professor might instruct his pupil.

"Dearest Lizzy, you must realise that no matter how this ends, you and Darcy cannot be. It is impossible to even consider. If your family is ruined, he will distance himself immediately. Did your father sign the articles yet?"

He had not, but I did not admit it.

"I am guessing he has not. Even better for Darcy—no breach of promise, no loss of reputation on his part.

"And the alternate is no better, is it? If I marry Lydia—and at this time, that is indeed an 'if'—your family's reputation will be saved. But for Darcy to be my brother? Me, the son of Pemberley's steward?"

He laughed loudly with his head thrown back and his hand on his chest.

"Darcy has lowered himself for you already. If your consequence diminishes further, he could not bear it. Connexions to a wealthy tradesman are not nearly as bad as connexions to…well, to me. He thinks me no more than a gamester and a profligate."

He taunted me then. "After all, what might it do to poor, dear Georgiana should Darcy become my brother? What would it mean to the vaunted Darcy name? Oh, he loves you, I am sure, but duty has been so firmly engrained in him that I cannot suppose he would sully his heritage, not even for you. There is a limit to all things, even love."

I wanted to deny him, to rebuke his hateful words. I wished to dismiss them as foolish nothings, the ramblings of a madman, but I found I could not. Mr. Wickham had voiced my own niggling worries, the very fears that had twisted and coiled within my gut since I first learnt of Lydia's folly.

"Have you told him?"

"Have I told him what?"

"Have you told him of me, of your sister…anything?"

I did not answer for a moment but finally admitted the truth. "No."

"And why not?"

I was silent.

"I think we both know the reason." Mr. Wickham chuckled. "You know what manner of man you have attached yourself to, and you know what is certain to occur should he learn of this unfortunate business. All I am asking is for you to remove yourself from him before he removes himself from you. Is it not better that way?"

I could not dispute him. It was true you had changed, but could that change be sufficient to overcome this? To be brother to the man you despised most in the world? It could not be, not when it affected more people than just you—Georgiana, most particularly.

I looked away from Mr. Wickham. In my mind's eye, I saw Pemberley, beautiful Pemberley, where I had already imagined our children at play on the lawns with happiness and love surrounding them. Your face rose in my mind, but I could not permit it; it was too painful to allow your dear visage entry into this vile circumstance.

I was stuck in a situation from which I could not emerge the victor. To refuse to do Mr. Wickham's bidding would mean my family's ruin; you could not bear such ignominy, and I did not wish you to. On the other hand, if I did as he wanted, he would become my brother. To ask you to be brother to Mr. Wickham was impossible. I had no good choice, and either way, there was no future for you and me.

Or was there?

"What if I agree to cry off and in the future…" I could not say more, could not give voice to my foolish hopes.

When he answered me, he was kind, too kind; it was akin to pity. I almost wished he had been derisive.

"If you and Darcy reconcile?" He shook his head. "You do not know him at all if you think this could be forgiven, not by such a man as Darcy. To forgive a woman who jilted him? Much less to forgive a woman who counts the likes of me among her family members! My dear girl!

"I am dreadfully sorry. I can assure you, though, there is no need to amend our agreement to consider the possibility of your reconciliation with Darcy. It is quite impossible. I might as well make a provision for what might happen if one of us were elevated to the monarchy."

Mr. Wickham, of course, did not know of the changes in your character. He had not seen the kindness you had bestowed upon my Aunt and Uncle Gardiner and the manner in which you had brought your sister to see me.

Then again, Mr. Wickham had no notion that you would be jilted by a woman who had already hurt you badly by a violent and unkind refusal only four months earlier. I felt that no man's heart could survive such hateful actions, even one who had much less pride than you have.

I could not bear to hurt you again, but I knew if I did not hurt you in this way, I should hurt you in another. I would be the ruination of your name, and I would wound Georgiana as well. I would take all that is most precious away from you.

At last, I said, "I shall not be cruel to him. I shall release him but no more."

Mr. Wickham smiled broadly, a delighted gleam in his eyes. He enjoyed my defeat very well. "Come," he gestured towards my aunt's small writing desk. "Let us write a letter together."

Visiting such unhappy thoughts—memories that Elizabeth had worked so hard to repress—drained her. When she turned from the window, it was almost a shock to find Mr. Darcy still there, utter disbelief marking his countenance. She sank onto the edge of a chair, wrapped her arms around herself, and watched as he paced about the room. The silence was heavy, and in her mind, she begged him to say something, anything, to relieve it.

"Wickham told you to jilt me?" He sounded amazed. "And you did it?"

"I had to," she said quietly. "He would not marry her if I did not."

"George Wickham bid you jilt me…and you did?"

"I…yes. I had no choice."

His breathing had grown somewhat ragged. "You mean to say that the letter you wrote to me was written at George Wickham's direction?"

"It was."

"You sat by George Wickham's side and wrote a letter releasing me from our engagement?"

"He…he sat by me and said…" She faltered when she looked at him, beholding the hurt rage in his eyes. "I did as I had to do to save Lydia."

Darcy flushed hotly red. He did not speak for many terrible minutes, but she watched as his jaw clenched and unclenched. At last, he spoke in that hate-filled, exacting tone she remembered from their argument at Hunsford.

"I should think it a great compliment that I believed the worst you had done was to be seduced by the likes of George Wickham. But no! Instead, I find you betrayed me in the worst possible manner."

"Betrayed you? Of course not! I had your best interests at heart."

"My interests! How can you say that?"

"Whether Lydia married or not, you and I could not be—"

"No? And why not?"

She took a steadying breath. "He said that either way you and I could not be. Whether my family was ruined or he was my brother, you would want nothing to do with me."

"Is that what *he* said? Oh, and yes, everything *he* said has proved so wholly accurate, has it not?"

"I had no good choice left to me," she cried, rising to her feet. "If I did as he bid, then I lost you, and if I did not do it, then still I would lose you, but my sister would be lost as well. I took the path of the greater good."

"Greater good?" He muttered a curse under his breath and turned away from her for a moment. "You did have another choice. You could have come to me instead of, once again, putting your faith in anything George Wickham had to say!"

"I did not put my faith in George Wickham; I was merely trying to save my sister! Tell me what good choice I had! You could not have suffered Mr. Wickham as a brother any more than you would have been bound to a ruined family."

"I was already bound! We were betrothed, promised to one another! Whatever problems you faced were my problems too! But you could not trust me! You proved yourself my enemy's consort. Ever since I thwarted his plans with Georgiana, Wickham has sought ways to revenge himself on me. How nice," he said with heavy sarcasm, "that the very woman who claimed to love me helped him do just that."

"I did what I had to do," Elizabeth protested through clenched teeth. "As you did for your sister, I did for mine! My family had no other recourse but ruination."

"Yes, they did!" he shouted. "We were engaged to be married. Do you not think I would have known how to deal with him? I have been doing it my whole life!"

"Yes! And my family would have sunk even lower in your esteem!"

"Instead, only *you* have."

For a moment, Elizabeth thought she might hit him. Her rage blinded her, and she stumbled towards the door with some idea of going to her bedchamber, eager to escape his hateful presence.

He was evidently of a like mind and also moved towards the door. "A loss of virtue, I could have forgiven. A child, yes, I would have forgiven that too. But this? This is willing perfidy. This, I cannot forgive."

He turned abruptly. "You have twisted me in knots and broken my heart in more ways than I ever thought possible. I regret nothing so much as the very day I first went into Hertfordshire."

He quickened his steps, vanishing from the room. She heard him speak a few words to Miss Darcy, who had waited all this time in the drawing room. Moments later, the door slammed as they exited the house.

As she had those many months ago in the parsonage house at Hunsford, Elizabeth sat down and cried for above half an hour.

Chapter Sixteen

Once Elizabeth finished her cry, she was left in a state of profound numbness. She sat for some time, staring at the fire in the drawing room and doing nothing more than observing how the coals would catch flame and burn hotter and hotter until they eventually receded into ashes. They would lie there then, as useless grey powder that would be removed by the parlour maids with no hint of the warmth that had once burned from them.

Such was love, was it not?

"I regret nothing so much as the very day I first went into Hertfordshire."

Those words rang in her head over and over again. It was done. Darcy knew everything, every part of the story, and he saw it as faithless perfidy.

She had not before considered it as such but now realised it was so. She had doubted him and thought his love lacked the courage required to conquer Mr. Wickham's hate. Too late, she understood what he wanted, which was for her to believe, *really* believe, in his goodness above all things.

"My enemy's consort."

Perhaps she was, though no one could ever say she had wished it so. It was a forced alliance, extortion in the purest sense.

It had never occurred to her to seek his help. Her first thought—no, her *only* thought—when she learnt of her sister's elopement was that Lydia must marry. She had given no thought to Darcy save for how the situation would affect his regard for her. As if the Bennets had not already shamed themselves enough in front of him.

But she had removed his power of choice. She had decided what he would prefer and acted accordingly. It now seemed, of the two of them, hers was the greater pride, the deeper arrogance, and the most selfish disdain for the feelings of others. She could not be surprised that he despised her.

When she had been there for a time—she had no idea how long—Jane and Caroline returned. They brought with them all the happy conversation of fabric, bonnets, and patterns, and they were thankfully insensible of the fact that Elizabeth sat before them like a deadened stump of a tree. She nodded and offered opinions on things she did not care about, and soon enough, she was able to escape to her apartment where she could think more of Darcy and how she planned to go on without him.

THEY HAD WALKED TO DAVIES STREET AND RETURNED HOME THE SAME way. Darcy's anger lengthened his stride, but his sister, who was silent and fearful, managed to keep apace. Indeed, he scarcely noticed she was still beside him, so consumed was he by thoughts of Elizabeth.

When they were in their vestibule, she timidly offered, "I am sorry. It seems my actions had greater consequences than any of us could have imagined."

"It was nothing that did not need to be said," Darcy replied. "Indeed, I wish it had been said many months ago."

Georgiana offered a wan smile before asking to be excused.

"You may be excused. But, Georgiana, do tell me you comprehend that these thoughts and suspicions we had of her were in error?"

Georgiana nodded, her eyes cast down. "We know what it is to have the family face ruin due to the imprudent actions of a young lady. She did not choose the best course, to be sure, but I do understand her desperation."

She went to her bedchamber, and Darcy went to his library where he sat in a chair and did not pretend he intended to read. For several long minutes, he permitted his indignation its due.

I changed for her. Did it mean nothing to her? How could she fail to see it?

But reason would intrude. How long had she been permitted acquaintance with the new man? A few hours, spread over three days. Not so much, not when one weighed them against the old grievances: the slight at the assembly, his disdain of her family, and all the terrible things he said to her at Hunsford.

Days of the new man versus months of the proud, taciturn creature she knew before. Was it any wonder she lacked faith in the change? Was it any wonder she still thought he would prefer the sanctity of his name over his love for her?

The scene she had described played in his mind: the hot August day, Wickham, arrogant and bold, Elizabeth holding the weight of her family upon her slim shoulders.

He lowered his head into his hand. Had he not trod the same path that Elizabeth trod and felt that same desperation?

When the horror of Ramsgate had unfolded before him, he would have done anything to save Georgiana and make that problem go away. He would have done anything to save his family name and see his sister spared the consequences of youth and imprudence.

How well he recalled the sickening fear. Even now, his gut would twist and a chill would run down his spine when he thought of the ruination that Georgiana—and by extension, the Darcy family—had faced.

He felt a sudden, deep pity for Elizabeth. At least he had the benefits of fortune and of being a gentleman, the head of his family, to aid him. She had no such advantages.

Could he truly despise Elizabeth for doing the same thing he would have done himself?

The image that had leapt into his mind as he stood in the drawing room at Davies Street was of Elizabeth and Wickham, cosily side by side, laughing and flirting as they composed the letter of his heartbreak. But now, with a calmer head, he knew it was not so.

He could see her now: not weeping, not screaming, not writhing. No, she would bear it with dignity and do what needed to be done or, rather, what she believed she had to do.

He cast a look at his mantel clock; it was just above an hour since he had left Elizabeth. The last time they had argued so bitterly, it had taken him days to begin to forgive her. Now it seemed an hour would do.

All of this might have been avoided. Yes, he would have been upset, but he would have known where to find Wickham, He would have given him some money, and it all would have been done. No months of despair, heartache, and unanswered questions. She had damaged him, and she had damaged herself.

Do I believe she loved me? Do I believe she loves me now? Yes, yes I do. We still love each other, but what can be done for such a Gordian knot as this?

He rubbed his head, which had begun to ache with his confusion. Not long after, his cousin was announced, saving him from further musings. Darcy recalled that he had a matter of some consequence to discuss with Fitzwilliam: the fact that he led him to believe Elizabeth had admitted to having Wickham's child.

Whistling cheerfully, Fitzwilliam entered the room. "Say, I was going over to Jackson's. Come along?"

"Would you care to explain yourself to me?"

"Explain myself?" Fitzwilliam looked perplexed.

"You painted the most absurd picture of her, and you encouraged my belief in it," Darcy replied darkly. "As you know, I despise nothing so much as a liar, and I intend to take my penance out on your hide."

Fitzwilliam closed his eyes a moment. "Is *her* Miss Elizabeth Bennet?"

"You know damn well it is."

"I did not lie," Fitzwilliam protested. "I merely said she could not deny it."

"She did not deny it because, I suspect, you never asked her. You deceived me into thinking she had given birth to Wickham's child!"

Fitzwilliam opened his arms. "So what if I did? Darcy, go find some whore that looks like her and get it out of your system. Throw in an extra tuppence or two, and she will even let you call her Elizabeth."

Darcy was on him within a moment, grabbing his coat and shoving his back against the door. "What has she done to you that you should bear such malice towards her?"

Darcy was larger than his cousin, but Fitzwilliam had the muscles of battle, and he shoved him off with relative ease. He straightened his coat while glaring at Darcy balefully.

"I could not bear to see her once again capture you, as seemed both likely and imminent. I needed to get you out of there and to a place where you might think with reason and good sense."

"I trusted you."

"You should trust me. The only person you cannot trust at present is *yourself*."

"I asked you a question and believed in your answer." Darcy glared, but his anger had seeped away.

"I know." Fitzwilliam swallowed and looked down. "It was not right; I grant you that. She has a hold on you like nothing I have ever seen! I did not believe I could make you leave her no matter how unhappy she made you, and thus, I did as I must."

"What's done is done," Darcy muttered. It was as close to absolving his cousin as he would allow. "We shall go to Jackson's later, and I shall exact my retribution on you there. For now, Cheapside."

Darcy rang for his carriage to be prepared. While the two men waited, Fitzwilliam watched Darcy, and Darcy watched his boots. "Why am I going to Cheapside?"

"To see George Wickham."

There was a short pause. "Wickham? Why?"

"It is above enough now. If I need to call in his debts and order his transportation to carry my point, I shall be happy to do so. I do not care whether Mrs. Wickham finishes her days on my charity; I shall see him hanged!"

Surprised by Darcy's vehemence, Fitzwilliam merely stood back and studied him.

"It was to the purpose of completing his revenge on me. It worked well, would you not say so?"

"What worked well?" Fitzwilliam asked. "His seduction of Miss Bennet?"

Darcy shook his head. "He never seduced Elizabeth."

With Fitzwilliam's eyes still intent on him, Darcy felt he needed to relate the whole unhappy tale. He did so in as cursory a manner as possible.

"Her sister is…was…somewhat untamed. High-spirited. Fell prey to Wickham's charms, found herself with a full belly, and chased him to Brighton to try and make him marry her, or so it seems."

Fitzwilliam pondered the information a moment. "And she clearly succeeded in her mission."

"He tried to slip away in the night, which she believed was an invitation to an elopement and joined him. They were found in London by Mr. Gardiner, the lady's uncle."

"This is the uncle in trade?"

"Who has warehouses in Cheapside where George Wickham is now employed," Darcy explained.

The carriage was announced, and the telling of the story paused while the gentlemen entered and settled themselves.

"'Tis a disgraceful tale but not uncommon, not where George Wickham is concerned" said Fitzwilliam. "The man likely has by-blows in any number of cities throughout England. And I do not see how any of it is revenge on you."

"When it came down to the very end, Wickham decided he would not marry Miss Lydia unless Elizabeth jilted me. So she did."

"I am shocked she would betray you in such a way. A Delilah to your Samson. Perhaps you should send her a lock of hair and convey that message to her." Fitzwilliam chuckled. "How did you learn all of this?"

"I called on her at Bingley's house. She told me everything."

"Everything?"

Darcy nodded.

Fitzwilliam digested this with an almost comically astonished look on his face. "Well, it must be to her credit that she has done that much. Why did you go to her?"

Darcy explained the circumstances whereby Georgiana offered Elizabeth the cut direct in Harding Howell. Fitzwilliam did not seem surprised, which, in turn, was no surprise to Darcy; he had suspected that Fitzwilliam already knew and perhaps had even encouraged Georgiana to do it.

"So are we now on our way to confront Wickham?"

"Yes."

"Well." Fitzwilliam gave a little exhale. "This will certainly prove to be a much more eventful morning than I had anticipated when I set out."

Although the men in Gardiner's warehouse were diligently going about their assigned work, they still cast curious glances at the two men who had entered. Fitzwilliam spoke to the first man he came across, asking after George Wickham, and the man told them where to find him.

Gardiner had given Wickham an ill-deserved position of some authority, it seemed, overseeing the warehouse and the men therein. They found him in a private office in the back, his coat off and his shirtsleeves rolled up, going about his business. When he saw them, a fleeting look of surprise crossed his face; however, as the gambler he was, he had no difficulty in quickly appearing unconcerned.

"This is certainly a shock," drawled Fitzwilliam. Darcy nodded, taking in the well-ordered stacks of paper, the many letters in process, and even a long list in Wickham's hand of tasks to accomplish. It seemed he had seized onto his new life with alacrity.

"What is this about?" Wickham asked. "As you see, I am in the midst of a busy day. We are not all gentlemen of leisure, you see."

"Pardon us while we recover from our amazement at seeing you gainfully employed." Fitzwilliam sneered.

"I would like to see *you* gainfully employed," Wickham retorted. "If there were half as many soldiers on the battlefield as there are whoring about England, we might get somewhere with the French—besides into the beds of their mistresses."

"I beg your pardon." A flush of anger heated Fitzwilliam's face immediately. "I have been shot and—"

"Yes, yes, shot at in the midst of war, imagine that. All I can say is that I am exceedingly glad for what time spent in the militia did for my card game. Day upon day of playing worked wonders for my purse. Could be the reason so many second sons favour the military."

Fitzwilliam seemed ready to attack him, so Darcy stopped their bickering. "This is not why we are here."

"Why are you here?" Wickham asked.

Darcy leant over the desk, splaying his fingers wide. "To challenge you. Tomorrow at dawn. An instrument of your choosing."

Wickham was thoroughly unmoved. "I have a wife and child, and I cannot be drawn into your silly games, Darcy."

"I shall happily support your wife and child forever if it means you are out of all of our lives for the same length of time."

"Well, this offer is a bit late in coming." Wickham smiled. "Where were you while I was in Brighton? That was when I truly needed you."

"It is no joke," Fitzwilliam said, stepping forward. "Do you have a second? Does anyone still hold you in enough regard?"

Wickham shot Fitzwilliam a strange look but did not reply. "I am not going to fight you, Darcy."

Darcy stepped back, frustrated and annoyed, unsure what he really wanted but knowing he was not getting it. A miniature on a side shelf caught his eye: an infant, a sweet little thing with curls around her face and rosebud lips. Darcy picked it up and studied it. He found himself smiling despite the circumstances.

"I want the truth concerning your marriage to Miss Lydia Bennet."

"Give us the story," Fitzwilliam growled. "Else you might find yourself pulling my blade from your chest."

Wickham rolled his eyes. "How droll you are. Darcy, put that back on my shelf."

Darcy did as bid.

"What would you like to know?"

"Was Miss Lydia with child in the summer of 1812?"

"My Emelia." One could not mistake the genuine fondness in Wickham's tone. "Such a sweet little thing, is she not? Yes, my wife was increasing then. I am even reasonably certain Emelia is mine. I think she has my mother's eyes."

"You never seduced Miss Elizabeth Bennet?" Darcy asked in a hard tone.

"Would that I had! There was a time when she was walking in the rain, and the muslin of her gown became transparent…" He smirked at Darcy. "I have always been rather fond of good legs and a firm arse on a woman. A bosom is delightful, but then you bend them over and cannot see it."

Darcy would not react to Wickham's vulgarity. "So you asked her to release me?"

"Not so much asked her as forced her," Wickham replied. He was obviously enjoying this little interview. "I told her I would abandon her sister if she did not write you a letter releasing you."

"Well, then," said Darcy in an even tone. "You had your fun, and now allow me to have mine—tomorrow at dawn, weapons of your choosing."

Wickham held out his hands, not the least perturbed. "For what? Last I knew, she was not yours to defend."

"She will always be mine to defend." Darcy leant over the desk, putting his face close to Wickham's. "Always. You have taken a great deal from me, but you cannot take that."

"I never took anything from you that you did not readily relinquish," Wickham replied coolly.

"Hardly true," Darcy replied as Fitzwilliam cursed behind him.

"Quite right, in fact," Wickham continued. "No one can ever take anything from a person unless that person permits it by thought, word, or deed."

Darcy straightened and stared at him, incredulous. "So you would like me to believe that all the times I have covered your debts and paid for your mistakes, I have wanted to do so?"

"Who made you do any of it?" Wickham raised an eyebrow in calm triumph.

"I did it for my father," he retorted, "so that he would not know how you had turned out and what you had done with the education he paid for."

"Your choice. You could have left me to choke on my own filth, yet you did not." Wickham leant back in his chair. "You paid my debts time and again so that my stain would not reach your name or that of your father. You covered my misdeeds for the same reason. You paid for my silence to guard your sister's reputation. Always, Darcy, it always comes back to your pride."

"There is no improper pride in wanting to honour my name."

"No improper pride, but pride nevertheless." Wickham stared at Darcy appraisingly, adding, "Just like pride stopped you from asking her."

"I beg your pardon?"

"When you received the letter, you must have thought it strange, believing that she loved you, yet she cried off. Did you not?" When Darcy had reluctantly nodded, Wickham continued. "So what stopped you from asking her?"

Darcy stared at him through narrowed eyes and said nothing.

"After all, was not your friend marrying her sister? You could have attended the wedding and talked to her, seen how it was for yourself. But I know why you did not. I know why you instead chose to remain at Pemberley licking your wounds."

Darcy did not speak but merely stared at Wickham through narrowed eyes. "Pray, enlighten us," said Fitzwilliam.

"She had your measure." Wickham kept his eyes on Darcy. "She knew that your name meant more to you than she did. She knew there would be degradation for you in either attaching yourself to a ruined family or in marrying into a family boasting the son of your father's steward to its credit. She could not bring you such harm, and once she realised it would pain you, it was done. Her decision was made."

"You made her—"

"I made her write a letter," said Wickham. "That was all. Only a letter. If you had gone to her—if she had explained it to you—I would be still married to Lydia and still spending my days in this infernal warehouse. I only forced Lizzy to write the letter; the rest was up to the two of you.

"And here you are, above a twelve-month later, still angry, still miserable, and all because you would not lower yourself to ask." He smirked and pointed his finger at Darcy. "You served revenge on yourself, my friend."

Darcy could scarcely help himself; he pounced across the desk, scattering Wickham's papers. Fitzwilliam grabbed him and pulled him back. "Darcy! We shall settle this as gentlemen."

"You want an apology?" Wickham asked. "Very well; forgive me."

It was the least sincere form of an apology Darcy had ever heard. "Never."

"I shall make amends," said Wickham smoothly. "What do you want?"

"I want you out of my life forever."

"Consider it done." Wickham sat for a moment, allowing a smirk to play about his lips. Eventually, he began to speak again, his manner oddly boastful. "I told her so, of course. She asked what might happen if she were to one day reconcile with you. I laughed at the very idea. I told her she might well forget any such fanciful notions, because Darcy would never forgive a woman who had done this to him. Your resentful temper; you have had it since boyhood."

Darcy stared at him for a long moment. It never ceased to bewilder him how jealousy had corrupted the man who had once been his dearest friend. He had never comprehended it, but as he looked on Wickham's smiling face, he realised he had but one avenue to victory.

"You are correct—yet not. See if I do not prevail over you even in this."

Wickham's grin slipped a bit. "What do you mean?"

Darcy allowed his own sneering grin to emerge. "She still loves me, you know. After all of this, these obstacles and trials, she yet loves me, and I love her. I have not the least doubt that we shall be happy together some day."

Wickham frowned. "A woman who loved you could never have done this to you."

Darcy smiled broadly. "You said it yourself, Wickham: she only agreed once she believed she would be hurting me. She loves me, and she wished for my felicity above her own. What joy there is in such a woman! Can you say the same about anyone?"

Wickham sat up straighter and gave Darcy a mean look.

"Mrs. Wickham? Can you claim to own her heart?"

"Yes," Wickham retorted.

"No." Darcy shook his head slowly, his eyes locked on those of his adversary. "She is with you because she has to be. You seduced her when she was barely out of her girlhood, and you left her with child. She had no choice."

"But she is, nevertheless, with me," Wickham spat, "and you are, as always, quite alone. Always have been, always will be."

"Much as I hate to admit it," Darcy mused aloud, "I believe you have the right of it. The extent to which you exact your revenge is wholly dependent on me. I may languish in my misery, or I may choose to conquer it—to forgive her and to beg her forgiveness, and then, at last, to pursue our happiness together."

Wickham was staring at him with a baffled, unhappy look on his face. "You would forgive her for jilting you?"

"She faced a rather impossible situation, did she not?" Darcy lifted his brow. "A situation that I, myself, am all too familiar with. I cannot fault anything she did. Bless her, she did what she could."

"She could have told you."

"I have not respected her family as I ought; I was too plain in my disdain of them. It can be no surprise that she wished to conceal this ugly truth from me."

"It will never do," Wickham pronounced in an uncertain manner.

Darcy adopted a pensive air. "You have given me excellent counsel. I shall put aside every notion of pride and do anything I can to bring us back together. Once I have her love again, then I shall truly have everything, and your revenge will not really be much revenge at all, will it?" He forced a little chuckle. "Come, Fitzwilliam. We have wasted enough of our morning here."

"You will never do it. You will crawl back into that study of yours—resentful, glum, and again thinking of how I have wronged you."

Darcy grinned broadly. "Miss Elizabeth Bennet will be called Mrs. Darcy before the summer, George. See if it is not so. And when that happens, I daresay, I shall scarce have time to spare you the merest thought."

DARCY AND COLONEL FITZWILLIAM MET MR. GARDINER WHEN THEY WERE leaving the warehouses and stopped to speak to him for some time, eventually agreeing to pay a call on his wife at home. They passed a pleasant half an hour therein; the conversation never did touch on their niece but instead centred on matters of business and political interest. Spending time with respectable, intelligent people and having a rational conversation of general interest helped Darcy to calm down from his vexation of the morning.

When they were again in Darcy's carriage and returning to Mayfair, Fitzwilliam stared at his cousin appraisingly. "That was certainly strange."

"Our visit to the Gardiners?"

"No, that was the most commonplace event of the day so far. I speak of our visit to Wickham."

Darcy cleared his throat. "No doubt you refer to the last part of it."

"I do." Fitzwilliam waited a moment, but when nothing further came from Darcy, he said, "Surely, you would not reconcile with Miss Bennet merely to best Wickham."

"I shall reconcile with Elizabeth because I love her. Any pain it causes Wickham will only be a pleasurable after-effect."

"Wickham should not be let off so easily."

"What can I do to him? I could beat him, but he would heal. I could see to him being sentenced or killed, but that would hurt those who presently depend on him." Darcy shook his head. "No, it would be the finest revenge of all to be happy where he wished for my misery."

"If you could be happy with such a woman!" Fitzwilliam leant forward. "Darcy, think of what you are saying."

"I know what I am saying. Believe me; I have never felt such anger as I did earlier this morning. I am certain she feels likewise of me."

"She is a Delilah!"

"Delilah was paid for her betrayal of Samson. Elizabeth gained nothing and lost everything."

Darcy thought once again of his sister and how, but for timely intervention, she might have been the one forced to be Wickham's bride. He had never told his sister what made him suspect her plans. It was a question in one of her letters about the terms of her fortune. She had never asked such things before, so when she did, the oddity of it made him uneasy. He had no cause to suspect the blackguard George Wickham; rather, he thought she was in love with someone merely inappropriate. In any case, he had felt disaster lurking at the edges and took himself off the next morning.

He still recalled the interminable ride to Ramsgate, the feeling of disaster gaining on him with every step. And then, the gut-wrenching, sickening shock, the panic when he learnt the truth. The devastation when he knew what she had done—and almost done—and the weeks spent praying it would all be well, that she would not be diseased or left with a child as a result of her indiscretion.

He considered no one else during that time; his attentions were centred wholly on how to fix his problem. He imagined that Elizabeth also thought of nothing but how to fix *her* problem and preserve her family's respectability.

"You are serious? You were not merely trying to vex Wickham?" Fitzwilliam gave him a sceptical look.

"I cannot say." Darcy turned his attention to the window. "I suppose it will depend on whether she is as willing to forgive me—"

"Forgive you? You have done nothing that was not wholly deserved! That woman is a blight upon—"

"Enough!" Darcy held his hand up to stop his cousin from further ranting. "You have overstepped your place in this matter. I know you mean well, and so I forgive you for deceiving me as you did, but do not think I shall be as generous next time."

"Very well," Fitzwilliam replied. "But, Darcy, pray think of what has come from all of this. At some point, you need to consider your best interests, and it is in your best interest not to see her again. Promise me you will do that much at least."

"I am only resolved to act in the manner that will constitute my happiness without reference to you or to any other person."

Chapter Seventeen

Some part of her expected a letter.

After all, the only time Elizabeth had ever argued in such a dreadful, violent manner was after his first proposal. The very air they breathed seemed to blacken with their rage that day. But the next morning, he had come to her with the letter that was the beginning of the end of her poor opinion of him.

She hoped he might do likewise now.

Elizabeth woke early every day for a week, going into Hyde Park and wandering around, hoping to see him. Hyde Park was quite large, but so was Rosings Park, and somehow they had found one other. So she would walk until she could no longer withstand the cold and then return to Davies Street.

After the week had passed, she realised there would not be another letter, and she considered writing her own. She sat at her little desk for above two hours one afternoon, seeking to compose something that would bridge the gulf between them. She soon came to appreciate that, although Darcy's letter had been effective, hers could not be. Darcy's letter had been aimed at clearing the misconceptions and misunderstandings between them. Hers would merely be begging for him to understand and forgive her. She surrendered the effort, realising anew that all between them was done.

There were some who believed that the winter months of 1814 would prove historic for the numbing cold that gripped it; Elizabeth was one of them. She spent many indolent days in front of the fire, reading and doing her best to abstain from thoughts of Darcy.

A Short Period of Exquisite Felicity

In the middle of January, Miss Bingley was the delighted recipient of an offer of marriage from Sir Edmund. Elizabeth could not have imagined her to be so girlishly thrilled, but she was, and Elizabeth felt glad for them both. Miss Bingley immediately set about making her plans and preparations, most of which involved new clothing. The wedding date was set for after Easter.

Less expected was the offer that Lady Sophie received from Colonel Fitzwilliam mere days later. Elizabeth learnt of it one day when Lady Sophie came to call. She tried to excuse herself from the drawing room, but Caroline urged her to stay, telling her that Lady Sophie found her refreshing. Elizabeth made a face but agreed to sit with them for a few minutes.

Lady Sophie had an air of triumph about her as she came in and took a seat, but she said little as tea was served. Caroline filled the silence with chatter about the fabrics and accoutrements she had seen and purchased. Elizabeth sat quietly and waited to hear something of interest.

"So," said Lady Sophie when Caroline had exhausted her subject. "I have a bit of news to share."

Caroline and Elizabeth waited with varying degrees of anticipation.

With a smirk and a nod, she said, "Our dear Miss Bingley is not the only lady to enter the state of matrimony this Season."

Caroline gasped so loudly that Elizabeth thought she had been set ablaze. "Oh, my dear! Do not say—"

"The colonel," Lady Sophie purred, "has at last come to the point."

"My sincerest wishes for your felicity," said Elizabeth while Caroline effused and exclaimed beside her. Much needed to be said after that: where and when he had made his offer, what he had said, and the way he said it.

"Our families are pleased," Lady Sophie concluded. "He is in need of my money, and my parents are just wild to be connected to the Fitzwilliams."

"Do you love him?" Elizabeth asked. The effect was immediate and dramatic; both ladies stopped speaking and stared at her for a moment.

"Of course," Lady Sophie replied with a grand wave of her hand. "He is rather dashing in his regimentals, is he not? And now, I may verify that he is just as dashing without them."

Caroline gave an affectedly shocked little gasp and shriek. "You did not permit him—"

"Just a quick little sample of the delights to come," drawled Lady Sophie.

This statement prompted more shrieks and exclamations from Caroline, along with several questions and confessions from both ladies that became increasingly explicit as they went on.

Elizabeth turned her head, embarrassed by the baseness of the conversation. Her squeamishness was noted by Lady Sophie. "Oh dear, we have offended Miss Bennet."

"Not at all, I assure you."

"I believe you once had some affection for my colonel, did you not? He told me something about a time at Rosings Park, his aunt's estate." Lady Sophie sighed. "Oh, dear Aunt Catherine."

Aunt Catherine? I never heard the colonel or Mr. Darcy refer to her as such. Elizabeth hid her smirk behind a cough and a handkerchief pressed to her lips.

"The colonel is an honourable gentleman, but if he perceived more than kind regard in my attentions to him, I fear he must have misunderstood me."

"You need not be missish on his account," Lady Sophie said with a feline smile. "He has told me that he once found you rather fetching."

Elizabeth felt herself blush and cursed herself for it. In a carefully even tone, she said, "The colonel and I have had our differences, and I must assure you, you have nothing to be concerned about from me."

Lady Sophie only smiled; then she lifted her cup to her lips and took a long sip. She gave Caroline an expressive look before turning back to Elizabeth.

"Yes, I have heard something of the differences between you."

Elizabeth stared at her coldly, but Caroline would not have it. She quickly turned the conversation back to pleasanter subjects, and so it remained until Lady Sophie departed.

ON THE FIRST DAY OF FEBRUARY, BINGLEY RETURNED HOME AFTER HAVING spent some hours at his club. Brimming with excitement, he found his wife, his sister, and Elizabeth sitting in the drawing room. "There is to be a Frost Fair!"

"A Frost Fair?" All the ladies were immediately enchanted by the notion.

"The first since 1789. The Thames has frozen solid by several feet, and already, some have set up their booths. There are skittles and puppet plays, dance barges and drink tents, even a whole ox roasted on a spit! And I have heard they will lead an elephant across the ice tomorrow!"

"An elephant!" Elizabeth exclaimed while the other two ladies gasped excitedly.

"But is it a respectable gathering?" Jane asked worriedly.

"Of course," Bingley cried out. "The regent himself will attend just as his father did the last one!"

Elizabeth's first inclination was to decline any part of it. She found herself with an uncommon lack of interest in society of late. She wished to be quiet at home with a book or her journal and her thoughts of Darcy.

She was no longer even slightly angry with him for thinking as he had. She still could not abide that he had thought quite so poorly of her, but her anger at his outrageous notions had dulled into acceptance. She knew he must think ill of her; therefore, the particular ill did not really matter.

More than anything, she found herself wishing that the whole tragedy could be forgotten. It would be, in time. And in the meanwhile, she wished to be left to her own devices.

"You cannot," Caroline scolded her. "Sir Edmund will be one of our party, and he is bringing Jolly. I believe you liked Jolly very well, did you not?"

Elizabeth nodded dutifully.

"Jolly is a splendid fellow!" Bingley cried. "He will make a most pleasing addition to the party! Lizzy, you simply must join us."

With a sigh, Elizabeth acquiesced. She dearly hoped that there was not some attempt afoot to ignite a romance between Jolly and herself.

They arrived at the river in the carriage that Bingley had given Jane on their engagement. A large vehicle, it clearly spoke to Bingley's desire for a house filled with children. For now, however, Baby Thomas cooed to his nursemaid at Davies Street while the carriage was occupied by six adults, all of whom were nearly as excited as children.

Having learnt more about Frost Fairs, Elizabeth found herself rather eager. Tales from the past seemed to be filled with the most fantastical of notions —until she laid eyes upon the spectacle.

It appeared that a city of sorts had sprouted on the icy Thames. A grand mall ran from London Bridge to Blackfriars Bridge with tents offering anything a person could desire, or so it appeared to Elizabeth's delighted eyes. This tent had a printing press busily producing souvenirs, that one had mulled wine and gin, and the next one had mugs engraved with the date. Books, toys, shawls, furs, and even bonnets were all there for purchase on the ice. And the food! Elizabeth saw the spit-roasted ox as well as mutton and meat pies, cream ices of every flavour imaginable, nuts, biscuits and cakes, oysters, and every manner of good thing.

What truly enthralled her, however, was the extraordinary mélange of people walking about. The watermen, in exacting their due, had settled on a price accessible to many people, thus servants and tradesmen rubbed shoulders with nobleman and aristocrats at this most unusual of affairs. Children dressed in rags ran alongside young lords and ladies while governesses and nursemaids fretted behind them. Elizabeth thought an entire year would not be nearly enough to take in all the sights around her.

When they first arrived, they did no more than stroll along the main thoroughfare, which had been dubbed the "City Road." Nearby, a barge, rendered immovable by the ice, had been made into a dance floor. Bingley saw it and his eyes lit up. Soon enough, he was waving farewell to the rest of them and taking his wife off to dance a reel or two.

Caroline was dedicated to lavishing attention on Sir Edmund; she scarcely spoke to anyone else. Elizabeth was left to Jolly, and fortunately, he was entertaining enough to remove all awkwardness from the situation.

He first proposed that she play against him at skittles, and Elizabeth was eager to accept the challenge. Every time she bested him, which was quite often, he would protest, saying she had cheated. She would counter by saying he was a poor loser, and they soon found themselves aching with laughter.

A great many tents were devoted to gambling, and many of them boasted as many ladies as gentlemen among the players. The ladies would play for little prizes, and Elizabeth, with Jolly's aid, found herself a winner at teetotum, earning a certificate that attested to her achievement.

It took little for Elizabeth to discern that Caroline would rather be alone with her suitor. She made several attempts to slip unnoticed into the crowd with him, but Sir Edmund always stopped and called after Elizabeth and Jolly. At last, they all stood together in front of a fuddling tent called City of Moscow; the owner no doubt thought himself a wit. Caroline proposed that she and Sir Edmund seek out some mulled wine while Elizabeth and Jolly purchased meat pies for them all.

"I cannot think the fuddling tent a decent place for you, my flower," said Sir Edmund, and indeed he was correct, for it appeared inhabited by many who had been there for a considerable time. Elizabeth looked away just as a clumsy, drunken sort of fisticuffs broke out among a few patrons near the doorway.

"What if you wait here?" Jolly proposed. "Sir Edmund and I shall see to the drinks, and then we can all find some pies together."

There ensued a little debate about whether Elizabeth and Caroline would be safer on the edge of the tent without the men or within it alongside them. With the former decided upon, Jolly and Sir Edmund issued instructions not to move and promised a hasty return before entering the tent.

As soon as the gentlemen were out of sight, Caroline demanded that Elizabeth tell her whether she thought Sir Edmund was the most gallant of all gentlemen; Elizabeth answered a dutiful affirmative. And the most handsome?—undoubtedly. She then wished to know whether her appearance was frightful?—certainly not. And whether Elizabeth thought Sir Edmund was violently in love with her?—of course he was.

The minutes passed long after that. Caroline had no interest in speaking to Elizabeth; for as much as they had formed an unanticipated truce, it did not follow that Caroline wished to befriend her. Elizabeth looked around for a while, relieved when she beheld a friend from Cheltenham, Miss Carrie Holmes, walking towards her.

"Miss Elizabeth Bennet," said Miss Holmes. "So lovely to see you and so well recovered!"

She was a charming and generous lady, and one Elizabeth had always liked. They had become friendly over a mutual love of reading and books, and it was not long before their conversation turned to like subjects.

"You must have already been to the booksellers' tents, I am sure! That one is the finest." Miss Holmes indicated the one closest to where they stood. "And I must say, I am something of an expert, as I do think I have visited them all!"

The two laughed lightly while Elizabeth glancing longingly at the tent. Miss Holmes was required to leave her then, and Elizabeth, believing there was still some time before the gentleman would return, decided a quick look could not hurt. She knew it was likely unwise to leave her group, but she was growing cold and had a wish to see which books were for sale. Caroline saw nothing amiss with her leaving. "I shall be right there," she told Caroline before slipping away. After all, it was only about four paces away.

There were a vast number of books that interested her, and she found herself reading the first few pages of one before moving to another and then another. She was reaching for *The Corsair* when a gloved male hand extended for the same; they touched and Elizabeth jumped back, looking up to see Mr. Darcy looking down at her.

"Oh!" She exclaimed. "Oh, I…my apologies."

"Not at all." He reached for the book and handed it to her. "Please take it."

"No, thank you." She gave it back. "I believe you were first."

He handed it to her again. "I was not, I assure you. In any case, I have already ordered it."

"I have no intention of purchasing it. You should take it."

"No intention to purchase it?" He gave her an unexpectedly kind smile. "Does the subject displease you?"

She was astonished by his smile and forced herself into a like expression before explaining, "I confess, I do not yet know the subject. Is it about a privateer?"

"Of sorts, or so I have been told. It is excessively popular; the entire first run was sold in a day. Over ten thousand copies, if the rumours can be believed. I am surprised to see it here."

"My goodness! It must be diverting indeed."

"One should hope," he agreed.

There was a brief silence, heavy with the weight of what had so recently passed between them. Elizabeth longed to escape even as she longed to stay. Reluctantly, she said, "I should return to my friends."

Darcy murmured something that she could not distinguish, and she turned from him, moving towards the exit of the bookseller's tent.

There was an empty space where Miss Bingley recently stood. "Oh."

Mr. Darcy had followed her, and from close behind, she heard, "Is something wrong?"

Elizabeth craned her neck, looking as far as she could in either direction. "I cannot find them."

"Who were you with?"

Dismayed, Elizabeth said, "I was with Jolly, Sir Edmund, and Miss Bingley. Mr. and Mrs. Bingley were also part of our party, but they went to the dancing barge. I should not have separated from them, but surely, they have not gone far. I shall find them quickly, I think."

"Will you permit me to help you?"

Amazed, Elizabeth looked up to see that there was less distress at the notion and more real interest in his countenance than she expected to see.

Nevertheless, she demurred at once. "No, I could not ask you to do that."

"I insist."

Well of course, he must offer. He can hardly send you out onto the Thames without an escort. He is likely scandalised that you are in here alone. "Truly, I am loath to be a bother to you."

"It is no bother at all."

"I am sure they are but a few paces down."

"I could not permit you to go off on your own, not in such company as this." He studied her and said in a lowered voice, "Surely it is better to endure the society of someone you despise than to risk your safety?"

Her heart cried out against the injustice in such a statement—*No! It is I who must be despised!*—but she gave no utterance of that nature. "I do not wish to be a trouble to you. No doubt you are here with a party of your own."

"No one who will miss me overmuch." He extended his arm to her, and after a moment, she accepted it. Relief rushed through her as she touched him; for a time, no matter how short, she was under his care and protection. They walked out of the bookseller's tent, looking for all the world—or so Elizabeth imagined—as if there had never been a cross word between them.

Chapter Eighteen

The wind bit at them as soon as they exited the bookseller's tent, stinging Darcy's cheeks and stealing his breath away, but he thought nothing of it. There was a warmth within him that he knew only when he had Elizabeth by his side. How easy it was to forget anything was amiss when she was with him! How little anything else mattered when he could look down and see her gloved hand on his arm.

They returned to the City of Moscow fuddling tent. Elizabeth looked around her, rising up on her toes to look down the City Road, seeking her lost companions.

"The gentlemen bid us wait here. Alas, I did not heed their directive."

The fuddling tent was not spacious, and being less occupied than previously, there was no difficulty in confirming that Sir Edmund, Jolly, and Miss Bingley were not within.

They exited the tent and spent several minutes searching the surrounding area. Darcy rather hoped he would not catch a glimpse of them; he was determined to make the most of this unexpected interlude with Elizabeth. He noted with satisfaction that she also seemed rather unconcerned. The crowd swelled with more and more people pressing their way onto the ice, though none appeared to be acquaintances of either of them.

"What was your next planned destination?"

Elizabeth shrugged. "Miss Bingley wished for gingerbread, but I believe that is sold by the strolling vendors."

"Perhaps we would do best to ramble about," he suggested. "No doubt we shall come upon them in due time."

"No doubt," she agreed. Darcy offered his arm again, but this time, she hesitated.

"My sister and Mr. Bingley probably remain at the dancing barge. If you would kindly escort me there, I can relieve you of the burden of protectorship."

"It is not a burden to me. Indeed I…"

He stopped, unsure what was better to be said or left unsaid. Their last meeting lay between them like a physical being. Her eyes were questioning as she sought his gaze, and at length, she bit her lip. He imagined that the recollection of their last meeting and the violent argument remained fresh in her mind. She had no idea where she stood in his regard, just as he did not know where he stood in hers. Neither of them was of a mind to speak plainly, certainly not here in the midst of a fair, surrounded by drunkards and laggards.

"If you wish to go to your sister and Bingley, I shall by no means suspend that pleasure. We can go there at once." He extended his arm in the direction of the barge, indicating she should precede him—if she wished to. "Or we could continue to walk about in hopes of finding the others."

She did not move. Her eyes searched his face, and he wondered what she saw or hoped to see.

"My only wish is that I not be an obligation to you."

"It is my pleasure to attend you. Truly, it is."

"It is my pleasure," she said in a voice so quiet he could scarcely hear it, "to be attended by you."

She blushed and looked away, directing his attention downriver. "We came from that direction, so perhaps we should go towards there."

He gestured, indicating they should move forward, and he again offered his arm as they began to walk. With a softly uttered, "thank you," she took it, and they went slowly through the crowd. The silence grew ponderous as they went, and he, in an attempt to remind her of easier times, said, "What think you of books?"

It earned him the hoped-for laugh even though it was more of an uncertain chuckle. "I like them very well. Too well, I think; books are what brought us to this predicament."

"I do not think this much of a predicament Miss Bennet—unless you believe in happy predicaments?"

A broader smile spread over her face as she looked up at him. "No, I do not think there can be happy predicaments. As a rule, predicaments require awkwardness and difficulty."

"Then I may assure you, it is no predicament to me." He delighted in her blush at his words.

They spoke then of books in a somewhat halting, nervous manner, but it soon became easier with both of them enjoying a subject that did not remind them of their past difficulties. Darcy was sorry when they came upon a little tent of souvenirs and Elizabeth expressed a wish to enter.

The tent held little toys, engraved cups, and the like. It was a pleasant time spent, Elizabeth exclaiming over the little bits of nothing that were, by virtue of the occasion, rendered into treasures. Several times, he wished that he had the right to buy her presents; she was so excessively diverted by all of it, and it would have been a delight for him. Alas, he could not, and he contented himself with observing her enjoyment.

There were other souvenir tents, and Elizabeth gave the wares of each careful study. Afterwards, they saw bull-baiting and dog racing and then a little puppet show, a humorous farce about a lady who fell through the ice.

It always amazed him how the least thing was enjoyable when he was with her. He had attended the fair on impulse with some other young gentleman from his club. Within moments, he had seen all he wished and was prepared to leave. Gaiety was too tiresome in his present state.

His wishes changed once he saw her. He had not intended to speak to her—much less be provided with the opportunity to devote himself exclusively to her amusement—but he was thankful that she had been put in his way. He now had no wish to leave; instead, he positively yearned to see every inch of the Frost Fair through her eyes, that he might know what delighted her.

When the farce was ended, they recalled their object was to find Elizabeth's friends. They increased their steps, peering into tents and looking all around them as they walked.

A man came down the centre of the mall, waving his arm and saying something about an elephant. Elizabeth immediately halted and turned to Darcy. "What is he saying?"

"Sir!" Darcy stopped him. "What is this about an elephant?"

The man explained that Maggie—an elephant well known among the *ton* for her performances in Covent Garden—was soon to walk across the ice.

He urged Darcy and Elizabeth to go to the spot immediately and observe an exhibition such as never was seen before and, surely, never would be seen again.

"An elephant," Elizabeth gasped, her face lit with delight. "I have never seen an elephant! But will the ice hold it?"

"This ice," proclaimed the man, "is three feet thick. It would hold ten elephants!"

"Shall we go see?" Darcy asked.

Elizabeth turned her shining eyes to him. He had forgotten this about her—the way both her pleasures and disappointments would be writ so clearly in her eyes. In this instance, there was only pleasure, and it filled him with a desire to see to her every happiness.

"I would like to go and see, but is it not down by—?"

"Blackfriars Bridge," said the man. "Down that way. I would hurry."

"Oh!" Elizabeth looked doubtful. "But surely, I should not. Is that not at the other end of the fair?"

"You will never see the likes of this again!" The man proclaimed and walked off to continue his shouting.

Elizabeth bit her lip, apparently undecided. Darcy longed to tell her to hang her friends and remain with him but knew he should not.

"Let us go," she said. "Perhaps they will be found down there as well."

"It is likely so," Darcy agreed.

The ice was uneven and grew ever more rough as they moved away from the central area of tents and stalls. Elizabeth clutched his arm tighter as they went, and he felt a frisson of pleasure from it.

They arrived just as Maggie stepped onto the ice to make her perilous journey. She was ridden by the beautiful Mrs. Lilly Tucker in a bright riding habit of such colour as to make her seem an exotic bird from another country. Mrs. Tucker smiled and waved as the elephant picked her way across the ice, which creaked and groaned as if it wished to give the crowd something to gasp about.

Darcy kept Elizabeth tightly at his side, telling himself it was for her protection. Elizabeth was enthralled by the great beast, even as much as he was enthralled by her. She watched the elephant with wide eyes and one hand pressed to her mouth, the picture of delighted astonishment. A particularly loud cracking sound made her gasp and giggle, and she looked up at him in almost child-like pleasure.

Maggie arrived at the other bank to great fanfare, her observers erupting into cheers and clapping, which did not alarm the animal at all. Treats awaited her, and it was only these that drew her notice.

"How amazing!" Elizabeth exclaimed. "I can say I have seen an elephant!"

"They do a delightful show in the warmer months called *Harlequin and Padmanaba*. I recommend it; it is a favourite of my sister."

"I think I should like it as well. I find elephants fascinating creatures. I once heard that they are one of the few animals that truly grieves when a member of their family dies."

"They are excessively intelligent," Darcy agreed.

The crowd had begun to disperse, but Elizabeth remained, still captivated by the elephant. "Are not they known to have extraordinary powers of recall?"

Darcy nodded. "I read somewhere once that an elephant may be separated from its herd for decades and still remember them."

Elizabeth smiled up at him a little wistfully. "Such a memory is both a blessing and a curse, I think. Perhaps I simply have too much I would wish to forget."

Darcy shook his head, his eyes fixed on the elephant. "Those who forget their past are doomed to repeat their mistakes. I would not wish to forget anything."

"Nothing?" Elizabeth tilted up her head to study him.

"Nothing," he said softly.

She turned her head quickly, resuming her study of the elephant. Darcy knew he had distressed her and, after a moment, lifted his hand. After a brief hesitation, he placed it on her shoulder and allowed his fingers to trace down her spine over her many layers of clothing to land at her waist.

"I cannot forget," he said gently, "but it does not follow that I have not forgiven. I have, and I can only pray that I am likewise forgiven."

Her eyes were wide and shiny with unshed tears when she looked up at him again. "How can that be?"

She could not go on and looked away from him once again.

After a moment, he cleared his throat. "I once thought it rather clever of me to possess an unyielding temper, but I now find I would rather be happy. Happiness cannot live side by side with resentment."

She smiled, though it was directed at the ice, and looked somewhat unsteady. "Happiness has much to recommend it."

"It does."

There was much more to be said, but it could not be said now, not in the midst of so many people. His stomach, due to the lack of nourishment therein, brought itself to his attention at this most inauspicious of moments; nevertheless, it made her laugh a little and broke the anxious moment between them.

"Shall we try the oxen?" he asked. "I understand it to be quite good."

They walked to where the ox roasted on a spit. They ate slices of the roasted meat as well as slices of mutton prepared in a like manner. Elizabeth thought, of the two, the ox was superior; Darcy did as well. They drank cups of mulled wine and then were tempted by gingerbread spread with treacle.

Elizabeth ate half of hers and passed the rest to Darcy. "If I have another morsel, I shall burst, I am sure!"

He liked the intimacy of the gesture, the sharing of a bit of cake together. "But there is so much more to be eaten. You cannot admit defeat now."

She laughed. "I fear I must. You know, I once knew a gentleman who had to leave an assembly because he had eaten so much at dinner, his breeches would no longer accommodate him."

"How positively dreadful," said Darcy with an embarrassed chuckle. "Such ungentlemanly behaviour to eat like a glutton! Perhaps he found it easier to eat than to talk that night."

She looked at him quizzically, but he decided that should be a tale for another time. "And you? Why did you leave the assembly?"

"I told Mr. Bingley I felt a fever coming on," she admitted. "In truth, I simply had no wish to be there."

He hoped his silence would serve in place of his asking why.

"Assemblies are a rather horrid thing when the person with whom you most wish to dance is the same one who is least likely to ask you." She gave him a small smile; it appeared rather forlorn.

"I should have done much better had I asked you to stand up with me."

"Perhaps it is best we did not. We were not then as disposed towards amicability as we are at present." She shook her head in a rueful but amused way. "You do always surprise me, sir."

"Do I? How so?"

All gaiety was gone when she replied. "The times when I most anticipate your anger or spite, you come to me with kindness and I am…I find myself quite undone by it."

"Now you know my secret," he said quietly.

A rush of people went by them, the crowd pressing and pushing before vanishing into the teeming avenue ahead. Elizabeth waited until they were afforded a small measure of seclusion before asking, "Do I?"

He nodded. "You have a great power over me. I find I am quite unable to stay angry with you."

"That is a wonderful power indeed," she exclaimed lightly. With more sobriety, she added, "I am glad. I would much rather be your friend than your foe."

"Always my friend."

HAVING EXHAUSTED HERSELF ON THE DANCING BARGE WITH HER HUSBAND, Jane Bingley thought she might like to partake of some of the treats offered by the various vendors. Bingley thought it a fine idea and was eager to sample Purl, a drink comprised of gin and wormwood wine that Mrs. Bingley thought sounded perfectly dreadful.

It was not until they came upon Jolly—who was with a Miss Blake and her brother but not Elizabeth—that they realised there might be some cause for alarm.

"Left me right at the fuddling tent," said Jolly, sounding a bit indignant. "Not a care in the world for old Jolly!"

"Lizzy would never do that." Jane looked to her husband in concern. "She is excessively attentive."

"Well, she must have gone off with Miss Bingley and Sir Edmund, for I can assure you, as right as I stand here, that I have not seen hide nor hair of the lot of them for above two hours now."

"Two hours!" Jane gasped.

"She is certainly with Caroline and Sir Edmund," said Bingley quickly. "There is nothing to be concerned about, I am sure."

They left Jolly, intent on seeking Caroline. They found her moments later, arm in arm with Sir Edmund and speaking in a manner most impassioned about the carriage he had purchased for her.

"Caroline," said Jane, interrupting them. "Where is Lizzy?"

"Lizzy?" Caroline looked around and smirked a little. "I do believe she and Jolly have taken themselves off somewhere."

Bingley stepped forward. "I think not. We saw Jolly a short time ago, quite vexed that you had left him back at the fuddling tent. He is with Mr. and Miss Blake now and swears he has not seen Lizzy for some time."

Caroline's eyes went wide, and Sir Edmund stepped in to protest. "She must have gone off with him. We did not see her anywhere, I assure you!"

At this, Jane burst into tears. Stories abounded at the Frost Fair about ladies who went missing, pickpockets, tales of ruination, drunkenness. Suddenly, all that had seemed so festive and gay looked menacing. She felt her husband wrap his arm around her, but even he could not disguise the fear in his voice.

"When were you at the fuddling tent? Where did you last see her?"

Alas, the two lovers did not have precise answers to these questions. It might have been half an hour ago…or perhaps it was an hour. Two hours, as Jolly had indicated, seemed rather absurd…then again, maybe it was not. Sir Edmund was sure Elizabeth did not enter the fuddling tent, but Caroline was equally certain she did. "Still on Jolly's arm," she insisted. "Right by his side the entire time."

It was clear that Caroline wanted Jolly to be the villain and remove the responsibility from her, but Bingley would have none of it.

"You were meant to stay together," he insisted. "Not to leave one another."

They argued for some time, vainly attempting to determine some facts about where and when Elizabeth had last been seen. Throughout, Jane wept, certain her sister had met some dreadful fate, until she could not bear the stupidity of it all.

"No matter where Lizzy was or was not," she said, raising her voice, "what we must determine is her present location! We must find her!"

ALTHOUGH THEY HAD NO SUCCESS IN FINDING THE PEOPLE THEY WERE looking for, they did succeed in finding the one lady Darcy least wished to see: Miss Lacey. She stood with her sister in the crowded avenue, watching an actor perform. Darcy hoped he might go past unseen, but it could not be so easy.

"How do you do, Miss Bennet? Mr. Darcy?" Miss Lacey turned from the play and greeted them, though with some evident discomfort. No doubt she felt it as much as he did.

Elizabeth dropped Darcy's arm, and the two ladies chatted while Darcy stood to the side, feeling awkward. Their conversation was mostly around the Frost Fair itself, each lady telling the other what she had seen and what else she wished to see. Miss Lacey looked almost exclusively at Elizabeth with only occasional darting glances at Darcy.

Miss Lacey was quick to excuse herself from the conversation, promising to call on Elizabeth at Davies Street very soon. Elizabeth replied with all due eagerness to receive her visit, and they parted company.

Darcy offered his arm at the same moment she reached for him; they smiled at one another in a cautious manner. They walked for a few minutes in silence until Elizabeth spoke, her tone high and a bit uncertain. "I should not ask this, perhaps, but—"

"I have no qualms to speak of it. It was merely a game. A stupid parlour game."

She looked up at him in confusion; evidently, he had not understood her question.

"Were you asking about Miss Lacey? About"—he looked around him and lowered his voice—"when I kissed her?"

"Oh." She blushed deeply and lowered her face. "No, I am sure it is none of my business."

"A parlour game," he repeated firmly. "No meaning attached to it whatsoever."

She gave him an abashed smile. "That is none of my concern, I am sure. I only wondered whether you…whether you ever thought about marrying her."

Now it was his turn to flush red and stammer about. "Oh…well…no, not in any serious way, but—"

"I thought about her marrying you. As much as I hated to admit it, I thought she would make you an excellent wife. Certainly better than Lady Sophie or the like."

"Well…yes, better than that choice to be sure but…no, I did not form any true design on Miss Lacey."

She said nothing to that, and as her head was lowered, her bonnet obscured her countenance and made it impossible for him to comprehend her sentiments.

He lowered his voice. "We have a great deal to talk about, likely many more questions than these to ask one another."

She hesitated for a moment. "Perhaps you will call on me?"

They were interrupted by a shout, something that sounded like, "There she is!"

A Short Period of Exquisite Felicity

A small crowd stood just ahead of them. Darcy first noticed Mrs. Bingley sitting off to one side near a fire, crying into a handkerchief while Miss Bingley stood beside her, patting her shoulder. Men were gathered around Bingley, all of whom appeared to be talking at once.

Elizabeth gasped when she saw them. She dropped Darcy's arm and ran to her sister. "Jane! Jane, I am here, forgive me, I—"

"Lizzy!"

The moment she was seen, she was surrounded, and everyone spoke at once, welcoming her with relief and joy at her good health.

"So many go through the ice below Blackfriars—"

"Heard of one lady separated from her party who is yet to be seen—"

"And then we went to the tent where the man who wrote *Frostiana* is printing copies for we were certain you would want—"

"And I told Bingley that the last I knew you were—"

Mrs. Bingley was unwavering in her belief that Elizabeth was sure to be stricken with pneumonia. She obtained a blanket and wrapped her sister tightly, so much that Elizabeth protested that she could hardly move. With dire proclamations about the warmth of Elizabeth's brow and the shivering she had noticed, Mrs. Bingley began to move her sister towards the nearby carriage.

"I think we must summon the apothecary straightaway."

"Jane!" Elizabeth laughed. "I know you feared I had gone through the ice, but I did not do so! I am no more exposed to the cold than anyone else."

Mrs. Bingley would have none of it and continued to push her towards the carriage, but at the last, Elizabeth broke away, shaking the blanket loose from her shoulders. With a light step, she ran back to where he stood. "Mr. Darcy, sir, I wished to say that I am obliged for your assistance." She offered him a curtsey.

He took her hand and bowed over it. "I assure you, Miss Bennet, it was my pleasure."

She did not wish to leave him; he knew it, could feel it in her touch. He did not release her hand nor did she pull it from his grasp. They looked at each other—serious but pleasing looks—until he heard Mrs. Bingley fretting behind them. "You had best get in the carriage," he whispered. "Else your sister is likely to summon a physician to treat you at once."

With a little nod, she agreed and turned away. Darcy watched her go, the first real happiness he had felt for some time swelling in his chest.

Chapter Nineteen

Colonel Fitzwilliam found Georgiana sitting in the drawing room, staring mournfully at a piece of needlework on her lap. She did not look up when he entered, and he took that as a sign of her distress.

He gently chucked her chin. She moved her head away with a jerk but granted him a faint grin. "What are you doing here?"

"Well, where should I be?" He sat in the chair closest to her, stretching out his legs until his boots nearly reached the fire.

"You came to see my brother, I am sure, but he is gone to the Frost Fair like anyone else who has the desire for any bit of amusement."

Fitzwilliam disregarded the angry dejection in her tone. "Has he? Good for him; I should have gone myself, but Lady Sophie did not like the idea."

She pouted. "It sounds enchanting—all the exhibits and the food. I daresay I could spend a week there and never grow tired."

"Why did not you go?"

"Because I am not permitted to stir from the house."

"Still?"

"Yes, still!" Georgiana expelled a breath forcefully. "He was quite angry with me for the way I treated Miss Bennet."

"But did you apologise?"

Georgiana nodded. "Yes. I am certain he has told you all about that day. I am confined to the house and not permitted a moment's pleasure for an entire fortnight."

"All for the likes of Miss Bennet." Fitzwilliam shook his head. "I have concluded she wishes for his fortune. Her father died, and with the threat of employment looming—"

"Employment?" Georgiana looked at him quizzically. "Why should she need a position when Mr. and Mrs. Bingley have taken her in?"

"Oh, well, the Bingleys cannot be expected to put her up forever." Fitzwilliam waited until she looked at him before adding, "He loves her, so I daresay, he would marry her for whatever reason she wanted him."

Georgiana sighed wistfully. "I never knew he was such a romantic."

"I never knew he was such an idiot." Fitzwilliam paused, rubbing his hands together slowly and cracking his knuckles. "No matter how justified her reasons, I cannot think it likely for two people such as Miss Bennet and Darcy to ever have happiness together."

"It certainly did not seem so from the violence of their argument. I am sure I never heard anything like it."

"Quite a row was it?" Fitzwilliam chuckled even as his mind spun in all directions, trying to imagine what he could make of it—how he might extricate Darcy this time. Miss Bennet's claws were sunk deep indeed, and thus far, his efforts had yielded little result. He had prevailed upon Darcy's reason, urged him in the direction of other ladies, and even tried to warn Miss Bennet off, but she proved more difficult to frighten than he expected.

He needed time to think and plan but knew not whether he had that time. Darcy's resolve was already faltering when they had gone to see Wickham, and from there, it was a short distance to forgiving and loving her once more.

"Cousin? It seems you left me." Georgiana was staring at him in a concerned way.

"Forgive me; I was just thinking of what I could do about this."

"Do about what?"

Fitzwilliam rose from the chair, determined to go find his cousin. "A soldier never leaves a wreck behind him, and I am afraid this problem of Darcy's has become quite a wreck."

THE DAY AFTER THE FROST FAIR, DARCY CALLED AT DAVIES STREET. He had dressed more carefully than he would have admitted, and he had bursts of nerves fluttering in his stomach and chest, making him feel like the greenest of green lads. He waited in anxious silence in his carriage for his coachman to appear with a summons from the house.

There was much to be said between them. They had moved easily—*too easily?*—from a violent argument into amiable wanderings through the Frost Fair. It was far too reminiscent of things at Pemberley.

In the torturous, protracted days immediately after she had released him, he had heartily regretted that they had not discussed more when she was at Pemberley. He had expected her spite—as likely she had expected his—but they had come to an understanding with only the merest scrap of conversation about their past difficulties. It was a mistake he would not repeat.

The coachman gave the quick one-two knock on the carriage door that was his custom, and Darcy's heart leapt; he would see her now. "The ladies are not at home, but Mr. Bingley would like to speak to you."

"Very well."

Darcy was surprised when his coachman moved from the door and his friend stood in the opening. "You do not object?"

"It seems I cannot." He offered a smile, and Bingley climbed into the carriage and settled himself across from Darcy.

"Lizzy has fallen ill. I fear the Frost Fair might have been a grave mistake."

"Surely not," said Darcy even as a frisson of alarm shot through him. "What is it? A fever?"

Bingley nodded. "We hope it will not become pneumonia, but we are exercising every caution."

"Has the apothecary been summoned? A doctor? Shall I send a note to my doctor? Perhaps I should send the carriage for him?"

Bingley lifted a brow and gave Darcy a queer sort of frown. "Darcy, I am able to care for her properly, I assure you."

"I am sure you are."

Bingley leant back, one leg crossed over his ankle, and studied his friend in a critical manner. Darcy did his best to meet his friend's gaze with equanimity, but a strange discomfiture assailed him. He wanted to drop his eyes but would not permit it of himself.

"I wonder how it came to be that you were alone with Lizzy all day yesterday."

"All day? A few hours only."

Bingley did not appear impressed by this clarification.

"I came upon her in the bookseller's tent, and your sister and Sir Edmund had inadvertently left her. So I accompanied her to find them."

"Sir Edmund mentioned that he saw you just before they lost her."

Darcy said nothing to this charge, but his face heated. He hoped he was not turning crimson.

"Said you were in the souvenir tent and just behind them when Lizzy was playing teetotum."

"And if I were?"

"Were you following her?"

"No."

"Seems rather coincidental that you should have been in three places at the very same time as her party."

"What are you saying, Bingley? Of what do you accuse me?"

"I accuse you of nothing." With a sigh, he relented a little. "You must comprehend how strange it all seems to a brother. I am sure if there were some man who came in and out of Miss Darcy's life, you would want to understand the truth of it."

"The truth of it is very simple: coincidence. It might seem unlikely, but we were in the same places at approximately the same times. There is no more to it than that."

"I refer to more than the Frost Fair, Darcy. I am not a fool. I see that you and Lizzy, for whatever reason, enjoy pretending to dislike one another, but I have long understood that there is much more to it than that."

Such a simple statement for such complicated goings-on! Yes, indeed, there was much more to it than that, and dislike was as inaccurate a term as could ever be.

"We have been friends for a long time, and I well know that you revolt against exposing your private thoughts and actions to the world. But now I speak to you not as your friend but as Lizzy's brother, and I say it will not do. If your intentions are honourable—"

"Of course they are!"

"Then all must be laid bare." Bingley levelled a serious look at him. "Nothing hidden nor closeted. I shall not countenance it. Whatever has gone on before, these suppressed feelings or understandings will be no more. I know you would want nothing less for Miss Darcy."

Darcy levelled an equally serious gaze on Bingley. "I comprehend you perfectly."

After a brief silence, Bingley shifted, clearly intending to leave the carriage. "We shall remove for a bit when Lizzy is equal to it. A brief time in the country to be certain she does not develop a more serious malady."

"Leave town? Where? When will you return?"

Bingley smiled faintly, paying no heed to his friend's queries. "I shall be sure to send a note once we are again in town."

Darcy strode angrily into his club, hoping to find Colonel Fitzwilliam. Moments later, he found his cousin alone at a table in an out of the way area. He was reading the broadsheets and did not notice Darcy had joined him until Darcy blew out his breath in an explosion of angry air.

"You would not believe Bingley! Evidently, he thinks marriage has turned him from a pup into a tiger."

Fitzwilliam lowered the paper and chuckled. "Bingley will be sixty and still not a tiger."

"I know it! Yet the audacity of him—positively enraging." Darcy explained how Bingley had nearly demanded that he declare himself right then and there.

"Well, stop recognising him, then," Fitzwilliam replied in an uninterested tone. "Why not be done with all these Bennets, Bingleys, and Wickhams altogether?"

He did not deign to reply. Fitzwilliam was growing tiresome with his persistent entreaties to forget Elizabeth. Darcy was afforded a convenient interruption when another gentleman came to speak to them. Another followed him, then another, and a pleasant half an hour was passed in conversation and laughter.

Fitzwilliam took up his newspaper again once the men had gone. "And what did you say to him?"

"To whom?"

"The Prince Regent." Fitzwilliam rolled his eyes. "Bingley, of course."

"I told him nothing. What right has he to ask such things of me?"

With a chuckle, Fitzwilliam replied, "The right of a brother. Is not she under his care?"

Darcy paused a moment. He had never before considered it, but how differently things might have been had only someone known of his intentions towards her. Not merely for their brief engagement, but even going back to his first offer! Had anyone understood what he was about, the results could have been quite different.

"Very well, I grant you that. It is not out of order that he should ask about my intentions."

"And what are your intentions?"

The question indeed! He had determined the answer to himself, but to say it aloud was another matter.

"I shall marry her."

It was liberating and terrifying to say it, even just to Fitzwilliam. Darcy's pulse quickened and a light sweat moistened the palms of his hands.

"Despite her alliance with Wickham?"

"Wickham is her sister's husband, nothing more."

To this, Fitzwilliam said nothing. Darcy expected some expostulation from him but received none. With a small twitch of his brow, his cousin returned to his reading and after a time, Darcy did likewise.

As it was, Jane was not wholly incorrect in her anxious fluttering over Elizabeth's health, for the day after the Frost Fair, Elizabeth found herself afflicted. It was merely a cold, but Jane was not of a mind to take any risks. Elizabeth was settled into her bed under strict orders that she must not stir. Both the apothecary and a doctor were summoned, and the housekeeper devised some horrible-tasting potion that placed Elizabeth into a long, dreamless sleep.

Inasmuch as being confined to her bed frustrated her, it also gave her time to think of Darcy, and she used her time wisely. She spent hours recalling their time at the Frost Fair, lingering rather shamelessly on the moment he had placed his hand on her back and lightly traced her spine. An innocent, brief touch, given through many layers of clothing, yet it had nearly undone her. There was a tenderness, to be sure, in all he had said to her, in speaking of forgiveness, but there was more—something indefinable.

But no, she could not be so missish as to pretend she had no notion what it was. Underneath the tender feeling, she had felt...well...plainly said, she had wanted more of his touch, wanted more of him. *Wanton thing*, she scolded herself half-heartedly.

Still, that pleasurable recollection led to another, thinking of times she had kissed him and he had held her. Was it any wonder her fever lingered on when fuelled by such remembrances as these?

At last, she was equal to leaving her bed only to learn that Bingley intended to take them into the country. It was Caroline who informed her of it while complaining to Lady Sophie.

"Leave town now! Can you imagine, my dear? Is there any notion more absurd?" Caroline rolled her eyes. "If my sister will not have me with her and Hurst, I do not know what will become of me. I shall be most exceedingly displeased, and I shall make sure Charles knows it with every breath I take."

"Think of when we are married," Lady Sophie pronounced in dire tones. "Then you are likely to be always in the country. A man can hardly play with his horses in town, can he?"

Elizabeth almost pitied Caroline for the look of trepidation that came over her countenance. "Sir Edmund loves being in London."

"He does, but not as much as he likes being with his cattle. You must realise it, Caroline, that we ladies do everything we can to find a husband. We spend so much time in town, at parties and dinners and balls, all for the purpose of marriage, and then once we achieve it, everything changes. Off we go into some country estate, no more parties, no friends, no shopping for beautiful gowns—"

"People do wear clothing in the country," Elizabeth offered, but the two ladies disregarded her. "They eat dinner too."

"Rather ironic, is it not?" Caroline joined her friend's lament. "We seek something all of our lives that, in the end, is rather a grim fate."

"You and Sir Edmund will retire to the country so he will be able to breed his horses and his children all in one spot," said Lady Sophie solemnly. It was amusing though, and Caroline fought between laughing and being distressed. She finally gave way to giggles, and Elizabeth joined her.

When Lady Sophie had departed, Elizabeth went to seek the truth of the plans from Jane, only to learn that, alas, they were to go into the country as soon as the arrangements were complete.

"I think I might do best to remain," she ventured.

"Nonsense," said Jane briskly from her place at her escritoire where she was writing furiously. "You are the largest part of our reason for going: to be sure your cold does not worsen."

"I am perfectly well," Elizabeth protested, but Jane's ears had gone deaf to her. With a sigh, Elizabeth was resigned to hoping that Darcy would somehow know she was in better health and come to call. Alas, he did not.

A Short Period of Exquisite Felicity

The Bingleys were to make their home in Rotherham, at a lovely place called Beckett Park. It reminded Elizabeth of Netherfield with the exception of not having Mrs. Bennet and Mr. Collins nearby. The house itself was similar, albeit older, and Jane had undertaken substantial redecoration. Elizabeth smiled to see the results of her sister's efforts, for they were like Jane, cheerful and pretty.

Jane and Bingley spent many days looking over what alterations had been made and planning for more. In the course of it, they urged Elizabeth to plan the refitting of her own apartment. In darker moments, she took this encouragement to mean they believed she would be always with them.

He had not called on her, and naturally, he could not write to her. She did what she could to learn whether he had written to Bingley, but short of a direct enquiry, she could not tell. Elizabeth asked her brother what news came from town, who had written, and what was said until Bingley remarked, "I had not thought you so interested in the goings-on in London, Lizzy." She realised then that she must cease; she was making a fool of herself. Darcy had ample opportunity to call on them or write, and he had done neither.

"The next time I see Bingley," said Darcy to Colonel Fitzwilliam, "he will count himself lucky if I do not box his ears."

The two gentlemen were walking from the boxing establishment to Lord Matlock's town house. There was a warmth and cheer to the early spring day that contrasted notably with the foul humour on Darcy's face.

"What has he done now?"

"He has taken Elizabeth off into the country, and it seems he will hold her there until autumn!"

"Likely not." Fitzwilliam yawned widely. "In any case, we shall be soon for Cotgrave."

"Cotgrave? I do not think so."

"You swore to me you would!" Fitzwilliam stopped in his tracks and turned to his cousin. "You promised me your aid!"

"Promised you? I do not think I—"

"Come, Darcy, you cannot leave me to go alone! I scarcely know a hay bale from a dovecote! You promised you would help me."

"Did not you and your father already survey it? I would hope neither of you would be fool enough to purchase something without a thorough examination."

"We viewed it as potential purchasers," Fitzwilliam replied, somewhat frantically. "Only seeing whether there was anything to keep me from buying it. Now that is done, and I shall view it as an owner. Darcy, I must have your assistance in this!"

It was true; he had told his cousin he would attend him into Nottinghamshire, but now? Darcy held up both hands. "But this week? Why would you want to go now? It is much better we should wait and—"

"No, no, I must go now."

"Why?"

"To see the plans and arrangements for spring. I cannot simply arrive in June and expect that all would have been done."

Darcy winced. "Yes, but it has such a tendency to rain in March. Travel grows complicated in the spring with all the mud."

"It is scarcely a three-day journey from London," Fitzwilliam replied. "We shall hardly be there a week, and you will be back just after Easter. I am sure Bingley will return then too."

Darcy wished to refuse, but he knew that, when his cousin was of a mind to have him, there could be no adequate reason. "Take Saye," he suggested.

Fitzwilliam laughed. "Saye knows even less about estates than I do. You must recall that you promised—do you not? And there is scarcely an amusement to be found in town at present."

Darcy sighed, and put his head in his hand. "The timing could not be worse."

"You promised me, Darcy," said Fitzwilliam beseechingly. "I would not insist if I were not in such need of your assistance."

"Very well," Darcy agreed unhappily.

The men entered the house, and Fitzwilliam left him to go to his bedchamber and refresh himself. Darcy, hearing music from the drawing room, took the liberty of seeing himself in. He found Saye lolling about while his wife played on the pianoforte.

Darcy!" Saye sat up straight. "I have been nearly mad to see you! I have heard a report of a most alarming nature."

Darcy greeted Lady Saye and made himself comfortable in a chair at the viscount's side. "Oh?"

Saye pressed his lips together for a moment. "It concerns Miss Lacey."

"Ah."

"She has accepted an offer of marriage!" Saye leant towards Darcy, his eyes wide with delighted horror—no doubt hoping for some outburst from Darcy.

"Mm."

"That is three grunts that stood in the way of proper responses. Say something, man! Are you distressed? Angry? Jealous? Will you challenge him?"

"Challenge who?"

"The dastardly brute who has stolen your lover!" Saye cried out. Then he calmed and added, "Though perhaps you should not call him out. It is Basely after all, and I went to school with him. He is not a bad fellow, and I think if he understood—"

"Miss Lacey was never my lover, and Basely is welcome to her. I wish them every happiness."

"Wish for her happiness?" Saye cried out with incredulity. "Lord above! That is no disposition for a scorned suitor!"

"I am not a scorned suitor," Darcy protested.

"Saye," Lady Saye called from the pianoforte, "let Darcy be concerned about his own ladies."

"I would, except that Darcy appears singularly incapable of liking anyone. How am I to see him married by Ascot if he does not…" His words died as he gave Darcy a penitent look.

"See me married by Ascot?" Darcy lifted a brow. "By whose order?"

"My father has commissioned me to find you a wife. He wants to see us all settled."

"Your father should not meddle," Lady Saye opined as her fingers flew over the keys. She was excessively talented; she barely missed a note even though she paid no attention to either the music page or the song.

Darcy gave his cousin a careful appraisal. Although he felt the need for such things rarely, in the matter of Elizabeth, he thought it would do well to have another in his service—a helpmate of sorts.

Saye was not one he would customarily rely upon. The viscount was selfish and could be quite rude, indolent on his best days and positively neglectful on the rest. Nevertheless, Saye was passionate about love and love matches; he firmly believed a wealthy man of position ought to have anything his heart desired, and the devil take the hindmost to any who opposed him. Darcy hoped that somewhere within these sentiments—and with the promise of payment—Saye might prove a helpmate for his nuptial plans.

He spoke with careful indifference "What business is it of his lordship's whether or not I should marry? Is he paying you to find me a wife? Have we sunk so far?"

"'Tis not truly a payment." Saye moved uncomfortably in his seat.

"'Tis a bet," Lady Saye called out cheerfully.

"Hush, woman," her husband admonished. "I shall let you know when we need your tongue in this."

"Five hundred pounds if you are married by Ascot," said Lady Saye.

"I receive five hundred pounds just to marry?"

"No, Saye does," remarked his wife gleefully.

When her husband scowled at her blisteringly, she gave him a wink and blew a kiss. Saye grinned, pretending to grab the blown kiss out of the air, and giving his wife a wicked leer, he tossed one back at her. He mouthed something that Darcy could not see, but he observed Lady Saye blush scarlet.

"In case you forgot," said Darcy, "I am still here. Why should *you* profit from my endeavours?"

"Will you not profit from a wife? Perhaps not profit of the pecuniary sort or, I should say, not merely pecuniary. Do I not deserve some small portion for my assistance?"

"Ah!" Darcy grinned. "So you will help me? Splendid." The situation was proving to be even better than he dared hope; nothing could induce Saye more than the promise of easy money.

"You proved singularly incapable of settling the business yourself, and who better than I to direct a young man in the ways of love? Now, what about that Miss Edmunds? You like her."

"No, not even a little."

"Lady Sarah Asbell? She has a fortune of twenty-five thousand pounds, you know."

Darcy screwed up his face to communicate his distaste.

"Ah! I know…now, do not say no, just consider the lady—"

"Saye, I beg you would stop your unceasing wagering. I cannot think of anyone I know who loses as much as you do." Darcy gave a heavy sigh. "Who could I marry when my one true love…the woman with whom I could share every sort of joy…"

Saye gave him a blank look until he seemed to recall something. "Oh, yes, Miss Ellen Bassett, that lady from Herefordshire."

"Miss Elizabeth Bennet. From Hertfordshire."

Saye leant back in his chair, his fingers forming a tent beneath his chin. "What was it about her again? There was something we did not like about her…I cannot quite recall…"

With a sigh, Darcy quickly summed up the whole of it for him.

Saye made a regretful clucking noise at the end of it. "George Wickham! He is at the bottom of every bad thing that has ever happened to you, Darcy; I do declare it."

"It does seem like it," Darcy agreed.

"She should have asked you to take care of it. You would have put old George in his place before an hour had passed."

"Indeed, but never mind that. All has been resolved in that quarter, and now I must see that she will be received well in town and amongst my relations."

"Ah." With a pensive frown, Saye drummed his fingers on the arm of his chair. "You put me in a difficult spot, Darcy. No name, no fortune—just the sort of person I usually despise."

"Her name will be Darcy, and her fortune will be mine," Darcy said pointedly.

"That is true, I suppose." Saye nodded thoughtfully. "And being friends with Lily will make her agreeable amongst the ladies. Lily!"

"Yes, dear?"

"Miss Althea Barrett—"

"Elizabeth Bennet," Darcy corrected him tiredly.

"She is one of your dearest friends for many years now, and in fact, this notion of her marriage to Darcy was all your doing."

"Of course," said her ladyship, undisturbed by such demands. She continued merrily with her song.

"There you are—done and done. Now, when will you propose?"

"There is more. Neither your brother nor my sister is inclined to look favourably on the match."

Saye made a rude noise with his mouth that sounded like flatulence. Lady Saye looked over at him for a moment, giggled, and continued playing. "That is what I think of his opinion. Marrying a useless bit of muslin like Lady Sophie Woodbridge for nothing more than a fortune and a fu—"

"Very well," Darcy said hastily with a significant look at Saye's wife. "Your meaning is not lost on me."

"Do you know what your problem is? You are too indulgent. A few tears and Georgiana has all she wants from you. You need to sit her down and tell her: if she does not behave like an adult, then she will remain at home for another year. There are two Darcys left in this world, and heaven forbid there is a feud between you. She has to trust you to know your own heart."

"Saye!" Darcy looked at his cousin with no little amount of astonishment. "That is positively sage advice. I scarcely know how to look."

"We cannot allow those two to stand in our way. There is money to be made here, Darcy. I shall even send a bit of it your way—how's that? It is you who will be shackled, after all; I think you deserve a bit of the gain."

"You are ever the soul of generosity." Darcy grinned. "Well, then, I think the plan is laid! As soon as I am returned from Cotgrave, we shall make a go of it."

Saye leant over and gave Darcy an affectionate clout on the arm. "Another man down!"

Chapter Twenty

It was Bingley's intention to return to town after Easter, but as the weather grew warm, he became restless, longing for the amusements of London. "Hyde Park is simply charming in the spring," he told the ladies. "How pleasant it would be to have a walking party!"

Jane was of a mind to agree with him, and before March had drawn its last breath, they were travelling again. The days had lengthened, so they made good time, stopping their last evening in Milton Keynes, only fifty miles from their destination, an easy distance to dispense with on the morrow.

Fifty miles of good road. Elizabeth smiled for the remembrance, but it was followed by a pang of regret. Such an innocent time that was; he had not yet made his first proposal. Had she only seen then the man he really was, how much pain might have been avoided! She wondered when the most tangential of subjects would stop inducing thoughts of him and regrets for the mistakes she had made.

The next morning dawned colder than the one before, and Elizabeth shivered in the small sitting room that had been set aside for the Bingley party. They had planned an early morning departure, and the inn still had a hushed feel to it. The maid saw her and hurried to stoke the fire, but Elizabeth assured her it was not necessary as they were certain to be on their way soon.

Bingley entered from the adjoining room as she spoke. "Lizzy, I am afraid I have some bad news. Jane is not well this morning, and I fear we may need to remain for some time. My apologies."

He did not look wholly distressed by the notion, and Elizabeth suspected she knew why. Jane's morning illness had been a sign when she was increasing with Baby Thomas; it was likely such signs might accompany the announcement of another child.

Elizabeth smiled and shook her head. "I have a good book, Charles; I shall shift for myself. Do not suffer any anxiety for me. Shall we stay the day do you think?"

"I think not. A couple of hours rest should see her set to rights."

Bingley returned to Jane, and Elizabeth returned to her bedchamber to retrieve her book. The maid stoked the fire in the sitting room, and Elizabeth settled in to read in comfortable silence. It could not last; Elizabeth enjoyed solitude only in small doses, and the time soon began to wear on her.

She rose and walked around a little, hoping to quietly remind her sister that she was there, but the Bingleys' room remained silent. She had no interest in disturbing them, and after some time spent pondering the wisdom of the matter, she decided to take a walk.

She gathered her things, left word with Jane's maid, and hurried down the stairs towards the front of the inn. Although it was still rather early —the breakfast hour if one was in town—the vestibule was now crowded with travellers coming and going, creating a hubbub of clatter and chatter.

And there, in the entryway, he stood: a gentleman, tall and elegant, a man who caused her to halt her steps with a pounding heart and a soul gone incandescent. *Is it? Could it be?* It surely could not be him, yet no other man could look so refined, so imposing, and so utterly... *Darcy!*

She watched him as he spoke to the proprietor of the inn and made some motion to a nearby manservant. She had moved towards him without realising she did so, only stopping when she was within the vestibule, no more than a dozen feet away.

But what could she say to him? Their intimacy at the Frost Fair, followed by silence for several weeks, rendered her uncertain. Should they speak here in a vestibule filled with strangers from all places and stations in life? Surely not. But would she be an utter idiot to walk away unseen as part of her wished to do?

Indecision froze her for several long moments until trepidation won. She felt not yet equal to speaking to him and decided she would fall back until she could gain her equanimity and meet him with graciousness and poise. She took a small step backwards, her eyes still on him, quietly planning her retreat.

Alas, it could not be so. A small cry was heard from somewhere behind her knees, and she cried out as she stumbled over a child who had evidently decided to hide behind her skirts.

Mr. Darcy turned at the sound, exclaiming, "Miss Bennet!" while the child at her feet began to wail. Elizabeth attempted to make her stumble into an awkward sort of curtsey, feeling herself turn bright scarlet.

"Sir!" she said over the child's screams. "How do you do?" She attempted to appear composed as she picked the child up into her arms, patting his back soothingly. "I…ah…we are travelling. I am travelling with my sister and brother."

Darcy offered a small bow and some words of greeting over the child's wails. "You must be travelling as well."

"I am with Colonel Fitzwilliam." Darcy sounded bewildered. "We stopped here last night on the way to Cotgrave, and Fitzwilliam…well, he is unwell this morning. He requires additional rest."

He reached out and lightly patted the child on his back. "This is…this must be Miss Wickham."

"Miss Wickham?" Indignation rose quickly. "No, of course not."

"No?" He looked surprised. "Who is it, then?"

"I am sure I have no idea. A child who was playing a game in my skirts. Am I to be considered the owner of every child who stands near me?"

A nursemaid hurried up to them; it was she who had lost the child, and she stammered out apology after apology as Elizabeth handed over her charge and assured her that it was no trouble.

"Forgive me for misunderstanding the situation. He looked like…his hair…"

"Yes, I know what you think," she murmured sarcastically. "Yet another child from one of my many liaisons, I suppose!"

He looked at her earnestly while she did everything she could to avoid his gaze, overcome by awkwardness and anger as well as some understanding that she was being silly. At last, she muttered, "I beg your pardon."

"Your bitterness is well deserved."

"As is your misapprehension." She gave a little shrug, still not meeting his eye.

After some moments, he spoke. "It seems there is much to be said between us."

"There is," she agreed. "We want only for time to say it."

"True." He looked pensive a moment. "I am at my leisure now if you are."

After only a moment's hesitation, she agreed.

A walk outside was considered until Darcy spied an alcove off to one side of the vestibule that he thought would serve them well. It was hidden enough to give them privacy but had an open door to answer any concerns for propriety.

They were soon settled together at a small table within the room. Darcy ordered a light repast, and Elizabeth removed the coat she had donned for a walk. When they were settled, each looked to the other to begin.

"You did not call," she said simply.

"I did. You were ill, and then you were gone."

Their tea came, and they paused a moment, allowing the servant to do his work. Elizabeth then poured tea for them both while Darcy watched her intently. They remained silent; there was too much to be said to know where they ought to begin. Elizabeth was the first to find the silence insupportable.

"How could you think that I had fallen to the charms of George Wickham?"

He lifted his cup and swallowed deeply, wincing as the tea scalded his throat. "I think any woman, no matter how witty or discerning, may find herself at the mercy of a practised seducer. Is not my sister the very example?"

There was something in his countenance that suggested this was not the whole truth.

"Your sister was young and knew not what he was. But you had told me the truth of him, and I was not a young girl of fifteen."

"That is true," he agreed softly. "It was rather stupid of me to have ever imagined you would…but I did not know what to think."

"I can easily comprehend that you must have wanted for reasons," she admitted. "I had given you nothing to explain my sudden change of heart. But truly, no matter how you must have hated me, this was your best explanation? Were there no other possible answers?"

"Indeed, there were many other possibilities, first and foremost being…"

Darcy picked up his cup and took a small sip, then he settled the cup carefully back in its saucer and wiped his mouth with his napkin. He stared into the cup as he spoke in a flat, deceptively disinterested tone.

"My chief reason—the one that tormented me many long nights at Pemberley—was the simplest: that you remembered you did not love me, nay, that you did not even like me. That perhaps the circumstances of our engagement had merely been the work of a moment—the effect of my house, the roses, and a summer day beside a pretty stream—and once you were away from all of that, you realised your feelings for me had not changed. Perhaps you had recalled that you thought I was selfish, conceited, and the last man in the world whom you could ever marry."

He drew a deep breath and released it. "I would have much rather believed someone else came between us than to imagine that…that you simply did not want me."

A lump entered her throat as he made his confession. To every outward appearance, he was unaffected, and it was this that made her understand just how deeply affected he was.

"But I told you at Pemberley," she insisted. "I told you that my prejudices had fallen away and I was in love with you."

"You had, but on later reflection, I deemed it too good to be true. The happiness had been of such short duration that I thought it a dream or the product of my imagination. You had disliked me for so long—and liked me for so little—that it was easy to believe I had misunderstood you." He sighed again. "As I have often misunderstood you."

She reached over, allowing herself the most ephemeral of moments to touch his cheek. "You did not. You did not misunderstand me when I told you I loved you."

"I suppose it must be given to mistrust, then."

"Misunderstanding and mistrust; it is these that seem to confound us over and over again."

"Trust is important," he agreed. "I believe I would much rather trust my wife than love her."

Surprised, she laughed. "How could you not wish to love your wife?"

"I never said I did not want to love her. I said only that given a choice between love and trust, I should choose trust."

"I do not think you could have one and not the other. I think to love someone you must also trust them."

"Love and trust are entirely different objects. Indeed, it is entirely possible to have one without the other."

It seemed they would soon be off on one of their fabled arguments, but Elizabeth did not wish it. There had been more than enough dissension and strife between them. "I think I should prefer both," she said mildly.

He paused for a moment; evidently, he had been prepared for an argument. In an equally agreeable tone, he said, "I do believe it would account for the largest share of happiness."

"But you do not trust me." She felt her eyes grow moist. "Perhaps you think you never will."

"You do not trust me—"

"I do. I do trust you."

"And I do not know whether you ever will."

She did not know what to say to his assertion.

"If you had trusted me, you would have come to me with this business of your sister and Wickham, and I would have helped you. Who more so than I know what it is to see a sister persuaded by that blackguard? Who more than I would want to help you?"

Elizabeth took a shuddering breath. It was true, now that she thought of it. She had acted alone, entirely alone. She had taken the whole of it on herself, and indeed, the thought had never even occurred to her to involve someone else.

"I did not think," she admitted. "All I could do was look at the disaster in front of me: my father dying, my sister with child and about to marry a reprobate, the possibility for ruination of my family. I was running as fast as I could just to stay in place. I never meant to betray you. Never. When Wickham came to me and bade me to release you, in truth, it seemed an act of mercy. I thought I would sacrifice my happiness to save everyone else."

"And your family, they did not try to stop you?"

She shrugged. "They were not at home when it happened."

"But did you not tell them later? When they returned home?"

"No."

"Not your aunt? Your sister?"

She shook her head.

This appeared to surprise him. He sat back and studied her countenance for a moment, and she became flustered under his gaze. "Why should I have told them? There was no point; nothing could be changed or helped. It would only have distressed them."

"Have you ever told your sister I proposed to you in Kent?"

"Yes, I told her as soon as we were both back at Longbourn."

"Which was when? And did you tell her all of it?"

"We were both at home in the middle of May, I believe. I told her that you had proposed to me, and I told her about Wickham. I actually said rather little; Jane's spirits were low, and I did not wish to distress her further."

"Did she know how we argued? That I hurt you and said cruel things?"

"No." Elizabeth sighed. "I did not want Jane to know that you had acted the principal part in separating her from Bingley."

"What about your aunt? Did you tell her?"

"No, she was busy with her own family."

"You often have reasons enough to keep your silence."

"I beg your pardon?"

"You have no true confidante, no one who sees the real Elizabeth Bennet, not even your most beloved sister."

"No…no, that is not true," she protested. "Jane is my confidante. I tell her everything."

"No, you do not. You just told me of things you never told her."

"Just because I did not—"

"It is true," he insisted gently. "When there is something to laugh about or be angry for, you are open and expressive. But when something hurts you? It is concealed or ridiculed."

"I disagree, but I do not think it has any meaning for our conversation."

"Yes. Yes, it does."

"How so?"

"Elizabeth, I have bled for you." He leant towards her with sudden ferocity. "Yes, I have been stupid, and I have been unintentionally cruel, but never have I withheld myself from you. From that day at Hunsford when I told you I loved you, I have held nothing back, good or bad. Most people would call me reserved. Most would say I was careful and controlled—but not you. You know every inner piece of me, yet I do not have nearly as much from you."

She did not know what to say to that except a murmured, "I am sorry."

"I do not want an apology." He moved his chair closer to Elizabeth's, putting one finger beneath her chin and forcing her to meet his eye. "I am a selfish, greedy lover, and I refuse to content myself with such as you will give me. Do you understand? If there is to be any future for us, I must have all of you, not just the bits you have seen fit to allow me."

A future. How she wished that could be! But hope, every time it appeared, was too quickly snatched away, leaving more sorrow in its place. Could she dare hope again?

She allowed him to feel her intent gaze as she lay within the depths of his. She permitted her eyes to slide along the contours of his countenance and linger on his lips. It would be impossible after such an inspection for him not to feel her true regard. It swelled and softened within her, and she sighed at the pleasurable pang it produced.

"After all of this," she said wistfully, "a future seems impossible to comprehend."

"I think quite the opposite. After all of this, to live my life without you is the impossibility. I still love you." His voice had grown hoarse. "I do. It has never altered, no matter how angry and hurt you have made me. But I fear that without more, without trust in one another, it will always end in problems and strife. You *must* trust me—trust me with all of you."

She was left breathless by his words. He spoke of things she wanted so badly, and it seemed that they were within her reach. She could have what she wanted, and she could make him happy as well. *Tempting, tormenting notion!*

"I shall," she promised. "I shall trust you with everything."

Darcy smiled, took her hand, and brought it to his lips, kissing it with lingering tenderness. Then he released her, sat back, and crossed his legs, looking at her expectantly.

She watched him for a few moments. "What?"

"What do you mean?"

"You seem to be awaiting—"

"I am awaiting you. Trust me. I would like you to start now."

"Oh! Well, I do not…" she stammered, feeling prickly heat rise up her neck, "I have…there is nothing to confide—"

"Elizabeth." He reached into his coat and withdrew a letter. He laid it on the table between them.

Her letter. With a pang of anguish and trepidation, she recognised her writing. It was difficult to sit there and see her malfeasance waved about in front of her. It compelled her to look when she wanted to run away from it. It fixed her in her seat, her hands folded in her lap, wondering how something so destructive could appear so small and unassuming.

Darcy laid his fingers on the letter, directing her to various things he evidently wished her to see. "This has been with me since the day I received it. You see these marks where I have crumpled it in my fist—sometimes in sorrow and sometimes in anger. Here is a mark made when I tossed it into the fire.

"And here..." He unfolded it, and she saw the main body of it, brief as it was. There were marks made by drops of water—*tears, Lizzy, they were tears*—that had fallen upon it.

She swallowed hard and tore her eyes away; the knowledge that she had made him weep both humbled and horrified her, but it was too much to be considered at the present moment.

He folded it again and carefully put it in his pocket. "Now that you have seen what I felt, perhaps you will tell me about all you felt and thought as well."

"Yes." The word came out in many syllables from the quavering of her voice. "I shall."

Elizabeth could not speak for several moments and sat staring at her skirt. She had gathered a bit of it into her fingers and played with it, worrying it between her thumb and forefinger. "It is difficult to know how to begin."

"Begin with anything," he said gently. "Tell me how it all came about."

"I was terrified that the scheme would not work, that the gossip about Lydia and my family was already too far gone or that he would abandon her. Lydia would have been lost forever, and I was furious at her for doing this to herself and furious that my parents had indulged and spoilt her, never saying no to anything she wanted. I was frightened and sad and alone...so very alone."

"Why were you alone?"

"No one knew," she murmured. "Wickham came to make his demands when everyone else was out. I had not yet told anyone of our engagement —you will recall we decided my father should know first—so it made no sense to tell them that I had been forced to end it."

"No one? No hints, however small, to your aunt?"

Elizabeth gave him a faint, rueful smile. "Strange, is it not? Only you and George Wickham know."

"I must confess: I told my cousin in a letter that we had come to an understanding, but only because I knew he could be counted on to keep his silence. Yet Mr. and Mrs. Gardiner were with us in Lambton and at Pemberley; do you mean to say they suspected nothing?"

"I have no idea what they knew or did not know. My presumption would be that they thought whatever had arisen between us was cut down by Lydia's situation, but we never discussed it. So I was angry and sad, but—"

"Angry? With Wickham?"

"Yes," she uttered in a meek voice that broke in the midst of the word, and she said no more.

"Elizabeth?"

A tear fell, followed by another, and she bent her head and pressed her hands to her eyes to stop them. "No, not Wickham, not really. How can one be angry at a viper for behaving as a viper does?"

"Then who?" He pressed her. "Who else made you angry? Your sister?"

She would not answer for a moment.

"Who?"

"Papa," she admitted. "The truth is that I do not know whether I have yet forgiven him."

Her tears dried as quickly as they had arrived. "He never took the trouble to check her." The words rushed and tumbled from her lips with such force that it left her gasping for air. "Never. He let Lydia do as she wished, and when I begged him not to let her go to Brighton, he laughed at me. He made a joke and asked me whether she had frightened off some of my lovers! He and Mama were indulgent and indifferent by turns, but when it came down to it, I was the one who was required to sacrifice for their folly. It was not fair."

She stopped to take a breath and quiet herself. Darcy said, "No, it is—"

"If you could have seen her in London, laughing and happy, delighted with her accomplishment! There was nothing of repentance about her; she thought it all quite clever of her! I was so resentful and angry…I cannot tell you how many letters were written, letters that I at least had the sense to burn when I was done, telling him of the rage I felt burn within me. I could not go home. I was not needed in London, but every feeling in me revolted at the idea of returning to Longbourn. I was too afraid of what I might say to him, what terrible truths might be laid bare. So I stayed in London, and my father…Papa died."

She inhaled a deep, calming breath. "He died, and my only thoughts were angry ones towards him for his failures as a parent, not only to Lydia but to the rest of us as well. I could not…I did not grieve him as I should because my heart ached and my anger occupied every bit of me. Is that not

A Short Period of Exquisite Felicity

the most terrible, selfish thing you have ever heard?"

He watched her as she rose, took five or six paces, and sat again.

"I wished my family to be saved from ruin." Her voice was low and controlled. "I wished no ill on any of them, and indeed, I love them, I love them all so very much. But how is it fair…?"

Darcy waited, his eyes dark and sober upon her.

Elizabeth smoothed the wrinkles she had made in her skirt as the thoughts and feelings she had repressed for so long bubbled their way to the surface. "Jane married Bingley, and she has everything she ever wanted: happiness in marriage, a son, and perhaps another child on the way. She is so happy; no one could possibly be as happy as my dear Jane. Mary, too, is content with her situation. We believed she would never marry, but she surprised us all. Kitty and Mama are still at Longbourn, much as they ever were. Do you know that Mama does not even give way to Mrs. Collins? She has remained in the mistress's chamber! I declare, I cannot think how Charlotte endures it."

Her voice began to shake. "No one else, Mr. Darcy, no one but me has paid any price at all for Lydia's folly! Their situations have all improved! Even Lydia herself. To be sure, I would not want such a husband, but Lydia did, and she got him. Their daughter is precious, their house is charming, and they maintain themselves in style enough.

"I resent that. I resent it very much. I was consigned—no, I consigned myself, I shall admit that much—to bear all the ignominy and shame for a mistake that was not mine, and I resent it. I resent the happiness of them all, and I am jealous, just eaten up with my jealousy for what they have and what I do not."

She lowered her face into her hands for a moment, breathing deeply to calm her nerves and slow her pounding heart. "I fear my character has been irrevocably altered. I used to be kind, and now I am jealous, resentful, and bitter."

There was a long moment; then she felt his hand, large, warm, and excessively comforting, rest on her shoulder. To feel his touch consoled her more than she could have imagined, yet she was afraid to look at him. Her character had sunk—she could not pretend otherwise—but it would sink still further because there was more information yet unknown to him that would provide additional evidence of her rotted disposition.

After some minutes had elapsed, Darcy offered a reply to her censure of her inadequate character. "I was furious with my father when he died. Pemberley was ill prepared to change masters, and although I had been taught almost from infancy, I was not ready to take charge. I had just received my degree from university, and my friends, all of them, were enjoying grand tours and the Season while I dedicated myself to tenants and crop reports. It was my duty, and I never would have done less, but that does not mean I did not have moments where I resented it. Including…"

She knew what he intended to say even if he was reluctant to speak of it. "Ramsgate?"

He nodded, not looking at her. "The situations were not quite the same, of course. The largest share of my feeling was guilt, but unlike you, I had the ability to act, to prevent her from going. The truth is, it was a moment of inattention. She wanted to go, and I did not see the harm in it, though I might have, had I given the matter due consideration. My father gave her over to me, and I failed. In the most critical juncture, I failed."

"You did not. I do not see that."

"I did," he insisted. "I did fail. I failed my father; I failed Georgiana. And now, I have failed you. I could have protected you and your family from Wickham, and I did not."

"You cannot take responsibility for Lydia's situation," she protested immediately. "You had no notion of any of it."

"If I had made known what he had done, no one in Meryton, not even your father, would have permitted their daughters anywhere near him."

It was an ideal moment to tell him, yet she hesitated. She did not wish to provide further proof of her inherent corruption.

"You must believe me when I tell you that you should not feel guilt on that score." Her voice dwindled to a shamed squeak. "I am loath to tell you more, but I fear I must. There is one more bit that I have not yet shared."

Chapter Twenty-One

Elizabeth rose from her chair and went to the alcove window. There were people everywhere: travellers, tradesmen, ladies, gentlemen, and servants. In her former good spirits, they would have been of great interest to her, but today, she barely saw them. She just wanted to keep her back towards Darcy whilst she confessed her misdoings in this affair that Lydia had begun so many months ago.

"I am certain that whatever it is cannot be so terrible." She jumped, not realising he was standing behind her.

She smiled in a wan, abstracted way. "Could we perhaps walk out? This room has become too full of the weight of my secrets."

"Of course." It took them a few minutes to gather their things, but before too long, they were outside. By unspoken agreement, they left the busiest part of the town and made their way to the outskirts, where a charming clearing beckoned.

Soon, they had outstripped any who might overhear her, and she knew further delay was not possible. Darcy had already made several enquiring looks in her direction.

"When I was in London, awaiting their wedding—"

"Mr. and Mrs. Wickham?"

"Aye." She licked her lips and inhaled deeply. "The day before he came to me, I received a letter from my sister Kitty, or at least I believed I did. It was addressed to 'Miss Lydia Bennet,' but my aunt's housekeeper misread it as 'Miss Lizzy Bennet.'"

"I see."

"Alas, I did not look at it closely before I opened it and began to read." Elizabeth sighed. "In the letter, my sister Kitty wrote of Lydia's…the father of Lydia's child, then still unborn."

"Of Wickham?"

For a moment, Elizabeth could not speak. "Lydia was uncertain."

"Ah."

"There was another man, not identified in the letter, one who…I must assume he had been also in Brighton or perhaps Meryton. He had…well, obviously, he had lain with her, but he had been clear from the first that marriage between them was impossible.

"Kitty thought…" She sighed. "Kitty thought it best that Lydia stay her course, to become Mrs. Wickham and forget anyone else who might have had a claim to the child. It seemed certain that this other man, whoever he was, would not own up to any bit of it—even if we could find him—and there was Wickham unaccountably willing to help us patch things up.

"God help me, but I…I closed up the letter and placed it on Lydia's bed, and I have never said a word of it to any other soul."

"Was this before or after Wickham…?"

"Wickham paid his visit to me the next morning. You can imagine how desperate I was, how fearful that it was all coming apart. If he had learnt the truth, if he had abandoned her, I was sure we would never find this other man, much less induce him to marry her."

She gave Darcy a bleak look. "So I went along with the deceit of Mr. Wickham and permitted him to marry my sister because of a child that, in all likelihood, is not his. He is living a lie, all so that my family and I would not need to suffer disgrace."

For some dreadful, long minutes, Darcy said nothing. They walked while Elizabeth felt all the weight of what she had done, and Darcy…she knew not what Darcy did. Thought about how horrid she was, in all likelihood.

"Wickham has acknowledged the girl as his own," he said at last, "though he did say to me, perhaps in jest, that he was reasonably certain she was his. Maybe he had his doubts and has chosen to disregard them. I know many men who have done similarly. If you must know, I think it a rather sweet irony. No doubt there are men in this world who are raising his bastards, and now he has a child and knows not its true father."

"It cannot signify," said Elizabeth miserably. "Full honesty would have been the honourable course. Have you not said that disguise of every sort is your abhorrence?"

"Hmm, yes, I did say that, just as you once said you would never dance with me." He gave her a consoling smile. "Things change; beliefs must alter as we grow older. Not every situation is as black and white as we supposed it should be when we were younger."

"But if I had told someone—"

Darcy stopped on the street and made her look at him. "If you had told someone, your family would be ruined, your sister would be living on the streets, and your niece could be starving or in the foundling hospital. Instead, there is a lovely young family comfortably situated near Cheapside."

"But Mr. Wickham—"

"Wickham was paid and far more than he deserves. He has a good enough living, a pretty wife, and a lovely daughter. He has no cause to repine; it is a far cry from a soldier's lot, I assure you." Darcy sighed. "Elizabeth, sometimes the most honourable thing comes from what is best for everyone. All parties have gained in this matter—your sister, your family, and even Wickham. Perhaps it is not his child, but perhaps it is; we have no way of knowing. Should you have jeopardised the future of so many for a mere possibility?"

"Does it materially alter your opinion of me, to know I am capable of such a thing?"

He pondered it. She watched as he cast his eyes towards the sky for several excruciating minutes. Then he looked at her and said simply, "Not at all."

Not at all. With those three words, the guilt that had weighed on her these many months melted away. Her lips lifted in a smile, and she felt her spirits rise within her. He was correct; things could not have ended so well otherwise. Jane would not be married to Bingley, Mary would not be married to Parker, and she would not be here with Mr. Darcy.

They continued their leisurely stroll, and wanting to leave the less pleasant topic behind, she asked, "You think Lydia is pretty?"

"I think you are pretty," he said, neatly evading her dangerous question. "And she resembles you, so naturally, she must be pretty."

"Well done, Mr. Darcy," she teased.

The day could not have been described as warm, but the sun shone in a manner that promised spring would eventually come. Elizabeth did not mind; the cool air gave her reason to tuck herself closely to his side.

"Your uncle must have paid him a great deal," said Darcy absent-mindedly.

"Above three thousand pounds, I think. Not all paid to him directly, though, but mostly in the form of debts paid off and so forth."

Darcy gave her a surprised look. "Three thousand pounds? I should not have imagined it was so little. I, more than anyone, know that three thousand pounds to Wickham can be spent in a few years, and that was when he was a bachelor. I should not have thought he would take her for less than ten thousand."

Elizabeth gave a little moan. "Perhaps he realised my uncle did not have as much to give, and it made him reasonable. In any case, he was also given his position at my uncle's warehouse. He does have some authority there, and he works harder than any of us imagined he would."

Darcy scorned that notion. A few minutes later, he said in an abstracted tone, "Perhaps the man in question held some authority…" He shook himself and looked at Elizabeth. "Never mind that."

"Colonel Forster?" Elizabeth smiled wanly. "I have considered it myself. If nothing else, I must wonder at the ease with which Wickham left his regiment. There were no consequences to it, at least none that I know of. It seems *that* business was patched up as well."

They walked a little farther, Elizabeth considering all Darcy had said, and he enquired about her illness.

"I came down with a cold that worsened into pneumonia—some feared it was consumption. It waxed and waned for some time. I truly think my lowness of spirit kept it upon me. When it was evident that I was not improving, I was sent off to Cheltenham with Mrs. Gardiner's sister. It was… it is a time I can scarcely bear remembering.

"The physician was an older man and very kind, but he believed frequent bleeding was the way to set things right. I cannot say which weakened me more: my melancholy or his treatments. I could not eat, although I knew it was to my benefit, and even a short spell out of doors fatigued me."

"That must have been excessively difficult for you. I know how much you dislike being kept indoors."

She could not immediately reply for the remembered unhappiness that had been stirred up within her.

"Truthfully, I did not care. I did not care about much of anything in those days, even my recovery. I could not foresee any happiness in my future. I had loved and lost, and it seemed that I must settle into the inevitable fate of unhappy spinsterhood."

"But why? Did you not ever consider coming to me and telling me the truth? Once he had married your sister, when it was done, what hold did he have over you?"

"Only my fears," she admitted softly. "Mr. Wickham, alas, made a great deal of sense in all he said to me."

"How so?"

"I used to laugh with Jane about the contradiction we faced between our hopes and our possibilities for the future. I always wished to find a man who was sensible and of exemplary character. A man who"—she slid a sideways glance at him—"made my heart quicken simply by entering the room."

Darcy gave her a faint smile, and her heart demonstrated its readiness to respond to him with a happy skip.

"A man who would receive my heart and give me his in return. I wished for it. I wanted it more than anything. But I must own that I never truly believed I could have it."

"Why not?"

"What man of sense would want me?" Elizabeth tried to make her words sound less painful than they were. "Not when I had such little to recommend me as a wife: no fortune, poor connexions, an indifferent education. Jane may at least claim extraordinary beauty, but I am only me."

They walked on for a few minutes, their pace slow. "Mr. Wickham said our union would pain Georgiana. He said it would damage your family name. He said...he said, 'There is a limit to all things, even love.' I believed him not because I doubted your character or your love, but rather, because I doubted my ability to inspire the sort of love that could conquer such obstacles.

"I could not bear the idea of hurting you, but I also could not bear the notion of marrying you in the face of scandal and then see your ardour for me dim. I was a coward, and I ran, but I did believe I was sparing both of us greater agony."

She could feel Darcy studying her even though her bonnet obscured her view of him. She wanted to say all that could be said on this subject, wishing it would never be spoken of again.

"Having once known such affection as this, I could not imagine ever consigning myself to life with some other man. I knew it would be better to remain alone."

Darcy was silent for a moment and then admitted, "I once went to Cheltenham."

"You did?" So great was Elizabeth's astonishment that she stopped walking and turned towards him. "You were in Cheltenham?"

"In January, I believe it was. I had decided I would confront you."

The idea of it made her smile a little. "How did you know I was there?"

"A letter from Bingley. He wrote to inform me that he was betrothed to your sister and to ask me to attend the wedding. In the letter, he mentioned you were in Cheltenham, but I had no direction beyond that."

"I wish you had found me."

"It is likely better I did not; I was in a fury, and who knows what might have happened."

Elizabeth could not imagine anything worse than what *did* happen. After all, did they not have months of anger and despair? Had not her very reputation been called into question? Had there not been stolen kisses to account for? But she spoke of none of this. "Now you know all. There is nothing more to learn of this affair."

"I thank you for entrusting me with this. It could not have been easy to say so much."

"No, it was indeed rather difficult." She stopped a moment and sighed. "But if there is anything you want from me, I want to give it to you. I can still recall how affected I was at Pemberley when you greeted me and my aunt and uncle with such kindness. You were so altered, and the idea that it had been for me was...I loved you for it. And I realise now that I, too, must change."

He laughed. "Pray, do not speak so. I would not know what to do if you were anything other than my spirited, impertinent Lizzy."

His teasing—and the fact that he had referred to her as *his* Lizzy—made her laugh. "I do not think I could change any of that," she admitted. "But if you want to see my misery, infrequent as it is, then I shall show it to you even though it goes against all my natural inclination."

"*My* natural inclination is that when someone I love is unhappy, I do what I can to fix it. You must allow me that. I do not intend that you should ever have cause to repine, but if you do, you must tell me, and I shall fix it or share it. Just, please, do not hide it from me…never again."

"I shall not," she promised him.

There had been much said, and there was yet so much to consider. They wandered the town together for a time, speaking of matters of no consequence: what might happen with the weather, the prettiness of the town, and the comforts offered by the inn.

Speaking of the inn made Elizabeth think of their past. "Strange, is it not, that we should find ourselves at the same inn in the same small town? Like at Pemberley where, if you had not decided to ride ahead of your party, we should have missed you entirely."

Darcy agreed. "There seems to be a grand scheme to unite us as if Fate itself had an interest."

"Fate?" Elizabeth teased. "I should not have thought you a believer in such things."

"When it comes to you and me, I shall believe in whatever might be of use in bringing us together. In any case, here we are."

"Here we are," she agreed, turning her face up to him.

He lightly touched her cheek with his gloved finger. "What now?"

"Now, I shall return to town, and you will go to Cotgrave. How long will you stay?"

"Not long, yet far too long. I never had much sympathy for these violent young lovers who steal their brides away from their families, but I must admit, I begin to see the advantages."

"Would you make off with me?" Elizabeth asked lightly. It was no easy question for the implication it presented.

"I believe I would," he answered gravely, but her heart was no less delighted with the admission.

"I would go," she whispered. "Quite willingly, in fact."

He chuckled but quickly became sober, his eyes dark and grave upon her face. His gaze moved from her eyes to her lips, and she knew he wanted to kiss her. He would not, however—not on some town street surrounded by dozens of people.

Before the temptation grew too unbearable for either of them, she whispered, "Where is a rose garden when you need one?"

It took him a moment, and then he smiled. "We do have a decided lack of privacy here."

"It is rather open."

He considered her for a moment more. "Come."

With a series of furtive looks around them, he took her hand, and they strode quickly back to the inn, going behind it to the stables. They slipped into this partly underground lair, where hundreds of horses, some recently ridden and others well-rested, were kept.

"I hope you know where we are going." Elizabeth looked around the shadowy maze. "I have lost my bearings entirely."

He gave her a crooked grin. "Perhaps we shall be lost for days together. Would you mind?"

She smiled at him. "Not at all."

They entered a little nook, dark and secluded. Elizabeth's heart, which was beating fast from her efforts to stay apace with him, began to pound for an entirely new reason. Darcy's intent was plain in his eyes, but he restrained himself, merely taking her hands in his so he could gaze at her.

"I cannot offer a rose garden this time. Only a stable beneath the ground, smelling as unlike a rose as anything could."

She laughed, but he silenced her by drawing her into his embrace. For several long moments, they could only look at one another.

He lifted a hand to caress her cheek as he lowered his lips for a tender kiss—the kiss of a lover, a man showing her without reserve that he loved and wanted her. Elizabeth knew she was too eager and too desperate to have more of him; she pulled him as tightly as she could against her and barely permitted him breath between kisses. He appeared equally desperate, pressing one hand against the small of her back while the other cradled the back of her head, cleaving her to him.

Her senses were filled with him; she heard nothing, saw nothing, and felt nothing but him, and it was sublime. She scarcely realised he had pulled away when she murmured, "I have been so hungry."

"You are hungry? Let me—"

"No, no." She laughed weakly, still entranced by him. "I have hungered for this, for you."

His forefinger traced her lips, and his eyes grew soft as he bent to kiss her again.

And then she sneezed. She jerked away violently as a series of sneezes and croaks overcame her, causing her eyes to run along with her nose. Part of her hair began to fall as Darcy exclaimed with concern beside her. She did her best to avoid sneezing on him and hoped she did not look too horribly undignified.

"The hay," she explained when she could speak. "It happens like this sometimes. It is why I do not often ride."

She hoped it would abate, that their more pleasant activity could be resumed, but as her nose and eyes continued to run, she realised that the attraction of kissing her had waned.

Darcy must have understood. "Come, let us get away from here so you can stop."

"No, no," she protested with a thick, syrupy voice. "I am sure it is almost done."

He laughed and took her hand again, leading her back through the shadowed, shaded maze of the stables at a quick pace and eventually bringing her out to the daylight. She sneezed and wheezed nearly the entire way while doing all she could to conduct herself somewhat elegantly but fearing that she failed quite miserably.

She was mortified, imagining what a fright she must appear. Hoping to restore herself, she slid a hand into his coat to find the inner pocket where she knew he kept a handkerchief. It felt stiff, but she paid no mind to it, pressing it to her eyes and rubbing at her wet cheeks.

"Elizabeth, wait—" Darcy broke off and began to chuckle.

She opened her eyes, realising too late it was not a handkerchief in her hand but rather a piece of paper. With a few deep breaths to calm herself, she looked at what she had ruined: a licence for the marriage of Fitzwilliam Darcy to Elizabeth Bennet. It was not new but dated from September 1812. He had, she supposed, kept it as a memento of sorts.

Darcy withdrew his handkerchief from a lower pocket and went to a rain barrel nearby to wet it. He rubbed at her cheeks, and the force he applied made Elizabeth realise he sought to remove more than tears.

He managed to find whatever hairpins were dislodged, and he helped her fix her hair reasonably well, even if he did stab her once or twice. Soon there was nothing left of the storm that had seized her but the faint grey of ink on her cheek and a slight pinkness around her eyes.

"Thank you," she said in a hoarse whisper.

He looked down at his handkerchief and, with a wry grin, explained, "I moved my handkerchief to a different pocket after I obtained the licence because I did not want to"—he looked down at the crumpled, wet paper still crushed in Elizabeth's grasp—"wrinkle it."

It began with her giggle. She laughed once, briefly, then again as he began to chuckle with her. Soon they were both beyond saving, heaving and laughing at the incongruity of the situation. "Forgive me," said Elizabeth. "I fear I have quite ruined it."

He reached over and laid his hand on hers, the crushed paper between them. "It is no matter; we shall need a new one."

Her soul alit at his words, but she needed to ask, wishing to be certain. "Are we going to marry?"

His eyes were warm and soft upon her, and he nodded slowly. "Yes, we are."

No flowery, impassioned declaration could have made her happier. Indeed, it was almost too much to bear, such happiness arising on the heels of so many months of despair. Her face broke into a broad, beaming smile that was matched by the one on the countenance of her lover.

"I was thinking, as I stood here, how I might ask you. As you know, speaking the right words has never been my strength."

"I do not need pretty words and declarations. A smeared bit of paper will do well enough for me."

"It is not very romantic."

She disagreed. "It is romantic. It is by far the most romantic thing that has ever happened to us."

HAPPINESS, WHERE THERE HAS LONG BEEN DESPAIR, IS A STRANGE FEELING, and Darcy knew not how to manage it. *We are engaged.* He repeated it silently to himself over and over again, but his mind and his heart would not wholly trust him.

"I shall inform Fitzwilliam that he will need to do without me in Cotgrave," he declared.

"That should do much to rectify his present ill will towards me," she said ironically and smiled a little sadly. "I do hope in time to regain his good opinion."

"He is all bluster, I assure you."

"Colonel Fitzwilliam rightly despises me. The ferocity with which they disdain me is only a compliment to you."

"It is not a compliment to me if it serves as an obstacle to my happiness," he said warmly. "Hang any member of my family who seeks to come between us. Have we not had troubles enough? If they love me, they must want my happiness, and my only hope for true happiness resides in you."

"I do hope that Colonel Fitzwilliam and the rest of your family can be induced to accept me as your wife. I cannot abide the notion of separating you from them." She reached out and lightly touched his chest. "If the colonel expects you to attend him into Cotgrave, you should. I do not intend to be a wife who makes you shirk your duty."

Hearing her refer to herself as his wife could only bring heartfelt delight and, on its heels, a realisation that he had not yet kissed her, at least, not since she had accepted his rather strange offer of marriage.

"We have been engaged for some time now, yet we have not sealed our understanding with a kiss."

"Oh no!" She looked mockingly horrified. "It can scarcely be called an engagement if we have not even kissed."

"We had better get to it immediately."

"Our last kisses did not end well. I should not be the least surprised if you wished to forgo any more."

Once again, he gathered her into his arms and allowed his lips to touch her lightly on the forehead. Her skin was sweet in a way he could not define—the essence of honey and flowers and all good things. "You should always be surprised if I ever forgo the opportunity to kiss you."

"What if I am ill?"

"I shall still want to kiss you."

"What if I have an extraordinary number of spots all over my face?"

He chuckled. "I shall still kiss you."

"What about when I am old and my hair is grey and my lips have wrinkles?"

"I shall take you into the rose garden, and we shall spend whole days kissing and reminiscing about the days, these days, when first we loved one another."

She made a little face. "Shall we? I think we probably have a great deal we would like to forget."

He smiled down at her, feeling wistful and wondering whether she could see it. "Even the most troublesome journey, in my experience, is rendered charming by the joy in the destination. I daresay, all of this will acquire beneficent hues as time passes."

"I hope so."

She could say no more, for he kissed her as he promised he would. The sun was on his back, and she was in his arms, and he thought that if he died at that moment, he could not complain, for his felicity was complete. He loved her even as he partook of her love, and for them, in that time, it would do.

Chapter Twenty-Two

"Let us go find Bingley," said Darcy when their kisses reached an end.

"I hope nothing of the last moments made you think of Mr. Bingley," Elizabeth teased with an impish grin.

"Only that I would like to have an audience with him for the discussion of a most particular matter." He ran a finger lightly over her cheek.

"I do not require my brother's permission to marry."

"Do you think he would deny my suit?"

She laughed. "No, of course not."

"Bingley told me shortly before he took you off that he would not abide secrecy where my courtship of you was concerned. I am only acting as he would like until such time as I can take you from his house to mine."

The idea of that made her smile, and so they returned to the inn, intent on making their engagement known. It seemed hardly possible, but the vestibule of the inn had grown even busier, travellers pressing against each other at the desk, hoping to obtain lodgings. Servants of the inn wove among them, darting into the adjoined tavern to bring refreshment to those awaiting a change of horses or taking a rest.

Elizabeth noticed Mr. Bingley almost immediately when she entered. He was descending the stairs from the rooms above where he and Jane had remained most of the day.

"Lizzy! There you are." He pushed through the crowd to reach her. "I daresay Jane is feeling a little better but…" His smile became quizzical as he espied the tall gentleman behind her. "Darcy? What do you do here?"

"Charles." Elizabeth stopped and permitted Darcy to draw up beside her. "Mr. Darcy and I would like to speak to you privately. Perhaps in the sitting room upstairs?"

Bingley's face shaded with trepidation in a manner almost comical; he gestured to Elizabeth to lead them towards their rooms. When they arrived at the small sitting room, she suggested he ask Jane to join them. Bingley did as bid, and moments later, Jane, pale and worried looking, emerged.

"How do you do, Mr. Darcy?" Jane curtseyed and invited them all to sit.

Darcy sat next to Elizabeth on a small sofa while Jane took the remaining chair, Bingley standing behind her. Elizabeth spoke first, her voice clear and firm. "Mr. Darcy has made me an offer of marriage, and I have accepted him. We wanted you to be the first to wish us joy."

"Marriage?" Bingley did not appear acquainted with the idea. "That seems…hasty."

"Hasty?" Darcy laughed "No, I assure you, it is anything but hasty."

Elizabeth began to explain everything they did not know about their complicated romance. As she spoke, she found, surprisingly, that Darcy's proposal at Hunsford had taken on the hues of an amusing anecdote. Jane and Bingley stared at them somewhat amazed, with Jane gasping at some of the things Elizabeth had said to Darcy. In the midst of it all, Elizabeth found herself teasing him.

"For your future reference, in the course of a marriage proposal, yes, some flattery is not unanticipated. A compliment to my eyes might perhaps have done better than an insult to my relations."

"I hope I shall never need to make another proposal—I have, after all, done it thrice—so I shall tell you now that your eyes have the power to enchant me."

Elizabeth smiled and permitted her blush to inform him how pleasing she found his compliment. "Well done, sir."

"And for me? Or is the flattery meant only for the lady?"

"Insufferable man! I told you before that my heart quickened when you entered the room!"

"If I may interrupt you," Bingley said awkwardly. He and Jane had been forgotten as Elizabeth bantered with her lover, and she was quickly recalled to her purpose.

She continued telling them everything, even the parts she knew must distress them, though she found Jane was not much concerned about Darcy's attempt to separate her from her husband. "Well, it hardly matters now, does it?" she said in her reasonable way.

However, Jane was aghast when Elizabeth explained all that had transpired between Darcy, Georgiana, and Wickham. "Would that we had come to you when Lydia ran off! You must surely have known what was best to do!"

Elizabeth exchanged a look with Darcy. "Yes, well…about that."

This was the part that was still too close to be smiled at. The fact that Elizabeth and Darcy had been engaged for nine days was a source of no little astonishment to Jane and her husband, though Bingley had suspected some attachment when they were all at Pemberley so long ago.

"You loved him even then?" Jane asked, her eyes wide with amazement.

"I did." Elizabeth's breath caught. Tears were close, but she was resolved to retain her equanimity. "Yes, I surely did. It was an excessively happy nine days, even amidst all my worries for Lydia."

There was silence when Elizabeth, keeping firm grasp on her emotions, recounted the day that Wickham visited Gracechurch Street for the purpose of forcing her to release Darcy.

She could not remain calm, however, when she told them of the letter; the image of it was seared into her mind's eye. Slow fat tears began to make their way down her cheeks as she related their conversation and how she and Wickham wrote that letter. She did not say anything, however, of her suspicions about another gentleman; she decided that could not have anything to do with their present circumstance.

She could not look at Darcy as she recounted the hateful details. It was an enormous relief when he, in a manner hidden from the two across the room, laid his hand on her back and used his thumb to caress and console her.

Jane's eyes had filled with tears too. "Oh, Lizzy, we never knew! You suffered so much, and none of us knew of it. Why did not you tell us?"

Elizabeth could not yet reply. Jane pressed a handkerchief into her hand then sighed in a fondly exasperated way and looked at Darcy. "That has ever been Lizzy's way, to take things on herself for her family, even if it means she will suffer for it."

Elizabeth felt rather than saw his eyes tender upon her. "She will have a husband now, and I intend that she should never again be anything short of exquisitely happy."

When Elizabeth had finished the story, and all the questions were asked and answered, the little group fell silent.

Jane spoke at last, declaring that her sister's engagement was the happiest, wisest, most reasonable end to it all. She rose and kissed Elizabeth's cheek, offering her sincerest wishes for her felicity. Mr. Darcy also rose and kissed Jane's hand, and Mr. Bingley came up behind them and wrapped Darcy in a fierce embrace. Elizabeth suspected that Darcy pretended to dislike it much more than he actually did.

"Is Miss Bingley's wedding soon?" Darcy asked when all such felicitation had ended.

"The week after Easter," said Jane.

"Ah. There must be many plans afoot."

"Caroline does have some grand schemes," Bingley agreed.

They settled themselves again and spoke of Caroline's wedding, Rotherham, Pemberley, and all manner of things, but soon Elizabeth wished the other two gone. Although much had been discussed, there were yet words unspoken, and Elizabeth quickly found herself driven nearly mad by the chatter of the Bingleys.

"It is a lovely day," she said, giving Jane a look. "The market had much to recommend it."

"Hmm." Jane continued to speak to Darcy about the ball Sir Edmund would hold for Miss Bingley.

After about five minutes longer, and several pointed looks in Jane's direction, Elizabeth said, "Charles, you would be amazed by the stables. So many horses! I declare, I have never seen the like."

"You went to the stables?" Bingley frowned. "Lizzy, the ostlers do not suffer ladies down there."

Elizabeth sighed.

Her words launched Bingley into a discussion of travel—the condition of certain roads and whether or not this route was faster than that. Elizabeth stared intently at Jane until Jane finally looked at her. Silently, she mouthed the words, "Leave us!"

After four or five tries, Jane appeared to comprehend her.

"Charles," she said suddenly. "I think I am in great need of some air."

"Are you?" Bingley leant back and slid his hand beneath his waistcoat to scratch his stomach. "You should have gone out with Lizzy before."

"Perhaps, but I did not, and I would like to walk."

Bingley smiled at her but did not seem inclined to move. He turned to Darcy. "For myself, once I am in Hertfordshire, I like to go to Yorkshire by way of—"

"Will you walk out with me, my dear?" Jane's smile took on a strained look. "Now?"

"I would prefer not to…" All of a sudden, Bingley caught the meaning of Jane's look. "Well, certainly! I was just sitting here wishing for some air myself."

It seemed to take ages for them to assemble their coats, gloves, and hats, but at last it was done, and the couple took themselves off for a tour of the marketplace.

When they had gone, leaving the door just slightly ajar, Elizabeth sat in contemplation of Darcy. He looked different now from the way he had appeared for so many months; he looked like her husband. There was everything familiar in him, yet the promise of so much more to be known. *How elegant and handsome he will be when his hair is grey and when there are lines on his cheeks and around his eyes!*

He sat down next to her and took her teacup, placing it on the table in front of them. He took her hands in his and stared at her, a faint smile on his lips as he beheld her.

"Why do you smile so?" she asked as she felt a blush spread over her cheeks.

One hand rose. and Darcy's long fingers slid into the curls by her temple. "I behold my beloved," he murmured. "How could I stop myself from smiling?"

He astonished her by continuing to look at her for what seemed like an eternity. Her lips were parted, and she wanted his kiss more with every passing second. *Will he have me beg?*

Just as she thought she might, his lips, warm and velvety, touched hers, bestowing kisses that were slow and seductive. He was leaning over her a little, and she laid back and pulled him down. A need she scarcely understood wanted to feel his weight on her.

Needing a moment to calm her nerves, she pulled back a little. "For so long, I have felt that I have had nothing to anticipate, and now there is everything. I am quite eager for it all."

He also pulled back, running his hand through his hair and taking deep breaths. "Marriage."

"Marriage. And children, of course."

"Children," he agreed. "I hope we have more than two."

"If I am my mother's daughter, I think we shall."

"Two is not enough to adequately fill Pemberley, particularly if any of them are as quiet as I am. Pemberley requires laughter and singing and perhaps a high-spirited boy or two that we can scold for running down the halls."

"I can hear us now." She adopted a stern tone. "If you run down that hall once more, you will be locked in your bedchamber for a fortnight! You will knock your ancestors right off the walls!"

"Excellent," he said. "But a fortnight for running in the hall? That seems rather hard."

"Perhaps, though one cannot undervalue the importance of properly subduing wild animal spirits."

"Very well." Darcy slid his arm around her. "But maybe just a day or two if it was the first offence?"

She lifted her head to receive his kiss. "Unless he knocked his ancestors off the walls."

He gave her two lingering kisses. "Oh, that will surely happen. I have done it myself a number of times."

Several kisses more and Elizabeth was quite prepared to abandon all good sense. "Promise me you will never stop kissing me," she whispered.

"Always," he vowed. "We shall be old and grey and still scandalise the servants."

She smiled at that idea.

"I am not fond of becoming engaged and then going off with my cousin."

"It will be best to oblige him, I think. I hope, one day, that my friendship with your cousin and your sister can be restored."

"Fitzwilliam and I shall be speaking of it even as the carriage begins to move, I assure you."

"It is my wish that, once he understands my heart, his hatred of me will relent."

"He is a reasonable man above all," said Darcy. "I am certain it will."

There was a noise in the hall, and they turned their heads, waiting until it was gone. Darcy leant into her again, his lips soft against hers, then becoming harder and more persistent. "Will they walk far?"

"No," she whispered. "But they are slow."

Darcy chuckled against her lips and slid to his knees on the floor, placing himself between her legs. He wrapped strong arms around her, pulling her to the edge of her seat, his mouth possessing hers, hot and needy. Her skirts bunched and tangled between them, so she tugged them up just a little and placed her hands on his posterior, pulling him tightly between her legs. There was still ample material between them, but she felt the heat of him, hard and urgent upon her centre.

Their mouths were mingled together, and his hand on the back of her neck kept them so. His other hand fell to her bottom pulling her tighter and tighter against his lower body. It could not long remain there, however, and left her backside to slowly drift between their bodies, first grazing her breast then seeking it in a more determined fashion. She sighed with pleasure; she found his ferocity rather thrilling.

"Tell me you love me," he demanded in low tones.

"I love you more than anything else in this world."

"Tell me you will never again leave me."

"I shall not," she vowed breathlessly. "I swear to you, I shall not."

"For nothing?"

She paused, drawing back and looking into his eyes. "No matter what happens during this small separation of ours, I love you, and it is my intention to marry you. Let nothing else sway you or introduce doubt into your mind, and if I should vanish, pray, come find me."

"Always," he promised, his lips searching out the sensitive skin of her neck. He worshipped her neck, kissing every inch of it; she was astonished by the pleasure it afforded.

He murmured in her ear, "Bingley would like us to marry after the Season."

"No," she said, her tone hoarse. "Let us marry as soon as you have the licence in your hand."

He offered a few lighter kisses then pulled back to look at her. "What of the breakfast or the…your gowns? Ladies like to purchase all the lovely things they will need as a bride, do they not?"

"Not this lady." She kissed him again. "The only thing this bride needs is her husband. I can buy clothes later."

That made him chuckle. "Alas, we do need to consider the other wedding, which must be soon upon us."

Elizabeth sighed. "Miss Bingley and Sir Edmund."

"And Lady Matlock has planned a ball for Georgiana's coming out. It is to be held later in May."

She gave him a rueful smile. "How difficult is the life of fashionable people! That we might be simple country folk, able to marry on a whim!"

"That would be rather agreeable, would it not?" He gave her a long, gentle kiss.

"A June bride is something to be admired, I think. It is not quite the end of the Season but near enough to satisfy my brother."

"In the meantime, I shall do my best to court you properly."

"When can we begin? How long until you return to London?"

"Nine days," he said, a sudden constriction in his throat. "We shall be gone for nine days."

"Oh." They were silent for several minutes.

"We had before," she said, "nine days of exquisite felicity upon which misery did intrude. Now we shall have nine days of unhappiness that will be broken by the bliss of our engagement. We need fear for nothing."

"That is true, but I find I dislike it heartily nevertheless."

"I shall write to you every day. Twice a day."

"And if I can find courage sufficient to open them, I shall reply." He attempted a faint smile to make his words seem like a jest, but it was plain they were not.

He needed some reassurance, she realised—a startling notion in such a man as Darcy—and she would give it to him. But what? She thought about it for a moment then reached behind her neck and unclasped the necklace she had worn since the age of fifteen. She looked at it a moment; it was a topaz cross, and when her father gave it to her, she believed it the most elegant thing in the world.

Darcy was watching her, but he still seemed surprised when she pushed it into his hand. "Keep this until we are again together."

By his lack of protest to the gesture, she knew he was pleased.

"It was a gift from my father, and it is excessively dear to me. I have worn it every day since age fifteen."

"He did love you very much. There was never any doubt in my mind which daughter was his favourite."

"I know," she agreed. "Even though he did not always listen to me, I do know he loved me and mostly respected me."

"Few fathers would heed the advice of their daughters, no matter how much they esteem them. It means nothing about what he thought of you or how dear you were to him. He never would have wanted you to pay such a high price for his inattention to your sister. Forgive him, and be as happy as he would have wished you to be. Resentment is a ponderous weight for anyone to carry."

She gave him a kiss on the cheek at such kind words. "I shall be happy, and I shall make you happy too."

"I am already happy."

"I shall be happier once you have permitted me to fix the correspondence that proved so troublesome to us."

"Correspondence? Oh, the letter."

On her nod, he produced the hateful missive from his pocket. "Would that I had smeared the ink on this earlier!" she exclaimed.

"I confess, I would not mind seeing these words erased."

"I believe I can do even better than that."

After retrieving the small writing kit that travelled with her, she scrawled across the older part of it, "retracted!"

She then wrote:

My dearest Fitzwilliam,

It will indeed be my honour to become your bride at the earliest date upon which such an event may be arranged. Until then, sir, you may be assured of my respect, my love, my trust, and most of all, my most fervent desire to marry you to the exclusion of any other consideration.

Yours & etc.
Miss Elizabeth Bennet

Chapter Twenty-Three

Astonishingly, Fitzwilliam slept through the entire day and had no notion that the Bingley party was in Milton Keynes, or that such an alteration in his cousin's life had occurred. If he thought Darcy was uncommonly agreeable—if not rather impatient to return to town—he kept it to himself.

Elizabeth's first letter awaited Darcy where they next broke their journey. He was shocked by the pulse of trepidation that immediately soured his stomach when he saw it. "That looks like a lady's writing," Fitzwilliam teased as they sat in the tavern. "Is it from Miss Lacey?"

"Heaven forfend," he answered shortly. A moment later, he shoved his chair back and rose. "Beg you would excuse me; I need to speak to my man." He left the tavern, intent on reading the letter in privacy.

Ridiculous. Obviously, this is not a letter intended to...there were circumstances she faced...we have a deeper comprehension of one another now...I have her necklace.

His remonstrance to himself could not calm the pounding of his heart nor the sick fear that made the hand that held her letter shake. At last, he was in the bedchamber with the door safely bolted behind him. He sat in the chair beside the fire, closing his eyes while breaking the seal. After unfolding it, he sat for several moments until he felt equal to beholding it.

Fitzwilliam,
 I love you, and it is my dearest wish to marry you.

A Short Period of Exquisite Felicity

I fear I have not learnt the proper manner in which one is expected to write to her betrothed. What can I say but that which I have already said many times over? I love you deeply, and I am sorry for the trouble I have caused. I hope, in years to come, we might forget the pain and think only of the lessons we both have learnt from it.

I believe a proper letter from a traveller should inform you of my journey, but alas, I cannot. I saw no sights, I heard no news, and even eating was a trial. All of my senses were filled with you, and I had no wish to displace you. We are safely now in London, and I am insensible of anything other than that.

Are we really to marry? I find myself beset by doubt that such felicity can be real. I am afraid I must have dreamt the whole thing, and I pray it is not so. In any case, I have already written to my mother and my aunts informing them of my happy news. I fear you may be honour bound now, sir!

I hope you and Colonel Fitzwilliam rest well at the Royal Swan tonight and find yourselves safe in Cotgrave on the morrow. I fear I shall not be easy until I hold your letter in my hand.

Eternally and Enthusiastically Yours,
Elizabeth

It was short—did she never write a letter of any substantial length?—but it served every purpose for him. A broad grin came over him while he read it the first, second, and even the tenth time, and he was grateful he had read it in seclusion. No doubt he looked like a saphead.

My Elizabeth,

How astonishing it seems to be able to write those words. You have never left my mind for above two years now, yet to have the privilege of writing to you is extraordinary. There is so much I long to say, yet I scarcely know where to begin.

I curse Fitzwilliam for the timing of this trip, for it is just now when I should most like to spend time with you. I learnt something surprising as we strolled the Frost Fair together: I so much enjoy myself when I am with you; it is quite out of the common way for me. Although I think you are the most handsome lady of my acquaintance, as well as the kindest and most witty, I wish to marry you most of all because I simply enjoy spending time with you, more so than any other person I know, gentleman or lady. Does it surprise you to know that, while we walked at Rosings, I would divert us onto paths that would take us away from our destination merely to extend the time we were together?

There is little to say of the Royal Swan save that the servants know their business and the stew is hot and plenteous. But you are not here; therefore, it is wretched.

In the days we have been apart, I have thought of no less than twenty subjects I wish to discuss with you. I have contemplated our home in London, and I wonder what you will think of it. It astonishes me how easily I think of it as our home now, even though you have never set foot in it. I long to hear your opinion of everything.

Do not fear for your acceptance by my family. I believe I have hit upon a plan, and I shall introduce you to my cousin Viscount Saye as soon as I return to town. He is a bit of a rattle and was a rake in his former days, but since his marriage, he has become a proponent of love matches. Indeed, he has made us all nearly sick with his many effusions about his wife, but now I know how he feels. Love can be rather an extraordinary thing, and it has the unusual quality of making the bearer think he invented it. Indeed, I find it a struggle to keep from crowing my joy to Fitzwilliam, but I believe it might be a conversation best had on our return journey.

I am eager to hear the felicitations of your mother and aunts. I cannot fear being honour bound, not when my heart, my mind, and my soul have been already bound to you for so many months.

Yours in every way,
F. Darcy

There was too much feeling within Elizabeth to be easily withstood upon reading the first proper letter from her love. She was immediately ashamed that her own had been so brief, but she knew not how to tell him all that she felt.

My Fitzwilliam,

I have struggled to form the appropriate salutation on this letter: Should I write My Fitzwilliam? My Darcy? My Beloved? But I have decided it is of no import, for the only bit of real consequence is the word that declares you are mine.

A Short Period of Exquisite Felicity

I wonder, as I sit here, what you are doing at this moment. In truth, I have not the least idea. It is a strange thing to know you love someone yet know so little about them, about the daily routines that bind them.

I wish I could know everything about you, yet I am pleased I do not. I have tried these many years to sketch your character, and although I understand the goodness of you, there is still much to puzzle me exceedingly. I happily anticipate many years of discovering everything about you.

I am eager to know everyone of importance to you. I have great hopes for the colonel in due time. I am certain that, once he sees my regard for you is certain and unwavering, he will relent. He strikes me as a fair and just sort, and surely he must know that it will serve us best to be friends.

I have been considering this notion of friendship. It might surprise you to know that, while I am eager to be called your wife, I am nearly as joyous to know we are once again friends. It grieved me so much at Netherfield that I no longer had the right to that title. I am most pleased to have it back in my possession, my dear, wonderful friend. Can there be anything more delightful than someone who will be your friend for life?

There was more this time, much more. Indeed, Darcy was pleased to see she had written two pages complete in a neat, feminine hand. She recounted some of her time at Beckett Park, but it was the part about friendship that stayed fixed in his mind. He had often imagined her as his wife, and far too often as his lover, but it was this idea of friendship that warmed him most. Could there be any better friend than the one you can trust? The one who shares your hopes and wishes, and who remains when all others have gone?

My Dearest, Loveliest Elizabeth,
You have given me a wonderful picture of Beckett Park. From what you have said, it appears ideally suited for Mr. and Mrs. Bingley. I am glad that it is not far from Pemberley. If I am correct about the roads, it is no more than half a day's travel. It must surely be pleasing to know your sister will be so close.

I have considered your charge that you know little of me; indeed, this is an area in which I have had considerable advantage. I met you in your home, among your neighbours and friends, and learnt of your girlhood habits. I know you like a morning ramble and to read in the afternoons. I have observed that you are excessively good at chess and whist, but you have rather poor luck at vignt-et-un and lottery. I believe your favourite colour is yellow.

I hope it will console you to think that as your life will change, so too will mine. Indeed, I know not what our future will bring us. Most recently, I have whiled away my days in town visiting my club, seeing a few friends and my cousins, and attending a few concerts and plays. Alas, these last were likely a misuse of my time for, while my eyes were fixed on the stage, my thoughts were fixed on you, and I fear I did not gain a bit of sense from what I saw. Perhaps when I return to town, we shall see them together.

Elizabeth shook her head, staring at the pages in front of her and imagining herself going to the theatre with him. Indeed, she did enjoy plays and concerts and all manner of amusements, but the notion of sharing them with him could only raise her anticipation. So many things to share, she mused. Walks, books, and friends will all be shared. She enjoyed a secret little smile at the imagined pleasures their commingled life would bring.

It was late at night when she finished her last reading of his letter, and for a moment, she sat in the chair within her apartment and sighed. She was positively lovelorn and wished for nothing more than to see him returned again. She wished for her tenure with the Bingleys to be done and to move on to the next chapter in her life.

She rose and paced, wanting to reply to Darcy yet unable to do so; she was too disquieted to settle down at her escritoire. She consoled herself with the knowledge that, in two days, he would leave Cotgrave to return to London.

She stared out the window, wondering whether her gaze was aimed in the general direction of Cotgrave. What was he doing this very minute? Was he staring at the moon and the stars and thinking of her? A romantic notion, but she did not take Darcy for a stargazer. Was he at some neighbourhood dinner or party? Did he wish she was beside him?

She forced herself to sit at her desk and pen a letter to him, one that would be sent with the earliest letters of the next morning. On later reflection, she thought it likely that tiredness had contributed to the frankness of her missive, for she held little back from him. She could only hope he would be pleased that she had entrusted him with her innermost musings.

It is late at night as I write to you, and I find myself in a great agitation of spirit, thinking of you and all the happiness we are soon to have. I have contrived to write cheerful letters, but tonight I am too much unsettled to present a guise of light-heartedness. I hope you will not faint from my candour.

I find that I am excessively unhappy without you, and I fear I always shall be whenever we are parted. The days remaining until your return loom large before me, comprised of hours I must fill with things of no consequence. I know not how I can manage it.

I can think of nothing but how much I long to have your arms around me, to hear your voice whispering in my ear, and your lips pressing against mine. I am shocking, I know, but I have vowed to give you the plain truth of me, and this is what I feel.

She stopped, sat back, and looked over what she had written. It was too naked, she feared. Too much bare truth. Could she speak so to him?

Slowly, she took up her pen once more, dipped it in the ink, and set it on the paper.

I love you with every fibre of my being, and I am thankful that we have arrived together at this understanding. The lonely days can now be numbered, where before, they were infinite. It frightens me to know how very near I was to losing you.

Please reassure me that I shall see you soon and have the joy of feeling my fancies made into reality.

Darcy leant back in his chair, breathless from her words. Another short letter yet filled with so much meaning that it was nearly a book.

He chuckled as his eyes again traced the passages describing her agitation. Yes, he understood her even though she did not understand herself. He had been likewise agitated by her many times over—it was desire, simply put, and he thrilled with the idea that she felt it for him even now in her innocence.

Yet it could not be said that she felt only desire, could it? She had told him that she loved him, needed him, in a manner profoundly different from any way she had said it before. Oh, but this was a precious letter indeed! He sighed to relieve the pleasurable pang that tightened his chest.

You cannot know how happy your last letter made me, to know that you feel as I do. This assurance of our bond is exquisite felicity indeed. You will never lose me, Elizabeth; this I vow to you as surely this day as I shall on our wedding day. You are too much a part of me; I cannot lose you without losing myself.

I cannot think of these last months with anything short of abhorrence for the pain and misery we have both endured. But I shall be grateful for this: in finding ourselves passed safely to the other side, we now know what it is to persevere. Our love has been tested and tried, perhaps unfairly, but nevertheless, we have triumphed. Can there be anything else before us to tear us asunder? I think not.

I count the moments until I see you, my beloved girl. I eagerly anticipate the day, not so far hence, when our official courtship might begin in earnest. But even so, will you please give me the relief of naming the day when we may, at last, be married?

DARCY PLACED A LETTER ON THE SALVER WITH THE REST OF THE OUTGOING mail—all of it belonging to him save for one thin piece Fitzwilliam had penned—and turned towards the hall. Fitzwilliam met him coming from the opposite direction.

"Darcy, there you are. I need to go into town..." He stared down at the substantial bit of mail on the tray.

"Do you? I shall go with you. Perhaps we can stop at the shop with the—"

"What is all of that?"

"All of what?"

"Those letters." Fitzwilliam lifted a brow. "Quite a few there."

Darcy chuckled. "Oh, just wait! You will see for yourself soon enough that the management of your estate requires..."

He watched as Fitzwilliam plucked out his letter to Elizabeth. Fitzwilliam examined it carefully before placing it back where it had been and looked up at Darcy.

"Wish me joy, Cousin. Miss Elizabeth Bennet has agreed to be my wife."

"Has she indeed," said Fitzwilliam in a toneless, neutral voice. "Perhaps this time her resolve will not fail her."

Darcy permitted the slight to pass. "It is my hope that whatever you hold against her may soon be laid to rest."

"Do not place any wagers on that," Fitzwilliam replied coolly.

"I pray you will not make me choose betwixt you."

"You would choose some insignificant bit of muslin—"

"You speak of my future wife," Darcy growled. "This is enough now. Your concern for me was admirable, but your stubbornness in adhering to it in the face of my obvious happiness is not."

"Obvious happiness? More like obvious foolishness. Then again, fools are often happy; they are too stupid to know their own misery."

Darcy's jaw tightened at the insult, but he would not give way to anger. "Miss Bennet and I have both made errors on the path that brought us to the place we are now, and we have addressed the misunderstandings that caused such anguish between us. We have a better comprehension of one another, which will serve us well in the married state."

Fitzwilliam took a step closer to Darcy.

"I shall not keep company with the likes of Miss Bennet or her husband. You might think I shall soften, but I assure you, I shall keep my word." Fitzwilliam spoke calmly, but his flushed skin and a tic in his eye announced his growing agitation. "I would be perfectly happy had you announced an engagement to anyone else—and that includes Georgiana's former governesses and the upstairs maid at Pemberley."

"You disappoint me. I should not have believed you thought so little of me."

"I think meanly of *her*. It says nothing to what I think of you. For you, I have nothing but pity."

"Is that it? Or are you merely stubborn? Perhaps you are too proud to admit you are wrong about her or about my happiness with her."

"That is unfair and untrue."

"Then what is it?" Darcy's frustration permeated his voice. "Why does my choice of a wife bother you so much? What has she done to you?"

This prompted a bombardment of criticism, curses, and epithets from Fitzwilliam before Darcy held up a hand to stop him.

"Enough of that, Fitzwilliam. She has done you no harm—"

"She has harmed someone I hold dear and—"

"Yes, yes." Darcy glared. "But it is no longer of any consequence. I shall marry her, and we shall be happy with you or without you. I should vastly prefer the former, but if I must, I shall content myself with the latter."

"You cannot marry her, Darcy."

"I can. And I shall."

There was silence while both gentlemen contemplated the yawning breach that was opening between them.

Fitzwilliam dropped his eyes. "I need to think on this." He turned on his heel and left Darcy in the hall.

"Idiot." Fitzwilliam strode rapidly to the master's rooms, resisting every impulse towards violence. Darcy knew not what he did, but Fitzwilliam knew it could not stand. He would not permit this absurdity to continue.

Entering the bedchamber, he violently and rapidly ripped the bedcovers from the bed, throwing them onto the floor. Then he kicked them a few times and tossed a pillow on top. It was an old habit from his school days. It relieved a man's need to destroy without actually ruining anything.

He went to the window and stared unseeing over the lawn. For a long time, he permitted his mind to roam free. He was a trained military man who had won far greater and more complicated battles than this, and he was certain he could and would prevail.

When the answer arrived, it was so obvious that he nearly laughed aloud. "Yes!" He pumped his fist in the air. "Yes!"

A seasoned soldier knows when it is time to call for additions to the troops.

Rubbing his hands gleefully, he sat at the desk, removing the necessary items for a letter. He sat for a moment, savouring the blank page before him. Then he picked up the quill and carefully dipped it in the ink. He would not blotch or smudge, for he knew well how the recipient of his missive despised carelessness.

He began writing with utmost deliberation.

My Dearest Lady Catherine...

Chapter Twenty-Four

It was not an easy journey back to London. Fitzwilliam was disinclined to make himself agreeable to Darcy, choosing instead to while away the hours with his nose in a book or his face covered by his hat, ostensibly asleep. After the first day, Darcy ceased his attempts to draw him into conversation and instead passed the time with his own books and flights of fancy.

It was Darcy's intention upon returning to London to see Elizabeth immediately. Therefore, he did not stir from the carriage as it waited outside the Matlock town house whilst Fitzwilliam took himself indoors and the footman removed his trunk. It was late for a call, but Darcy hoped for the privilege afforded a relation at Bingley's house, for that was what he was soon to be.

As it stood, his intentions did not signify.

Caruthers, the Matlock's butler of long tenure, was dutiful and hesitant at the door of Darcy's carriage. "Sir, you are needed inside. His lordship respectfully asks for your attendance."

"Pray, tell Lord Matlock business calls me home. I shall wait on him tomorrow."

Caruthers appeared distressed. "Sir, do oblige him now. I assure you, it is a matter of urgency and importance."

Darcy sighed loudly to convey his annoyance before recalling the fact that it was not Caruthers who vexed him. With a smaller sigh, he alit from the carriage and strode into the house, where he was arrested immediately by the cause of the inconvenience.

Lady Catherine de Bourgh stood in the middle of the vestibule, quivering with what appeared to be either rage or apoplexy. When she saw her nephew, she threw her hands into the air. "Darcy! At last!"

Lord Matlock stood beside his sister. "There you are, Darcy. Come sit down in the drawing room."

"What is this about?" Darcy frowned at his relations. "I have been away from home and naturally am most eager to return—"

"To your mistress?" Lady Catherine lifted a brow. "Will you be chasing down to Davies Street tonight in search of Miss Elizabeth Bennet?"

Darcy drew himself up to his full height. "I beg your pardon?"

Lord Matlock came between them. "Come now. Let us go into the drawing room. Catherine, civility please; nothing can be gained from such coarse behaviour."

With that, Lady Catherine allowed herself to be swept into the drawing room, Darcy following reluctantly. The beginning of a headache was already pinching at his brow, but he knew there would be much more to come before the evening concluded.

Darcy assisted his cousin Anne to a seat with Lord Matlock at her side. Lady Matlock, from her settee, urged Lady Catherine to join her, but her ladyship chose instead to stand in the middle of the room in the attitude of a prima donna preparing to enact a tragedy. "I have been," she uttered with great solemnity, "to see that girl."

"Who is that?" Darcy asked with as much feigned sedateness as he could muster.

"Miss Elizabeth Bennet." Her mouth was pinched as if the syllables were sour. "Such impertinence and cheek has been heretofore unknown to me!"

Fitzwilliam entered the room with Saye hard on his heels, and he settled into a chair where he had a view of both Lady Catherine and Darcy. He smiled with the delighted anticipation of someone about to enjoy a show.

"She had the insolence to claim she would marry you."

"Ha!" Saye crowed with delight. "See there, Father, I told you I could do it!" He was ignored by everyone save his lordship, who muttered something about filial affection and the abhorrent lack of it among the younger generation.

Lady Catherine continued her enraged rant from the middle of the room. "I had hoped to find her reasonable to the circumstances. I hoped she would act with prudence."

"What are the circumstances as you see them?"

"Firstly," said her ladyship briskly, "that we, as a family, shall not recognise her. Should you be determined to pursue this mésalliance, you would do so against the express wishes of your family, and we would not condescend to receive either of you."

Darcy slowly paced to the window, putting his back to Lady Catherine. "And what did Miss Bennet say to that?"

"Miss Bennet is a pitiable creature; it astonishes me that I once thought her clever. She is determined to fix you, Darcy, and she cannot see that quitting her own sphere would be to her detriment. Then again, foolish behaviour is not unknown to her. I do not suppose you knew this, but she refused Mr. Collins, my former parson, when accepting him might have secured her place at Longbourn!"

"And it is fortunate she did, for her place will be with me at Pemberley."

Lady Catherine sputtered for a moment. "She is determined to ruin you! I told her that her name would never be mentioned by any of us! Can you guess what she said to that?"

"I cannot."

"She said she had once been fool enough to be persuaded to put her attachment to you aside in favour of the considerations of others, and she would not do so again! I told her she was an obstinate, headstrong girl and —can you imagine?—she said I might well add selfish to my list, for she intended to be selfish when it came to you."

Darcy was glad to have his back to her, for nothing could have prevented the beaming grin from spreading over his countenance, which likely would have astonished his relations. He was the picture of sobriety when he turned.

"I am sorry to learn that you have offended the future Mrs. Darcy in such a way. I had hoped to remain on good terms with my relations; but alas, it seems you will force me to sever my connexions."

"You would surely do no such thing."

"Indeed, I shall," he replied calmly. "Lord Matlock, does Lady Catherine speak for you as well?"

"She does not," said his lordship.

All heads that had not been pointed in his lordship's direction moved there rapidly. Lady Catherine immediately began to sputter and protest, but her brother forestalled her with a raised hand. "Catherine, you have had your share of the conversation, and now I shall have mine. Darcy, it does not excite me to imagine that, with all the suitable ladies who have been set before you, you will choose to marry beneath you."

"I am a gentleman, and she is a gentleman's daughter."

"*Was* a gentleman's daughter," said Fitzwilliam, finally entering into the conversation. "Her father has been dead above a twelve-month. She lives on the charity of her relations."

"And what is that to you?" Darcy retorted, his mastery over his anger slipping.

"I told you, Darcy, I would not disguise my feelings for the lady. She is nowise your equal, she will corrupt—"

"You must cease in your unjustifiable endeavours to separate us!" Darcy thundered to his cousin. "It is done! I shall marry her, and for any who oppose it, I am happy to depart from you. This interference has gone far enough."

He glared around the room. "In case any of you have forgotten, I am my own man, and I answer to none of you. I have afforded you the regard occasioned by virtue of being my nearest relations, but if you go on in this way, my regard must end. I shall marry Miss Elizabeth Bennet with or without the approval of anyone in this room. This is my final conversation on the matter."

With that, he turned and strode from the room, leaving the house only moments later.

ON THE NIGHT HE WAS DUE BACK, ELIZABETH WAS OF NO USE TO ANYONE. She was racked and distracted, sure he would come to her that night and equally certain he would not. Of his aunt's visit she dared not think; it had not been a scene in which she acquitted herself well. Rather, she had been stubborn and, at times, decidedly impudent. She was just so tired of obstacles that she had quite lost her grace in dealing with them.

She had settled on the latest hour she believed he might come, and when that hour passed, she resolved to retire. Elizabeth soon found herself in her bedchamber, though she knew sleep would not soon find her. Not bothering to undress, she settled into a window cushion that overlooked the street, a book in her hand. For some time, she stared out, watching as carriages came and went, their occupants returning home from their evenings of parties and other sorts of enjoyments.

A Short Period of Exquisite Felicity

Davies Street was rather more bustling than she might have expected, but at last, she noticed a gentleman emerging from the darkness. He was tall and walked slowly, and her eyes fixed on him—first uncertain and then sure—as he paid special notice to Bingley's front door.

Her heart quickened, and she moved to undo the latches on the window, struggling to open them. She called out, "Darcy!" even though the window was still secured.

He certainly could not hear her, and she uttered a mild oath as she tugged harder. The latches would not give way, and she pushed and pulled with increasing desperation. "Open, you foolish metal…"

She groaned, realising it was a lost cause, and groaned again when she saw Darcy walking away. With one last heave and an unrefined curse, she abandoned her efforts at the window.

In a trice, she had jerked the door to the bedchamber open and was flying on silent feet through the quiet halls of the house. She did not go to the front door, choosing instead to use the door that Sir Edmund had found quite useful for clandestine meetings with Miss Bingley. It permitted her to emerge at the side of the house, and she ran around to the front.

"Mr. Darcy!" she cried out in a hushed sort of exclamation. "Sir! Wait!"

He stopped and turned around slowly as if disbelieving he was sought. Then he beheld her, and his face, though shadowed, lit with pleasure.

At once, she saw herself as he likely saw her: unkempt, undignified, and rather brazen in her approach. An attack of nerves, uncommon and ill-timed, beset her, but she would not allow its interference.

She went to him directly, wishing she could fling herself into his arms and kiss him senseless; alas, it was not prudent. The future Mrs. Darcy must exhibit some understanding of propriety, no matter how she disliked it. Too many passers-by were on the street, and too many interested persons went by in carriages for her to do as she truly wanted.

He immediately took both of her hands, gazing at her with a look that left no doubt he felt just as she did. "You are here," she said warmly as he caressed her hands with his thumbs.

"I did not dare call on you. I thought surely the house would be abed."

"Some part of me must have anticipated you. The most hopeful, eager part."

He drew her hands to his lips, kissing one then the other, even as his eyes remained fixed on hers. "You told her you would not be persuaded from your attachment to me."

"I was rude to her," she confessed in a whisper. "I did not afford her much respect."

"She did not behave in a respectable manner. I am mortified to call her my aunt."

"It will not do; I wish for your relations to accept me and perhaps, in time, to even like me a little."

"They have not endeared themselves, have they? But I am with you and for you, and they can choose to like you or to leave us both. I shall countenance no less for you, for *our* family, the one we shall make together."

She wanted to kiss him for that, but propriety stopped her. "There are too many people on this street."

"Far too many," he agreed softly. "Would that I could whisk you away!"

"I would like that."

There was so much more to be said and done and felt, but it was, in all respects, impossible. Eventually, there was a quiet moment on Davies Street, and he leant in, kissing her tenderly on her lips. There was a damp chill in the air, and her feet, in their highly imprudent house slippers, were growing wet and cold, but the shiver that raced up her spine had only to do with him.

He must have felt it too, for he held her tight, murmuring, "Never again. Nothing will be permitted to get between us, and we shall not part again."

IT WAS FAR TOO EARLY WHEN SAYE ARRIVED AT DARCY'S HOUSE THE NEXT day. As he had lingered with Elizabeth for far too long the night prior, Darcy was not yet down to his breakfast. Saye did not mind, showing himself into Darcy's dressing room immediately.

"They are all in an uproar over there," he announced.

"About Elizabeth?"

Saye waved his hand. "Elizabeth is old news. Shortly after you stormed out, Anne had her own news to announce. Seems she has held a secret for some time and was only hoping you would go first so her mother would be enraged at you instead of her."

"Our cousin has her own nuptial plans?"

"The man's name is Beverton; he is forty and a barrister."

"A barrister? Nothing to object about in that."

"Oh, you can be sure Lady Catherine objects," Saye replied with a chuckle.

"Anne was not to be swayed. Lady Catherine said he had no estate and no land, but Anne said he would have a great deal of land just as soon as they married. You should have seen our aunt's face! I thought the old bird was like to die at once! Generally, one must leave the house for such diversions as these."

"How nice," said Darcy drily, "that we could all entertain you so."

"Our aunt says the entire family is sunk, and it is all on your shoulders."

Darcy shrugged it off. "Let them blame me, but I shall not tolerate disrespect towards my wife. See if I do not mean it. We have had too much vexation and grief already, and anything that comes in my way will be dispensed with summarily."

"Regardless," Saye said with a little yawn, "you have already been pledged the support of my wife and me—"

"Only because you want your father's money."

"True, but what does that signify? I think I should meet the girl. Shall we go over there?"

The two gentlemen arrived to find Davies Street humming with activity. Miss Bingley's wedding was only days away, and there were breakfast dishes to be prepared and packing to be done. Saye greeted Elizabeth with as much kindness as his customary airs would permit and undertook a short interview.

"So, your younger sisters have married before you?"

"Two of them have."

"Your mother should not have permitted them out before you wed."

"Perhaps not, but what if I had never married? Should they have remained spinsters as well?"

"An excellent point. Why did you think you would not marry? Was it because you were pining for Darcy?"

"Of course." Darcy could tell she was trying not to smile.

"But were you not mad to marry? You have no fortune to live on, if I am not mistaken."

"Having lost Darcy, I had decided I would never marry." She smiled at Darcy wistfully. "No fortune, no material comfort could ever be sufficient to induce me to accept another, not when I knew I had broken the heart of the very best of men."

"Ah." Saye looked silly for a moment, seemingly unable to form a rejoinder. It was then that Darcy knew Elizabeth had won Saye, not just his support—which Lord Matlock had purchased—but his true regard. This was not common with Saye, but she had done it, and he repressed a victorious grin.

"Have you thought about wedding cake?" was the best response Saye could devise. "Make sure the icing is white, for I cannot eat any other."

They were soon talking and laughing as three old friends would. By some manoeuvring—Darcy could not say how it happened—he found himself edged away from Elizabeth whilst Saye joined her on the settee.

"This wedding day cannot come soon enough," Elizabeth said, speaking of Miss Bingley's nuptials.

"Oh? Has Miss Bingley been much in anticipation?" Darcy asked.

Elizabeth gave a mischievous little wink. "I believe *much*, if not *all*, has been *anticipated* between them."

It took Darcy a moment to understand her, but when he did, it made him laugh, though not nearly as heartily as Saye did.

"A dangerous business, indeed, and I speak as one who has seen the stricter side of Bingley," Darcy said.

Elizabeth told them, "I should have deeply pitied Sir Edmund had there been any consequence to his clandestine business."

"Oh, yes. Sir Edmund would have faced violent censure from not only Bingley but his own family as well."

"That is true," Saye agreed. "They are the only people I know who are as pious on such matters as my father."

"Is Lord Matlock very strict?" Elizabeth asked.

"Oh, yes," Darcy told her. "My father was too. With so much at stake in their patronage of the church, they both felt it a duty and a moral obligation to be upright and to have families that behaved properly. Lord Matlock has been forceful with us all on the subject of marriage."

"I had no idea," said Elizabeth. "But I can only approve. I should hope our sons would behave with so much honour."

"Our sons?" Darcy smiled at her. "Shall we have more than one?"

"One would do, I suppose." She turned to face him. "But two might be even better."

He had to remind himself not to kiss her sweet lips, so charmingly curved into a little smile, but he drew nearer to her, far too close for polite society. "Then two daughters too, I must hope."

"To be sure!" she exclaimed with a little laugh. "But what if there are five, as in my family?"

"I should like it very well as long as they are all like you."

"I have a son." Saye loudly interrupted their little flirtation. "I am sure my Lily would like a daughter soon, but I do not know that I could bear it. So many rakes these days! I shall like to hang them all by their ball—ah, by their fingernails."

"I only hope some of the men who were required to chase you off will still be alive to watch you protect your daughters," Darcy told him. "I think it well deserved."

It was on Saye's invitation that Elizabeth joined him and his wife, along with Darcy and Georgiana, to see *Aladdin*. Although Darcy did not think it worthy of great acclaim, it was well worth seeing Elizabeth's enjoyment. Lady Saye, pressed into service as the future Mrs. Darcy's particular friend, warmed to Elizabeth quickly, and the two ladies showed all signs of becoming intimate friends.

Georgiana was perhaps not yet entirely disposed towards approving Elizabeth. Her demeanour was best described as quietly watchful, but with each passing day they were together, Darcy saw the development of regard that he hoped would later turn into true sisterly friendship.

Lady Catherine had departed for Rosings in a fit of pique, refusing to be in society with an upstart. No one much minded her leaving, and indeed, Anne, who chose to remain behind, blossomed without the constant oppressive effects of her mother's censure.

Darcy, who had for some time known he would be happy, began at last to really feel it. He suffered an almost embarrassing lightness of being. That is, he might have been embarrassed had he the slightest concern for anything but his love. He woke with a smile on his face, predisposed to think the day a good one, and he laid his head on his pillow at night filled with fond remembrances of the day and hopeful expectations for the future.

There was but one thing to mar his felicity: the continued disdain of Colonel Fitzwilliam. Darcy had not spoken to his cousin since their return from Cotgrave, and the last time he saw him, Fitzwilliam turned his back and walked in the other direction to avoid him.

Elizabeth was too observant to have missed his distress, and she introduced the subject at Miss Bingley's wedding breakfast. "You have not been in company with Colonel Fitzwilliam of late."

Darcy forced himself to grin in what he hoped was an easy manner. "I am too busy with my beloved to concern myself with him, and he is occupied with his intended as well."

But Elizabeth would not be deceived by his words. Her eyes studied his countenance while her lips pressed together. "I cannot like having divided you from him."

"He is behaving in an irrational and unjust manner. I cannot comprehend him, and I can only hope he will soon see reason."

"It will not do."

"It must do, at least for now."

"I would like to speak to him and explain—"

Darcy shook his head. "Absolutely not."

Elizabeth laid her hand on his arm. "Perhaps he can be made to understand—"

"You do not owe him any explanation or justification."

"Pray, allow me to speak to him?"

"My love." Darcy brought her hand to his lips for a brief kiss. "I cannot allow it. He will likely be rude, or at least impertinent, and I would not have him hurt you for anything."

"I can withstand his rudeness. His words cannot hurt me; however, seeing the breach between you and knowing I am the cause of it does pain me. Please, will you not allow me an audience with him?"

Darcy did not like the idea, but he apprehended immediately that Elizabeth would not be gainsaid. Her beautiful dark eyes stared up at him, begging him; her words were gentle, but her eyes were not. He gave a little groan. "So this is how it will be?"

"What do you mean?"

He lightly touched her cheek with his thumb. "You turn those eyes on me, and I am under your power."

A smile broke over her countenance. "Is that so?"

"Very much so."

"You should perhaps not have told me that, Mr. Darcy." Her eyes turned still more beseeching. "Please grant me an audience with your cousin. Let us not permit the breach to stand."

Darcy sighed. "Very well. I shall arrange a meeting between us, and you may say as you wish. However, if he is too unkind or rude, I shall not permit it to continue. Pray, do not expect too much from it; my cousin is as stubborn as he is unreasonable."

DARCY CALLED AT LORD MATLOCK'S HOME THE NEXT MORNING, WHERE he suspected he might find them at breakfast. Lord Matlock had already taken his meal and left the house—he did not suffer town hours, no matter how much he was there—but Darcy found Lady Matlock sipping coffee beside her son.

Darcy offered the appropriate courtesies to his aunt while Fitzwilliam lounged in his seat, regarding them with wary eyes.

"Will you have something with us?" his aunt enquired.

"Some coffee will do. My purpose was not to interrupt your meal; I wish to speak to Fitzwilliam."

She was already pouring him coffee and smiled at him with fondness. "I see. Well, as I am not one to linger where I am not wanted—"

Both men protested immediately.

"No, no," she said with a gentle smile. "I must be about my day. Darcy, I would like your bride to call on me this week. I have a note for you to take to her that I shall leave with my housekeeper."

Darcy nodded, and his aunt quit the room.

Fitzwilliam remained silent as his mother departed and showed no inclination towards speech in the face of the silence she left behind.

Darcy smiled. "Where have you been keeping yourself, Cousin? I have seen you but rarely."

Fitzwilliam shrugged. "I have been where I usually am. I think you have not seen me because you have been otherwise engaged."

Darcy chuckled in a forced manner. "I cannot deny that. I have been more in Davies Street than at my usual haunts; such is the fate of an engaged man."

Fitzwilliam did not respond to Darcy's attempt at light-heartedness, instead regarding him with a flat, uninterested mien.

"Elizabeth is much occupied today in helping Miss Bingley—Lady Hynde rather—settle into her new house. I thought I might go to my club. Will you join me?"

"No," Fitzwilliam spoke coolly. "I do not think I shall."

"Some other place, then? What of Angelo's? Or Jacksons?"

"I thank you, no."

There was a heavy pause in which Darcy considered his cousin's displeasure. He decided that to speak frankly would have to do. "It seems you intend to make good on your promise to have no part of me."

Fitzwilliam nodded slowly. "I am a man of my word, Darcy."

"As you wish. My bride cannot comprehend it, however, and would like an audience with you. I can no longer be assured your heart is soft enough to receive her, but I promised her I would mention it to you, and so I have."

"She wants to speak to me?" The colonel chuckled in a low way. "Such pluck! She is ever the courageous one."

"Never mind." Darcy rose. "It is clear you can do nothing but be cruel to her, so forget I asked. I only did it because she insisted; I think it a stupid idea."

"She can hardly anticipate my welcome."

"No, but she is still hopeful enough to think you a fair and just man."

The colonel remained in an attitude of deep contemplation for several moments. Finally, he sighed, seeming to come awake. "Very well, Darcy. I shall speak to her at the ball."

Chapter Twenty-Five

In honour of Georgiana's first Season, Lady Matlock had planned a ball to introduce her niece to her circle of friends and acquaintances. The arrangements had been the subject of much conversation, and Elizabeth anticipated something grand, though as she approached the door of the elegant facade, she realised that she could never have imagined such as she saw in front of her.

Lady Matlock's "circle" included most of London if the stream of persons entering was any indication. Looking around her, Elizabeth thought it must surely be hundreds of people, all of them laughing and gay, wearing their finest attire and most dazzling jewels.

Almost inadvertently, her fingers rose to touch her necklace, a fine emerald and diamond creation Darcy had given her only a few days prior. "Given to my mother to mark the occasion of my birth," he told her. It had been rather amazing to imagine herself wearing such a necklace, but looking around her, she was pleased that she had. She almost appeared to belong there.

Elizabeth had arrived with the Bingleys as Darcy had been obliged to escort his sister to their aunt's home some time earlier. He had promised to open the ball with Georgiana; Elizabeth's would be the supper set, which pleased her well enough. She hardly cared about any other dances but that one as she desired to dance with Darcy and Darcy alone.

Lord and Lady Matlock greeted her in a somewhat friendly manner; they were not yet prepared to welcome her as a relation, but their warmth did increase every time they met. Elizabeth thought it satisfactory. Following her greeting, Mr. Bingley took his ladies into the main rooms where the ball was being held. Movement was slow due to the number of people crowding around them, but at length, they arrived at their destination.

"Very lovely," Jane said as they surveyed all the people mingling in the ballroom. "Lizzy, do observe the flower arrangements. I do not think I have seen their like."

"Neither have I. So many roses! And so early in the season too."

"Quite fortunate, is it not?" came a deep voice from behind her. "For I am excessively fond of roses."

Elizabeth whirled to find Darcy staring down at her with the hint of a grin on his lips. She responded with her own grin. "As am I, but alas, it is not a garden."

He leant down and whispered into her ear, "I could make do." He gave her a tiny, secret kiss on her ear before straightening.

"Shocking behaviour, sir!" she teased him, noting that Jane and Bingley had quietly melted away into the crowd.

"Not nearly as shocking as I would like to be. Your beauty is almost too much to be borne tonight."

His heated gaze caused her to blush, and she dropped her eyes. She had given way to vanity in the selection of her gown; it was the palest cream, and the sleeves left her shoulders exposed, setting off her neck and bosom in a spectacular manner. "I hoped my gown would please you."

He placed his hand on her upper back in just such a way that it was hidden from observers yet permitted him to stroke the bare skin of her shoulder with his thumb. "You please me," he murmured. "I wish I could steal you away."

She laughed a bit weakly at the sensations he was inducing with his maddening caress. "That might make Miss Darcy's first dance a rather awkward affair."

With a deep, forced exhale, he dropped his hand and straightened, taking a small step away from her. "Yes, it surely would. Duty calls, does it not? And generally at the worst times."

She reached down and squeezed his hand. "At least, I have our dance to anticipate."

He grasped her hand and pulled it up between them, bowing over and kissing it. "I shall count the moments."

"Ho there, Darcy! Best get yourself under regulation, my boy." Saye had arrived with Georgiana clinging to his arm. "Almost time to dance with your sister, and therefore a wretched time to be making love to your lady."

He tweaked a brow at Elizabeth. "You turn up well. Have you a partner to open?"

"Ah, no, not—"

"Perfect. You are with me." He sighed heavily. "It seems I am to be a bachelor at this do."

"Where is Lady Saye?" Darcy asked.

Saye waved his hand irritably. "Indisposed. This monthly nonsense, always the most vexatious times!"

He made his voice into a high, ladylike simper. "Do not touch here, stay away from there, and by the by, I shall take to my bed for all the day!" In his usual voice, he lamented, "It is too much for a man to bear!"

Elizabeth looked at Georgiana and rolled her eyes. "Yes, it is unfortunate how the *gentlemen* do suffer in such times as these."

Georgiana smothered a little smile, and for a moment, she appeared almost easy. Her calm was short-lived, however, as the musicians played those few notes that signalled the dancers to the floor. Her eyes went wide, and Elizabeth saw the sudden stiffness in her posture. She gently placed her hand on the girl's arm.

"I hate the idea of everyone staring at me," Georgiana said in meek tones. "I wish I could just be out with none of this ceremony and fanfare."

"It will be better after this first dance," Elizabeth told her. "And indeed, it is really just the first minutes of the first dance—just get through that much, and all will be well. They will return to their own concerns then. And you look beautiful; no one could fault your loveliness."

Georgiana did look pretty in a gown of such pale blue as to seem almost silver. To enhance the effect, she wore a silvery overdress and pearls around her neck. "Thank you, Elizabeth," she said with a little sigh. Then her eyes flew even wider. "Oh! I called you Elizabeth. Forgive my presumption if you will…Fitzwilliam calls you Elizabeth and Lillian does too…I…but I should not presume—"

Elizabeth touched her arm again. "I am pleased that you call me Elizabeth. Are we not to be sisters?"

Georgiana nodded and gave Elizabeth a true, warm smile. "We are. I do hope you will call me Georgiana?"

Elizabeth nodded, and the two ladies exchanged a quick embrace.

"Well, this is a charming scene." Colonel Fitzwilliam and Lady Sophie joined their group, and the colonel drawled his greeting in a way that made his displeasure apparent.

Strangely, it was Lady Sophie who eased the tension that had arrived with them, greeting everyone and exclaiming over the beauty of the ladies. The colonel stood back a bit, regarding it all with cool solemnity. He did not remove his gaze from Elizabeth, staring at her with flat, disgusted eyes that she felt even as she turned her back on him.

There were dances to arrange then, with Saye and the colonel deciding when they should dance with their young cousin and warning her against various gentlemen they thought she should avoid. With that bit of business concluded, the gentlemen claimed their partners and moved to take their places within the forming set.

Saye was in all ways a diverting partner. He was vastly handsome and a superior dancer, and Elizabeth earned the envious looks of more than one lady. He was filled with amusing anecdotes and pleasant conversation, and more than once, she missed a step for laughing. The set passed quickly, and too soon Saye was escorting her from the floor.

She would not dance with Darcy until the supper dance, but she saw him much engaged with Jane, then Lady Sophie and Miss de Bourgh. Nor did she not lack for partners, finding herself dancing every set.

It was after the fourth that the colonel found her. "Miss Bennet. I understand you wish to speak to me.

Surprised, she said, "Yes, I do, sir."

He shrugged with open hands. "So, let us talk."

Elizabeth looked at the crowd around them. She did not like the idea of speaking without privacy, but on the other hand, going off somewhere with him made her uneasy.

"Not here obviously." He gestured. "Follow me."

Elizabeth glanced around the room again, seeking Darcy. He was, alas, nowhere in sight, likely introducing his sister somewhere. It seemed she was on her own for this hapless tête-à-tête. "I do think Mr. Darcy wished to—"

"Darcy is otherwise engaged; are you coming or not?" The colonel had already grown impatient with her reluctance. She nodded, hoping that Darcy would somehow know to join them.

A Short Period of Exquisite Felicity

The colonel led her through the throng in a manner that would have appeared perfectly correct to an interested observer. He took her down a hall towards the back of the house and up a staircase. Elizabeth heard the sounds of the party die away even as her trepidation grew. Where was he taking her? She cursed herself for not finding Darcy.

Just as she opened her mouth to insist Darcy join them, Colonel Fitzwilliam opened the door to a handsomely appointed study. Elizabeth entered the well-lit room lined with books. A table with a chess game in process was positioned by a window, and a well-worn leather chair was behind a desk piled with papers and journals. Elizabeth swallowed against a sudden lump in her throat; it reminded her of her father's library.

With feigned nonchalance, she strolled into the room, looking around her and going to the chess board. She studied it for a moment, seeing a relatively quick path to victory, and wondered who belonged to each side. Her musings were interrupted by the sharp click of a door being locked. She jumped and turned to look at the colonel.

"A precaution," he said with a smirk. "Would not do to have someone burst in on us and come to some wrong ideas about what we were about."

Elizabeth nodded, not taking her eyes off of him. He stared at her just as intently until she had to drop her eyes, and she turned her attention back to the chess board. Idly, she moved a pawn back and forth, just to give her hands something to do.

"I suppose you would like the opportunity to explain your cruelty," he said. "You may say what you like to me; however, do not think it will change my opinion of you."

A moment of anger flashed hotly within her and her hand tightened on the chess piece. How tired and vexed she was that this man continued with his spite! But to lose her composure would do no good. *This is for Darcy.*

She took a moment to ensure she was calm, and she even managed a small, tight smile. "I have always thought you a fair and rational gentleman, and I hope I shall find you so now."

He barked a mean laugh. "I am sure you did. Your charms might have beguiled Darcy into forgiveness, and even Georgiana, but they will not work on me."

"Yes," said Elizabeth evenly. "Mr. Darcy has forgiven me, and for my life, I cannot comprehend why you persist in despising me."

"There is an easy answer to that: he is a fool, and I am not. I do not intend to relent, Miss Bennet, no matter what you say. He said you wished to say your piece to me, and so I shall hear you, but it will change nothing."

"I am sorry to hear that. I had hoped one day we might again be friends."

"Friends?" The colonel shook his head. "No, Miss Bennet, I shall never be your friend, nor shall I cease my efforts to make Darcy see that marrying you will be his ruination. If he continues in this folly and persists in attaching himself to so low a family, then I cannot help him. But I shall be damned if he drags me down with him."

His remarks about her family brought back that searing rage. He knew nothing of her family; who was he to speak so? But again she controlled herself. Cool heads must prevail if she had any hope of success.

"It grieves me to think that two men as close as brothers should be so divided."

"Precisely," the colonel agreed. "Can you truly be happy knowing you have been the cause of a breach between Darcy and his family? We shall see how much he loves you when everyone else turns against him.

"Your parents and Lord and Lady Saye have been quite kind to me, and Georgiana and I are fast regaining our friendship. It seems, sir, that you alone stand against me. So who is the cause of this breach? I daresay, it is you."

He did not seem to take note of her words. "It will take little time for anyone of discernment or wit to reject you and, by extension, him. You are due to become Darcy's humiliating mistake, and you will be spending your days in Ireland just as soon as we can bring him to his senses.

"Do not depend on my family or Georgiana to defend you when he becomes unhappy with you, and do not mistake it: when this little infatuation of his is done, he will be unhappy. You are nothing more than the toy he was denied; therefore, it became his passion to have it. Now that he has it, he will see it is flawed and cheap—a mere nothing."

Flawed and cheap? How she longed to set him down as he deserved!

"I see what you want here. You wish to scare me, to make me think I shall bring him misery and cry off. Is that it?"

"Precisely, and if you have half the sense—"

"Do not waste another moment of your time considering it. I am not letting go, Colonel Fitzwilliam. Never. You may tolerate me or not, but I shall not let go. You will need to find a way to accustom yourself to the notion that the only person who can put me off is Mr. Darcy, and he has decided to love me."

"He is made foolish by lust and longing," the colonel retorted.

"That is your opinion, and you are certainly entitled to it; however, I know you are wrong. He loves me, Colonel Fitzwilliam, and I love him. That is why I stand here, willingly subjecting myself to your insults. I know that the absence of your friendship affects him, and I want to do everything in my power to fix the situation for him."

"Alas, it is not within your power."

"Mr. Darcy told me that you know what Mr. Wickham required of me, the choice I was forced to make. Surely, you are compassionate enough to understand my sorrow? I do not mean to say you should agree with me, only to understand. Can you not put aside your prejudice against me to consider that much?"

"I shall agree that you faced a difficult choice. The facts remain, however, that you hurt my cousin, wounded him deeply, and I am certain you will someday do it again. Yes, it will be under different provocation, but you are what you are, Miss Bennet—charming, to be sure, and witty, but with a stubbornness and a conceited independence that will make you a bane to any man and, most particularly, to a man like Darcy."

Although privately she revolted against any show of weakness, she would, for Darcy, allow her vulnerability to be seen.

"I cannot deny your charges. I am, or have been, most of those things. But I pray you would believe me when I tell you I have changed." She clasped her hands in front of her and, in a tone just short of begging, said, "I do intend to make him happy. You may depend upon it; I shall be a good wife to him."

The colonel's blue eyes studied her in an inscrutable way until he dismissed her coldly. "No. You will never make him happy, and if I have my way, you will never have the honour of calling yourself Mrs. Darcy."

Despite everything, his unrelenting spite hurt her. She wished him to believe she was, at heart, a good person, and she had hoped they might come away from this meeting with at least the promise to begin anew. But it seemed there would not be a second chance with the colonel.

She studied him, suppressing the sigh that would signal her defeat. He was the picture of male assuredness with an easy stance and a calm countenance. He appeared immovable in his dislike, and her anger was once again roused by it.

"Mr. Darcy and I shall marry," she said with more firmness. "It is going to happen, sir, whether you like it or not. And yes, I do comprehend that you do not like it."

"It is abhorrent to me."

She disregarded his words. "All I ask is for time to heal the breach between us."

"Time?" He chuckled. "Yes, some time would do very well. You would like time to persuade me, and I would like time to persuade him. Why not postpone these ill-fated nuptials a year or so, and give us both what we wish for?"

Elizabeth imbued her words with as much confidence as she could. "You could delay my nuptials ten years, and I have no doubt that my Darcy would still love me."

He did not like when she said 'my Darcy'—she saw it in the curl of his lip—so she resolved to say it more often.

"*My* Darcy could only be frustrated at such obvious machinations. Come, Colonel, you are a man of sense and education. Will you not see that all of us are best served by reconciliation?"

The colonel observed her for some minutes and she, unable to bear his gaze, again lowered her eyes to the board, touching this piece and that with as much nonchalance as she could muster.

"You like that chess game, do you?"

"I do."

"Then let us play a game. The winner will obtain what they would like: for you, a chance to prove yourself worthy of my cousin, and for me, time to persuade him of your lack of worth."

"How much time?"

"One year—to give him time to regain his senses."

"One month."

"Six months."

Elizabeth lifted a brow. "Three."

Colonel Fitzwilliam acceded with a chuckle. "Very well. I do not think it should require even so much as three. My influence over him is not inconsiderable."

Elizabeth only smiled at this bit of foolish puffery.

"'Tis the power of an elder cousin. He followed me while still in his dresses; he learnt to catch fish from me. I taught him how to beat George

Wickham, though not hard enough, I fear. Yes, elder cousins, particularly those who are more like elder brothers, are always revered. Very well, Miss Bennet, you have arranged your stake. Let us sit to our game."

"Darcy!" Saye beckoned him from across the room. "Come here, I must speak to you."

Darcy hastened to his cousin, who tugged at his arm and directed him towards a relatively deserted corner. "Is something wrong?"

"Shh!" Saye looked around carefully.

"Is Georgiana—?"

"She is well; do not think of that." With a grand sigh, he said, "Though I do fear she is at risk of obscurity among the *ton*."

"What do you mean?"

"This ball, held in her honour, is proving to be a rather…forgettable affair."

"Forgettable?"

In earnest tones, Saye whispered, "No one is doing anything even remotely scandalous! Who invited all of these very proper people? Not a thing of interest is happening here!"

Darcy laughed. "And that has raised your alarm? The party is too well behaved?"

"It is distressing." Saye shook his head. "For above an hour, I have sought out dark corners and servants' closets. No one is doing the least illicit thing."

"Forgive me, but I shall count my blessings if there is no breath of scandal to be had tonight." Darcy chuckled.

"That," Saye pronounced haughtily, "would be utter disaster. Let me send a note to Frobisher; he will—"

"No!" Darcy exclaimed. "He will arrive with numerous harlots on each arm!"

"What about Lady Bart's sweet young thing? That boy we saw her with at the theatre. They danced together earlier."

"Her nephew."

"Nephew!" Saye rolled his eyes. "What sort of namby-pamby dolt wastes a dance on his aunt?"

"The sort that stands to inherit her fortune."

Saye cursed. "Darcy, we must save this party. Something must happen; otherwise, I fear we are in grave danger"—he looked around a little wildly—"of *no one* talking about us!"

"Your mother's parties are always worthy of at least one morning's conversations."

Saye groaned and rolled his eyes. "One morning? This is the sum of your aspirations? Heavens above, Darcy! Even a literary salon gets one meal's notice! My mother and your sister deserve conversation for at least a week!"

"I thank you, but I shall be happy to avoid the sort of conversation you seem to crave." Darcy gave his cousin an affectionate pat on the arm. "Can you tell me where Elizabeth has gone? Is she dancing?"

Saye shrugged, concern still wrinkling his brow as he scanned the room searching for scandalous behaviour of any sort. "I suppose she is."

"What do you mean, you suppose?"

Saye had already lost interest, his eyes drifting over the crowd. "Oh! Look there…Mrs. Strathleigh dancing with Mr. John Pennington. Were they not once lovers?"

"Brother and sister. Elizabeth? Have you seen her?"

"I think my brother took her off. Well! Look over there! I believe that is Cuthbert, and where he is found—"

"Took her off? Where did they go? To dance?"

Saye sighed and turned his attention to Darcy. "Am I her governess? I am sure I do not know."

Darcy growled with frustration and left his cousin at a quick pace. It took some time—his aunt's rooms seemed to be growing more crowded by the minute —but after a while, he found Lady Sophie, who had not the least notion of where her intended was. "It has been above an hour since I have seen him. Pray, when you find him, tell him I would like to be sure of a partner before supper."

A sense of foreboding filled Darcy; he had not liked this idea of Elizabeth's to speak to Fitzwilliam, and he had only agreed presuming he would be present at the discussion. Now Fitzwilliam had taken her off to who knew where, and although Darcy reminded himself that his cousin was a gentlemen, it would not do. He still feared for what might be done or said that would not be easily undone when cooler tempers prevailed.

IT WAS EVIDENT FROM THE BEGINNING OF THE GAME THAT COLONEL FITZwilliam was vastly less adept at chess than he believed he was. Elizabeth, who had played extensively with her father from girlhood, carefully allowed him to take her to what seemed an untenable spot, then she came back in a way that, to him, might seem rather like witchcraft.

As his frustration grew, so too did his tendency to insult her. He again made mention of her low connexions, her stubbornness, and her keen ability to induce misery upon undeserving, good men. His sly remarks angered her, but she would merely reply, with a little smile, "How thankful I am that *my* Darcy does not think so."

By his countenance, no insult against his person could have vexed him more. He grew increasingly flushed and tugged at his neckcloth rather incessantly. More alarming was his drinking, first from the flask in his coat and then from a decanter retrieved from his father's desk as the game wore on. His growing drunkenness did nothing to improve his game or his temper.

The match was not a long one, yet the colonel had accused her of illegal manoeuvres no less than five times. Fortunately, Lord Matlock kept a book for just such tactical questions. She was, by her estimation, three moves from finishing him when a knock was heard at the door along with a rattling of the latch. "Fitzwilliam?" Darcy's voice was heard from the other side of the door. "Are you in there? Have you seen Elizabeth?"

"It seems *my* Darcy wishes to join us."

Fitzwilliam clenched his jaw. "Must you speak so?"

"How do I speak?"

Fitzwilliam made his voice a falsetto. "*My* Darcy this and *my* Darcy that." In his usual tones, he added, "It seems to me that you want to persuade yourself that you have him."

Elizabeth gave him a tight smile. "I think we are both persuaded that he is mine, and so will he remain. But he is here. I shall admit him, and you can hear it directly from him." She rose and went to open the door.

Darcy looked almost wild with his breath quickened and his eyes darting about the room. "Are you well?"

"Perfectly so," she said with a smile. "I have been playing chess with your cousin."

There was another knock, and the door opened to admit Miss de Bourgh, who appeared rather tired. "Might I join you for a moment? I am quite exhausted from all the dancing!"

"Please do," Elizabeth said, and Anne sat in chair by the two chess players. "Are you well? Shall I summon Mrs. Jenkinson?"

"I just need a little rest. I am used to a quiet life and usually asleep by this time of night, but here I am at a ball!"

Having not been much in company, Anne appeared to be rather insensible of the underlying anger and frustration in the room. She chattered on cheerfully about her dance partners while Fitzwilliam glared at the chess board, whispering drunken curses about the unfairness of the arranged pieces. Elizabeth made a move after which he stared at the board in a near stupor for some minutes.

"I wonder whether you know the family of my intended husband," Anne enquired of Elizabeth. "They are from Hertfordshire. His mother was a Soames, and their estate is called Whitehall."

"Indeed, I do know it," Elizabeth replied. "It is not far from my home. When one leaves the London road for the town where I live, it is right there."

"It is good to know that there is something of distinction in Hertfordshire," said the colonel. "I have never been there myself, but from what I know of it, I presume it has a low and excessively confined, illiberal sort of society."

"Fitzwilliam…" The warning was clear in Darcy's voice, but Anne interrupted him.

Speaking gaily, she said, "But you have been there! You told me so yourself."

Fitzwilliam lifted deadened eyes to regard her. "You are mistaken, Anne. The most I have ever seen of Hertfordshire is likely some coaching inn, and even that was too much for my liking."

"But I remember it clearly! It was after a visit to Rosings—the time Miss Bennet was with us—and you said you were going to London and then on to some little place in Hertfordshire. Even then I wondered whether you would see Whitehall! What was the name of that place? Maryville? Merton?"

"Meryton?" asked Elizabeth, her curiosity aroused. "Colonel, you must have had business in Meryton."

"I have not been to Hertfordshire," the colonel repeated with a strange obstinacy.

"Meryton!" Anne had the air of one who solved a great riddle. "For business with another military person, a man called Forster. I remember you wrote it in a letter to me—confined and unvarying society. No one leads a smaller life than I do; I read all my letters so many times over that I have quite committed them to memory! Except the names do escape me when I have been so rarely to any place myself, but once I marry, I am determined that I shall—"

Anne continued on in an animated fashion, but Elizabeth stared at Fitzwilliam with Darcy behind her, his hand clenching her shoulder. There was a sense of some great beast within the room, previously hidden but now straining towards the light. Elizabeth's heart pounded in her chest as she watched the colonel, who refused to look up at his observers. The chess piece that had been in his hand since the game was interrupted was dusty, and Fitzwilliam traced its grooves and indentations with his finger, vainly attempting to remove the dust.

"What did you do in Meryton, Fitzwilliam?" Darcy asked in a benign sort of way with nothing of censure apparent in his manner, but the colonel coloured deeply. Then, with a rapidity of movement that caused Elizabeth to gasp, the colonel hurled the chess piece into the wall. "I thought she was a whore!"

Anne shrieked and fell silent, and Elizabeth found herself strangely aware of her own breath. She almost missed Darcy's quiet question. "You thought *who* was a whore?"

There was a terrible silence, pregnant with anticipation, until the colonel rose from his seat with a force that caused the little chess table to topple, spilling its pieces all over the floor. He seemed not to notice. He began to pace, going to and fro in the limited space, his agitation suffocating the room.

Elizabeth's eyes were fixed on the colonel, but from her peripheral vision, she saw Darcy step forward. "Fitzwilliam? What is this about?"

The words nearly tore themselves out of him. "I had...I had some business with Colonel Forster that April after we left Rosings Park. You stayed in London and I...I went to that nothing town, stupid with its insignificance."

He paced in a stumbling, shambling way, the story emerging in fits and starts. "These bounties, you know...an excellent means for a wounded soldier to earn some money...you get so many to enlist and then...never mind that. I concluded the business and..."

Frustrated, Fitzwilliam could only point at Elizabeth, thrusting his arm out as if it had been set afire. "I have called you a siren, Miss Bennet, and truer words I have never spoken."

"Me?" Elizabeth could not follow his thoughts.

"I admired her, Darcy, but I could not afford to have her. I could not afford to love her. You knew that. Did I not say it even at Rosings? I said it,

I did. I said it to her, and I said it to you. You would never have looked at her had not I seen her first!"

Darcy stiffened. "I met her the autumn prior, Fitzwilliam, and—"

"And nothing!" Fitzwilliam shouted. "You left her, but when I liked her, you had to have her. That is your way, is it not? Take what I like just to show me you can have it but I cannot!"

Darcy looked at Elizabeth. "He is wrong. My attachment to you began long before Rosings and has nothing to do with anything he might have felt. Indeed, I had no idea he—"

"I regretted her; she lingered in my mind, so I needed to…I wished her out of it. No sense repining, is there? A man does as he must…hair of the dog and all that."

Elizabeth had no notion of what he meant, but Darcy did, and his eyes narrowed. "You acted on the advice of Aristophanes?"

The colonel, still pacing, muttered, "If this dog do you bite, soon as out of your bed, take a hair of the tail the next day."

Elizabeth looked at Darcy, but Darcy would not look at her. "I understand you completely, Fitzwilliam. Pray, continue your tale."

"So there I was in some terrible tavern in Meryton and saw a pretty young girl, looking a bit like Miss Elizabeth Bennet but taller and more stout—"

Elizabeth did not understand for a minute, and then, suddenly, she did. Gooseflesh prickled her arms. "Not Lydia!"

"She was clearly no stranger to a good time…I thought it all an innocent diversion. I should not have imagined, never could I have thought…but no, surely, I was not the first she had. I would stake my life on it."

Darcy muttered a quiet imprecation, and Elizabeth closed her eyes and pressed her hand to her eyes. *Oh foolish, foolish Lydia!*

"Would that I had perceived her as a lady! But what lady, what young girl would hang about in a tavern full of soldiers? She said she had not before known a man…I doubted it…"

"She was but fifteen!" Elizabeth cried, but her words were not heeded.

"I knew not, of course, what other men might have…but nevertheless, I thought it prudent to muddy the waters, so to speak. Wickham was lingering about so I encouraged him—"

"Encouraged him?" Darcy asked with a hard voice.

"In the way Wickham is best encouraged."

Darcy rolled his eyes and sighed with disgust. Elizabeth looked up at him, and he whispered, "Money."

"He paid Wickham to seduce Lydia?" Elizabeth's whisper was quiet but horrified.

"I left Meryton thinking I should never see her again. I was ashamed for how I had used her, but no one caught us…she seemed so much older, so worldly, there in the tavern, and I could not have imagined…but then, there she was at Brighton."

"You went to Brighton?"

"Any soldier not on the Continent was in Brighton, I assure you."

"Lydia went to Brighton," Elizabeth said softly.

"Ah, yes, is no pleasure withheld from her? Still as brazen and bold as you please and quick to tell me she had not had her courses."

The room was silent and still. Elizabeth was sure she could not even breathe.

"You are the father of Mrs. Wickham's child," said Darcy in a flat tone.

"No," said Fitzwilliam, his eyes as wild as his tone was stern. "No, no…it could not…no, I am but one possibility. In any case, a few days or maybe a week afterwards, Wickham was facing a possible disciplinary action, and he decided to run. He played a few hands with me one night, and I let him win; I had no doubt he would take his winnings and be gone. I told her where to find him, and the next anyone knew, they were eloping.

"I met him in London and persuaded him that he had left her with child. He did not completely believe me, not at first, but I made my own contribution to your uncle's offer—"

"My uncle knew of this?" Elizabeth exclaimed with a shriek.

"No." Fitzwilliam stopped pacing and shook his head. "No, he believes his was the principal part in it all, but I do not think George would have been so willingly domesticated had I not intervened. A little money, and I arranged for his troubles with his regiment to go away.

"But Wickham is, alas, never properly grateful. He learnt somehow of your engagement to her—"

Darcy drew up. "And how did he hear of my engagement, Fitzwilliam?"

Elizabeth whispered, "Wickham said his brother—"

"Wickham has no relations," Darcy interjected, and Elizabeth fell silent.

Fitzwilliam's energy was depleted and he sat down, hard, into a near chair, staring at nothing into the space in front of him.

"You received my letter," said Darcy quietly. "I told you, only you."

Fitzwilliam would admit nothing. "He wanted to extort more money from you."

"Who hit upon the scheme to take that which means more to me than money?" Darcy's stare was dark and unrelenting, and Elizabeth, observing it, felt vastly fearful of what must soon be known.

"A good soldier leaves nothing behind," Fitzwilliam said. He stared with dead eyes at the floor and spoke as if by rote. "Nothing. Take the wounded and the dead off the field, let the rain wash away the blood, and you do not go back. Never do you go back."

In the terrifying silence, Darcy made one short utterance.

"You did this to me."

Fitzwilliam's head jerked upwards, and he glared fiercely at Darcy. "I needed no by-blow lurking about! Much less your being uncle to the damned thing! Why would you wish to be connected to such a family? Young ladies lurking about taverns! I wished for you to be separated from her, and I wanted it done and done for good. I thought if she did something as dreadful as this that you would surely end any association with her, and then I could forget the entire mess. And we could all forget that we ever knew any Bennets in any manner."

Darcy was wild-eyed and pale. Elizabeth expected him to rain blows upon his dastardly cousin or expel rivulets of hateful curses upon him. He did neither but merely stood in frozen silence.

"I am a man with a man's needs," the colonel said to no one in particular. "I should not be forced to pay for one night's indiscretion with my life."

"But Lydia does," said Elizabeth. "The girl who is likely your child does."

"The child is well cared for, and so is your sister. She could have come upon the town or been secluded from the world, but instead she is a respectable married woman."

"No thanks to you."

He glared up at her, his ferocity waylaid by a drunken belch. "A great deal of my money went into that arrangement, I assure you."

Elizabeth considered him a moment, this man who was quite possibly the father of Lydia's baby. His blue eyes, so unlike Lydia's brown ones, and the fair hair; she had wondered anxiously how Lydia's child could be so fair when both her sister and Wickham were darker. But she had done all she could to dismiss such concerns, disregarding the guilt that such thoughts brought her.

But she would waste no more time contemplating such things as these. She would permit herself only one small condemnation of the colonel as she departed.

"You are a coward, Colonel Fitzwilliam, a miserable, lowly coward. I pray that I should never see you again."

With that, she took Darcy by the arm, intent on leading him from the room. "Anne, come with us, please."

Chapter Twenty-Six

They left the colonel still sitting in his father's library. Scarcely had the door closed behind them when they found Saye, who had a strange expression on his face. After some moments, Elizabeth realised it was shock.

"You are no doubt surprised to find me here" he said by way of a greeting. "Such a dreadfully dull party! When I heard people in the library, I hoped I might find the Earl of Tooleywag making free in there."

"The Earl of Tooleywag? I fear I have not yet made his acquaintance," Elizabeth replied, and Saye laughed weakly.

"No, I suspect you have not, at least not yet."

"What did you hear?" asked Darcy, and Saye sobered, looking uncharacteristically grave.

"I heard it all. The whole execrable story."

Elizabeth looked up at Darcy; the shock had gone, and instead, his countenance bore an expression of agony. She could not bear it. She wrapped her arms around his waist and pressed her cheek to his chest. He said nothing to her, but she felt the soft weight of his cheek on her hair for the briefest of moments. He did not speak, and she did not require him to, believing silence was likely his preference.

Saye cleared his throat. "This is neither proper enough for polite society nor scandalous enough to interest me, and therefore, I beg you would stop."

They parted, and Elizabeth gave Saye a contrite smile that he waved away impatiently.

"I must, of course, tell my father."

"Yes." Darcy gave a resigned nod. "I can scarcely bear to imagine what he might do."

"Will your father be much aggrieved?" Elizabeth asked.

Saye gave a wry chuckle. "He has always threatened that, should we father a child out of wedlock, we would be removed from the family comforts. I suppose this will teach us whether he will indeed carry his point."

"It is of no consequence," Darcy said. "What is done is done."

"That," Saye pronounced, "is for his lordship to decide. And if my father ever discovered that I knew this and kept it from him, I would be in for my own share of his anger. As I am excessively fond of my hide, I shall not trouble myself to conceal my brother's misdeeds."

So saying, he began to move away from them but paused a moment, shocking Darcy by throwing his arms around him and giving him a brief but tight hug. "Damned poor doings," he said and strolled away.

Elizabeth stood in the dimly lit hall with her beloved, hardly able to imagine what he must be thinking or feeling at this most disastrous of times. She glanced up at him and was surprised when he offered a faint smile.

"I believe I owe you a dance, Miss Bennet."

She slid her hand into his. "You do, indeed, sir, but I do not mind forgoing a dance for the mere pleasure of your company."

"I cannot think of this now. Let us dance and pretend to be merry for my sister's sake if none other."

With a nod, she allowed him to lead her down the stairs and into the crowded rooms. It was no easy matter to make their way to the dancers, but at last they arrived. It was the middle of a set, so they waited in sombre quietude amidst the gaiety. Several people came up to them, those who had not yet been introduced to Elizabeth or those who wished to extend congratulations on their engagement. Darcy was short in his replies, saying no more than was required to be polite.

The dance called was one they had danced at Bingley's first ball at Netherfield. That seemed so long ago, and it made Elizabeth smile to remember it. It was strange to see Darcy looking much as he had then but with such a different understanding between them. She could comprehend him now and knew what lay behind his mask of reserve.

"I remember," he said, "when we danced this dance before, we spoke of Wickham."

Elizabeth closed her eyes and groaned a little. "Pray, do not remind me how impertinent I was! The worst sort of fool is the one who fancies herself clever, and I did indeed think myself clever to speak so to you."

He smiled at her admission, but it faded quickly. "I remember telling you that Wickham was able to make friends with ease but far less able to keep them."

"I do remember."

"Ironic, is it not, that I of all people should say such a thing?" He could say no more as the dance required him to move away from her.

It was some minutes until they met again, this time to pause a bit in their exertions. She knew not how to respond; he had been spectacularly unlucky in his choice of friends.

"Having known what it is to lose you, I must say that I feel Colonel Fitzwilliam's is the greater loss."

"At present, it does not seem so."

"Perhaps not," she acknowledged. "But there is no one I have ever seen who matches your goodness or your care of those you love. He will regret what he has done; do not mistake it."

Darcy nodded but seemed rather unpersuaded.

Elizabeth did not intend to accept further invitations to dance, but Darcy urged her to. There was not much left of the ball; she was engaged twice, and it was done. Darcy had spoken to Bingley in the interim and persuaded him to allow Darcy to see Elizabeth home. After some token protest, Bingley agreed, realising that to turn Elizabeth over to Darcy's care meant he would see his bed sooner.

"The evening is fair," said Elizabeth. "Perhaps a walk would do?"

Darcy was silent as they set out. Lady Matlock's balls were famed for ending with the break of day, and the sky had begun to brighten. Elizabeth could just make out the contours of his countenance set into the mask of the reserved man she had known back in Meryton so long ago. *I thought he was haughty, but perhaps he was only suffering the hurt of deception and treachery.*

"I think being an adult will not be as wondrous as I believed when I was young," she remarked.

"Why is that?"

She considered her words carefully. "It used to be that scarce a day passed when I did not spend time laughing and talking to Charlotte Lucas. Indeed, if we missed a day, both Jane and I would be nearly mad to see her, and when we did, such stories and laughter that would come! We could hardly make our lips and tongues move fast enough to tell it all. I could never have imagined…"

Their pace, slow to begin, slowed even more.

"My mother always said that the Lucases were artful people, out for what they could get, but I thought it was her usual silly bluster. In this case, however, it seems she knew something I did not. Charlotte was determined, absolutely determined, to have Mr. Collins. It showed me something about her I cannot like."

"And now she is situated nicely at Longbourn."

"He was eligible, Charlotte was seven and twenty, and she needed to secure her future. One might say she was desperate, and desperate people do act in their own interests."

"I see what you are doing. But, alas, your example will not do."

"No?"

"Mrs. Collins might have acted out of her own interests, but she did not bring you pain in so doing. She did not gloat for your loss, nor did she rejoice in her advantage over you."

She looked up at him and saw a stoic countenance. He inhaled deeply then exhaled in a controlled way before speaking again, his tone quiet and sedate.

"They were once my closest friends, Fitzwilliam and Wickham. We were playfellows and schoolmates. I can remember the three of us having fun together, scampering and frolicking as young boys do. I could never have imagined that they would one day betray me. Both have tried to take from me that which I most value."

They walked slowly and silently for some moments.

"I begin to see your way of it," he admitted at length. "Being grown is vastly overrated."

"Oh, I do not know about that," said Elizabeth lightly. "I begin to think I am wrong. After all, adults do have many advantages."

"Pray, remind me of them."

She slid her hand free of his arm, moving to stand directly in front of him. "A child can neither fall in love nor do this." She lifted on her toes and kissed him.

"That is an advantage." A weak shadow of a smile flitted across his countenance.

They had arrived at Davies Street. The pearly light of the early morning and the mists of the day seemed to envelop them in an enchantment, and they stood motionless for a moment within it. Elizabeth's eyes moved over his face, seeing real sorrow within his dark eyes.

She touched his face briefly. "Pray, allow me the honour of being your dearest friend?"

"You already are my dearest friend."

"Shall I be your companion too? I cannot shoot, but I daresay, I could observe while you do it."

This time he laughed. "I think I must rely on others to be my companions in these gentlemanly pursuits."

"Indeed not! What is it that you like to do with your gentleman friends that I could not do?"

"Go to my club."

She laughed. "Very well, I grant you that. But what else? I can play chess, and we do like to read similar things."

"You do not fence."

"You can teach me."

"What about boxing?"

She gave him an impish grin and a gentle punch to his arm.

"Of course, my favourite thing to do is ride." He cocked a brow, challenging her.

"Oh-h-h." She sighed. "Well, I suppose I could learn."

"Would you? Would you learn to ride for me? Or should the violent sneezing spill you from the saddle?"

She laughed. "Oh, yes, there is that."

"Never mind all of that. I am sure we shall find more than enough to divert ourselves."

There was something in his manner and tone that made her blush, and she hoped he did not see it as she smiled up at him.

"I wish it were not so long until I could call," he said.

"Are you not tired?"

"Not at all."

She shook her head. "Neither am I."

They looked at one another for some time, which seemed to stretch infinitely until Elizabeth, with hopeful uncertainty said, "You could come in for a bit."

He smiled and shook his head. "And have the servants tell Bingley? No, I could not."

"As Miss Bingley and Sir Edmund taught me, the servants are either unaware or indifferent."

"I could not dishonour you so." But he took a step closer when he said it, and she knew he was tempted.

She took his hand and tugged at him. They would need to go around the house to the little door on the side with its exceedingly convenient staircase. "Nothing of that sort. Just some time spent together." With a grin, she added, "As friends."

They entered on silent feet and hurried quietly up the stairs. Elizabeth could hear, at a distance, the kitchen servants stirring, albeit in a languid way; they knew the occupants of the house would be slow to rise that day. At last, they arrived in her bedchamber, and she quietly closed the door behind them. He stood, seeming very large and masculine among her things.

He watched her closely as she removed her pelisse and her shoes, and because she thought it might please him, she undid her hair, allowing it to fall down her back. He approached, his eyes fixed on her and his movements determined. In a trice, he slid his hands up into her hair, brushing her scalp as his lips fell on hers.

They kissed for a long time, moving from fevered to languidly impassioned and back again. After a while, they moved to sit on her bed, and from there, it was short work to lie upon it. For such a reserved man, he spoke to her quite a bit while he kissed her, asking her whether he should stop and telling her how beautiful, how tempting he found her.

They reached the point where a decision needed to be made, and he flung himself away from her with such force that it nearly sent him off the edge of her narrow bed. Elizabeth had decided she was quite done with maidenly virtue, but Darcy was more prudent. "Not now, not when we both must scurry away afterwards."

She turned towards him, leaning on one arm. "So dare I suppose that you will not make a habit of scurrying away from me once we are married?"

He laid there, his arm over his eyes, breathing deeply for a few minutes before turning to her and mimicking her posture. "No, I intend to be there as long as you will have me."

"How very well that sounds." She ran her finger lightly over his jaw, and he closed his eyes in response. They lay like that for some time, Elizabeth wishing her fingers that soothed his skin could do the same for his cares and heartbreaks.

The house had slowly awakened around them, and they soon heard the sounds of Jane's maid bringing her mistress her morning chocolate.

"I need to leave before I am discovered," Darcy murmured, eyes still closed while Elizabeth gently stroked his face. "It seems Bingley is one of my few remaining friends; I do not wish to find myself in his disfavour too."

So they rose, and she straightened his waistcoat and helped him into his coat in what she thought a wifely manner.

"Just a bit above a fortnight now," she said.

"Yet still far, far too long."

She smiled. "It will pass in a wink."

"I hope so." He kissed her again, deeply but with resolution. "These partings grow more insupportable each day."

It was with no little surprise that Darcy heard Colonel Fitzwilliam announced a week after his cousin's startling confession. He considered refusing him entry, but in the end, his curiosity won out over his spite.

He stayed at his desk, rising as manners dictated when his cousin was shown in.

Fitzwilliam did not look well; he was tired and worn, wearing wrinkled clothes and smelling of spirits. Darcy observed it but felt no sympathy. He gestured towards a chair, and Fitzwilliam sank into it. For several moments, neither man spoke.

At length, Darcy asked, "What do you want?"

"I am leaving for Upper Canada. I wished to say farewell."

"Upper Canada? The war?"

Fitzwilliam nodded.

"I thought you intended to sell your commission."

Fitzwilliam shook his head.

"Then I shall wish you Godspeed," Darcy replied.

There was another pause that Darcy bore with solemn humour.

"Lady Sophie cannot be pleased with this turn of events."

"Lady Sophie has chosen to release me. It seems her father finds much to object to in my…in this business with Miss Wickham."

"So you did tell her you had fathered a child?"

"I do not know the girl is my child," Fitzwilliam shot back at once. "Nothing is sure."

Darcy shrugged.

"In any case, my father felt it needful, and so I told her." Fitzwilliam shook his head, clearly still feeling himself the aggrieved party.

"And your estate?"

"Will still be there when I return."

Darcy leant back in his chair. "It seems your affairs are all settled."

"Save for this one." Fitzwilliam sat up a bit and leant forward. "For what it is worth, I did not realise the strength of your attachment to her. I thought your fascination would pass, that this notion of love would soon give way to a wish for a more distinguished match."

Darcy felt an angry clench in his gut but managed to reply calmly, "Then you, it seems, knew very little about me and understood even less."

"So it seems. But I do wish you joy." Fitzwilliam rose. "If I am killed or die over there, pray, do your best to remember me fondly."

"I think that to recall you fondly must be beyond my generosity at this time. I should do best to think of you as does my intended—the most pitiable and weakest creature I have ever known."

"Pitiable?" Fitzwilliam did not like this; his jaw tightened and his lips pursed, but he was quick to regain his composure. "I suppose I am. My family has removed their support, I am poor and despised, and your Miss Bennet, with her kind heart, would naturally pity that."

"The only consolation to us is that our love triumphed over your selfishness. It has shown us that nothing can divide us, and in that, we are made happy."

"You have indeed found a treasure, Darcy. I do not begrudge your rather lofty joy and can only pray I may one day find the like."

"I doubt you ever will." Darcy remained seated. "You must love to be thusly loved, and I am not sure you are capable of it."

On the eve of the wedding, Jane came to her sister's bedchamber. "Mama has threatened to come speak to you about marital duties, so I told her I would do it."

"And for that, I am exceedingly thankful." Elizabeth laughed as they sat. "Am I too late?"

Elizabeth glanced at the mantel clock. "Late? No, I was getting ready for bed, but I assure you, I expected—"

With great deliberation, Jane rose and bent down, retrieving some small object from the floor beneath Elizabeth's bed—a pin, long and with an enamelled head engraved in a design of various spirals and swirls.

"Have you taken to wearing cravats?" Jane asked with a small grin on her lips and one brow raised.

"No." Elizabeth summoned the greatest degree of hauteur possible. "But I have taken to buying a gift for my soon-to-be husband."

"Mm. Have you given him this gift as yet?"

"Not yet."

"Have you given him any other gifts?"

Elizabeth rolled her eyes. "If you have something to tell me, perhaps you will get on with it? I am not of a mind to be here all night."

And so Jane began, and amid the halting and blushing (and some unfortunate hand gestures that Elizabeth begged her to cease immediately), she managed to say her piece to her sister.

"But I must conclude by saying this," Jane announced as she rose and went to the door. "If our fifteen-year-old sister, who lacks sense and ability, could manage it with no assistance whatsoever, then so will you."

And upon this horrifying thought, Elizabeth took to her bed on her last day as a maiden. Her final thought as sleep began to claim her was that she must speak to her husband about his tendency to grow distracted and leave things strewn about, much to the detriment of all.

THE DAY IN WHICH MISS ELIZABETH BENNET AT LONG LAST BECAME MRS. Darcy was all things perfect. The wedding was held at St George's with the breakfast at the Bingleys' house on Davies Street. "A wise arrangement," Elizabeth told Darcy. "Then my mother will not be induced to excessive comfort in your house."

"*Our* house," he told her, already enjoying the sound of those words.

The wedding night, by contrast, was positively dreadful. He had been too fast and too fierce in all ways, and she, delicate and small as she was, had suffered for it. She tried for some time to pretend all was well, but he soon realised it was not so. He had asked whether he should leave and she, looking a bit ill beneath her brave disguise, said, "No, no, you can stay if you would like."

And so he left her.

But should I return to her? Was I a brute to abandon her? Maybe she wishes for solitude? Has she cried herself to sleep? Darcy sighed heavily and kicked angrily at the counterpane.

He knew not how long he lay there fuming and stewing when there came a soft knock on his door. Darcy had nearly persuaded himself that he had not heard it when the door opened quietly. A feminine voice whispered into the darkness, "Are you sleeping?"

"Elizabeth." The word, breathed at a daytime volume, seemed thunderous. He leapt from the bed and went to the door, flinging it wide.

His wife—what joy there was even to think it!—stood before him in a simple nightgown, with her hair flowing around her shoulders and a smile on her lips. "Did I disturb you?"

He took her hand and led her into his bedchamber. "Disturb me? Certainly not."

"You were not asleep?"

"How could I sleep?" he asked in a voice filled with self-loathing. "Not when I…"

She was looking at him with wide eyes, trust, and complacency. He sighed and placed a kiss on her forehead. "Forgive me, please. I should not be the least surprised if you would forbid me from your bedchamber forever."

Shockingly, she laughed. "That is a rather dim view of things."

"I hurt you," he said earnestly. "I know I did. And it pains me to think that I did so to you, my wife, the person who I have so longed for and—"

"I do not believe that it could have been avoided. No doubt my anxiety made it worse. I think we do ourselves an injustice when any moment in time is swelled in importance; it can only be less than what our minds have made it."

She dropped his hand and moved towards his bed. She stopped at the edge, resting one hand on the post and giving him an impish look over her shoulder. "I am perfectly well now."

She smiled and crawled onto his bed. Having arrived at his pillow, she gave it a few thumps with her fist. "Oh, this is very nice. May I have this one?"

"Oh, do you mean you…? You would like to spend the night in here?"

"Am I invited?" She smiled in a beguiling fashion as she slid her legs under his covers.

"Of course. Or we could return to…"

"Alas, my bed is not serviceable at present, and I am not of a mind to call the maids from their beds to restore it."

"Right." He began his own ascent into the bed, moving carefully. He had slept on the right side of this bed for near to a decade, but if she wanted it, she would certainly have it. He settled onto the left side, stretching out, careful to keep to himself.

He lay in the darkness, awake and exquisitely alert, hearing her breathing. *Is she awake? Should I talk to her? Or should I try to sleep?* He would never sleep this night, of that he was certain. *What is she doing over there?*

Hushed tones came through the darkness. "It seems to me that you and I begin everything in fits and starts."

"The first proposal I made is surely an excellent example of that belief."

"Just so." She rolled over and placed her hand on his chest, stroking it lightly. "The second was much better but ended in disaster, unfortunately."

"But the third time was perfection itself."

"It was sublime," she agreed.

"You also refused me the first time I asked you to dance."

"What?" Her ministrations to his chest stopped for a moment. "I did not."

"Yes, you did. When Sir William Lucas forced it upon us at his party."

"Sir William Lucas—oh, *that* party! You did not really wish to dance with me. You were only bending under the discomfort of his entreaty."

He smiled but said no more of that. "The second time was at Netherfield, when I asked you to dance a reel with me."

"When did…oh, the first week Jane and I spent at Netherfield. You surely did not wish to commence a reel then and there while Miss Bingley played?"

"I did, indeed, and you refused me quite cruelly. 'Tis a wonder I had the courage to ask a third time."

"But we did dance that third time." He thought he could see her smile in the darkness. "Our success comes in patterns of three."

"It seems that it does."

"We would then be quite silly to stop at one—would we not?"

A Short Period of Exquisite Felicity

An unexpected jolt of hot desire jerked through him. Such simple words but so inflaming! But no, surely she did not want...not when she must still be in some pain?

"What do you say, Mr. Darcy? Shall we suffer ourselves a repeat of our earlier poor performance?"

"But you must be...that is to say, do you not..."

"I think if we proceed a bit slowly—"

"Oh, I shall, to be sure. Very slowly. But I cannot bear the thought of hurting you. Do you not still—?"

"Only the smallest bit. I daresay, the activity might be soothing. Shall we not try?"

He took his hands and smoothed the hair back from her face. "I do love you, Mrs. Darcy, and I am, as always, yours to command."

"Very well." She smiled again and kissed him. "Then I shall command it."

Epilogue

1817

Given their habit of doing things in threes, Elizabeth supposed she should not have been shocked at their lack of success in having children in the first and second years of her marriage. Oh, there were certainly times of hope—followed by times of increasing despair. Jane continued to serenely birth child after child. It seemed she was forever increasing, or in confinement, or recently churched.

The halls of Pemberley were, however, far from silent. The Darcys had been approached with a startling request during the first year of their marriage. The Wickhams had the support of a wealthy patron to become courtiers, and as it was the dearest wish of them both, they had no intention of permitting the inconvenience of a child to stop them.

Little Emelia became, therefore, something of a saving grace to them. She was quite a bewitching young thing, almost shocking in her childlike beauty, but with a captivating manner as well, even at the most tender of ages.

Nevertheless, as pleasing as she was, she could not answer for their want of Darcy's heir, and on this, the eve of their third anniversary, Elizabeth hoped she might be able to give him just that. She had missed her courses for three months, and she was often ill in the mornings. She had managed to conceal these symptoms from her husband, not wishing to raise his hopes yet again. But now she had felt the little flutters within her that announced the presence of a little soul to bless them.

As they sat to breakfast, she decided she could wait no longer. He looked rather dear that morning, frowning at his newspaper whilst he attacked a rather large plate of bacon and eggs. A full salver of bacon sat only inches away from her, but nevertheless she reached out, stealing a piece from his plate. It had the expected result; he lowered the paper and gave her a brief severe look followed by a smile.

"What do you have planned today?" she asked with a smile.

"Well…" He turned and looked out the window. "I did think I might ride over to Matlock and look at that field that has his lordship so worried, but now it is raining, and I think we are due a good soak. I fear you must be required to entertain me, for nothing else will do."

Elizabeth looked down at her plate, feeling suddenly shy. "I am rather busy today working on a very particular undertaking, but it does not follow that your society is unwelcome."

"What sort of undertaking? Perhaps I could help."

"You already did."

"Did I?" He looked pleased with himself. "Then I shall help more."

"I fear you cannot. Not at this stage."

His brow wrinkled, he leant towards her. "No? Why not? What is this enterprise of yours?"

Elizabeth took a moment to look around her, wishing to imprint upon her memory every bit of this momentous occasion. "I daresay, it is something of a Christmas present for you."

"A present for me?" He leant back, looking happily confused. "In June?"

She nodded. "It is a present that requires some time to complete, but it is worth every second of the effort."

He thought about that for a moment. "Is it something you are sewing for me?"

She laughed. "No, there are no needles involved in the making of this."

In the face of his continued confusion, she could tease no more. She rose from her chair and went to his side; after a moment, he understood her intention and pushed his chair from the table a bit, permitting her to sit on his lap.

She took his hand and laid it gently on her abdomen. "Here is your present. Safe and warm and kicking my insides just as he is meant to do."

A deep flush overtook him, and she felt his hand grow hot and tremble the slightest bit. In a hoarse voice he asked, "Is it true, my dearest Lizzy? After all this time, shall I at last be a father?"

It roused her emotion to hear his so prominently displayed, and she turned her head, pressing her face into his neck. "I have not wanted to raise your hopes, not until I knew. And now I do, I know. I feel him, he is hale and strong."

In that, she was nearly entirely correct: the baby was hale and strong and at times made Elizabeth gasp by the strength of the kicks to her innards. However, she was wrong in that the baby born to them in late autumn that same year was not a son but a daughter they called Rose. Though Elizabeth had wished to give Darcy an heir, her husband was delighted just to have a healthy child. Elizabeth only hoped it would not be impossible for her to give him a son.

It turned out that she need not have worried, for by the following Christmas, she had given him his heir, young George Darcy, who was followed two years thence by Thomas.

"Threes," said Elizabeth. "We do everything in threes."

1827

Major Fitzwilliam sat by the window in his old bedchamber at Matlock, watching as the girl, just turned fifteen, strolled about the garden with the young Viscount Saye. There was something in that young buck of his brother's that he did not like—an insolence and an arrogance. Then again, could a son of his brother behave any differently?

She was beautiful, this young Miss Wickham, almost startlingly so. The fair hair of her youth had not turned but had taken on a coppery hue. Her face was the face from which all others should be formed, perfect in shape and symmetry. Her eyes, however, were truly arresting. They were a deep blue, nearly violet, and ringed by thick lashes. Fitzwilliam thought he had never seen their like.

There was a great deal in the lovely and charming Miss Wickham to be proud of. Not only unusually beautiful, she was unequalled in her kindness and the strength of her character. She had uncommon compassion for the poor, she played the pianoforte better than any lady he knew, and she spoke French as one who was born there. Yes, Miss Wickham would be the pride of any father, to be sure—should the father be willing to admit to her existence.

Fitzwilliam clenched his jaw at the old, never-forgotten memories.

But she was Darcy's joy now. She had lived with the Darcys for many years, since the age of three when Wickham somehow contrived to secure the position at court and asked Mr. and Mrs. Darcy to take her in for a few years. The Darcys, ever the souls of generosity, had done so.

A few years had turned into twelve, and Fitzwilliam did not anticipate any imminent change to the arrangement. The Wickhams vastly enjoyed their years at court, and as they were strangely unencumbered by the arrival of any further children, they saw no need to surrender their licentious way of living for one more domestic.

Similarly, Fitzwilliam had not found himself the proud father of any children. Any *more* children? Nay, *any* children. He knew not why; he had married when he returned from Upper Canada in 1815, a sweet girl who saw fit to forgive his past escapades. Her inability to give him an heir grieved her, but they kept themselves contented enough with just the two of them, and his estate would make a fine gift to his brother's second son someday. He had always held a special fondness for the boy.

No, there were no children for him, which seemed as persuasive an argument as any against this notion that Emelia was his child. Then again, Mrs. Wickham had never again fallen with child either…a puzzling business that.

Fitzwilliam shook his head, seeing the two young people turn a corner in the gardens. He supposed he never would know the truth of Emelia's parentage—but what could it matter now?

1832

HAVING NOT SEEN HER YOUNGEST SISTER FOR MANY YEARS, ELIZABETH Darcy was amazed to receive Lydia's card one morning at the house on Grosvenor Street. "Madam," said her manservant. "Mrs. Wickham was quite particular that she would see you alone. You and no one else."

Elizabeth lifted a brow. Lydia did not wish to see her daughter? She frowned at the card, but this was a grievance of long standing, and it did no good to think of it now. As courtiers, Lydia and Wickham led a life that was single to the pursuit of their pleasures, and one could not expect now, when Lydia was a middle-aged matron, that she would be any different from the self-indulgent, silly girl she had always been.

With a grave countenance, she told her butler, "Show her in."

Although Elizabeth had not seen her for many years, Lydia was Lydia still, yet with a great deal of Mrs. Bennet as well. Her clothes were fashionable and of the finest quality, but her bosom strained alarmingly at her bodice. Her jewellery was too large and ostentatious, and she styled her hair in a manner much more suited to a young maiden than a middle-aged matron. She was all that Mrs. Bennet might have become with a more generous allowance.

The two sisters spoke for some minutes in the manner of strangers with a shared history. Mrs. Wickham showed as much interest in her daughter as she did for any of the Darcy children, and soon their common subjects were exhausted.

"We saw your husband a few days ago," said Lydia at length. "On Bond Street. I congratulate you, Lizzy; he is still a handsome man, is he not? We must laud ourselves for having managed to capture two such handsome men, who are still, in these years beyond the prime of their lives—"

"Yes, yes," said Elizabeth, stifling her natural impatience. "Very handsome, indeed."

"And," Lydia's voice turned sly, "if your husband is anything like my Wickham, never one to tire of his husbandly duties. I declare, it must be something in the waters of Derbyshire! For Wickham will never forgo—"

Elizabeth pressed two fingers to the bridge of her nose. "Lydia, is there a particular reason you wished to see me today? Not that the pleasure is unwelcome, but it was unanticipated, and I confess I have much to do for a dinner we are hosting for Emelia."

Against all inclination, she offered, weakly, "Of course, I should be honoured to have you and Mr. Wickham attend…the invitation is late, I know…but naturally—"

"No, no." Lydia shook her head. "That is not why I am here. I am here because of something your husband told Wickham. He believes Emelia might receive an offer of marriage from Mr. Denny."

"We do think so," said Elizabeth calmly. "Young Denny is a fine gentleman, of exemplary character. His father, as you know, is Sir Frederick Denny who we—"

"—knew back in Meryton." Lydia sighed and tossed herself dramatically back into a lazy posture. "A baronet! Who could have imagined it!"

"Yes, well." Elizabeth sighed, thinking it was a dreadful time for Lydia to become vainglorious. "An aunt died, leaving him a little fortune that he invested well, and his efforts at the end of the war earned him the favour of King George so…yes, he is rather grander than he was when we knew him.

His son is a fine young man, a little young perhaps but—"

"I shall not allow Emelia to marry him," Lydia pronounced dramatically. "The very notion is abhorrent."

Elizabeth took several measured breaths before she replied. "I know that you had hoped your place at court would raise Emelia's expectations—"

"No, no." Lydia shook her head, her ringlets bobbing and tossing around her. "It is not that."

"Then what it is?"

Lydia did not answer for a few moments. She lifted her cup of tea to her lips, tasted it and grimaced. "Do you have anything else to drink, Lizzy? How about a touch of sherry?"

With a sigh, Elizabeth rose and went for the sherry she kept in the sideboard. She poured her sister a small glass.

"Do me about twice that, if you please." Lydia smiled, looking eager, and Elizabeth, gritting her teeth, complied. She brought it back to her sister and watched as Lydia tossed it back like it was nothing. Lydia handed her the glass. "A little more, dear sister. I have a story to tell you, and I cannot tell it without proper fortification."

Restraining her wish to sigh again, Elizabeth went for another glass, pouring generously, and went back to her seat.

"What a mad, bad time that was! The war and the soldiers, all of us so young! Ah, the romance of it all, I can scarce bear my longing for it."

"If you mean the sort of times where young men are leaving their homes and families to be shot and killed, then no, I must disagree. I am happy to see that sort of thing gone."

Lydia laughed loudly at this although Elizabeth had not intended any amusement. "True, true. But you must remember the gentlemen, how fine they all looked in their regimentals! Oh, my dear Wickham out-swaggered them all, but I daresay, there were quite a few of them I liked very well."

"Yes, I do remember your enjoyment of the lot of them." Elizabeth paused a moment and then prompted Lydia a bit. "So, you are speaking of the time Meryton hosted the regiment—1812?"

"You and Jane were in London, and I recall how jealous I was! Remember, I went that summer to Brighton, but before that, in the spring, I should have thought I would go mad from the tedium. There was nothing at all, just nothing, to keep a young lady entertained. Stupid, dull Meryton! How relieved I am to be gone from it! And Kitty still at Longbourn; I cannot think how she bears it! She should have married that fellow, what was his name? The one with the—"

"The story? You had a story to tell me."

"Of course. It was spring, and a young lady likes a bit of romance in the spring. Come Lizzy, we are not so old that we cannot recall how it felt on those first warm days when the muslins got lighter, and the muddy roads meant you could lift your skirts a little as you walked down the way. You must remember how it was?"

Elizabeth pursed her lips a moment before replying, "No, I must say, lifting my skirts in the road was not something I aspired to. Lydia, allow me to come to the point on your behalf. I know all about your secret."

"You do?" Lydia's eyes went wide. "How?"

"A long, long time ago, before I married Mr. Darcy, his cousin confessed the whole of it to us."

"His cousin?"

"Major Fitzwilliam—though he was then a colonel."

"Colonel Fitzwilliam? Ah, yes." Lydia smiled dreamily. "Colonel Fitzwilliam."

"Yes, and if you believe that being the illegitimate, possible daughter of the brother of the Earl of Matlock—a daughter he has *never* recognised, by the by—means Emelia should marry a duke or marquess, then you are sorely mistaken."

"How droll you are, Lizzy. Do you not think all these years at court has shown me how it must be? That is not what I meant at all, and in any case, I do not think there is any possibility that the colonel sired my daughter."

Elizabeth drew up, inhaling sharply. "What?"

With that, Lydia indulged in a vulgar and far-too-detailed narrative of her relations with Colonel Fitzwilliam, abusing him gleefully on his lack of endowment and his unfortunate treatment of the bale of hay on which they had reclined.

When Elizabeth had suppressed the boiling nausea in her gut, she admonished, "Lydia, you should not speak so of the dead."

"He is dead?"

Elizabeth nodded. "He passed two years ago from pneumonia." When Lydia had no response, Elizabeth continued, "It seems he has not done ill by

Emelia all these years as we had supposed he did. We were angry that he left her nothing in his will, but it turns out, it should not have been expected."

"No, not at all." Lydia yawned. "But I am not finished with my tale. I had always fancied Denny as you know, and we began a little romance that year. It started in the winter, but it went on—oh, all the way into the spring. He was quite mad for me, Lizzy, always telling me that he knew not how he could bear the military life had he not the pleasures he found in me."

She smiled, lost in her thoughts. "Oh, if only you could imagine, Lizzy! Three, sometimes four times a day, in any and every place imaginable. I presumed to think we should marry but that was when I learnt—"

Elizabeth had been calculating ages and dates in her mind. "But his son! He must have been already married in 1812!"

With a petulant toss of her head, Lydia confirmed her suspicions. "Yes, some terrible little mouse who lived with his parents while he fulfilled his duty to the militia."

"Oh Lydia! He made you his mistress! With his wife and son waiting for him back at home!"

"Well, no one knew he had a wife, did they?" said Lydia crossly. "We had argued about it the same night I met the colonel, and there was my chance to show Denny what he must lose! You know how it was, Lizzy, the soldiers always did like me better than any of you! Of course, I did not know he was anyone special, but others did, and they said his blood was very high. I thought it would be fun—little Lydia from Meryton having a romp with the son of an earl!—and so it was.

"Soon we were all in Brighton, and I knew by then that I had a bit of trouble on my hands. Denny was no use at all, and there again was the colonel. He had been drunk as a lord that night in Meryton—him and Captain Carter and all those boys playing cards and drinking all night long—and he did not know he had spent himself on a bale of hay! Oh, what a fine joke it was! You should have seen his face when I told him I had been a virgin before him. Why does that puff up a man so? I shall never comprehend it."

Elizabeth, who had been in shock since the narrative took a turn towards Denny, finally was mistress enough of herself to say, "Lydia, you do not mean...are you telling me that Emelia is...that she is...?"

"She and Mr. Denny possibly are...well, I suppose they would be half-brother and half-sister, is that not right?"

Thoughtless, thoughtless Lydia! Would this tale never cease to haunt us all? Yet there was Lydia speaking for all the world as if it had been some harmless lark, something long past that was amusing and charming.

Elizabeth rose abruptly, walking to the window where she stood staring out at nothing. Poor, poor Emelia! She loved young Denny with her whole heart and soul! The two young people had laughed at the similarities in their hair and their eyes, never imagining any vile truth behind the matter.

"I knew you would understand, Lizzy." Lydia had come up quietly behind her sister. "I knew you would know just how to manage it, telling Emelia that she could not marry where she liked."

Elizabeth turned and stared coldly at the woman whom she could no longer manage to think of as her sister. How had this selfish, useless trollop come to be as she was?

Contriving to keep her voice from trembling, she said, "Do you have any idea how many have been affected by your actions? How much sorrow, how many heartaches, have been caused by your selfish, wanton behaviour? Where will it end, Lydia? How long until you stop being the silly girl ruled by animal spirits that you have always been?"

Lydia drew back, mildly offended. "Oh la, Lizzy, you have become as much an arrogant prude as your husband. Never mind all that—just see she is told before she ends up married to her brother." With that, she flounced out, and Elizabeth vowed it would be the last she ever saw of her or that foolish husband of hers.

EMELIA BORE THE NEWS WITH EQUANIMITY, MUCH MORE COMPOSED THAN Elizabeth had ever dared hope. "I confess I did at times wonder," she began but then stopped, blushing.

"What, my dear? What did you wonder?" Elizabeth held the girl's hand within hers and she squeezed it reassuringly. "Speak plainly, my child. There is nothing of this conversation that puts either of us at ease, but it is best to say it all now."

"I see sometimes how Uncle Darcy looks at you," she said, blushing fiercely. "Even now, when you are both so old—"

So old? Elizabeth's brows shot up, and she opened her mouth to protest but then thought better of it.

"Still, one cannot deny the…the feelings—"

A Short Period of Exquisite Felicity

"Yes, I do understand."

"Well," she said, still unable to meet her aunt's eyes. "I simply did not feel that way. I love Denny—I do truly love him—but ours was never like that. So to know that perhaps some part of me understood that ours was a different sort of attachment...well, it does make a great deal of sense to me."

"I am so proud of you for bearing this upset with such reason and good sense," Elizabeth told her. "And yes, I must say, when the love you share is the right sort of love, you will know it, and I daresay, it will last for all your life."

"What are you saying, Mrs. Darcy?" The ladies lifted their eyes to see Darcy leaning on one shoulder against the door frame.

Elizabeth felt the familiar quickening of her heart that she always had when she saw him. She rose and went to him, kissing him on the cheek although it was not their custom to be so free with such endearments in front of the children. "Emelia and I were speaking of love."

"Then I must have my share in the conversation," he said with an easy grin. "For it is, above all subjects, a particular interest of mine.

Acknowledgments

Getting any book from the manuscript stage to publication takes a whole team of people, and the team at Meryton Press is by far the most talented and delightful group any writer could be fortunate enough to have. For my editor, Gail Warner, there just aren't enough superlatives to sing her praises fully. I was also very blessed to have the assistance of Ellen Pickels in the final editing stage and Zorylee Diaz-Lupitou in the cover design and marketing stages. Finally, I would like to thank Michele Reed for her oversight and guidance.

My beta readers for this book were an absolute dream team. Kristi Rawlings, Sarah Pesce, and Janet Foster, your assistance was invaluable and much appreciated!

I would also like to thank all of the readers and commenters at A Happy Assembly. Your contribution is much more than any of you probably realize, and it is greatly appreciated! Of those. I have to give particular acknowledgement to Jan Ashton, Claudine Pepe, and Vickie Lewis for being great friends, always willing to toss around writing ideas.

A special acknowledgement to Kari Holmes Singh for making a generous donation to the Texas Hurricane Relief effort of autumn 2017 in exchange for an appearance in the book (as Miss Carrie Holmes).

Last but certainly not least, I want to thank my daughters and husband, Allie, Lexi, and Tom D'Orazio for all their love and support, and also being willing to grab a bowl of cereal in lieu of a proper dinner at times. Also thanks to Roger, Brenda, Jason, and Missy Ilgen for their support and to Linda D'Orazio for her assistance in proofreading.

CPSIA information can be obtained
at www.ICGtesting.com
Printed in the USA
LVOW03s2013050318
568697LV00006B/1447/P

9 781681 310237